MEGHAN WILLIAMS P.

The Sound Carries

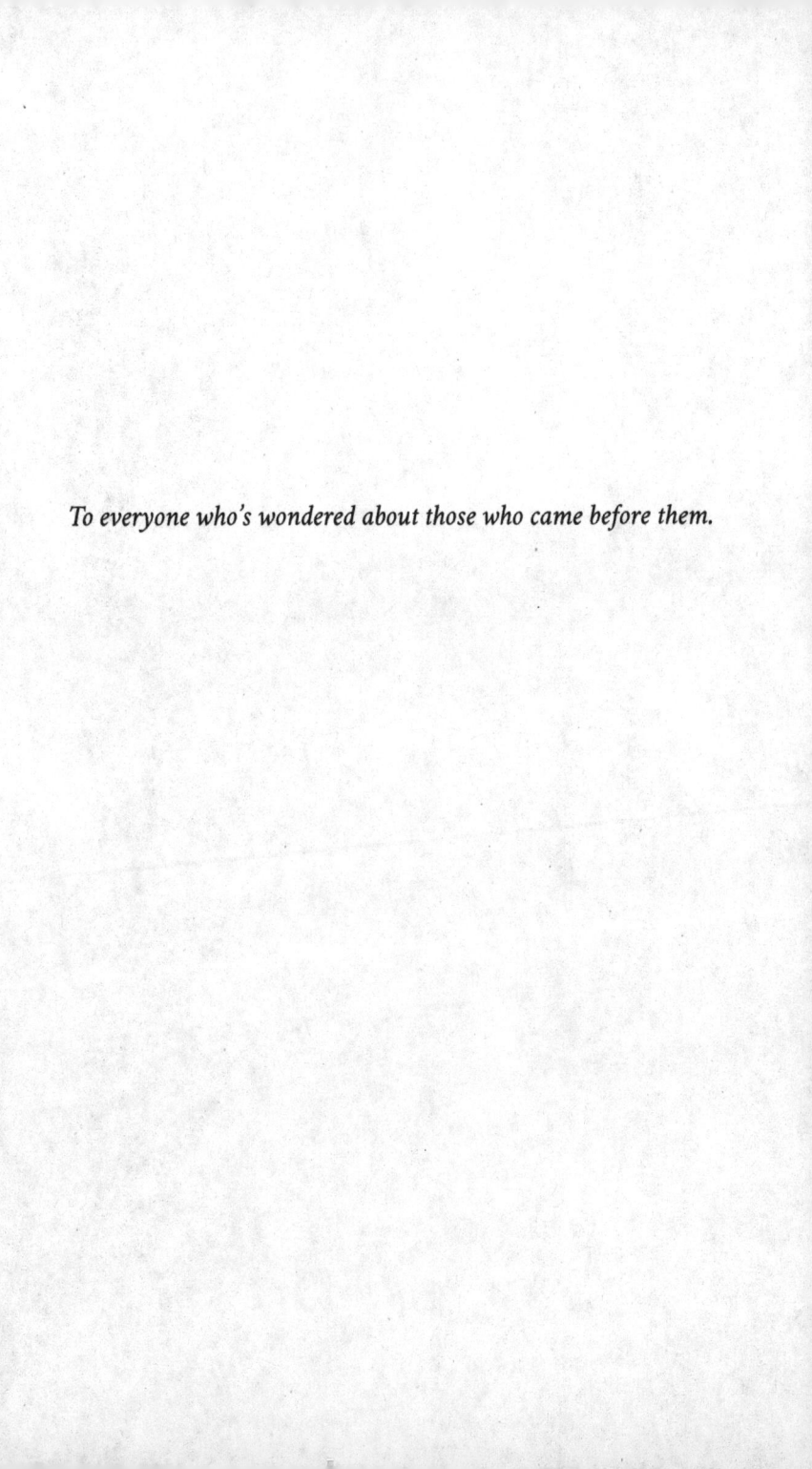

To everyone who's wondered about those who came before them.

The bird fights its way out of the egg.
The egg is the world. Who would be
born must first destroy a world.

Prologue

Neither Miriam nor Richard grew up in Hope Springs. The twists of life that led them there, after tangling them up with each other, were nearly untraceable in their complexity, unfathomable in their vastness. To their children, it would seem like they had always lived there; their roots plunged deep into the rich soil at the base of the Cascades. To them, the young couple was a towering pine—and they were birds perched at the branches, ready to fly away.

It wasn't that the children didn't like Hope Springs. It was a peaceful town not far from one of the state's best universities. A good place to launch but not the most exciting to land. That was all well with Miriam and Richard. They hadn't been looking for excitement when they found Hope Springs but for refuge.

The first prerequisite Miriam had when selecting a house was the land. Much like any other part of the world, the western United States had been drenched in blood and rancor years before, once and twice, and once again. Miriam didn't expect to find land at peace, but she wanted to find land she could appease. Somehow, they had made it past the never-ending plains of the central continental US and emerged at the other side if not victorious, at least feeling disillusioned enough to settle.

The Hope Springs community was fairly open to them,

barely out of their twenties, heterosexual, and familiar. It didn't matter what gods lay behind Miriam's dark eyes; her skin was fair enough, and her head was uncovered. The couple would never speak of their past to any of their new friends or coworkers, and after the first few months, nobody was ever interested enough to pry. Soon, they grew into the town's customs, lending a hand for school fundraisers, attending local football games, and helping set up for yearly festivities. But first, they had to find a house.

The Victorian sat at the end of a short cul-de-sac off Willow Street, which fed into one of the town's main roads. Other than its convenient location, the house had white window panes, stone roofing, and two enchanting flowering dogwoods, one in the front and one in the back. The place would have sold for a fortune in any other city, but nothing cost a fortune in Hope Springs. It was the nineties, and Miriam had carried a worn-out blue backpack on her lap all the way from the east full of twenty dollar bills. If the realtor found the arrangement suspicious, she didn't let on.

It was in this house that the couple would go on to raise not one child but four. Cara, their first, had nestled deep in the center of Miriam's body even before they journeyed cross-country. Cara was expressive from the moment she was born. From the womb, according to Miriam, who had to put up with her incessant kicking. Miriam was unmistakably present in the prominence of her nose, the roundness of her face, and the texture of her hair; however, her most striking feature, her periwinkle eyes, mirrored her father's.

After Cara, came Ada. Months after the second daughter was conceived, thick rivulets of blood streamed out from between Miriam's legs, a sure sign, she thought, that the life in her womb had come to an end. Before the couple could mourn, however, the doctor put an ice-cold stethoscope to her stretch-marked belly and listened. There, hidden behind her mother's frantic heartbeat, was the little pitter-patter of Ada's twelve-week-old heart, pumping along. When the second daughter was born, she had brown skin that reminded Miriam of her father. Though it would fade into a softer olive by the time she was a teenager, her dark eyes and thick eyebrows would always remain reminiscent of a family her mother had long ago left behind.

The third child and their only son seemed to appear between one second and the next. Cara was six years old when they brought Gage home. And it wasn't until seven years later, when Richard received a phone call from a lawyer in Detroit, that a ten-month-old Meena would be hand delivered to their doorstep and placed with the utmost care and a sigh of relief into their open arms. At that moment, Miriam and Richard knew their family was complete.

1

Ada was dreaming about towering ivory spires and a red moon when the song woke her. It infiltrated her dreams and brought her consciousness back to her bed. Suddenly, she could feel the sheets wrapped around her legs, her head pressing into her pillow. She opened her eyes.

The light of dawn had not yet found the cracks between her window frame and her blinds. Her clock read four thirteen AM. For a disorienting moment, she couldn't even hear the singing anymore. Then, there it was again, as clear as day. She looked over at Cara's sleeping figure. Her sister hadn't even budged.

She listened for noises in the hallway, telltale signs that other people in her household had been jostled awake by this melodious voice, but there were none. This seemed odd. Ada was one of the deeper sleepers in her family, and the sound had been loud enough to wake her up. It seemed to reverberate through the very air. A low, steady humming. Try as she could, it was impossible to pick out words. Finally, convinced it wasn't coming from inside the house, she rose and headed for the window.

Blue light illuminated the road and unlit houses, the

clustered trees, and the sprawling mountains in the distance. Nothing stood out immediately—there were no lit windows nor cars driving by—but as her eyes adjusted to the dawn, beyond the neighborhood and Jackson Drive and even beyond the forest, she saw one figure towering far above the rest. Specter-like from the distance, Ada was perplexed by the sheer size of it. The more she stared, the more it began to look like a woman, a woman five times as tall as the Cascade Mountains.

Doubting her own senses, Ada walked over to Cara's bed and shook her. "Hey," she said. "Hey, wake up. I think there's a giant outside."

Cara mumbled and groaned, annoyed, but Ada didn't give up.

"What?" Cara finally snapped, cracking open an eye. "What time is it?"

"I think there's a giant outside."

"What?" Cara pushed herself up on her elbows, her expression twisted in annoyance.

"Come look. Tell me if you see it, too."

Reluctantly, Cara sat up, the cold air hitting her like a bucket of ice water. "I swear if this is a joke, you're so dead."

Ada walked over to the window. It was almost five, and the sky was beginning to brighten. "There by the mountains, can you see her?" She stepped aside to give her sister space.

Cara stared for a moment, completely expressionless. Then, "Holy shit. Did you tell Mom and Dad?"

"No, I just woke up," Ada said with a sigh of relief. "Can you hear her?" she asked wide-eyed.

"What?" Cara tore her eyes from the silhouette.

"Can you hear her?" Ada said again. "She's singing."

2

"No, I can't hear her. You should get Mom and Dad, like, now." Cara held steadfast by the window as if the giant would disappear if she turned away.

Ada reappeared minutes later, groggy parents in tow. Too late, Cara realized they could've let their father sleep. A non-practitioner, Richard would see nothing even as he crowded around the window with them.

"Jesus," their mother said, catching sight of the figure. "I haven't seen a giant in ages." Noticing her husband staring blankly into space, she patted him on the arm. "There seems to be a giant standing right over there by the mountains."

"What's it doing?" he asked, gaze fixed somewhere on the horizon.

"She's just standing there." Miriam shrugged. "Time moves slower for them, you know, being so big and all."

"So she's just going to stand there?" Cara jumped in.

"Well, I don't know, dear. We'd have to ask her."

"Can you hear her singing?" Ada asked again, hopeful.

"Singing?" Her mother turned to her, startled. "I can't hear anything."

"Am I hallucinating, then?" She wrung her hands. "Her singing was what woke me up."

Miriam stared at her for a moment, then turned back to the giant. "Do you see how hazy she looks?" The girls nodded. "It's because she's behind a veil. Do you remember I taught you about magical veils before?" She turned to her husband to explain, "Magical beings put up barriers between themselves and the human world to live undisturbed. It's like creating a parallel dimension running along the same space and time. Some are separated by small degrees and are actually quite easy to stumble through, but others, like the giants' realm, are hard to traverse."

"How did she get here, then?" This was Ada, already forgetting her original question.

"And why?" Cara added.

Miriam shook her head. "Again, we'd have to ask her. It is quite strange for her to be here, but because she is still partially behind the veil, we can only see a hazy silhouette and shouldn't be able to hear anything she says." She turned to Ada. "Maybe you're a gifted traveler if you are able to hear her even now."

"A gifted traveler," Ada mumbled under her breath.

"That might be the case. It would certainly explain why you can hear her when no one else can," Miriam said. After a pause, she asked, "What is she saying?"

"I can't make it out. It sounds like humming."

Miriam assessed the situation.

"I don't think giants speak English in the first place," she finally said. "Let me think about how we can communicate, and we'll talk again tonight. For now, see if you can get a little more sleep, girls. You still have classes to attend today."

* * *

Ada rushed down the stairs with her backpack in hand, heading for the door. Cara was waiting for her in the driver's seat of their Jetta, having come down a few minutes before.

"Bye, Mom!" she called. "See you later."

"Have a good day," she could hear Miriam reply as the front door slammed shut.

In the car, Cara shook her head.

"What?" Ada asked, settling into her seat and adjusting the

4

air vents. It was February, and the morning air was frigid. "We're not even late. It's just seven twenty-eight," she said, pointing at the dashboard clock.

"Yeah, barely," Cara replied shortly as she pulled out of the driveway.

"Hey, she's still there," Ada said, leaning forward to get a better view. From the car, they could only manage to see the bottom of the giant's legs, stretching up into the sky like skyscrapers. "What do you think she's waiting for?"

"What makes you think she's waiting for something?" Cara asked and turned onto Jackson Drive.

"What else could she be doing, just standing there?" Ada asked, sinking further into her seat.

Cara glanced at her sister stone-faced. "You know time passes slower for them."

"Oh yeah, cause they're so big." Ada sat back. "That's wild, but still, how much time would be a long time for her to be standing there? A week? A month? Should we ask her?"

"I don't think she'd be able to hear us," Cara mumbled.

"But I can hear her. She can probably hear me."

"She's so tall, you'd have to fly up there or something."

"Yeah, I guess so." Ada was silent for a second before muttering, "I'll ask Mom."

Cara sighed. To her, most things Ada said or did just sounded like trouble. Cara was a precision instrument. A scalpel. A fine point pen, extra fine. She needed specificity, clarity, predictability. The same propensity often rendered her inflexible and overly sensitive.

Even so, she always had a clear view of who she was and where she was going. After high school, she enrolled in one of the country's top plant biology undergraduate programs, located conveniently within a thirty-minute commute from their house. She minored in Latin and Hebrew, despite her counselor's attempts to convince her otherwise, and graduated with honors. Now, she was completing a master's program at the same university and working part-time in a tenured biochemistry professor's lab.

Ada, on the other hand, had only agreed to attend college so close to home because her mother just short of begged her to. For the life of her, she couldn't understand why. Miriam and Richard were doting but not overprotective. Cara had turned twenty-four in July, and Ada twenty-two in November. Cara had already been at the university for six years and would probably stay and teach there if they gave her a job. Already in her last semester of undergraduate studies, Ada couldn't wait until she never had to step foot on campus again.

A creature of habit, Cara prickled at change and hated surprises. In her mind, she saw no real reason to leave her beloved Hope Springs, cradled in the curve of a mountain, shrouded in foliage and fog. Just like her parents, she felt safe, protected. Nothing within her sought more.

Even Gage, who would be graduating from high school that Spring, had selected their university as his first choice. Granted, he would likely receive generous financial aid, but Ada could not understand her family's complacency. Their home was beautiful but small. Safe, but boring. She loved it dearly, but she would give anything to know something more.

Rarely did they leave the state. Miriam signed off on field trips reluctantly when they were growing up and still seemed anxious when Gage had to travel anywhere for a soccer game. Ada had first noticed when she was twelve and had since wondered what in the world was her mother so afraid of?

It seemed that the very things that excited Ada frightened Miriam. Once Ada graduated, there would be no holding her back. She would move to a city so big it would be impossible to find her in the crowd. Maybe she would move halfway across the world. There was only one place she was wary of: wherever her mother had come from. In recent years, she had realized how strange it was that she didn't know where that was.

Miriam talked vaguely about living in New York, but any casual observer would see that her stories didn't add up. Ada had found writing in Arabic in her mother's drawer before, and heard her talk about going to the coast of the Mediterranean Sea as a child. That was the extent of the clues her daughter had to go off of.

Ada, so desperate for novelty, was sure she was dreaming when the giant appeared before her eyes. That she had somehow willed this being into existence. That her desperate longing for the strange and unusual had called the giant forth from behind the thick veil. Or that she had dropped a seed between the frozen Cascades and watered it with her thirst, and from it had grown this colossal visitor, this looming presence. So focused was she on the giant that she didn't hear a single word her professors said that day.

***

Cara wouldn't be done at work until after five, so Ada took the bus home. When she arrived, the house was empty. Her parents were at work—her father owned a flower shop and her mother a construction company—and her younger

7

siblings were at their respective classes. Sitting down at the dining room table, Ada opened her computer determined to find a way to communicate with their otherworldly visitor.

Thankfully, she knew exactly where to look. It was their mother's life's work, transmitting magical knowledge into an encrypted online database for preservation. Always being added upon by a community of hundreds of practitioners around the world, the site was accessible by referral only. Its wisdom was not for the random peddler. Needless to say, Miriam's children took it completely for granted.

Ada had been searching for little over an hour and gone off track, clicking into a description of time jumps when she scrolled to the related terms at the bottom and saw the words *astral projection*. Clicking the link out of curiosity, it wasn't long before a word caught her eye. She read it in her mother's voice, *traveler*. "Projection spells usually require three or more practitioners for the safety of the subject." The description began. "However, some practitioners possess remarkable skills in traversing dimensions and are often referred to as travelers. These persons may have the ability to slip in and out of their physical forms at will. Travelers may have an affinity for other transportive spells. See also: *planetary links, wormholes, rifts in spacetime.*"

If she really was a traveler, and that was why she could hear the giant's voice, this entry was exactly what she was looking for. Further into the page, it said beings disconnected from the human world by twenty or more degrees, such as giants and titans, experience many more physical dimensions than humans would, including the plane of astral projection. Because of this, it is much easier to contact them within a state of projection, as communication becomes intuitive rather than linguistic.

Engrossed in her research, Ada jumped when the front door opened, and her father walked in with Meena in tow.

He had brought back a big bouquet of pink, purple, and red flowers from the shop. His way of giving a second life to those on the verge of wilting he could no longer sell in good conscience. "Hey, sweetie," he said, leaning down to kiss the top of her head. "How're you doing?"

"Good," she mumbled. "What are those?"

"Mostly begonias, some anemone, and rhododendron," he replied.

Meena sat in the chair across from Ada, pulling out her homework. She always completed it as soon as she got home.

"They'll last a couple of days, not much more. Can you put them in water, please?" their dad asked.

Ada got up reluctantly, shutting her laptop and following him into the kitchen. She would have to wait for her mother to get home in a few hours to discuss her findings. In the meantime, she helped her dad prep for dinner, chopping vegetables and picking herbs.

Cara arrived first, replacing Ada as the sous chef, then Miriam and Gage, who had just finished soccer practice. He had joined the team his senior year of high school, an odd move but overdue given his stellar performance. Their parents liked to say they didn't understand why it took so long, but his sisters knew he would much rather stay home playing video games than train after school for hours. It was a wonder his friends had managed to convince him.

Ada let her mother set down her things and greet the rest of the family before broaching the subject.

"Mom, did you come up with a way to talk to the giant?"

She didn't wait for an answer before continuing, "Cause I think I did."

"Oh, no, honey. I was so busy today I completely forgot. I'll look into it tonight," Miriam replied, apologetically stroking her hair.

"It's fine. I actually found something that might work," Ada repeated, the excitement seeping into her voice.

Miriam's busy hands paused as she focused her attention on her.

"Really? What is it?" she asked.

"Astral projection," Ada blurted. Miriam's brow immediately furrowed. "It says communication is intuitive, so it doesn't matter that we don't speak her language."

"Honey, no," her mother said, already turning away.

"No, listen! You said I was a gifted traveler, and the spell only takes three people." Ada scrambled, but her mom was still shaking her head.

Cara snorted, coming up behind her, snack in hand.

"Are you an idiot?" she asked. "You can't just cast an astral projection spell. It takes years of practice. People dedicate their lives to it."

"Sweetie, I'm sorry, but astral projection spells are risky even for seasoned practitioners." Miriam seconded. "If I agreed to try, it would take months to prepare you for your first attempt." Ignoring Ada's protesting gaze, she continued, "I promise I'll look for another *safer* way to communicate with her this week, but any kind of projection is out of the question."

Knowing better than to argue with her mother at the end of a long day when fatigue and hunger abounded, Ada bit her tongue and kept quiet during dinner. Once again, she had become keenly aware of Miriam's unjustified fear. The sour taste of injustice persisted through the night.

Before going to sleep, she turned to Cara. "If you and Gage help, we can still try astral projection."

Her sister rolled her eyes. "Sorry, no," she said. "I don't want my body to be taken over by astral plane gremlins. Also, you know Gage has no interest in magic, so good luck getting him to join you."

"Shut up, astral plane gremlins are *not* a thing," Ada responded with her own eye-roll.

Cara scoffed, rolling onto her side as she said, "You suck at research, dude. Gremlins are the main concern when projecting, but whatever. It doesn't matter because we're not projecting. Mom will find another way to communicate with the giant, so just forget it."

Ada couldn't forget it, and she tried. The giant's voice seemed to grow louder and clearer at night. Memories from earlier in the day raced through her mind.

Travelers, the wiki had said, could slip in and out of the astral plane at will. Laying in her bed, Ada tried to concentrate. All she had to do was separate her consciousness from her body. *Magic is a witch's will*, Miriam would say to them when they were younger. All they had to do if they wanted to practice their magic was concentrate all of their energy on their thoughts and will them into existence.

Without any instructions or guidance, Ada could only rely on instinct. She visualized herself like a spirit, a soul overlaid on her body. Drawing on meditation methods, Ada forced herself into a state of hyper-awareness, zeroing in on her toes, feet, ankles, leading to the crown of her head. *My body is but a vehicle.*

In her mind's eye, her body shimmered and rippled like water. It felt like she was rising, floating. Light flooded her mind's eye, so bright it was blinding. Then, suddenly, a thick dark fog enveloped her. She was being suffocated; buried alive, the air around her thick like mud. She tried to dig through it, but as soon as she parted the sludge, it would reconstitute around her again.

She ventured a look back from whence she came and saw a ray of light breaking through the darkness. Concentrating, she willed her body to follow it, trusting nothing could be worse than where she was then. With a start, Ada awoke in her bed. Her body felt too warm. Feverish. The giant's song filled the dawn-drenched room.

2

The following day, Ada's mind kept wandering toward the fog that had enveloped her the night before. Her muscles had felt strangely sore when she woke up, like she had done an hour of kickboxing after quitting years before.

Thinking about it objectively, she felt that she had boggled the projection attempt somehow, and her consciousness had entered a plane it shouldn't have. Or it was all a dream. Neither theory was convincing. Ada had started self-identifying as a traveler from the moment she understood what it was. It had just felt right when her mother had said it. She might have lacked evidence to prove it, but there wasn't any to the contrary yet, either.

Determined, Ada searched for spells that would let her better control her projection, her research bleeding into class periods and lunchtime alike. She jumped into an archive of transportive spells and their complimentary incantations, or boosters, as Miriam called them. After bookmarking an acceleration spell and finding a booster for intuitive communication, Ada then turned to the term that had been bugging her since her little heart-to-heart with Cara before bed: *astral plane gremlins.*

Of course they were a thing.

A heavily stylized image graced the upper right side of their page. Heavily stylized, Ada assumed, because it said within the first paragraph that, being creatures purely of the astral plane, they had no shape humans could perceive, instead appearing as shadowy blurs. The picture on the page was exactly what you would expect a gremlin to be: small, wrinkled, and irritated. However much she sympathized with their adverse representation, the more she read, the more she came to regard them as a real threat.

They originated from the Mistlands, whatever that meant, and had gotten stuck in the astral plane because of a failed bid to reach the Midlands, the earthly realm where humans lived. The journey was nearly impossible to make in the physical plane, but the Mistlands were apparently so terrible that the gremlins, desperately hoping to escape, left their bodies behind and traveled to the Midlands as specters in hopes of encountering an underprepared projecting practitioner they could rob of a physical body.

In the astral plane, the ties spirits have to their earthly vessels glow like stars. Most projector protection spells focus on dimming or completely hiding that light from everyone but its owner, who must keep sight of it if they ever want to find their body again. As she read, Ada's skin pricked with goosebumps. She had seen the light from her body quite clearly the night before and was sure any gremlins in the vicinity had as well. She added finding a spell to conceal it to her to-do list.

Spells were made up of basic symbols and natural elements, sometimes also movements and phrases. When combined together, they were larger than the sum of their parts. Cara's unnatural talent for memorization served her well during their magical training, but Ada sometimes struggled. She was the type that had to understand the reasoning behind why some things were included while others were not to make them stick.

Once she understood how the puzzle pieces fit, Ada loved mixing them up and creating new combinations. Because of this, her magic was a patchwork of Eastern and Western traditions, religious imagery often alongside their pagan counterparts. This was a core tenet of Miriam's magic education: interdisciplinary and cross-theological experimentation. After all, when magic is the witch's will, it matters not whether she uses crystals or crosses, rhyme or reason, English or Thai. But as much as Miriam encouraged them to learn outside of traditional confines, Ada's eclectic style bothered her.

While she allowed her daughter to improvise spells fairly often, she drew the line creating new symbols of her own. It was something Ada would do often as a child until her mother's warnings grew more heated. It was dangerous, she explained, because of the lack of consistency. Made-up symbols weren't guaranteed to do the things you wanted them to do. Ada might have gotten away with it for a while, but spells could go wrong with a single misplaced brush stroke.

When she found scribbled spells on her fifteen-year-old daughter's notebook pages, Miriam ripped them out and burned them, threatening to feed Ada a magic-blocking potion so she could never perform spells again.

Ada, throat tight with righteous fury, slammed her bedroom door and searched the magic database for such a potion.

15

Unfortunately, she found many. Since then, she only traced such spells with her fingertip on nearby surfaces, where they left no trace. This kind of magic she only ever did alone.

* * *

Ada didn't head home after class that day. The bus deposited her in the deserted parking lot of a diner off the two-lane highway that led out of town. With overcast skies, its unlit neon sign and dirty windows gave it an abandoned feeling. Anyone else might have found it eerie, but Miriam and her children were frequent visitors.

Once the coast was clear, Ada crossed the road and stepped into the woods just opposite. Crisp leaves crunched underfoot as she made her way through the trees. A late afternoon breeze brushed the back of her neck, sending a chill down her spine. She sped up, knowing the brisk walk would warm her up in no time. The indie rock blasting through her earphones set the pace.

As the ground fell away, giving form to a hidden valley, a wide gray structure materialized in the far left, tucked away behind clusters of towering pines. It was a hunk of a building, short and to the point, nothing more than a big cement cube. As children, they would always end up at the clubhouse after school, purportedly for daily magic lessons.

The siblings probably spent more time reading comic books and playing than learning, but it was, nonetheless, the best setting for spell casting they had. The mezzanine that passed for a second floor was lined with shelves from end to end, floor to ceiling, and held all the ingredients a witch could possibly need, from dried bat wings to bakuli pods. The windowsill housed bunches of quartz, amethyst, and hypnotizing strings of orgone, all charging in the fading afternoon light.

The air was warmer inside, and the quiet emptiness as familiar as her own bedroom. Ada settled into the spacey first floor with a stick of charcoal and got to drawing the complex magical circles needed for astral projection. Incorporating all the booster spells she had researched was tedious work, and nearly an hour had passed by the time she checked and double-checked each stroke. Heart pounding, she stepped in the middle, laid down, and hoped for the best.

Every spell Ada cast felt empty at first. Whether it was rigorously scientific or absolute drivel, she had never felt what magic books called a spell's innate power. It was the same with this circle; until she instilled her energy in it, it held no power.

It was like a golem, all built and shaped, waiting for an incantation. A light bulb waiting for electricity. Spells always seemed to be waiting, holding their breath, until she decided to give them life. Because of this, she had never quite understood the way other practitioners wrote about magic, as if it had a mind of its own. The genie waiting to twist your every word into a terrible wish. To Ada, magic had always been forgiving and intuitive, easily responding to thoughts she had yet to put into words.

She lay in her circle and pictured her energy trickling from her body into the charcoal lines. The circle drank and drank and drank until finally, it started emitting a golden light, and Ada found that she didn't have to concentrate, at all. As if gravity's pull had been reversed, she drifted up from her body, weightless. Noticing a haze lingering around her that hadn't been present last time, she instinctively knew that it was the protection spell she had cast.

Her gaze directed upward, Ada willed herself to propel toward the giant. In a second, she was enveloped in the same darkness as before, squeezing her as if she were at the deepest depths of the ocean, the pressure almost unbearable. As soon as it had started, however, it stopped. She had traversed through it much faster, coming out the other side as she hadn't been able to before. Now, she could see the giant standing by the mountains, blocking the setting sun. The light passed through her like she wasn't really there, her body shimmering like the film of oil on water.

Ada propelled herself forward until she was a few meters from the giant's shoulder. The giant's eyes were fixed ahead. Remembering her intuitive communication booster, Ada tried projecting her thoughts.

Hello.

No movement. Ada flew closer, up to eye level.

Hello? Can you hear me?

If they had no way to communicate, Ada worried her troubles would be for naught. The giant didn't move. At the risk of seeming rude, Ada floated right up to the giant's eye, obstructing her view.

Can you see me?

The giant's eyes finally focused on her.

Yes.

The voice was like nothing Ada had ever heard before. In fact, she didn't think she actually heard it, at all. The giant's reply just appeared inside Ada's mind like a thought.

The giant's eyes became fixed, again, on the horizon. Except, Ada realized, they weren't fixed on the horizon, but downward…as if toward the town.

She whipped around to look in the same direction only to get the breath knocked out of her.

Have you come to look at it, too? The giant asked. *I haven't seen anything like it in some time. Since before the veils were erected, perhaps.*

Ada turned to look in every direction, anxiety starting to vibrate at her core. The astral plane offered unparalleled visibility. She could see more than was possible with the human eye. The beautiful landscape extended far beyond the misty Cascade mountains to the foamy grey waters of the seaside.

Then, *why?* Why? Where Hope Springs sat, when she should've had a bird's eye view of her house and the club and the school, why was it covered by a thick black layer of sludge? It blanketed the town like a super-condensed smog.

What is it? She finally asked.

The giant's eye shifted again toward her, moving as slowly as her monumental size required. *Well, it's darkness, isn't it?*

Why is it there? That's my home. Ada said.

She felt the pang in the middle of her chest radiate outwards like heat. This was how emotions worked in the astral plane. There was no brain to contain them. No neural network to confine them. The giant must've felt it, too, a tiny prick like a mosquito landing on her astral layer.

It has to originate somewhere. Usually from beings of the lower world: Mistlanders, most likely.

What does that mean? Ada asked, confusion emanating from her as clearly as her words did.

Don't you see the center? The giant asked. Ada turned to look at the blackness, and sure enough, it seemed to agglomerate in the woods. *They must be there. Kill them, and it will kill the darkness.*

Kill? Ada asked, confusion replaced by fear.

The only way to rid yourself of darkness is to destroy its source. This is something I thought Midlanders knew. The giant said.

I don't know anything about darkness. Ada replied as she bowed her head.

The giant considered what was in front of her.

You say this is your home, but travelers don't have homes. She said. *If you don't want to kill the darkness that shrouds it, you could always escape behind the veil.*

It occurred to Ada then that lies cannot exist within the astral plane. They give themselves away to others immediately. Yet, she braced herself, steeling her nerves and said, *I'm not escaping from anything.*

A transparent bluff. Ada wasn't someone people would hedge their bets on in a fight. Broad-shouldered but delicate, she took her magic studies less seriously than her morning skincare routine and had never learned anything more difficult than a healing spell for scrapes and burns. And yet, there was no doubt in the giant's words when she spoke.

Then you must kill them. Behind the veil, we could not see. Here, the magical energy is high, so the veil is thin. I noticed the darkness and came out to look. When I stepped into your world, I saw that the darkness is not just here. I see it in the distance, again and again, covering space like rain clouds. They seem to be multiplying, dividing like cells. Unbridled growth becomes malignant.

You have strong magic for a Midlander. Maybe you could defeat them. She said, and her eyes turned to Ada, squinting as if she was trying to get a good look. *That is a strange*

20

magic you are using, somewhat like a Titan's. You remind me of the Beginning—these words were accompanied by a tinge of nostalgia. *When the world was young, no two magics were the same. Then the Titans left, and the Midlanders saw only us. Because all giants use one magic, you thought you had to do the same.*

A hint of bleak amusement. She continued.

But Midlanders are not giants. For years, it seems they have tried to fit their magics into two or three molds. You have been fortunate enough to escape their oppressive machinations and more fortunate still to have received the gift of the Void, which few Midlanders through history have possessed.

Sensing Ada's confusion, the giant cryptically elaborated. *The Void. The Abyss. The Nothing. The There-Is-Not. The Swallowing Half.*

A half of a whole?

The image the giant projected into her mind was hard to interpret, except as, *The light?*

More than that. If the Void is the one who takes, this is the Half that Gives.

Every word tied Ada's mind into knots harder to undo than the last. *Can't you help us?* It was a desperate venture. She would have begged if she thought there was a chance the giant would say yes.

Why would I? We do not meddle in other creatures' affairs. I have done enough already. The Mistlanders are no threat to us. A ripple ran through the astral plane like a rumble; the giant was moving.

Where are you going?

The giant did not answer.

Her body disappeared behind the veil as if plunging into a

21

pool of water. Try as she could, Ada could not see beyond it.

She imagined what it would feel like to follow her for just a brief second, then was consumed with guilt. Turning back toward Hope Springs, she zeroed in on the source of the pollution and was soon gone, too.

Mist drifted over the Cascades.

3

Cara had gotten out early from the lab that day; the professor she worked with was attending a seminar a few towns over and she had no pending tasks. She was in her car just a few blocks from her home when her phone rang, interrupting one of her favorite songs. Slightly irritated, she used one hand to accept the call, trying to keep her eyes on the road.

"Hello?" she said.

"Cara." Ada's voice was just a breath. "Come to the club. It's an emergency. I'm not kidding. Gage is in danger."

Cara's first instinct was to treat anything Ada said as a nuisance, but something about her tone seemed off. "What are you talking about, Ada? Come home, and we'll talk."

"No." A loud clatter echoed as something fell at the other end of the line. "Shit."

"Are you okay?" Cara asked, concern growing heavier on her chest by the second. "Ada? Just wait for me. I'll be at the club in ten. Don't move."

"I'm fine," Ada said shakily. "I'll meet you by the highway, so don't get out of the car. We need to hurry. Call Gage. Tell him to set up a protection circle wherever he is and not leave it for any reason."

"Ada, you're not making sense. Why the hell would Gage need a protection circle?" Cara asked, beginning to panic. "Have you called Mom?"

"She didn't pick up," her sister said. "She must be at work. My phone is about to die. Call Gage, okay? I'll see you in ten."

The line went dead.

Cara cursed repeatedly, reaching for her phone.

"Hey Siri, call Gage." The phone rang and rang, but no answer. "Hey Siri, call Mom." No answer.

Worst-case scenarios ran through her head. Had Ada botched a dangerous spell and cursed Gage unintentionally? Could she have overheard some of unhinged classmates planning to hurt him? Cara pressed down harder on the gas pedal.

Within minutes, she pulled up by the path to the club, veering into the soft shoulder. There, she waited, cycling between calling their mother and brother with no luck. Ada's phone also sent her to voicemail, likely dead. Cara debated calling her father. She would regret it if this all turned out to be one of Ada's usual messes.

After fifteen minutes of watching the clock tick by and getting automated messages over and over again, she couldn't hold it any longer. She got out of the car and started walking purposefully down the forest path. It was almost seven at night, and the sun had set. Her way was illuminated only by the blue light of dusk and her phone's flashlight. Every passing moment amplified her anxiety.

"Ada?" she called. "Ada?"

Something moved in the periphery ahead, and she stopped, frightened. Something about its shape, however, convinced

24

her to take a few steps forward.

"Ada!" Cara yelled. Her sister was leaning against a tree, her knees buckled below, her shoulder braced against the trunk. "Are you okay? What's wrong? Are you hurt?"

Ada swatted her worried hands away.

"I'm fine," she said unconvincingly, her face scrunched with the effort of rising to her feet. "We need to get to Gage. Now. Someone's going to hurt him."

"What?" Cara exclaimed, much more concerned with helping her ailing sister. "Did they hurt you, too? We need Mom."

"No," Ada grunted and moved forward with Cara's support. "We don't have enough time. Text her to meet us by the soccer field. I'll explain on the way."

It took a full ten minutes to get Ada into the car, her limbs weak and uncooperative. "Are you sure you're okay?" Cara asked, glancing at her sister as she turned the car back onto the road.

"I have literally never been in so much pain in my life," she replied.

"Did they attack you?" Cara repeated. "Whoever is going after Gage?"

They were breaking the speed limit.

"No," Ada finally admitted. "Apparently, excruciating pain is a common side effect of astral projection."

Cara's face went blank for a second, then an angry glint appeared in her eye.

"What did you just say?" she asked and shook her head, shooting her sister a searing glare. "You did not. I am literally in awe at how reckless you are! You disobeyed our mother and have put yourself *and* Gage in danger. You don't deserve to practice magic."

"Hey!" Ada shouted. The effort sent a sharp pain through her diaphragm. "I didn't endanger anyone. Gage would be in danger whether or not I projected. And *because* I did, now we can protect him."

"I don't believe a word you're saying," Cara grumbled, but her foot didn't ease up on the gas pedal.

"Why would I ever lie about something like this?" Ada half-whined. "If you hadn't noticed, the giant is gone."

Indeed, the Cascades were unobstructed.

"Did you talk to her?" Cara asked. Her suspicions were waning. Her irritation wasn't.

"Yeah, she's the one that told me Gage was in danger," Ada said and sat up in her seat. The burning in her limbs starting to dull.

It wasn't the whole truth, but she knew that going into any more detail would just lead to more pointless arguments.

"Are you feeling better?" Cara asked after a moment of silence.

"Yeah," Ada said, leaning forward and pointing. "Pull into the parking lot there. We can walk from here."

"Where are we going?" Cara asked.

They were still a block from the high school, but she did as Ada said.

"The woods," she said. "They should still be at their camp. We have enough time to intercept them."

Ada had already thrown the passenger side door open and started walking as fast as she could with her limp. Cara scrambled out of the car behind her.

"Can you cast a stealth spell on us?" Ada asked. "We can't get caught."

Cara nodded, a knot growing in her throat, and held out her hand. They paused at the forest's edge while she outlined a simple spell circle on the soil underfoot and muttered an incantation under her breath.

"What happens if we get caught?" she asked, against her better judgment.

"Honestly?" Ada's tone of voice made Cara immediately regret asking. "We might die." Catching the look on her sister's face, she began to backtrack. "I'm kidding." Silence. "Actually, I'm not. But look," Ada said, turning to look her straight in the eye. "I have a list of defensive spells on my phone that we can use to trap them, and then Mom can help us deal with them. We just have to make sure they can't hurt Gage."

"Let me see that list."

* * *

"I can't believe you're criticizing my spell list right now," Ada huffed, treading carefully through the forest underbrush.

"I'm just saying, these are really advanced spells. You could have chosen some simpler ones," Cara said from close behind.

"All spells are simple, Cara," her sister said dismissively. "Have you ever met a spell you couldn't cast?"

'I usually stick to those I feel qualified to do," she griped.

"Then just think of it as a challenge, a step outside your comfort zone." As she spoke, Ada caught sight of a familiar sequence of trees.

"It's called a comfort zone for a reason," Cara started to say, but she was promptly shushed. "We have a stealth spell on us, you know?"

"Yeah, but they do magic, too," Ada whispered. "I don't know what counter-incantations they've cast around their camp. Would you be able to tell if our spell was undone?"

"Yeah, obviously. I would feel it."

"Okay, good," Ada said and advanced slowly toward the tree line.

If she was being honest, she would tell Cara that she wasn't sure where she was going, or who she was looking for, or how she was planning on dealing with them. All she could do was hope that she hadn't led them down the wrong path. That she would find exactly what she was dreading the most: the masked men.

"What the fuck?" Cara whispered, catching sight of the figures beyond the bushes. "What are those?"

"Be quiet," Ada hissed.

"We have a stealth spell," her sister repeated, but lowered her voice significantly. "What are they?"

Standing just a few yards away were what looked like two adult men with black wool masks pulled over their faces down to their necks. They were completely covered, wearing black turtlenecks, pants, gloves and shoes. Not an inch of their skin was exposed. Their heads were bowed together as if in deep conversation, but the girls were too far away to make out words.

"I think they're Mistlanders," Ada said.

"That is literally impossible." Cara scoffed.

"You know what Mistlanders are?" her sister asked.

"Don't you?" she shot back. "They're creatures that live beyond the veil, in the Mistlands."

"Wait," Ada said, giving her a perplexed look. "Where the giants live?"

Cara rolled her eyes. "No, you idiot," she said. "Don't you even know how veils work?" Seeing her sister's blank stare, she explained, "We have them to both sides. On one side, there's the giants, the Highlands, then on the other, there's the Mistlands. We're in the middle."

"Midlanders," Ada interjected.

"Yeah, the Midlands." Cara shook her head. "I can't believe you astral projected, and you don't know where your own two feet are planted."

Ada ignored the jab. "So, will our spells work on them?" she asked.

"Of course." Cara paused, mostly sure. "Let's create a circle around them. I'll draw the power zapping spell every three feet, and you draw the trapping spell every two. I'll go right, you go left, and we'll meet back here."

They set out. After drawing the sigils around the spells a couple of times based on the instructions, Ada quickly got the hang of it. By the time she was halfway through, she even considered adding her own adjustments, but her mother's venomous warning resounded in her mind and stopped her.

When they both met back at their starting point, Cara turned to her, holding out her hand.

"Ready?" she asked.

"Ready," Ada said and took it.

Their energy started flowing immediately, first clashing slightly, then merging.

As soon as the magic began to activate, the Mistlanders' heads snapped up. They felt it, too.

Cara willed her magic to travel quicker.

The Mistlanders jumped to their feet and started sprinting straight at them. Had the stealth spell had failed or were they aiming at the spot the magic was originating from?

It didn't really matter. They needed to finish putting up the circle before it was too late.

Cara felt their energy reach the furthest end. The circle was about to close.

Then, something rammed into her back with the force of a football player.

Both girls were thrown forward, their hands coming apart. The flow of magic faltered as they hit the ground. Their hands and forearms smarted from the fall.

Cara turned to see a third Mistlander standing behind them. The other two were pressed up against the barrier right in front of them waiting for it to come down.

"Finish the circle!" Cara yelled. "I'll distract him."

Ada barely heard her over the ringing in her head. The pain from projecting was nowhere near gone and was now amplified by her injuries. She was bruised and scraped, but even without Cara's orders, she wouldn't have let the spell fall.

She reached over and pressed her bloody left hand directly over the nearest trapping sigil, channeling her magic through it. The barrier stopped falling, instead rebuilding.

The Mistlanders noticed the shift within seconds. They turned to run to the gap still open at the other side. Ada was acting on pure instinct. The only spell she could cast that quickly was the type she would usually have to hide, but she had no other choice. She began tracing new symbols into the dirt with her dominant hand.

The imagery was rudimentary. First, two stick men, then lines across their limbs. The Mistlanders inside the circle crumbled. Their cries didn't sound human. Then, the noise was drowned out by a scream. Cara's.

A blinding light flashed from where she had been fighting. When Ada turned, she saw her sister floating a few feet off the ground. The Mistlander was standing in front of her. His hands were held out in front of his body as if they were keeping her afloat. From her body emanated a beautiful golden light.

No, it wasn't light. It was thicker. More viscous than water. More dazzling than sunlight. The image the giant had projected came to mind. *The Half that Gives.*

Her attention was forcefully brought back to the barrier. One of the Mistlanders was escaping. She channeled her energy into the spell with renewed force, closing the gap within seconds. Only one Mistlander was still trapped. She turned back to the one attacking Cara. After activating her made-up spell against him, he, too, fell to the ground.

Cara remained suspended. Ada rushed to her feet and ran toward her. The temperature rose the closer she got until it felt like the hottest day of Summer. A sound to her right gave away the escaped Mistlander's movements. He ran to his fallen comrade, the one that had extracted the light from Cara. Ada braced to fight, but they fled in the opposite direction of where she was standing. A colorful vortex appeared in front of them—a portal—and closed soon after they disappeared inside it.

Ada was left standing in the forest alone, staring up at her unconscious sister. The shimmering golden mass that illuminated the night was spreading out further from Cara's body. As she watched, it started fading and disappearing into nothingness. The sight was gut-wrenching.

She couldn't explain why, but tears welled up in Ada's eyes.

She had never heard of anything like this, but it all felt so wrong, like looking at a mangled body. She had to get this light back inside Cara, and she felt like she somehow knew how to. It didn't make total sense, but the situation was too dire to hesitate.

Ada took a deep breath and, just like the Mistlander had before, extended her arms toward Cara. She imagined the resistance of the mass against her hands, how it would feel to push against it; and to her relief, it started responding.

It gathered slowly toward Cara, but it was getting heavier by the second. Ada's wrists were sore. Her fingers were trembling. The tendons in her hands stood out as she funneled all her strength into them.

The golden light was responding, moving and collecting around its source. Just as she was running out of breath, the space between her shoulder blades painfully tight, it began to sink into Cara again.

Behind her, just then, a twig snapped.

The soccer team had been standing around one side of the field taking turns practicing penalty shots when a loud yell came from the forest across the street. They all paused to look, and Coach Byers had started shouting at them to concentrate when suddenly every light around them shattered. The field's floodlights, the streetlights nearby, the bulbs that lit the way to the locker room, all burst at the same time.

As they shrieked and jokingly grabbed at each other in the near-total darkness, the coach fished his phone out and turned on the flashlight. The boys followed the beam back to the bleachers, where more phone flashlights awaited. There, they started calling their parents and pretending to panic for social media content.

Only Gage remained quiet and removed. Just minuted before the scream, he had gotten a weird feeling. The wind carried over a familiar smell from the woods. The air felt electric. The hair on his arms was standing on end. Whatever was happening was undoubtedly magical.

When he finally reached his phone, his heart dropped. He had seventeen missed calls from Cara, three from Ada, and five from his mom. He pressed the most recent one to dial back.

"Gage? Honey, where are you?" Miriam asked frantically.

"I'm at the field still. I think there might be something going on in the woods," he said, careful not to let any of his teammates hear. "Have you talked to Cara and Ada?"

"No, I haven't. Stay where you are. I'm coming right now," she said and hung up without waiting for a reply.

Gage pretended to still be collecting his things while his teammates headed back into the locker rooms. When Coach Byers called out to him, Gage told him his mom was picking him up any minute and he might as well wait out here.

Sure enough, Miriam pulled into the nearby parking lot within moments, already having been on her way when he called.

"Have you seen your sisters?" she asked. "I think I saw their car back there."

"Not since breakfast," he replied, fastening his seatbelt. "I think I feel magic coming from the forest, though. That's probably them, isn't it?"

They pulled up by the Jetta and got out. Making their way through the dark forest, Gage wondered if his mom knew where she was going at first. Then, he realized the feeling in his chest was growing stronger. It was like an innate sense for magic. He could clearly feel them getting closer and closer to the source.

"Where's Meena?" he asked, trying to distract himself.

"At home. Safe," Miriam replied quickly.

Suddenly, the air seemed colder. The shadows of branches looming over them seemed more threatening. It hadn't occurred to him that any of them could be unsafe. He felt more like a child than he had in years. Was this the first time he had ever feared for his family's safety?

Before he could dwell on his thoughts, Gage noticed the air warming and the darkness dissipating ahead. A bright glare was peeking between the trees. It was as if all the light in Hope Springs had been taken and hoarded in that very spot. When his eyes adjusted, he recognized Ada standing with their back toward them, facing the brightness.

A thought darted through his brain: *that can't be good for her eyes*. It was like she was staring at the sun, both arms stretched toward it, asking to be lifted up. His mother gasped, but by the time he turned to ask what was wrong, she had run toward the light past Ada. When Gage followed her line of sight, he finally understood. It was Cara. She was running toward Cara.

Ada seemed to be in a trance, looking back and forth between Gage and Miriam as if not recognizing them. When they met his, Gage felt a pang of fear, immediately followed by one of guilt. His sister's eyes were wide and wild.

"Ada?" he whispered.

It took a second, but her face started registering other emotions. Confusion. Concern. Fear.

"Gage?" she asked and looked around to see Miriam behind her. "Mom? When did you get here? Help me get this back inside, Cara."

Back inside, Cara? Gage didn't understand. What were *they* even doing there? A sound to the right alerted him that they were not alone. While Miriam concentrated on Cara, adopting a similar stance as Ada had when they arrived, he followed a dim blue glow a few meters away. He thought nothing would've surprised him at this point, but he wasn't expecting to find a magical barrier with someone trapped inside. Or some*thing?*

Crouched at the circle's center, it could have been a black-clad mannequin. Gage inched closer to get a better look, but then it lunged. The creature's horrible face frightened him so much that he stumbled back and fell onto the ground. The barrier thankfully held, but it couldn't shield him from the image of the Mistlander aiming for his neck. Its head was devoid of hair, ears, and a nose. As if given only the bare necessities, the creature looked at the world through slits, breathed through slits, and bared its teeth through a slit of a mouth. Pale, corpse-like skin stretched taut against its bones, leaving little to the imagination. It seemed like a wretched, utilitarian existence. A creature unable to feel pleasure. But even this fickle shred of pity evaporated from within Gage when the Mistlander released its guttural voice.

"You worthless Midlanders will pay for your arrogance," he hissed. "The Haljo Empire will strike you in your most vulnerable hour. We will be contained no longer. The riches beyond the veil will not be kept from us." As he spoke, Gage noticed scribbles removed from the symbols the main circle was built on. "We will kill every last practitioner in the Midlands and rule over the useless masses."

Do it. A voice inside his head urged.

"You and your family shall never know peace again."

Shut him up.

"I will kill your sisters, your mother, your fa—"

Gage leaned down near Ada's spell, feeling her leftover energy in it, and drew a straight line through it. Just like that, the creature fell silent to the floor.

Gage dragged his shoe over the dirt, erasing the symbol, and ran back to his mother just in time to catch Cara as she fell back to the ground.

* * *

Cara woke up drenched in sweat. She tried to move her neck, to sit up, but her body felt heavier than lead.

"I think she's waking up," she heard Gage say. She was lying across the backseat of her mom's car, her head on his lap.

"Cara, honey?" her mom called from the driver's seat. "Can you hear me? How are you feeling?"

Terrible, she wanted to say, but instead, only a grunt came out. She tried again, "Bad."

"Yeah, I'm not surprised."

Geez, thanks for the comforting words, Mom, she thought.

"Your temperature is really high." Gage said.

He sounded uncomfortable, and Cara felt a little bad for him. She couldn't really remember what happened.

"We're going to the club," Ada told her from the passenger's side. "Mom will help you."

Cara's head was pounding. She brought a hand up to her forehead as if expecting it to be anything else than feverish. She felt like a meteor, burning as it traversed the atmosphere. She felt like she was about to disintegrate. Dissolve.

"We're almost there," Miriam assured her.

Moments later, the car veered onto the same soft shoulder Cara had parked on earlier that night. Ada helped her get on Gage's back, piggyback style. Cara thought of protesting, saying she could walk on her own, but she didn't have the energy to lie. Even holding on took more strength than she could muster, but she somehow made it to the club without falling.

"What the hell is this?" Miriam's voice was cold as ice and just as burning.

Ada froze. She had been in almost as bad a state as Cara after projecting, and it had taken all her strength to stand up and walk out to the road. She hadn't even considered clearing her circle and hiding the evidence from her mother.

"I astral projected," Ada confessed. It wasn't the first time she had incurred her mother's wrath, endured her glare. "I spoke with the giant, and she told me where those Mistlanders were. I went to see for myself and heard them talking about kidnapping a practitioner from the high school. Who else could it be but Gage?' She exclaimed, hoping the life-threatening events of the evening would somehow bury her transgressions. "So, I got Cara to come with me and trap them."

Miriam's clenched fists shook with rage. The vein on her forehead came to the fore. "Why didn't you wait for me to call you back?" she shouted.

"It would have been too late!" Ada yelled back. "I couldn't risk it. What if something had happened to him?"

They glared at each other silently for a moment. The air in the room felt fragile. Flammable. Gage's ears were ringing. Those creatures—Mistlanders?—were originally coming after *him*. A new weight crept onto his shoulders, responsibility coupled with a sense of injustice. He never used magic. He tried his hardest to live as if it didn't exist. Why would they target him, of all people?

Their mother sighed, exasperated. "We'll talk about this later. Help me gather the elements."

She was referring to the ingredients for a potion, one that would hopefully cure Cara. For such an important brew, it

38

was ready in under ten minutes. Miriam used a ladle to bring it to Cara's lips. Her temperature plummeted immediately and noticeably. She tried to sit up.

"Take it easy," her mother cautioned. "The potion will only lessen your pain."

Cara nodded, then voiced a thought that had been gnawing at her since earlier. "What about Ada? Does it not hurt anymore?"

"What?" Miriam spun to look at her second daughter with a face that said, *you're hiding more?*

"Nothing, nowhere," Ada said as she struggled against her mom's prodding hands.

"Oh, of course!" Miriam said, bringing the heel of her hand to her forehead. "From projecting. Your body must be unbearable."

"Well, it is much more bearable now."

Her mother ignored her. "Come, have some of this potion," she said. "There's a lot left."

Ada didn't refuse. The pain dulled but didn't disappear, just as Miriam had promised.

* * *

The siblings each went to their rooms as soon as they got home. Cara and Ada succumbed to sleep the moment their heads hit their pillows, but Gage's mind was reeling. Their parents were in the living room, deep in conversation. He could already picture how it would go; how his mom would vaguely explain the chain of events.

Miriam hadn't been there for half of it, for one, and she had always tried to keep the magical part of their lives out of Richard's sight. She set up all their tools and elements in the club, where he barely ever went, and seldom brought up their practice during mealtimes. None of their children understood why.

As far as they could tell, Richard was accepting and loving despite their differences. Gage didn't care enough to put his thoughts into words, but he had an inkling. Miriam was just like him, trying to be as normal as possible. The reasons behind it? Different from his, he was sure, and therefore unfathomable.

* * *

The next day, Ada awoke to Meena's little face looming over her bed.

"You're awake," she stated.

It took Ada a beat to respond, "Yes."

"Lunch is ready," Meena said.

"Lunch?" Ada looked at the clock on her bedside table: one thirty-five PM. Someone must have turned off their alarms.

Meena stood very still, a notebook hugged to her chest.

"What about Cara?" Ada asked, turning to see her older sister still nestled under the covers.

"She's asleep," Meena said. "Will you come down to lunch now?"

Ada was momentarily torn between her bed and growling stomach, but then she threw off her covers. It was impossible to say no to Meena.

"Let's have lunch," she said.

"You didn't make your bed," her little sister pointed out.

"I'll do it after I eat. You need energy to make a bed, y'know?

Downstairs, Richard was setting two big bowls on the table, curry and rice. "Good morning, darling." He glanced at the clock. "Or should I say good afternoon? How are you feeling?"

"Much better." Ada pulled out a chair. "This looks delicious. I'm starving."

"Not surprising," he replied. "You didn't have dinner last night. Worry not. Leftovers are in the fridge. You'll need your strength for the scolding your mother will give you when she gets home."

Shit. "Is she very angry? Are you?" Ada asked.

"I would probably be a whole lot angrier if I understood what's going on," he said. Ada smiled slightly at his honesty, but it was too early to be relieved. Her dad continued, "I'm glad you helped Gage, but not if it meant putting yourself at risk. You should have waited for us."

"I tried to call Mom! She didn't pick up," she protested.

"You should've waited," he repeated, his no-nonsense tone of voice clearly drawing a line. "Or you could've found Gage and gotten to safety. Not sought them out."

Ada's throat tightened, but instead of feeling apologetic, she grew defensive.

"What if they attacked?" she asked. "I was supposed to do magic in front of all his stupid teammates?"

Her arms were waving wildly by now. She hated being scolded by her father, seldom as it happened. It had been a high-pressure situation, and she did the best she could. So what if she was a little reckless?

"You weren't supposed to do magic at all!" Richard cried. "Your mother might have made it in time. We'll never know. Instead, your sister is bedridden and is having issues with her magic."

He was far more upset than he had let on earlier. Guilt glued Ada's eyes to the floor.

Cara's voice broke the silence. "I'm not bedridden," she said as she took a step down the stairs. "And why are you saying I'm having issues with my magic?"

Her sudden appearance stunned Richard momentarily. He sighed.

"Come sit, honey," he said, his face softening. "You had your magic pried out of you, but they managed to get it back in. We don't know anything for sure. Your mother is afraid it may have lasting side effects."

"That was her magic?" Ada said in a shocked breath.

"I feel fine," Cara said, but her tone was unsure. "I'll try some spells, I guess, see if they work out…"

"Your mother thinks it's best if you rest for now. You don't want to exhaust yourself," Her dad started.

"How can they even do that?" Cara interrupted, her tone rising. Outrage covering for her fear. "*Pry* my magic out of me? That's barbaric."

"They were Mistlanders—"

"They're monsters. Where are they? I want to see them!" She stood from her chair, face reddening. This was her magic. Her *magic*.

"Cara, sit!" Richard barked. "They're not here. Two escaped, and the other one is dead." The room went silent.

"Dead?" Chills ran down Ada's arms. "Did I…?"

Her dad looked at her blankly. "Did you what?"

"Well." She searched his eyes but saw he knew nothing. "Nothing. Never mind."

Cara sat back down in her chair.

"Aren't we having lunch?" Meena asked. She had been waiting for them in her seat the entire time, not seemingly tuned into their conversation at all. The notebook was open beside her plate; she had a pencil in hand.

"We are," Ada said, grabbing a serving spoon. Changing the topic.

They started eating, but Cara was feeling worse by the minute. She couldn't handle the suspense.

"Apologies in advance," she said, much to the others' befuddlement. Then she dipped her finger into the curry and drew a sigil on the table.

"Cara," Richard started, his tone defeated. Before he could continue, the rice in the bowl multiplied and started to overflow, spilling out onto the tablecloth. Ada let out a sigh of relief.

Cara cleaned the incantation off with her napkin.

5

C ara and Ada were waiting for their mother to return from work. After failed attempts to concentrate on television series, books, and homework, they ended up sitting silently in the living room. The air was heavy with unasked questions.

It was Cara who broke the silence, "What exactly happened yesterday? Can you tell me again from the beginning?"

Her sister's uncharacteristic sincerity was jarring, but Ada humored her. The narrative started in her bed when she first tried astral projection. Cara interrupted her when she got to the part where she came across the Mistlanders for the first time. They had said they were after a kid at the school that smelled like he was from the Aaron clan.

"Aaron?" Cara was confused. It was Miriam's maiden name, one she never brought up in front of them. They only knew because they had seen an old ID of hers from before she married Richard and took the Leiva name. Shortly after they asked their mom about it—her reply a brisk, *I no longer answer to that name*—Cara found the cut-up pieces of the card in the kitchen trash.

Ada nodded. "First, I thought there could be another practitioner in Hope Springs, but I don't know anyone else named Aaron...They started talking about snatching him from the soccer field. It was too obvious." After another moment of silence, she added, "I'm glad your magic's fine."

"Me too," Cara muttered.

When Miriam arrived, she took her time setting down her bag and greeting Meena before sitting down with them. Her daughters waited anxiously, unsure of what to expect. Ada predicted they would get a stern talking to, but her sister was doubtful.

Miriam hadn't scolded them in ages—they were adults, after all—but if she was really mad, she would have woken them up before going to work. Cara had a feeling their mom was putting this conversation off.

"How are you feeling?" she asked, finally settling into a chaise. "Any residual aches?" They shook their heads. "Good. That's good."

Before she could continue, Cara's overflowing sense of dread spilled from her mouth. "I'm sorry about yesterday. We could have handled that situation much better. We were just worried about Gage and didn't know if we—"

"Cara." Miriam stopped her mid-sentence. "Please, I'm not here to lecture you."

Cara's suspicions had proven correct. Rather than angry, Miriam looked apologetic. The girls were baffled. Her next words did little to clear things up.

"It might be best if you live with your aunt for a while," she told them.

"We don't have any aunts!" Ada snapped. She wasn't actually sure of this. Miriam had technically neither confirmed nor denied it before.

"You do," her mother said, frowning. "Although, it is more

accurate to call Amit an old family friend."

"When exactly are you talking about?" Cara asked sharply.

Her meticulously planned schedule was running through her head. The professor she was working with had promised she could attend a conference with him that Summer. Would they be back by then?

Miriam pressed the heel of her hands into her eyes. "I thought we would be safe in Hope Springs."

Safe?

"Safe from who?" Ada asked.

"Everything," their mom said. Her characteristically great posture was faltering. She seemed defeated. It was unsettling. "I don't know how the Mistlanders found us, but they've seen Cara's magic and won't leave you alone now."

"Why?" Cara asked.

"Your magic is special, baby," Miriam started.

"What do they want with it?" she interrupted.

"We're not one hundred percent sure," their mother answered with a shake of her head. "But they won't stop until they have it. They don't care who they hurt in the process."

"What happens to me if they take my magic?" Cara asked.

Miriam hesitated. "You'll be normal."

That isn't too bad, Ada thought, but as it crossed her mind, she immediately knew she didn't mean it. Knowing she was different, special, had gotten her through the toughest moments of her life.

"Amit?" Ada asked, repeating the name her mom had said earlier.

"I've known her since we were children. She's very dear to me. You'll be safe with her," Miriam assured them.

Ada frowned and asked, "And you'll be safe here? What

about Meena and Gage?"

Miriam had been hoping they wouldn't ask that question, but she had an answer prepared. She reached over and tucked a strand of her second daughter's hair behind her ear.

"I can protect them," she said. "It's just hard to protect everyone at once."

Cara built up the courage to say, "The Mistlanders said Gage smelled like an Aaron."

Their mother visibly flinched.

"My family," she said, then corrected herself. "The Aaron family has been practicing magic for centuries. They are well-known in the practitioner world."

Ada's voice was barely more than a whisper. "Did you run away from them?"

Miriam's silence spoke volumes, but her daughters weren't sure of exactly what it was saying.

"What about school?" This was Cara, of course.

"You can apply for leave. You can finish when you come back. When it's safe again."

Safe.

"Where does she even live? Where are we going?" Ada asked, barely keeping herself from whining.

"I'm not sure. She moves around. It's the only way to stay safe," Miriam said.

Safe.

"When are we going?" Cara asked. She was growing more stressed by the minute.

"Amit will be here tomorrow," her mom replied.

"Tomorrow?" Ada exclaimed.

"Does Dad know?" Cara asked.

"He knows it's the best option. We just want you to be safe."

Safe.

"Will we really be safe?" Cara asked.

Her mom sounded confident when she replied, "It's our best bet."

Cara bristled. Her plans were crumbling before her eyes. Venom seeped into her tone. "A bet implies risk, hazard, chance. Uncertainty."

"Cara." Miriam's voice broke.

Sensing her exhaustion, her impending collapse, her daughters paused their interrogation. Gave her a brief respite.

* * *

Amit's family was in the business of changing. Assimilating. Blending in. They were masters of disguise. Putting up façades. Smoke and mirrors. They modified and replaced, shifted and shaped, nudged and shuffled and inched their features into others, remodeling their bodies like houses, gutting them, sanding them down, rendering them unrecognizable even to their own eyes. After all, isn't the body just a house for what lives within?

Their physical shapes being as mutable as they were, their education focused exactly on that which was within: strength of character and knowing oneself beyond a specter of doubt. The shell that contained them could transform endlessly, but as long as their essence remained unchanged, they would continue to be themselves, or so the philosophy went. However, this left little room for personal growth, crises of identity, or self-discovery. And this was exactly what Amit stumbled onto at the tender age of eleven: self-discovery.

Suddenly, her world evolved, upgraded, so to speak. To

use a common metaphor, it went from black and white to the nuanced, nauseating realm of Technicolor. It was terrifying. The previously innocuous principles of behavior which ruled over her and everybody else's lives revealed themselves to be arbitrary and cruel. The familiar became strange, or was it she who did?

For years, she pretended not to notice. She listened well and obeyed, hoping that if she played her part well enough, if she managed to fool everyone else, she would be able to fool herself, too, and the damage would be undone. Somehow, she hoped, she could unsee what she had seen and forget all she had learned. The mise-en-scène would be restored, and they would all proceed with their happy lives.

Unfortunately, hiding her true self sent her into the darkest depths known to man, and by her seventeenth birthday, she had veritably lost her mind. She exiled herself to a dim room somewhere in the mountains with nothing but a vague resolve to end her own life. In a fit of desperation and rage, mostly fueled by her feelings of injustice against the world and her inability to accept her fate, she committed what her family considered the ultimate taboo. Relieved of the weight that had dragged her down so far, she returned to her home, determined to lie no more.

Her father rejected her and stripped her of his name. Her mother didn't say goodbye. The rest of her family watched from the windows as she left the estate for the very last time and laughed. The only person who cried for her was Miriam. Only she railed against the unfairness of Amit's suffering, the hypocrisy of her clan, and the burden of her misfortune. Only Miriam told her that she loved her and that she would miss her, and that she hoped that one day they would meet again. That alone gave Amit enough courage to continue to live.

And so she did, wandering aimlessly through space and time, having lost the sense of purpose instilled in her since birth. At times, the freedom was intoxicating in its sweetness. At times, she wished she was dead. Never did she want to go back. She didn't long for her mother's touch or her childhood home. Sometimes, she had dreams about Miriam, her one childhood friend. She imagined her married, living in one of the Aaron homes, maybe with children, still under her mother's thumb. They would never see each other again, and it was for the best.

But here she was now, cold and tired in Oregon, walking up to the only house in the cul-de-sac with a light still on, tensed as if prepared for an ambush. Before she could knock, the door swung open, and she was suddenly face to face with her own colossal cowardice, that which she had so doggedly dodged for decades. It gave her a warm embrace and invited her in.

* * *

Gage woke up to the buttery smell of pancakes. His room was closest to the kitchen, so he had learned to distinguish the sweet and savory smells of common breakfast foods, his willingness to get out of bed often dependent on what was on the menu. On the rare occasion both Miriam and Richard were busy, all scents were conspicuously absent, which meant cereal.

Usually, pancakes were reserved for special occasions since his parents insisted on making them from scratch. Gage approached the kitchen tentatively that day, unsure if he had to wish his parents a happy anniversary or if he'd gotten one of his sister's birthdays messed up.

"Good morning, sunshine." His dad glanced up briefly from the stovetop. "You better hurry. It's already seven-thirty."

He nodded and took a seat at the table. His mom came down the stairs not long after, already dressed for work.

"Morning, honey," she mumbled, kissing the crown of his head and then serving herself a plate.

"How's our guest?" Richard asked.

"Still asleep, she got in late," his wife said.

"Your friend?" Gage asked. "What was her name again?"

"Her name is Amit."

Meena came down soon after to have half a pancake before swimming lessons. She was mostly home-schooled by Richard, but her parents proposed dozens of extracurricular activities to her every year. She had recently participated in art classes, birdwatching excursions, and yoga.

While there were some classes that she would only take for one or two years, the only one she had never dropped was swimming, which she would practice in the public pool. No one swam as fast as she did.

Gage got up from the table to brush his teeth, but before he could make it to his room, Miriam called to him from below the stairs, "Can you skip practice today? We're not sure at what time the girls are going to be leaving."

"Yeah. Okay."

"Shake your sisters awake for me, will you?" Richard added.

A few minutes later, they emerged in varying states of sleep.

"Yum," Ada mumbled. "Pancakes."

"Hey, sweetheart," Miriam said, walking her dish to the

sink. "Are you all packed?"

"Almost," Cara replied promptly.

"I'm not," Ada admitted after a beat, slumping in her seat.

"Well, you better get on it," their mother said pointedly.

* * *

They were both upstairs packing when they heard the door to Meena's room creak open and froze. Meena had slept in their parents' bed last night, and only one person was left in the house. Out emerged a tall, thin woman with a thick mane of black hair, a sharp gaze, and a pierced nose. She was wearing loose black clothes and was holding something in her fist.

"Hello," Ada said. "Would you like some breakfast?"

"Sure," Amit said and headed toward the stairs.

The girls looked at each other and followed.

Once in the kitchen, Ada took the leftover pancake batter out of the fridge, and Cara turned on the stove behind her.

"Would you like anything else? Eggs, bacon…?" Ada asked.

"No, thank you." Amit settled, straight backed, into one of the tall chairs by the countertop.

Ada turned to help Cara only to be swatted away.

"How old are you?" Amit's voice startled them more than it should have. *Twenty-two, twenty-four,* they replied. "And your siblings?"

The line of questioning continued. Did they work? What were their majors? Plant biology—useful for potions, Amit posited—and linguistics and anthropology—not useful for anything, Ada joked self-denigratingly. How long until they graduated?

Then they sat in silence as she ate. The sisters trained their eyes on the plate, the glass, their hands. Confronted simultaneously with a relic from their mother's clouded past and a fixture of their unpredictable future, they were having a hard time staying in the present.

"Where do you live?" Cara asked, trying to turn the tables. Her attempt failed. Amit looked up apprehensively.

"Why?" she asked.

"Well, " Cara said, faltering at the unexpected response. "I was just wondering where we're going."

"Oh, yeah. Not to my place."

They waited for her to continue. She didn't.

"So, where are we going?" Ada pressed.

Amit chewed for a moment, mulling it over. "Somewhere remote," she finally said. "Middle America, maybe? Wouldn't be the first place anyone would look for magic…"

Fair enough, the sisters thought.

"Can you train us?" Cara's question seemed to catch even her off guard when she blurted it out.

Ada looked at her like she had grown a third eye.

"Train?" Amit asked. "As in practicing magic? Didn't Miriam?"

"She did, but it's…ongoing," Cara said. That felt like an accurate enough description. "We haven't covered everything yet."

Ada nodded, and her sister could tell they were on completely different wavelengths even before she spoke, "I ask her to teach me things all the time, and she refuses."

"That's because you always ask about weird, dangerous stuff," Cara snapped. "Sometimes it's so obscure, she might not be familiar with it."

Amit scoffed. Noticing their questioning glances, she said, "Miriam had a particularly thorough education. I'm sure she's familiar." She had the last bite of her breakfast before answering Cara's question, "I can teach you the fundamentals. What discipline do you specialize in? You're Aarons, so pre-historic?"

"No," Cara said with a frown. "She taught us the basics of everything. We haven't specialized yet."

Amit agreed to talk to Miriam when she got home from work. "Knowing her, she had a learning plan in place for you two," she told them.

Ada understood that it was unreasonable to resent Amit for knowing a side of her mom that she didn't, but she couldn't help it. It smarted, especially when Miriam seemed so reluctant to share. Ada wondered if everybody her mother had grown up with was this reserved, this mysterious.

She kept stealing glances at their new acquaintance, trying to square her alternative aesthetic with the buttoned-up image she had of her mother. It must have been the fourth or fifth time when she found Amit staring right back at her. Flustered, Ada jumped into action, clearing the plates and heading upstairs to pack.

6

Miriam and Amit were talking in hushed tones in the living room that evening when the girls dragged their bags down the stairs. Amit had told them to keep it as light as possible: some pants, a few changes of shirts and underwear, comfortable shoes, no surplus. Richard sat with Meena at the kitchen table looking at her recent drawings. Gage was upstairs in his room.

Ada stayed in the kitchen, relishing the remaining moments with her family. It was the first time she was leaving Hope Springs indefinitely, no return booked. Cara headed back up and waited.

She was sitting at the edge of her bed as the afternoon light dimmed and retreated from the window. The shadows played across the room, her face, made her almost unrecognizable in the mirror. Cara was a precision instrument. A scalpel. A fine point pen. She knew where she came from, who she was, where she was going. At least, she used to. Her mother's voice echoed in her head, repeating the same word over and over again, *safe.* Her eyes started to burn the way they always did before she cried.

If Hope Springs wasn't safe anymore, what was? Was there anywhere safer than hidden by the foliage, the fog, the mountains? Where would she be more protected than at the dining room table, surrounded by her family, her clan? How would she feel secure when the safety net she relied on was suddenly pulled out from under her?

No plan. No schedule. No certainty. Suddenly deprived the comfort of her color-coded notes, her flashcards, her day planner, Cara had never felt so vulnerable, left with no option but to follow a stranger into the unknown.

She could hear Ada's voice faintly from downstairs, light and facetious as always. Her sister had always wanted more, something different. She was probably excited to finally leave and live somewhere new, even if she wouldn't admit it. Ada wanted to escape, but Cara saw clearly that they had nothing to escape from. Until now.

Now, they were fugitives. Dare she say, refugees. Being displaced from her home, nothing felt too dramatic. She wiped her tears just in time. Gage appeared at the doorway, voice hoarse, donning an incredible bedhead. He must have taken an after-school nap.

"What's up? You all packed?" he asked.

Cara gave him a small smile. "Just about."

"See you downstairs?"

She stood from her bed and stretched, enough wallowing. "Let's go down together," she said.

Amit stood from the sofa when they entered the room. "Are you ready?" she asked.

She stood awkwardly to the side, arms crossed, gaze averted, as they hugged and kissed and teared up. When all was said and done, Cara and Ada grabbed their bags and started to the front door before Amit stopped them.

"We're headed this way," she said and gestured to the back

door.

Cara had noticed the conspicuous absence of a car in their driveway but chalked it up to Amit having taken a taxi or rideshare. Of course, she hadn't.

They stepped out into the backyard. Everyone else went back to their routine, getting started on dinner, turning on the TV, but their mom still stood by the window. Cara tore her gaze from Miriam's backlit figure in time to see Amit pick up one of the dogwood's fallen branches. The tree was still bare from the winter's relentless attack.

She turned back to them, saying, "I spoke to your mother. I know she hasn't taught you much."

The girls balked. This was news to them.

"We've been learning magic for twenty years!" Cara protested.

She was exaggerating; they hadn't begun lessons as toddlers, but in her outrage, she thought it sounded better than the alternative *over ten years.*

"You have been shown only the most superficial layers of magical practice. Miriam was of the opinion that you didn't need to know many of the topics we were taught growing up, but I think she did you a disservice. She thought this would protect you, but instead, it has left you underprepared and uninformed." The girls were speechless, so she continued, "Now you're up against Mistlanders, and who knows what else…" Shaking her head, she sighed. "I will be taking over your instruction from now on, and this is your first lesson. We will open and travel through a rift."

Ada's ears perked at the word. She recognized it from her recent research.

"When you open a rift, you are tearing through the space-

57

time continuum to arrive at your destination," Amit said. "She drew a large circle around them, setting up for the spell. Before she could continue, Cara, who was still reeling from being called ignorant earlier, interrupted.

"This sounds more like science-fiction than spell casting," she said.

Amit's glare was piercing. "How should I put this in simple terms?" she mused. "When it comes to magic, Cara, you have been taught street smarts, but you have no book smarts." Ada winced, knowing this hit her sister where it hurt. "If you internalize anything today, let it be this: magic and science are thoroughly intertwined. Science studies the nature of our reality, and magic concerns itself with altering it. You can break rules you are not familiar with, but can you bend them? Can you twist them? Your practice is limited by how well you understand the world and its properties. Do you understand?"

Cara was fuming—Amit's tone reminded her of all the men in the biology department who would talk down to her, some with less advanced degrees than her—but she nodded. She had been the one to ask for lessons, after all. Just as in school, the condescension motivated her to prove everyone wrong. In this case, that meant becoming the best pupil Amit would ever know.

Amit began to draw sigils on the soil between them. "As I said, the rift tears the spacetime continuum, creating a path to traverse space, time, or both. However, I would strongly advise against attempting to traverse both. There are sparse records of practitioners achieving it in recorded history, and all the accounts are unreliable. Anyone who's attempted it in the last few millennia has failed."

"What happens if you fail?" Ada asked, eyes wide with fascination.

"You can die, but most are stuck in a state of limbo," Amit replied.

"What's limbo?" was the quick follow-up.

"Limbo isn't a place," Amit said, then paused. "We are three-dimensional beings, yes? When we create a rift from one three-dimensional space to another, we are traversing a compressed amalgam of one- and two-dimensional spaces as well. That's what we refer to as limbo. The question of what happens there is widely debated. No one has lived to tell the tale."

"You can't use magic to escape these spaces once you're in them?" Ada's throat was dry. This sounded exactly like the kind of place she would wind up after some reckless stunt.

"As I said, you must know your reality in order to manipulate it. If no practitioner has made it back, we can only guess that the rules limbo is governed by are so different from our world's that magic doesn't have the same effect. Or that people die before they can attempt to escape."

Amit shrugged. This was old news to her, but she had offhandedly blown the sisters' minds. As much as they hated to admit it, it was starkly apparent how much she had to teach them. Even now, as she drew the magic circle, Amit broke down into core components out loud for them.

"Now, *I* activate the spell," she said pointedly when she was done.

They watched, mesmerized, as her magic flooded the spell circle, and the air began to glint.

"Wow." Ada looked around wide-eyed. "There's hundreds."

It was as if someone had dipped their brush in glimmering

multicolor paint and gone wild. Rifts appeared suspended at different heights as far as she could see.

Amit and Cara both gave her odd looks, but it was the way her sister said her name that made her realize something was wrong. "There's only one, *Ada*," she said.

"What? But they're everywhere!" Ada said with a wave of her arm.

"You must be a traveler," Amit interjected, a novel glint in her eye.

It was the first time Amit seemed even mildly interested in something they had to say.

Ada jumped at the validation. "Did my mom tell you I astral projected?"

She nodded. "It's worth exploring. You should pay close attention to this spell since you may be using it in the future."

"How does it know where we're going?" Cara asked.

"It doesn't," Amit said and tapped her temple. "The caster does."

Approaching the rift that hung, defying gravity, straight ahead, she gestured.

"After you."

* * *

They were somewhere in the central United States. Amit wouldn't tell them where exactly. Some town called Deer Creek, maybe? That might've just been the name of the nearest paved street. For some reason, the GPS on their cell phones didn't work. They suspected an interference spell that stopped satellites from finding them.

"Why can't we know where we are?" Cara had asked the

first night after they arrived.

"If the Mistlander who drew out your magic kept any, they could harness it. If they do it correctly, they could access your mind and dreams." Amit lowered her voice solemnly as she said, "It's quite difficult to guard against those who seek to invade dreams."

They woke the next day and went to the kitchen to find a note scrawled on a ripped paper towel. *Went to get food.* Ada's stomach was grumbling, so despite the foreshadowing, she pulled open the refrigerator, the pantry, and the cupboards to find them empty save for basic kitchenware.

"Do you think this is an Airbnb?" she asked.

"I don't think our *guardian* knows what an Airbnb is," Cara grumbled, settling on one of the tall stools by the counter.

They were staying in a big white farmhouse with peeling paint that only contributed to an aura of abandonment. The rift had left them about a quarter of a mile away from its front entrance, and they had struggled to drag their suitcases through the snow. One of the advantages of being a traveler, Amit explained, was their greater precision compared to differently talented practitioners.

The house wasn't as dilapidated on the inside. There were probably six rooms, three of them now in use; a door to the basement very noticeably in the kitchen; and a big hanging handle in the middle of the hallway outside their room, the kind that, if pulled on, reveals the creaky steps up to an attic.

"This doesn't seem haunted at all," Ada had said sarcastically while pretending to pull on the discolored string.

When Amit returned with groceries, it was in an old, dirty pick-up truck. The girls heard the sound of the engine and jumped up from their perches, rushing to a window to see who this way came. When they noticed the familiar face, they went out to help her carry their sustenance.

"Did you go into town?" Cara asked upon noticing the unfamiliar supermarket name printed on the flimsy plastic bags. Amit grunted an affirmative.

"Whose truck is that?" Ada asked.

"No one's. Ours."

The girls met each other's eyes at this slip-up, shooting telepathic question marks at each other.

"Okay...Can we go into town?" Ada looked at Amit expectantly.

"No," she replied shortly.

"What are we supposed to do in this house all day, then?" Cara complained.

It was the first real smile they had seen Amit don, except it was sickly sweet, sarcastic. "We'll be having a fun few weeks of intensive practical magic lessons," she said.

The smile immediately fell, and her face became as enigmatically devoid of emotion as it always was.

Ada scowled, but only briefly before her face twisted with distaste.

"Ugh, what's this?" The bag she had started unpacking was filled with fractions of cows and pigs tidily encased in plastic wrap. "We aren't going to eat this, are we?" she asked and held up a package labeled *Beef Kidney*.

"I originally bought them to recreate some traditional British dishes, but they could also be useful for your lessons," Amit said off-handedly.

Shocked as they were at that she was even capable of joking, neither laughed.

"Are you British?" Cara asked, ignoring her little sister's

squeals.

"No." She frowned. "Do I sound British?" *Kind of*, Ada muttered, barely audible.

"Where are you from?" Cara followed up immediately.

Amit's accent was indecipherable.

"The same place your mother is from."

"New York?" Ada chimed in from across the kitchen, where she had quietly began putting the various animal parts away.

Amit raised an eyebrow. "No."

"That's what she's always told us." Ada's voice faded.

It wasn't that Amit's answer was a surprise, but confirming that she had been lied to her whole life— and by her mom at that— remained startlingly unpleasant.

"Well, I'm sure she has her reasons," Amit said.

She was clearly uninterested in what these may be. She turned away from them and pulled out plates and utensils like she was fixing to make breakfast.

"So, you won't tell us either?" Cara asked. She didn't know Amit enough to feel betrayed, but it did sting a little bit.

Amit said that she was not in the business of revealing other people's secrets, and that was that.

Cara went to the parlor while Ada helped Amit cook. She approached a bookshelf first, tracing a few spines, but none caught her attention. Then, she walked over to the large window at the back of the room. There was a small table with two rickety chairs where she sat and looked out at the frozen landscape.

The shrubbery was overgrown and spilled indiscriminately into the fields, the yard, blurring the border between the property and the woods. If this place had once housed a family, enough years had transpired that their traces had been expunged. The only other signs of life were a small herd of cows—could she call four cows a herd?—that walked around and rested by utility poles and fences, occasionally pecking at the frozen ground.

* * *

That day, Amit introduced them to the concept of active and passive spell words, then recited two hundred of them in languages from Spanish to Hebrew—which gave Cara the chance to demonstrate what she had learned for three years in college—and Mandarin Chinese—where Ada's one semester tryst resulted in no great contributions. She then gave them two days to memorize them, tsking at their complaints.

"Miriam and I would usually only get one, but I'm being lenient since it's your first lesson."

The active words were usually along the lines of *combust, swallow, bury, lift, illuminate,* and *guide.* Passive words included but were not limited to adverbs—*quickly, painfully, quietly*—and adjectives—*powerful, nimble.* Although sometimes, Amit told them, those considered passive could become active. "So be attentive to not only your choice of words, but the order in which you use them," she cautioned.

Ada studied intermittently that evening before entrusting the rest to her future self. This was Cara's thing after all; color-coded notes, flashcards, quizzes. It was no surprise that Cara stayed in the living room cramming by lamplight while Ada went upstairs, brushed her teeth, and lay down. Within minutes, she was asleep.

In her dream, Spring had sprung. The trees surrounding the house were lush and green, boughs bent with the weight of ripe red apples. The breeze carried the smell of overturned dirt. The bellows of cows rang out briefly, then grew fainter. There were people speaking. She realized she was standing on the porch, so she spun and walked back into the house.

Clearly, this dream was from a time when the place was much better cared for. There were fresh flowers in a vase by the entryway, just beginning to droop. The windows and floors were clean, save for some pollen that was starting to form a thin film near the open window. Most notably, there were strangers in the parlor.

As Ada approached from the front hall, she noticed a small boy sitting at the top of the stairs, head between the railing, listening. From her position, she could not see the people who were talking; a wall obscured them. Eyes fixed on the child, she perked up her ears, attempting to hear, but to her confusion, the words sounded garbled and proved impossible to understand. As she rounded the corner, entering the open space encompassing the parlor, three people came into sight, all in button-down shirts and slacks. Two sat at the small table by the window while the third stood above them, facing away from Ada and the boy. Although she couldn't quite make out any of their faces, she finally heard one sentence clearly.

"Where is Leto Roche?"

Ada opened her eyes. The question resounded in her ears. *Where is Leto Roche?*

It took her a moment to remember where she was. She was in the farmhouse. Cara was downstairs in the living room studying; she could tell because the light was still on. She could see this from her position in the hallway facing the stairs. A handle was dangling in front of her; the steps to the attic were half-pulled out above her. She made the mistake of letting her eyes wander to the dark entrance, gazing into the blackness. Her heart jolted straight up into her throat, and she stifled a whimper, taking off down the stairs to her sister.

Cara could hear her coming before she ran into the room. "Hey, I thought you were going to sleep," she said.

"Cara, this place is super haunted." She fell to her knees beside her on the couch, frantically grabbing her older sister's arm. "I'm not even kidding."

"What are you on about?" Cara was preparing to dismiss her until she noticed the tears rolling down her cheeks. She sat up, asking, "What happened?"

Ada told her both about the dream and waking up below the attic. "I've never sleepwalked before in my life. You know that! There must be something in there trying to lure me up."

"Okay, slow down. We don't even know if ghosts are real," Cara tried unconvincingly. If they were going off of past experience, it was more likely than not. "We need to tell Amit. She'll know what to do."

"I don't think I can fall asleep tonight," Ada said.

The idea of yielding control of her body again frightened her to the point of feeling sick. Her stomach was twisting, and her pulse hadn't slowed down. "And we still have to close the attic door."

"It's fine. I'll do it, okay?" Cara said exactly what she needed to hear. "We'll draw a salt circle around your bed, too. Nothing will get through."

"Can't you stay in my room with me?"

"Yeah, of course. I just want to go over these a couple more times."

66

"Okay."

Amit found them sprawled across the living room the next morning.

"Hey, wake up," she prodded them cautiously, noticing the notebook jammed between Cara and the cushions. "Why did you sleep here? Did you study all night?"

"No," Ada replied groggily. "There's a ghost in the attic."

"What?" Amit asked. She had noticed the open attic stairs on her way there and pushed them back up, closing them. "Did something happen?"

The girls took turns sitting up and yawning, then Ada told her what she had gone through last night, asking, "Do you know who that is? Leto Roche?"

"Not really, but it sounds like she used to live here," Amit said.

"I'm pretty sure she did," Ada said with a knowing nod. "One of the men was her husband, and that kid was theirs."

"You said you couldn't hear what they were saying," Cara said, shooting her an accusatory side-eye.

"Yeah, but..." Ada hesitated. She knew that whatever answer she gave would be unsatisfactory. "I could tell," she finally said.

Amit hummed and said, "I see."

Ada had resigned herself to not being believed when Amit continued, catching her completely by surprise.

"You may be a more gifted traveler than we originally thought," she said.

"What does *this* have to do with traveling?" Cara asked.

"The realm of the dead is just that, another realm," Amit said with a shrug. "The most powerful mediums in history could even traverse physically past the veil. It's not common, but there are accounts of travelers that were also talented mediums and possessed a certain ease in contacting the living past."

"But I didn't contact it. She contacted me," Ada protested. "I think…" Speaking the words aloud felt like a jinx, but she said them anyway. "that she wants me to find her."

"That isn't your responsibility," Amit replied sharply. She frowned and added, "Either way, judging by where you sleepwalked to, she's in the attic. There, mystery solved."

Ada sought out her sister's gaze. "Can we check?" she asked.

Amit agreed to go with them after breakfast, but signaled they were going over pronunciation afterward. As Cara pored over the words while munching on granola, Ada's progress was impeded by thoughts of the men from her dream. She was starting to feel nauseous again.

They headed up after washing the dishes. Amit pulled down the stairs and climbed up first. Cara, caving to Ada's pleading gaze, went next.

By the time Ada ascended, Amit had located the sole lightbulb, and Cara had made her way to the window at the far end, pulling the curtain open to let white winter light trickle in through the murky glass. Now devoid of darkness, it looked more dusty and sad than foreboding.

"So?" Cara said, gesturing to their surroundings. "Do you feel anything?"

"Not really," Ada said as she turned three-hundred-and-sixty degrees, waiting for something, or someone, to catch her eye.

They split up, rifling through the hordes of things stashed above the house. Amit kicked a few things around while Cara gingerly thumbed through items near the surface. Ada started reading the marker scrawl on the side of the boxes.

Cormac's toys, one said. *Jeff's books. Leto's hats. Baby clothes. Baseball cards. Grandma's albums.*

"Oh."

Cara and Amit's heads snapped up. Ada was facing the far end of the attic, her eyes trained on the distant wall. Her stare didn't falter as she took step after step toward it.

"What is it?" Cara asked and came up behind her.

On the floor was a big steel barrel, sealed.

"I think it's her," Ada said.

Amit went downstairs to get some elements, then returned to divine the barrel's contents. As Ada predicted, it was a corpse. The divination also revealed an anchoring spell on the barrel, which made it impossible to move by non-magical means.

Ada wanted to bury her, but Amit told her that the body was probably terribly decomposed by now, maybe even liquified. So, they drew a peace sigil on the drum instead. Amit must have thought the situation resolved after that, but Cara could tell her sister was unsatisfied.

Quiet and distracted throughout their lesson, she waited until they were preparing dinner to bring up her concerns.

"I believe Leto Roche was murdered," Ada said, stopping all activity in the kitchen in its tracks.

"And?" Amit asked in a thoroughly diplomatic tone. Her hands were hovering over the sink, dripping wet after just being washed.

Ada stared at her for a moment before saying, "She was murdered by her husband."

"Yes, most likely," Amit said and grabbed a rag to dry herself on.

Cara took the chance to voice her own concerns. "We're not telling the police, are we?" she asked.

"Of course not," Amit said, shooting her a look. "We're in hiding, and listen, the house is empty. The husband is presumably dead..."

Definitely not an Airbnb, Ada thought.

"What about the son?" she asked.

"Long gone," their guardian said emphatically.

"So, there's nothing we can do?" Ada pressed.

"Let's have dinner, yeah?" Amit suggested, already half-way out the door.

That was something they could do, and they did it silently, each lost in their own thoughts.

* * *

They both passed Amit's pronunciation test and moved on to learning the symbols associated with each word. For some, like Chinese characters, they even had to memorize the order in which the strokes were written or casting them would give unreliable results.

Soon, they were combining the symbols to create basic

sigils. By the end of the second week, they were well on their way to mastering spell circle formulation.

Amit must have been pleased with their progress because it was around this time that she allowed them to accompany her to the grocery store. They piled into the pick-up truck and drove for about thirty minutes until they hit the nearest town center. Seeing the deserted highway and shuttered stores, Cara wondered why their guardian had been so reluctant to let them out of the house. They would have probably crawled back on their own, anyway.

At the supermarket, each girl got a section of the shopping list and was sent on their way. Cara was taking her time picking out produce when she overheard the conversation other customers were having nearby. Words like *terrifying*, *twisted*, and *psychopath* stuck out, but she couldn't make out whole sentences.

She absentmindedly turned an apple in her hand while she listened. Could it have to do with Leto Roche? Improbable—Leto was stashed in a steel drum in their attic. Cara quit stalling and met back up with Amit at the checkout line. She had nearly forgotten about it when a gossip rag caught her eye.

Second body found by Deer Creek. Could a serial killer be terrorizing this sleepy town? The headline proclaimed.

"What's this?" she asked, picking it up and showing it to Amit.

Amit replied promptly and unemotionally, sounding almost practiced, "Two girls have disappeared from the surrounding area within a year. Both bodies were found at the nearby river, mutilated, etcetera. The people are freaking out."

72

"God, that's terrible," Ada said with a scrunched nose.

Cara looked at the paper again. It had garishly included a photo of the crime scene, though from a considerable distance. A panel with the zoomed-in picture revealed a severed foot lying on the river's bank. It was hard to tell exactly since the image was so pixelated, but it looked like something had been drawn on the bottom. After failing to decipher it, she looked back at the original picture. Her breath hitched.

"Hey," she said. Goosebumps had risen on her skin. "Doesn't this look like a sigil?"

Amit snatched the magazine from her hands. The cashier, a pockmarked blond teenager, glanced up at the small commotion but continued scanning their items. If he had heard anything, he didn't let on.

She scrutinized the image intensely, then shoved the magazine back in the slot it had come from. The girls looked at each other but stayed quiet. Once they had paid and were walking toward the exit, Ada pushing the cart, she spoke.

"You're right. It was a sigil," Amit said.

"Are you serious?" Ada hissed, then looked around before lowering her voice. "Did they find us?"

"No," she replied simply.

They passed out the automatic doors to the parking lot.

"There's another practitioner here?" Cara asked when she saw that they were alone.

"It would seem so," Amit said.

As the below-freezing air hit them, permeating through clothes, skin, and bones, Ada started hobbling furiously towards the car. Having discovered early on that her method of running at high speed towards the nearest heated place inevitably ended in slipping on the icy ground, it was all she could do to carefully shuffle her feet one in front of the other. She was making some progress when Cara's voice stopped her.

"Is that girl okay?" she asked.

There was a young woman standing in the parking lot to their right, lightly dressed in leggings and a tank top. Upon closer inspection, they could see her clothing was ripped. Her skin was too pale.

"Oh dear," Amit said quietly, unexpectedly tender. "No, Cara. She's passed."

It took a minute for her words to register.

"She's a ghost?" Ada exclaimed, spinning to take a better look.

The sudden movement nearly sent her feet sliding out from under her, and she let out a yelp. Cara shushed her, but the girl didn't flinch.

"Yes," Amit said, pursed her lips, and started walking again. "There's nothing we can do for her."

"I thought it was hard for normal practitioners to see ghosts," Ada said, resuming her shuffling. "How come we can all see her?"

Amit unlocked the backseat of the truck and started loading the groceries. Cara came closer, partly to help but mainly to hear her response.

"She died recently, and before her time," Amit said. "So she has more energy remaining than average departed spirits."

"Why is she just standing there, then?" Cara asked, but she didn't dare look back.

The ghost looked hardly any older than she was. The thought made her throat tighten.

"Ghosts are remnants. They're not all the way here," Amit said with a sigh. "It's hard to explain their behavior because they don't think like we do. She might not even know that she is dead."

"And a practitioner did this?" Cara asked.

It felt like ice was seeping into her veins. She was suddenly keenly aware of a dull ache in her limbs, her joints.

Amit was already on the other side of the truck, climbing in.

"I chose this place because there are no registered practitioners within a hundred miles, not for years anyway," she said. "If this is a practitioner we are dealing with and not some delusional copycat, they're not in any registry or database."

"There's a registry?" Ada asked as she climbed into the backseat.

"Is that important right now?" her sister asked from the front.

"Well, are we in it?" she countered.

"You're not," Amit said. The engine rumbled to life. "Neither is your mother, or I guess her information hasn't been updated for years."

"Are you?" Ada asked.

"No," she said, pulling the car out of its parking spot.

Cara tried to turn the conversation to more pressing matters.

"So, what do we do about this murderer?" she asked.

"Nothing," Amit said.

"What?" Cara cried, slamming her hand down on the center console. "There's an unlicensed practitioner going around killing women for *who knows* what black magic rituals in our backyard, and we're supposed to just turn a blind eye?"

"Yes," she said. When Cara only stared at her in disbelief, Amit continued, "First of all, there's no such thing as black magic. Banish that notion from your brain. Practitioners can be evil, but magic cannot. *Second* of all, our enemies can track us down using magical energy. Even if they don't know we're here, if they see too significant an increase in the area's magical energy, they may come investigate."

Ada could tell from her tone that this was the real reason she was turning a blind eye, but something wasn't clicking.

"Wouldn't the murderer's magical activity increase the risk, too, though?" she asked.

Cara seized on this, exclaiming, "See! They're putting us in danger already!"

"If I had known Miriam was going to ask me to babysit a couple of brats…" Amit muttered a curse under her breath and shook her head.

When they got back to the house, she went straight to her room while Cara and Ada put away the groceries. They were giggling at a silly video on Ada's phone when Amit came back down. She set a big leather-bound book on the kitchen island and started flipping through its pages.

"What are you looking for?" Cara asked and peeked over her shoulder, already excited by the look of the text.

The pages were frail and yellowed. The content seemed hand-written.

"The symbols used in the spell," Amit mumbled. "They weren't very common."

The girls watched her for a few minutes, but soon grew bored. Amit was skimming page after page, going back to the index and searching one section after another.

Then Ada said, "You know, my mom put all of that online."

"What?" Amit asked, but her head still buried in the tome. Her tone and expression suggested that she didn't have time for whatever nonsense this was.

"Yeah, don't you have a computer?" Ada asked.

"Here, I'll get mine," Cara said, getting up from her nearby seat. "It's in the living room." She came back and pulled up their mother's database. The internet connection was slow, but by the time it loaded, Amit was still turning pages. "Hey, Amit. Look, I found it," she called.

Amit was clearly disgruntled, but after several interruptions finally looked up and said, "Girls, thank you for your help, but there's no way you can find any of this information online."

"It's literally our mother's life's work," Ada said and shared a look with her sister that said, *boomers, right?*

"Just take a look," Cara said, pushing the laptop in front of her. "It's like a wiki format. Type in whatever you're searching for here." She directed her to the search bar.

Amit complied, at first grudgingly, as if to please them. Then, her expression changed. She clicked on one of the results and started scrolling down the page. After a few paragraphs, she looked back at them wide-eyed. "Miriam did this?" she asked.

"Well," Ada started, "she established the website, but there are a ton of practitioners who contribute and edit entries. They're all vetted by Mom, though; they need three referrals from current members to be considered."

"This is insane," Amit said.

Her eyebrows had shot up in her forehead. She started clicking one link after another, almost like she was checking they worked at all. Her agitation caught the girls off guard.

"This could revolutionize how millions practice," she cried as she straightened up. Noticing their odd looks, she shook her head and said, "You don't understand. The practitioner community is extremely stratified. Most knowledge is contained in huge lexicons like these."

Amit gestured to the book she had brought down earlier.

She went on, "And the Committee makes it impossible for common practitioners to access first editions. If information can become widely available like this, it could overturn the entire class structure of practitioner society."

Ada chuckled uncomfortably at their guardian's uncharacteristic intensity.

"I didn't realize it was such a revolutionary act," she admitted.

Amit was beginning to cool down and took a moment to collect herself. She cleared her throat and said, "Your mother is doing very important work. This will definitely help us find the perpetrator."

The girls had smiled proudly at their mom's praise, but the atmosphere grew solemn again as they waited expectantly for Amit to peruse the website. After a while, Cara walked over to the huge spell book and, finding that she couldn't focus on the words in front of her, closed it after glancing over a few pages.

When she was done, Ada took the chance to satisfy her curiosity. Miriam had spell books when they were growing up, but she must have put them away after the database made them near obsolete in their household. It had been years since they had seen one.

Ada dragged it toward her and flipped it open to the first

page. The font to the introduction was tiny, so she kept flipping. Soon, she grew bored and slammed it closed. The cover was well-worn, however, and fell open again when she returned it to Amit's side. Stuck on the inside was a yellowed library card slot, an archaic symbol stamped on in blue ink.

Ada ran her index finger over it. It was a crest with Latin printed within. It looked so familiar. She was sure she had seen it within the last few days.

"Amit? Hey, Amit?" she called out.

"What?" Amit asked, not bothering to look up from the computer screen.

"Where is this book from?" she asked. Her thumb idly grazed the seal again.

"What?" This time, Amit looked up. "Why?"

"Is this a library card?" Ada asked, struggling to prop the book up. Not caring enough to hear the answer, she didn't wait for her response, "This symbol. I've seen it before."

"Where? Where have you seen that before?" Amit asked. She had turned in her chair to face her and deeply etched lines had appeared on her forehead.

"In my dream," Ada replied timidly. Seeing that Amit didn't get it, she elaborated, "The dream Leto showed me. Leto Roche? The men who came to look for her, the ones that were talking with her husband-slash-killer, they both had this symbol embroidered on their jackets. Like a badge or something. I thought they were cops, but is this like a practitioner thing?"

Amit stared back at her blankly, but the gears were turning in her head.

"Wait, of course they did," she said. "That barrel had an anchoring spell on it. Somebody must have cast it after Leto died."

The girls didn't get it.

"Yeah, and?" Cara asked slowly.

"Her husband could have cast it," Ada volunteered.

"That's the thing," Amit said, her gestures growing animated. "Leto's husband wasn't a practitioner. When I found this house, I checked the registry, and only one practitioner has ever lived here." Her tone grew grim as she said, "He must have stolen her spell book and killed her."

"Wouldn't he be too old today to be the serial killer, though?" Cara asked.

Her sister gasped dramatically and asked, "What if he's sacrificing women in exchange for eternal youth?

"It's nearly impossible for non-practitioners to cast complex spells like those," Amit said with a shake of her head. "They must give so much… As dark as it sounds, it would take more than two women for one to accomplish anything at all."

Ada's eyes had wandered over to the stairway during this exchange, as if pulled by an invisible force. Her finger was still tracing the symbol unconsciously, but her original question had been long forgotten. An image surfaced in her mind. Small hands gripping the balusters.

"What about their child?" she murmured.

"Whose child?" Cara asked.

"Leto's," Ada said, her eyes lighting up. "He would be an adult now, and he's half practitioner. Like us."

"Kind of like you," Amit said slowly. "It could be him, especially if he took his mother's spell books."

"We're not alike," Cara said and scowled. "We don't need sacrifices to practice."

80

"Not all halflings are the same," Amit mused, almost to herself. "Their affinity for magic differs. Some can't cast a spell to save their lives."

"Can we find Leto's son?" Ada asked.

The answer was yes.

Leto Roche always dreamed of America, the land of the free. She chased visions of James Dean, Marilyn Monroe, and powder blue Cadillacs all the way from a provincial French town behind the veil to Ellis Island, where her elation lasted the three days it took for her to run out of money.

A fellow practitioner she had met on the ship consulted with the Caribbean island gods that guided her and pointed Leto in the direction of a dingy café in the Bronx where magical folk liked to gather. It was owned by a small man with a permanent grimace who looked her over once and handed her an apron. As long as she didn't break anything, she could stay.

It wasn't happy work; that is, not until Charlotte arrived in a particularly foul-smelling ship from Scotland. She had red hair and a huge gap between her teeth. Leto adored her from the second she set sight on her freckled face. Charlotte was the kind of person who filled a room with her presence. Eventually, she filled Leto's life.

When she squeezed through stalls and tables in the narrow café, Charlotte often dragged men's coats with her, the suede catching on her ample bottom. Most regulars laughed it off until one day, she knocked over the wrong man's wallet. It fell open to the ground, and Charlotte saw something tucked away inside that she really shouldn't have. She scrambled to return it, but it was too late.

The two customers' eyes cut into her back like knives as she did her work, and they didn't budge even as the clock ticked closer to the end of her shift. She the metallic taste of impending doom and went out the back door in an attempt to dodge them.

It just so happened that Leto was off that day, waiting in their shared apartment for Charlotte to return. Eight o'clock came and went, and she thought she might have gotten the time of her shift wrong. It hit ten o'clock, the café's closing time, and she started pacing. At midnight, she ran out into the darkened road and searched every alley Charlotte could have taken on her way home. They never saw each other again.

All Leto was left with was the stories that Charlotte had told. Stories of the ancient gods in the Western Desert, Sasquatches and birdmen from the North, and about the wonders in the swamplands down South, where trees moved when nobody was looking and animals never really died. The blood of witches, she said, was so deeply soaked into the ground that it imbued everything with magic.

For months after Charlotte's disappearance, Leto felt like the world had nothing left to offer. She became so desperate for answers that, in a fit of recklessness, she presented a week's wages to a black market spell dealer in exchange for a faded scrap of paper supposedly containing instructions to conduct a séance. It was a miserable failure, she thought.

That night, she had a dream of tall green grass fields as

far as the eye could see. They blocked her view in every direction so that she was left with no option but to walk blindly through them, pushing them away with her arms, until she emerged in front of a beautiful white farmhouse. A tall man stood outside wearing a big hat and overalls, feeding chickens. A young boy sat with his feet dangling off the back porch. They looked up and smiled at her.

Leto came to see this dream as a message from Charlotte to keep carrying on, a promise of happiness if she would only keep living. The man in her dream walked into the café for a quick lunch the next day. His name was Jeff, and he had come to the city with his father, who wanted to look at some new machinery at a convention.

They were farmers and lived in one of the many states Leto was wont to forget existed. Convinced that the match had been ordained by forces beyond her comprehension, she fell in love with Jeff quickly and without caution. He took her back with him to his hometown, they got married, and soon she was with child.

* * *

Amit went up to the attic to find some of Cormac's old possessions for a scrying spell, then started setting it up in the foyer. When the sisters walked in, she was nearly done drawing the circle. A bowl of water, some dried herbs, and a couple of crystals were strewn around her.

Cara fidgeted by the entryway, building up courage. Then, her sister beat her to the punch.

"You know, Cara's probably the best scryer there is," Ada said.

It was true. Whenever Cara willed herself to find anything, she inevitably came across it. It had landed her into trouble at times as a child when she didn't know how to explain the mysterious circumstances surrounding it. It also meant that she had never lost anything she could be bothered to find.

Cara had an innate ability to scry with nary a spell or tool, but she had also studied up on widely used methods. She had hesitated in front of Amit, however, afraid to fail at the one thing she had never failed at.

That's why her voice came out in a stutter when she said, "I-I wouldn't say I'm the b-best."

"She's been scrying since she was a kid. Doesn't that mean it's her specialism or whatever?" Ada asked with a roll of her eyes.

"I don't see why we shouldn't give it a try," Amit said and moved away from the circle, gesturing for Cara to join her on the floor.

Ada perched herself on the sofa behind them.

After a cursory overview of the spell's components, Amit gave Cara the go-ahead. Cara reached for the bowl of water, pulling it closer. Used to carrying these spells out with little to no preparation, it was exhilarating to feel how the magical energy palpated around her. The ends of her hair hovered as if she had gotten too close to an old TV set. One of Cormac's toy cars was on her right side, a moth-eaten shirt on her left. All she had to do was press her fingers lightly to the shirt for images to appear before her eyes.

The first was of a young boy in bed. He was ill, slipping in and out of feverish sleep.

No, Cara thought. *Later.*

The boy was older, a burgeoning teenager, climbing into

the attic.

Later.

He was bigger now, kneeling like Cara, but in front of a book. Sigils were drawn out on every side of him: on the floor, furniture, walls. They covered every available surface. He pounded his fists on the floor until they bled. It wasn't working.

Later!

He snuck through a dark yard, approaching a window. He pried it open slowly. Someone lay in bed sleeping inside. He climbed up, over, and in, hitting the floor with a soft thud. As he approached the sleeping figure, their face came into view.

No, Cara flinched. *Not this. Later! Ah...Here he is now...*

* * *

The first five years Jeff and Leto spent together were unremarkable. Their son, Cormac, was a shy but bright boy. Their relationship was jovial, if less than intellectually stimulating. Everything changed the day Cormac fell sick. Pneumonia, the doctor said. He wouldn't survive save for a miracle.

Now, Leto could perform miracles fairly easily. She didn't so much debate whether to save her son or not, rather she hesitated to fool her husband. She could tell him their son was touched by the hand of a god they didn't often pray to, or she could reveal herself as a practitioner and open herself up to rejection, abuse, or exploitation. She had grown up hearing about such tragedies; practitioner society was rife with cautionary tales. But this was the man Charlotte had led her to. Surely, he would accept her as she was.

In reality, Jeff mistook Leto's confession as the ramblings of an anguished mother. Half-mad with grief, he didn't take notice as she gathered herbs from the forest and brewed them in the kitchen. The tonic's sickly sweet odor lingered for weeks. The next day, Cormac was relieved of his terminal illness, but a new affliction had laid its roots in Jeff's heart. He came to view everything Leto did with suspicion, refusing to eat the food she cooked, sleep in the same bed as her. He obsessed over the minor details of their first encounter, wondering if she had bewitched him from the start. Leto was at a loss. Her truth fell on deaf ears.

As the months passed, his suspicion warped into anger and his anger into violence. He hated that his wife had more power than him, that she could do what he could not. He could not have saved their son from the brink of death. He could not ward away illness by hanging strange contraptions on their windows. Even the things that had seemed wonderful to him before—how she could predict which heifer was going to bear her first calf that season, find the sweetest patch of wild berries, and calm down agitated animals with a song—seemed sinister. He could not love that which he didn't understand.

One day, after a particularly bad beating, Jeff went to his fields to discover that his crop was dying. It was infected with some sort of parasite, which ate at the leaves and left empty husks filled with dust in its wake. Convinced Leto had been responsible for this, calling down a pest to punish him for his brutality, he re-entered the house and killed her. Their son slept soundly just two doors down while he carried her to the barn and sealed her inside a steel drum left over from the last harvest.

He spent days with his mind on the barrel, the woman inside, sure that someone would find it, discover his monstrosity, and bring him to justice. The thought tormented him to the point that he forgot to feed his son, bathe him, or try to explain where his mother had gone.

Cormac, seven at the time, poured cereal, made peanut butter sandwiches, and convinced himself that his mommy had gone into the city and been delayed by incumbent weather or a railroad accident. His birthday was coming up, after all, and he had asked her for a toy train set. It really did no good to ask his daddy, who seemed incapable of speaking in full sentences anymore and had taken to playing a funny game in which he pretended Cormac didn't exist.

* * *

Balding and bespectacled, it was Cormac, all right. He sat on a lumpy couch, beer in hand, wearing a stained shirt, and watching wrestling on TV. His house was empty. He was alone.

Where? Cara asked. The spell answered by turning to his kitchen counter, where piles of mail sat unopened.

"1111 Beavertail Drive," she rattled off. "Crystal Creek, Nebraska."

She finally knew where she stood, but she had the feeling they wouldn't be staying for long.

Amit was plugging the address into her phone's GPS, the only one that still worked, when Ada asked something that had not yet crossed her sister's mind, "What are we going to do to him when we get there? Kill him?"

Cara sprung back to her feet as if propelled by the force of her alarm.

"Of course not!" she exclaimed. "Right, Amit?"

Amit avoided meeting her eyes, which unnerved her.

"I mean, we're not. Right?" Cara pressed.

Amit heaved a heavy sigh before saying, "Girls, let's lay out our options here. We can't turn him into the police force. Cormac is still a practitioner, which means they're not equipped to arrest him. We may just send innocent people to their deaths."

"What about the practitioner authorities?" Cara cried. "Can't we leave an anonymous tip?"

Amit shook her head. "Even anonymous tips are delivered magically, and all magic is traceable," she said. "Contacting practitioner authorities would mean announcing our location to them." She held out her hands, open palms facing up. "I'll let you choose; we can leave or kill him and leave."

"We can't just let him keep sacrificing girls," Ada said quietly.

Cara's head was spinning. She understood the rationale behind sacrificing one to save the few, but the idea of being the one to decide another's fate was paralyzing. There was too large of a margin for error for her to move forward.

"Can't we lock him up somewhere?" she asked, throwing her hands up in frustration.

"Who will concern themselves with feeding him, Cara?" Amit asked and gave her a pointed look.

Cara's head bowed forward as she wrestled with her moral compass. Noticing her defeated posture, Amit offered what she hoped was a bit of comfort.

"If we had turned him into the Committee, the practitioner authorities," she explained. "They would have also executed him."

"Really?" Ada asked, gasping. "Why?"

"Using human sacrifices in spells has unintended consequences," Amit said as she leaned back against the nearby sofa. "It breeds darkness as a byproduct. Not shadows, but a malignant energy that takes over the practitioner's mind. If they caught wind of someone who had already sacrificed two, there's no way they would allow it to fester."

They didn't quite understand the darkness Amit was trying to describe, but her underlying message came through loud and clear. Cormac had doomed himself from the start. Whatever catastrophic fate befell him, he was the cause of his own downfall. They needn't feel guilty for taking a life already condemned.

Cara still struggled. She couldn't imagine a dark substance emerging from a spell and compelling an otherwise sane practitioner to kill. She couldn't think of darkness as something to be contracted and spread. As something that could have a mind of its own. As a singular darkness. An original evil.

She knew everyone carried a little darkness inside, like an ember. Every person decided whether to feed it, stifle it, or let it run its course. Cara heard the crackling and popping of her own smoldering flames. It was sometimes a battle not to let it devour everything in its path—her relationships, razed to the ground in minutes by her arrogance. If this was what Amit meant by darkness, then Cara understood. But it wasn't.

"Where does this darkness come from?" she asked.

Ada recalled asking the same question of the giant and receiving an unsatisfying answer. Amit didn't offer anything better.

"It's like asking where our magic comes from," she said. "If you want to know, you're going to have to find out." She held up her phone screen, the path to Beavertail Drive clearly plotted. "It's ten minutes away. Are we going, or are we going?"

* * *

Jeff's paranoia eventually led him to Leto's armoire and the big, leather-bound book within. It took him a few days to actually find what he was looking for, but when he did, he zapped the barrel with a permanent sealing spell and dragged it up to the attic while Cormac was at school.

He anchored the drum to the spot with another spell and never worried about it again. He didn't get the chance. As soon as he landed back in the second-floor hallway, pushed the attic door closed, and turned to return the grimoire to its previous hiding place, his heart stopped beating, and he fell dead to the ground. What Jeff didn't know, of course, is that the price any minor spell demands from non-practitioners is often incapacitating, and two spells will surely cost their life.

Cormac had been left orphaned at the tender age of twelve after watching his father's mind steadily deteriorate over five years. He found his father lying in a pool of his own vomit with no visible injuries, a few feet from his mother's dresser in a room he hadn't entered in years. Suspicious and long having lost any lingering affection for Jeff, he rifled around before calling emergency services. Cormac left that house for good the next day, his mother's spell book taking up most of the space in his backpack.

Little did he know that he had hosted the architects of his family's self-destruction just years before when the Committee sent two high-ranking practitioners to pay Leto Roche a visit. Her fees were far overdue.

These two men had fervently petitioned their supervisor to be assigned to the case, claiming they had known Leto for years—which wasn't technically a lie. They told their supervisor that Leto had dated one of their friends, but the truth was that they met her as a waitress in a café in the Bronx working alongside a redheaded immigrant years ago. This they couldn't reveal as they were supposed to be in Boston at the time, hunting down the leader of a notorious organized crime group known for dismembering protected magical creatures and selling them on the black market. Instead, they were in New York, spending the big man's bribes.

Leto and Charlotte knew the café welcomed shady characters from all walks of life and had seen the men several times before, eating lunch with other practitioners with undeniable ties to the criminal underworld. When Charlotte accidentally discovered one of them was a Committee bureaucrat, catching sight of his ID when she leaned down to pick up his wallet, they didn't hesitate to get rid of her.

They lingered around New York for a while, but it irked them that Leto refused to stop searching for the redhead for months after they killed her. It was risky to murder two registered practitioners in such a short span of time—they didn't want to attract too much attention—so they concocted a plan so heinous, so wicked that none of their victims ever suspected external involvement.

It all began when Leto went to the black market to purchase a séance spell, and they saw their chance. It took a bit of cash, but they convinced the dealer to sell her a hex that would leave her mind vulnerable to psychic interventions. They planted the vision in her head that night after happening to see Jeff on the street that day, then they influenced him to enter the café for lunch.

It could have stopped there, but it didn't. Years later, after they had mostly cut ties with their illicit partners, the pair was considered for promotions that would significantly improve their quality of life. Climbing the ladder came with considerable scrutiny, however, and they grew paranoid, starting to obsess over every indiscretion they had committed. In a quest to tie up loose ends, they tracked down Leto and Jeff in their idyllic countryside home, observed her disdainfully, and conspired wickedly.

It wasn't difficult to make Cormac ill. Even less to poison his father's mind. It did take a bit longer than they expected for Jeff's violence to culminate in murder, so they infected his fields. They were sure they would never have to hear the name *Leto Roche* again, but the day came when the Committee noticed she hadn't paid her dues.

After a final visit to the farmhouse, they made sure Jeff's mind was scrambled enough that he would never reveal his story—putting it through the blender one last time. They couldn't believe their good fortune when he took his own life in order to keep their secrets sealed. Lady Luck was on their side.

9

"You don't have to come if you don't want to," Ada said, having noticed the unease on her sister's face. They were standing by the house's main doorway bundling up before braving the harsh winter air once more.

"If I don't go, you don't go," Cara said and shot her a look.

"What are you? My mom?" Ada sneered.

"Shut up, both of you," Amit snapped. "We all go, or no one does."

They all went.

It was a short drive. There was only one property between Cormac's shack and the farmhouse. He hadn't made it too far from home. The GPS signaled that they only had to turn down an unmarked dirt road, and they would arrive at their destination. Instead, Amit pulled onto the soft shoulder and twisted around in her seat to face them.

"This is the plan," she said. "I will cast a stealth spell so he can't see us approach. If a nullifying charm negates the spell, you are to immediately activate your defense spells, like I taught you. If I find myself incapacitated, this." She pulled a scrap of paper out of her coat pocket, a sigil drawn carefully on its surface. "Will be your best bet." She handed them each a copy. "It's unlikely to come to that. This should be a quick in and out. Then we can leave this place forever."

Ada's mouth felt dry. Cara's hands were trembling.

They got out of the car, shutting the doors gently, and started down the rocky, uneven path. Their feet caught on exposed roots, and Ada's ankle twisted more than once. That day had been the warmest since they arrived, meaning the snow had started to melt. Rather than slipping on the frosty ground, they found themselves trudging through muddy puddles, their jeans splashed with brown sludge. They were too tense to complain.

It took a few minutes for Cormac's house to come into view. It was a step down from his family home, small but not necessarily unwelcoming. Maybe it was because they knew the type of monster it housed, but the sisters couldn't help but find it ominous. To Ada's overactive imagination, every mound of dirt in the yard was a freshly dug grave, every unappetizing smell carried on the frosty breeze was a whiff of rotting flesh. Her heartbeat was racing, and it wasn't just from the physical activity.

They followed Amit, creeping past a beat-up truck and crouching lower as they got closer. A television's blue light illuminated the living room and streamed out the window nearest to them. Amit told them to stay put and went ahead, slinking through the shadows.

She reached the window and caught a glimpse of a middle-aged man reclining on a couch, mouth ajar, dozing. If what Cara had seen was true, there was no one else this could be but Cormac. Amit did find the absence of protection spells conspicuous, but chalked it up to his poor affinity for magic. She gestured to the girls to approach, drawing a sigil below the window as she waited.

"What's that for?" Ada whispered, forgetting about the stealth spell as always.

"It's a verification spell," Amit replied. "To verify that person is the killer."

"I saw it in my vision," Cara said. "I know he is."

"No matter. If we are to kill him, we must be sure beyond a shadow of a doubt."

When she finished drawing, Amit pressed her dirt-caked finger into the wall of Cormac's house and muttered her query in a language they couldn't quite place. Even with her eyes closed, she could feel Cara and Ada's stares boring into her, eagerly awaiting confirmation.

A familiar feeling tugged at Cara, distracting her momentarily and drawing her gaze past Amit toward the woods. There was a wavering apparition, identical to when they'd seen her in the parking lot. Except this time, their eyes met, and her arm lifted, pointing in their direction. Toward the house.

Cara turned back as a shadow fell over them. Something was blocking the light. It was Cormac, his face all but pressed against the window, eyes bulging, mind—Cara was sure by just looking at him—unhinged. Her whole body jolted with terror.

Amit finally spoke, "It's him."

Cormac's fist smashed through the window, shattering the glass and sending shards flying all around them. They jumped out of the way but fell on their sides and knees and had to scramble up to standing.

As per Amit's instructions, Cara and Ada murmured defensive spells as they ran away, putting some distance between them and the serial killer. Cara's fell around them like a shield, while Ada's solidified in front of Cormac, impeding his advance. Amit pressed her hand into the dirt and sent a curse through it. Had it worked, the target would have gone stiff, then fallen, stunned to the ground. It had no effect.

A beat too late, Amit realized—felt the energy of—the spell coming back toward her. She put up a nullifier, but it just managed to soften the blow. She was flung back a few meters and rendered unconscious.

"Shit," Ada blurted, fumbling to retrieve the sigil they had been given from her pocket. "Come on, let's do this quick," she said, then looked up to see Cormac just a few yards away, gaining ground. "You know what," she said, shoving the paper into Cara's hand. "You do this, I'll stall."

"Wait, what?" Cara reached out to grab her, but only managed to graze the slick coating of her waterproof jacket.

Ada had darted off to the side, toward the house. Cormac paused and started after her. She had never been the fastest runner. Her breath condensed like a billow of white smoke from her open mouth as she lurched forward to escape from her pursuer.

Having focused on studying, her lifestyle had been pretty static recently. Within five minutes of distracting Cormac, her legs were starting to tire of pushing their way out of the soft ground. With each step, she could feel the mud retracting and compressing, her feet sinking deeper than they should, her muscles working harder. She wanted to yell for her sister, but it would have been a waste of breath. Ada could feel the tingling of magic rising. She only had to hold out a little longer.

Cormac, on the other hand, seemed positively possessed.

Large as he was, his boots buried deep into the slush with each step. Every time he moved, he kicked icy mud at Ada's back. First, she felt it on her calves, like tiny pebbles falling against the fabric of her pants. Then, as she grew slower, the droplets started hitting her coat, then her hair. She yelped as she felt something graze her arm. Desperate, she called upon her magic. She funneled it into ground beneath her feet, willing it to propel her forward, begging it to weigh Cormac down.

Seeing a murderer chase after her younger sister did little to help Cara concentrate, but she forced herself to. Tracing the spell circle onto the ground with trembling hands, her fingers turned numb and bright red. Looking over Amit's template one last time, she checked off the elements.

Spirits, untethering, separation, life, afterlife. She ripped her gaze away only to see the gap in Ada and Cormac's twisted game of tag diminishing. Cara's breath hitched in her throat. She was starting to panic. Cormac was more agile than he seemed, and each time he reached towards Ada, his huge hand seemed to get closer and closer. Cara turned back to the sigil, frantically trying to complete it, when a yelp made her snap her head up again.

"Ada!" she yelled.

Cormac had grabbed ahold of Ada's hair and seemingly toppled down into the sludge shortly after. His firm grip had forced her down too, though, and she was thrashing her neck from side to side to free herself from it.

Cara found herself frozen like a deer in headlights, torn between running to her sister and casting the sigil. Before she could waste too much time, a white film obscured her vision. Startled, she jumped back to see it was the spirit that had warned her of Cormac's presence at the window. Two other specters stood beside her. One kneeled, moving her pale finger across a part of the spell as if attempting to trace a line. It took Cara a beat, but then she understood—the adjustment turned the spirit component of the spell from passive to active form, effectively giving them agency.

Let us, they were saying.

Cara didn't have time to think. She hastily adjusted the spell and imbued it with her magic. Instantly, the ghosts lost their human forms. Their auras blended together in a flurry of energy and lurched toward Cormac. His arms reflexively came up, trying to pry them off, when they enveloped his head and shoulders.

Ada took the opportunity to slip away from his reach, stumbling as she came to her feet and ran towards Cara. Cara rushed out to meet her, catching her just in time as her sister's knees buckled beneath her. Ada leaned her head against Cara's shoulder and tried to catch her breath. Instead, she found herself hyperventilating between stifled sobs. Cara tightened her arms around Ada's waist, eyes firmly glued on Cormac's spasming body.

At first, he seemed to resist the power that assaulted him, his stocky figure lumbering this way and that. Finally, he crashed into the side of his house, the impact enough to make every window rattle. Then, he crumpled forward and downward.

From a short distance, Cara could see his limbs still twitching. The white fog that had blanketed him slowly lifted and dissolved into thin air. Cara waited a few minutes, tentatively hopeful, somewhat expecting him to get back up. When he didn't, she squeezed Ada's arm gently.

"It's okay, Ada," she said gently. "I think he's dead. He's not going to hurt you."

Ada's breath had started to slow down, but when she pulled away from her sister's embrace, Cara saw that her whole body was shaking. Her clothes were soaked in muddy sludge, and there was a scrape on her cheek from struggling to get away from Cormac while on the ground.

"Really?" she asked, her voice barely audible. "What about Amit?"

Slowly, they turned towards the direction Amit had been tossed in. She was laying under the leafless branches of a sprawling cottonwood, motionless. Ada clung to Cara's arm as they walked over, bracing herself for more misfortune.

To their relief, their guardian had no visible injuries. Cara extracted herself from her sister's side for just long enough to ensure her vitals were solid.

"She seems to be stunned, but otherwise okay," she told Ada.

They both let out a sigh of relief. Another glance back at Cormac confirmed he was still down.

"Do you think an energizing charm will wake her?" Ada suggested, starting to settle down.

The adrenaline was leaving her system and, with it, it took her immunity to the elements. All she wanted was to change into dry clothes.

Cara took it upon herself to cast the charm, and it worked. When Amit's eyes blinked open, she was almost moved to tears. Amit, on the other hand, was briefly disoriented but otherwise unfazed. She came to her feet and grasped the situation within moments. All it took was seeing their pathetic states and Cormac's prone body a few meters away.

"What do we do with the body?" Cara asked.

"Nothing, we get the hell out of here," Amit said.

It was as if sweeter words had never been spoke.

Approaching Cormac one last time, Amit looked down and said, "They'll take care of him."

When they followed her, the girls saw tiny black worms crawling all over Cormac's lifeless body. They squirmed across his skin, hair, clothes. Ada lurched back instinctively, and Cara pressed a steadying hand on her shoulder. There were few things Ada hated more than bugs.

It was apparent in her tone when she asked, "Are those maggots?"

"Isn't it a bit too soon for decomposition?" Cara asked and leaned in to take a closer look. "And maggots are white."

"They're bottom feeders," Amit clarified. "Magical maggots, so to speak. They eat the magical energy creatures release when they die."

"So this happens to every practitioner when they die?" Ada asked with a shudder.

"Not unless they're consumed by darkness," Amit replied. "Magical energy isn't normally stored in tissue, so these little ones have no need to eat practitioner's bodies. Darkness, however, is different. It seeps into people's organs and bones. The bottom feeders will consume him in his entirety."

Cara noticed the creatures had begun to break skin in some spots, revealing the dark meat beneath. It was then that her stomach began to turn. Still, she was fascinated. It was a paradoxical combination of feelings she had encountered before in her biology courses. Things that could be gross and still exciting.

"So when you refer to darkness, it is a type of magical

energy?" she asked, turning to Amit.

"That's right," Amit said and hesitated as if deciding whether to say more. "We should go back and pack," she finally said. "Even unregistered practitioners' deaths are noticed by the Committee; they release too much energy. They will be here soon to investigate."

Ada lingered briefly after Amit and Cara turned to leave. Something on Cormac's exposed wrist had caught her eye; a tattoo. No, a sigil.

She realized that it had warded off Amit's attack, but it had likely cost one of his victim's lives. A new emotion rose in her core, temporarily overshadowing the fear and disgust. It was a cold superiority.

Cara had been right. Cormac was nothing like them, even if he was also a halfling. This was not a practitioner. He had no magic, only darkness.

* * *

Amit's urgency was contagious. They were given fifteen minutes to shower, pack, and meet downstairs. They followed her out the front door and waited, shivering on the porch, as she cast an erasure spell to rid the house of traces of their presence. She turned to Ada after stepping down onto the frozen grass.

"Open the rift," she told her.

Ada froze.

"I don't even know where we're going," she said.

"I don't believe in planning ahead," Amit replied with a grimace. "Makes you too predictable. Pick a place, any place. Do you remember the spell?"

Ada nodded; she had never memorized something so quickly. Crouching down, she used her finger to draw it onto the damp dirt. Her hand was tingling with cold by the end of it.

As she finished, she felt something wet land on her cheek and looked up. It was snowing. Growing up, snow days had been rare and short-lived. A snowflake glinted in the air in front of her, dancing and swirling like nothing she had ever seen before. The lump in her throat seemed to have become a permanent fixture.

"Where should we go?" she asked and straightened up.

"Why not somewhere you've always wanted to go?" Cara said agreeably, knowing they were all weary, seeing her own suppressed fragility mirrored in her sister.

"Wherever we go, we won't have time for sightseeing," Amit made sure to warn them. "We will also be going straight behind the veil, so choose sensibly."

Her words fell on deaf ears; Ada had already made up her mind. She activated the spell and approached the nearest rift. The thought crossed her mind that she should shut her eyes tightly, like when you blow out a candle to make a wish, but that seemed ridiculous. Instead, she walked through with eyes wide open.

* * *

"Paris?" Cara cried, delighted despite her best efforts not to be. "Very sensible," she joked.

Ada had caught sight of the Eiffel Tower peeking over some buildings and was stunned in place. Amit was unimpressed, as usual.

"Let's go," she said and turned to walk further into the alleyway they had appeared in.

"What? Where? I thought you said we didn't have a plan," Cara said, tugging her sister's arm to pull her along.

"We need to get behind the veil," Amit called out from over her shoulder.

"You mean, like, behind the veil where the giants live?" Ada asked. She was having a hard time lugging her suitcase behind her on the cobblestone street.

Amit stopped, turned and said, "God, I always forget that you don't know anything."

The sisters prickled but let the insult slide. It had been an eventful night.

Amit continued, "The veils between our world and the giants'—or the Mistlanders'—are what we call dimensional veils; thus, crossing them would be considered transdimensional travel. Travelers." She gestured toward Ada. "May be able to do that on a regular day, but we will not. Within the confines of our world, there are thousands of thinner veils erected by communities of magical beings at just a few degrees of separation. Elves, merpeople, faeries, you name it; they have isolated themselves from this noxious industrial human realm as much as they can."

"Will we be harder to find behind those veils?" Cara asked. She was uncertain about going where practitioners congregated and felt sure to stick out.

"Definitely," Amit assured her and started walking again. "The Committee may govern how practitioners interact with the human world, but they have much less control over independent veiled territories. Most view them as outsiders, and their desire to grow their influence as a threat

104

to sovereignty."

"And once we're on the other side, where do we go?" Ada asked, taking quick steps to keep up. "Are there hotels, or what?"

"There is lodging, of course. Inns," Amit said.

"Taverns?" Ada joked.

"Yeah," she said.

They turned into a tiny dead-end, and after ensuring there wasn't anyone around, she started drawing a sigil onto the wall.

"Wait, what?" Ada asked, laughing. "Are we going to medieval times or something?"

This, too, was partially a joke, but Amit fell silent for a moment before saying, "You were the one who chose Paris, not me."

"You've got to be kidding me," Cara said. "Does time advance differently behind the veil or something?"

"No," Amit answered, drawing out the syllable longer than usual. "Some veiled territories have technologies humans only dream of. Parisians choose to live this way."

With that, she walked right into the wall and disappeared.

10

The house on Willow Street had been quiet since Cara and Ada left. Their father still went to the flower shop every day, ferried Meena around to her assorted activities, and learned to cut his recipes down after they were forced to eat lentil stew for a week straight.

Their mother still spent most of her time at the office and construction sites, with the occasional hour at the club, and didn't really say anything about the girls or Amit. Meena hardly acknowledged their absence, but Gage found her in Cara and Ada's room playing with dolls once and Miriam found her taking a nap in Ada's bed on another day.

A couple weeks had passed in this manner when Gage's mom asked him to go to the club for her one Friday morning.

"I just need a couple of herbs," she told him.

"Can't you go after work?" he asked after grimacing reluctantly.

"We have dinner with the Nguyen's," Miriam said. She was already near the front of the house, keys in hand, ready to leave for work.

"Can't you go tomorrow?" he muttered, irritated with her and with himself.

"I'd rather have them today," she replied simply.

And that was that. He turned down his friend's invitation to get Mexican food after practice and jumped into the Jetta instead to drive down to the diner. It was a bit warmer now, and daylight was lingering later.

He was already inside and going through the list his mom had texted up on the mezzanine when something clattered loudly enough to be heard above the music in his earphones. Gage turned, removing the buds from his ears.

It was silent for a moment, and he thought it might be nothing until someone banged against the front door. The sound came twice, three, four times. He crouched down, heart racing. Was someone trying to break through his mother's barriers?

He pulled out his phone and called her.

"Hello?" Miriam's voice was muffled. They were probably already at the restaurant.

"Mom? I'm at the club," he whispered. "Someone is banging on the door."

"I'll be right there," she said.

Gage waited for her to hang up, but she stayed on the line. He could vaguely make out the excuse she was giving the Nguyen's. Something about the sink flooding. Richard would stay, and she would come back if it didn't take too long. She's so sorry and so disappointed she won't get to taste the duck! Richard will get it to go for her.

"Okay," she said, putting the phone up to her cheek again. "I'll be there in ten minutes. Talk to me. Tell me what's happening."

"I'm not sure," Gage said as he glanced at the door and windows. "I'm upstairs. They've banged on the door four times." He flinched as the sound resounded once more. "Five times."

"Who are they?" Miriam asked.

The call disconnected for a second when it transferred to her car.

"I don't know," he said when she was back on the line. "I didn't see anyone on my way here. Could just be some kids out in the woods trying to break in for a joke."

"Those kids would be bypassing some pretty strong concealment spells, Gage," his mother said. She had made an effort to sound calm in front of the Nguyens, but he could now hear her frantic breathing. "It's alright. That door is harder to break through than you'd think."

"Right," he muttered.

Gage knew theoretically that magic triumphed over brute force, but with how loud the slamming sounded, he couldn't shake the irrational fear that they would break through.

"I'm pulling into the diner," Miriam finally said nearly ten minutes later.

"Do you need me to do anything?" Gage asked. He hadn't practiced magic in months—years?—but he liked to believe he could still be some help. "The herbs or—"

"It's fine," she replied shortly. "Just stay put. Got it?"

"Got it."

"Okay," she muttered. "I'll see you in a bit."

The line went dead.

"Wait, what?" Gage stared down at his phone, mouth agape. "She hangs up *now*?"

Something hit the door once more. Annoyed, he rose to his feet and approached the stairs, eyes glued on the entrance. Slowly, he made his way down, waiting for any indication that his mother had arrived. From this perch, he could hear grunts outside.

He approached the peephole. When his mom arrived, was he really to let her face them alone? What if they had come for him again? He pressed his hands against the door, drawing his eye close to the glass piece. A few people gathered across from him, four, maybe five. It was hard to make out their features in the dark, but two were close enough to the entrance to be illuminated.

Two burly men stood well above six feet, fully bearded and dressed in grimy clothes. Gage gulped. At least they weren't Mistlanders.

This was new to him, he realized. He wasn't used to worrying about other people. Much less about his mom. It was hard for him to imagine her hurt or scared.

The men turned, looking behind them into the woods. Gage tensed. His hand rose to the doorknob. Miriam had told him to stay put. He let the flesh of his fingertips rest on the cool metal. His view was partially blocked, but he tried to gauge the situation through the reactions on the men's faces.

First, they stiffened, shifting their bodies to face away from him. He heard their voices raise, but the words were too muffled to make out. Then, at the periphery, blue lights appeared. His hand closed around the knob. He could make out a figure by the pines, walking down the hill. More shouting—had she said something?

Gage furrowed his brow, frustrated that he couldn't hear them, frustrated that he couldn't help. He held his breath for just a moment, then retreated from the door. He crossed the room to wait on the stairs instead. In minutes, the knob shook gently, and the door opened. There stood Miriam, the two men, and three young girls.

"Mom?" Gage said, standing. "Do you know them?"

"No, but we're helping them out," Miriam replied as she let the group in. "They're going to be staying here for a few days."

"What?" Gage snapped. "How can you let strangers into our house?"

"Gage." Her tone of voice in itself was a warning. "This isn't our house, and no one has been using it since your sisters left. You certainly aren't," she said pointedly. "What's the problem?"

He could see now that, other than the two men, the rest were young girls. They placed large backpacks on the floor by the entrance and seemed not to dare venture further. He glanced at them, at their curly hair—the smallest one was barely taller than Meena—and rolled his eyes.

"Whatever," he said. "Do what you want."

He could feel his mother glaring at him. He wasn't usually this bratty. These days, he couldn't seem to find his patience.

"I'm leaving. Maybe I can still catch some of my friends at Maracas," Gage said as he turned toward the door.

"You're not going *anywhere*," Miriam said, her tone low and threatening. "You walk out of that door, and you're not even *seeing* car keys for a month."

Gage returned her glower silently before acquiescing. He threw his head back, raising his eyes as high as they could go, and muttered, "Fine."

"Go get the inflatable mattress," she told him.

Miriam stayed in the club's tiny kitchen placing a kettle on the stove. The family sat behind her at a round table—the makeshift dining room. The girls were quiet while the men whispered between themselves. They were werepeople.

She noticed their trace as soon as she parked her car by the diner. She couldn't be sure if they had smelled Gage and followed him to the club or had just been drawn to the vicinity because of their magic. She didn't know how they had seen through the concealment charms, either. She would reinforce them before leaving.

After the incident with the Mistlanders, Miriam took three days off work and brewed around the clock, casting hundreds of spells and drenching their house with potions to keep it safe. She hadn't thought to renew the safeties on the club— only she ever ventured out there now—and she kicked herself for not realizing it before sending Gage to run her errands.

"I'm done," her son said, appearing beside her then. "Can I go now?"

Miriam mulled the question over, then said, "Wait ten more minutes. Can you serve the tea when it boils?" She gestured to the kettle. "I need to find out more about these people."

She could see the protest in Gage's eyes, but he nodded anyway, silently positioning himself to watch the stove. Miriam smiled softly, running her finger through the hair that flopped forward over his eyes, pushing it back.

"Thanks, love," she said.

He resisted the urge to push her hand away.

The men were standing around the sofa bed, tucking the girls in. Next to it was the inflatable mattress Gage had blown up—a relic of the days when his sisters used to have sleepovers there, when they were younger and closer.

They straightened and turned when Miriam approached.

"Will you come talk with me upstairs?" she asked.

It took a few more minutes for the kettle to whistle. Gage snapped the burner off the moment he heard it, hoping the sound wouldn't wake the sleeping girls. He poured it into the cups Miriam had prepared and headed upstairs. A few steps in, he started to make out some parts of the conversation.

"They drove us out of our city—" one man was saying.

"First, they threatened to expose us, then they almost kidnapped our youngest. We fought them off, but they came back with backup. Dozens of them..." the other added.

"Portland's a big city. There weren't enough practitioners to drive them off?" his mother asked.

"We tried to find someone, anyone, but..."

At this point, they came into sight. One of the men's heads was bowed, his eyes were closed, and he was holding his hand over his face.

"There was no one there," he said.

"What do you mean?" Miriam asked.

Gage had never seen his mother's gaze so fierce. He could hardly recognize her. Neither she nor the men reacted as he appeared.

"We must have messed the spell up—" the second man said as he tried to comfort his companion. He lay his hand on his shoulder, gently rubbing his upper back. "Or the other practitioners could be in hiding."

His partner seemed unconvinced. To Miriam, he said, "You should try it, the spell. I'm afraid you may be the only practitioners left in Oregon."

Gage tried to avoid their eyes as he set the mugs down. He realized that he could stay up here and listen to their conversation but chose to wait downstairs, instead.

"Ready?" Miriam asked, finding him in the kitchen a few minutes later.

The men's murmurs were still audible above them.

Gage rose from the kitchen table, locking his phone and slipping it into his pocket. He had forgotten how terrible the reception was at the club—he'd spent the last ten minutes swiping through old photos in his library. He came across one of Ada's twenty-second birthday just a few months ago and found himself fixated on the person standing next to her, her best friend, Isabel.

Had Ada said anything to her before leaving? It felt like he hadn't seen his sisters' faces in a long time. He glanced at the gaggle of children sleeping in the living room. He hoped they were safer where they are now.

"My car's at the diner, too," Gage said as he followed his mom into the woods. "I'm kind of tired, so I think I'll just head home. See you there?"

"I have to make a stop before," she replied. "But go ahead. I'll meet you there."

"Where are you going?" he asked. She was quiet for a second. "Mom?"

He couldn't see her face in the dark, but he heard her sigh.

"Jed said they were drawn to Hope Springs by a strong magical energy," she said.

"Jed?"

"Yeah, Jed and Bo."

Those sounded like fake names to Gage.

"So?" he asked. "You're going to go look for it now?"

"I think I already know where it is," his mom said.

Headlights briefly broke through the shadowy forest. They were close enough to the main road to see the flickering light from a broken streetlight by the parking lot.

She hadn't answered his question.

"So you're going there? Now?" Gage asked.

"Yes, I need to confirm my hypothesis," Miriam said, stopping to turn toward him. "It's not too far—should only take about thirty minutes."

"I'll go with you," he blurted.

She glanced at him, surprised. "There's no need. It won't be dangerous," she said.

"There shouldn't be an issue then."

They crossed the street. Gage stepped up to the passenger side of her car. He took his phone from his pocket and checked the clock.

"It's only ten," he said. "You can drop me off after to pick up the Jetta."

Miriam sized him up and smiled. "Sure, I appreciate the company," she said and got into the driver's seat.

They drove for a few minutes in silence, but Gage recognized the route.

"Are we heading to school?" he asked.

"Close," his mom replied. "We'll have to leave the car at the soccer field and go back into the forest."

Miriam pulled into the lot, turned the car off, and twisted around in her seat. She rifled through the random assortment of things that seemed to permanently occupy her car's backseat, then passed him a flashlight.

"Here," she said. "So you don't use up your battery."

It was like déjà vu. Same path, same darkness, same company. This time, there was no glowing sibling floating in the middle of the woods to guide them, but Miriam walked purposefully. She seemed so sure of where she was going that Gage found it strange at first, but then he felt the same pull.

At first, it was subtle, stemming from the pit of his stomach.

114

Once he noticed it, he didn't worry about keeping up with his mother. They were following the same scent.

"I knew it," he heard her mutter. She looked at him and asked, "Can you feel it?"

"Yes," Gage said. "Is that another practitioner?" he whispered.

"What?" she asked, laughing. "No, silly. It's through here."

She headed for a break in the tree line, stepping over some bushes and into a clearing. He followed closely behind, his curiosity building. What type of creature could be generating this powerful of a pull. If wolves were following it from the coast into the mountains... if even a fledgling practitioner like him could feel it... He stumbled into the clearing and found himself shin-high in grass. No, not grass. Swinging his flashlight around, he took a sharp breath.

"It looks different from how you remember it, doesn't it?" Miriam asked, crouching down to dig her fingers into the ground.

"Different?" he asked as he squinted, his eyebrows pulling together. "Have I been here before? I think I'd remember a place like this."

"You haven't been in a place like this," Miriam said. She turned, and the beam of his torch illuminated her face briefly before he aimed it away. "But you've been here before."

Gage took another look around. What he originally thought was overgrown grass was actually a dense population of wildflowers. They grew about two feet tall, their petals reaching out into the world like yearning arms. In all his years helping out at the flower shop, he had never seen any like this before. They all faced the same direction, but not how sunflowers do, seeking out the sun. Instead, they all faced inward, toward the center of the field.

"Did you see the trees?" Miriam asked, standing by one herself. "Fascinating. I've always wanted to learn more about glimpses of Eden."

"What of Eden?" Gage called, following her voice. He shone the light on the tree as he approached but couldn't quite make out what she was talking about.

"Here," she said, reaching out and guiding his flashlight down. "It's easier to see in the dark."

"Oh! It's glowing."

"It's her magic," she said. "Cara's magic."

* * *

The next day, Gage woke up to the smell of burning fat. Still a bit groggy, he thumped down to the kitchen.

"Dad?" he called out.

"Oh honey, you're up!" It was his mother, shoveling charred bacon from his father's favorite cast iron skillet. "Breakfast is ready. I was about to go wake you up. How did you sleep?" she asked.

He rubbed his eyes, settling into a stool by the kitchen's island.

"All right," he croaked. "Where is everyone?"

"They moved Meena's swimming lessons up this week. The instructor is going out of town, and we wanted to squeeze a session in before he left," Miriam said. As she spoke, she chose a couple of still salvageable strips and spooned some scrambled eggs onto a plate. "Here," she said and handed it to him. "Let me check if the toast is done."

He took it and started eating silently, then stopped and

added some salt. As he slowly came around to a fully awakened state, he noticed his mother staring at him. He took a pointed bite of his toast and stared right back.

"Will you come spend some time with me today?" she asked with a smile. "You'd be a big help."

"What do you need me to do?" he said through a forkful of egg.

"Don't speak with your mouth full," Miriam berated him. "I'm going to go conceal that magical spot in the woods we found yesterday, the glimpse of Eden. I could finish much faster with two pairs of hands casting instead of one."

"You know my magic skills suck," Gage said and sighed, pushing away from the table. "I'd really rather not get involved."

He could feel her eyes on him as he crossed the dining room toward the stairs.

"You need to be able to defend yourself, Gage," she said.

It was enough to stop him in his tracks—he'd had similar thoughts lately.

"You put a bunch of spells and charms on me," he reminded her half-heartedly.

"There are many powerful practitioners out there that can see through them," she replied.

"I won't go into the forest anymore," he said, jutting his chin out. "I'll stay here and at school. I'll even come home earlier, but I'd like to still go out with my friends."

"You can go anywhere you want if you just train with me a few hours a week," Miriam pressed.

He turned, meeting her eyes. She had crossed her arms, and her expression said that she knew how this was going to end.

"I don't want to be a practitioner," Gage said.

"I understand that," his mom replied, then pursed her lips. "I don't always want to be, either."

Her sincerity was disarming. Try as he would to distance himself from his family and rebel against them, the truth was that there was not much to push back against. He often ended up feeling embarrassed and small-minded.

"How many hours?" he asked, exhaling through his nose sharply.

"Just three a week," his mom said and stood up a little straighter. "We can do it all on weekends in the mornings, too, so you can hang out with your friends afterward."

Gage pretended to deliberate. They both knew he wouldn't say no. They both knew he couldn't.

* * *

Gage had an odd childhood memory that would always float back to the top of his mind. Sometimes, it would take weeks, sometimes years, but it would always unearth itself again. Sometimes, something would catch his eye, and the images would flash in his head. Sometimes, he would dream it again. And again. And again.

When he did, he would wake up feeling lost, disoriented, not sure if this was reality or if he had just left it. Over the years, he developed a habit of getting up and walking over to his parents' room to check they were still there. It didn't always make him feel more secure when he saw them. He would feel alienated for days to come. He noticed Meena would avoid him.

In the memory, he was maybe three or four years old. He

remembered his Elmo bedspread and the race car nightlight he kept nearby. He was bedridden with a terrible fever. His sisters would come by in the afternoon after school to sit by his bed and read to him.

In his dreams, they would read the same stories two and three times, showing him the same pictures again and again and again...His parents would be with him the rest of the time: his father during the day and his mother falling asleep at his bedside every night. In the morning, she would check his temperature, give him his meds, and kiss him goodbye again.

And again.

And again.

He had never brought it up to his family, but his mind always returned to that place, lying immobile in his bed, soft-edged shapes and figures blending together, his consciousness waning. In that place, he felt small and childlike. The days seemed like an endless loop. He felt like he had surrendered to the stillness.

* * *

Miriam and Gage spent the morning drawing sigils in the woods across from the soccer field. The magical energy the Mistlanders wrenched from Cara that day was highly concentrated, she explained. It interacted with the physical world and left its mark, as magic always does. Miriam knew of no way to turn it back to its previous state save for turning back time, but even that was a temporary solution and would require more effort than Gage was willing to put in.

They were stepping out from the cover of the trees when

he heard a familiar voice calling.

"Is that Gage?" It was Riley Cole. She was piling into one of her friends' cars. He kicked himself for forgetting about Saturday cheer practice. Now, he was emerging from the woods with his mother and no plausible explanation.

Before he could come up with an excuse, his mother stepped up. He cringed as soon as he heard her voice.

"If it isn't little Riley," Miriam sing-songed. She was grinning. "I heard you got an early acceptance into Berkeley. Your parents must be thrilled."

"Yes, oh my God," Riley said and laughed, ignoring the questioning glances her friends were shooting her from inside the car. "You two almost scared me to death when I saw you coming out of the forest."

Miriam chuckled. "I'm sorry, hon," she said. "I was just showing Gage one of my favorite spots. The path isn't too well marked, so I'd rather you kids don't go in there alone, but there's an absolutely magical patch just about a mile in where bushes grow heavy with wild berries. They're about to be in season, and I wanted to check if any were growing."

"That sounds amazing," Riley replied, smiling. "They must be delicious."

"I make some killer wild berry pie." Miriam winked before adding, "I'll have Gage bring you some when they're ripe."

Gage waited until they were back in the car to crinkle his face in contempt.

"Wild berry pie?" he asked, emphasizing each word so it sounded stranger than the last.

"What?" His mother glanced at him from the driver's seat.

"I'm sure it *would* be killer," he said and shot her a look. "As in, it would probably kill someone." His mom's laughter goaded him on. "Who knows what kind of spell you would end up brewing instead."

"Okay, okay," Miriam said and wiped the tears that had gathered in the corners of her eyes. "I get it already. I'll have your dad buy some berries from the farmers' market and make the damn pie."

"Good," Gage said, then chuckled.

* * *

A few days later, at school, Riley approached him to say, "Hi."

Last period had just ended. Gage was putting his books away and grabbing his clothes for practice. He looked up from his locker.

"Hey," he said.

"Um," she hummed, clutching her notebooks close to her chest.

He waited for her to continue.

"What's up?" he asked when she didn't.

Her friends were watching from across the hall. They were pretending to look at their phones, but he would glance at them every now and then to find one or two sets of eyes on him. Then they'd turn their gaze back to their screens, flustered, whispering and giggling under their breath.

Finally, having built up some courage, Riley got it out in one quick breath. "Would you like to go to prom with me?" she asked.

"Prom is almost a month away," was Gage's automatic response. He frowned, wondering if this was a prank. He knew Riley, though, and she was too nice to do something like that.

"Yeah," she said and ran a hand through her hair, letting it fall easily over her shoulder. "I just didn't want anyone to ask you first."

He tore his eyes from the dark strands.

The words slipped out of his mouth before he could stop them. "Sure. I mean, why don't we grab dinner first?"

"What?" she asked, almost as surprised as he was. "I mean, yeah."

They both laughed awkwardly, eyes dropping momentarily.

"Cool. Friday?" Gage asked, then shut his locker door roughly, bag in tow.

He didn't know where this confidence had come from. He had barely any experience with girls outside of the silly games high schoolers would play after stealing some of their parents' booze.

Riley smiled and said, "I'm down."

"Text me," Gage said, starting to take some backwards steps. "I'm going to be late to practice."

"Okay," she said mostly to herself.

The faint sound of her voice almost made him chuckle, but he caught himself.

Gage crossed the school's courtyard briskly, heading toward the soccer field. The early afternoon sun beat on his shoulders, and he resisted the urge to stop to pull his sweater off. It was barely Spring, but it was starting to feel like Summer.

"G-spot," Sam called out when he saw him coming down the steps to the field.

"Shut up," Gage said and punched him hard on the arm.

"What are you all happy and smiling about?" Sam asked.

They were best friends. He could read Gage like an open book.

"Nothing." Gage blew him off, walking past him toward the locker rooms. "Come on, I don't want to be late."

"Whatever." Sam scoffed but followed anyway. "I heard the cheerleaders saw you coming out of the woods with your mom on a Saturday morning. Something about a pie?"

"Yeah, I don't know," Gage said dismissively. "You know how my mom is. She likes a lot of weird shit."

"You say that, but I think it's better to like pie than this," he said, then held up Gage's towel. "Weird ass anime."

"Goddamn." Gage snatched it back. "You know that was a gag gift."

Sam ducked out of his reach, eyes glimmering with mischief. "Then why do you use it so much?" he asked.

"I only have so many towels, okay?" Gage shot back.

"Yeah, yeah…" They fell silent for a minute as they started changing. "Real talk, though. I heard Riley was planning on asking you to prom," Sam said.

"She did."

"Bro, what?" Sam paused, shocked. "What did you say?"

"Yes," Gage said, laughing.

"Of course." His friend nodded. "Who in their right mind could say no to that sweet face?"

"Shut up," Gage mumbled.

"I'm not even fucking with you. I'm just shocked you didn't consider this something worth sharing," Sam said, his voice going higher as he placed a hand on his chest. "With your own best friend? I am offended."

"Shut up!" Gage yelled.

They heard the coach yell outside on the field and picked

up the pace. Within two minutes, they were jogging outside, apologies ready.

"Look who decided to join us," Coach Byers said. "What an honor."

Another senior on the team called out, "I heard you have a date with Riley on Friday, G-Spot. Living up to your name?"

Gage rolled his eyes. This would be a long day.

11

Behind the veil, Paris looked like time had stopped centuries ago. Small stone houses with wooden beams and tiled roofs lined the path, dramatic feats of Gothic architecture towered in the distance. The sisters looked around, fascinated.

"I feel like I'm in a movie." Ada gushed.

Amit led them to a building with a sign over its door, *Auberge des Balances*. A tipped scale was carved above the letters.

"Don't let anyone hear you speaking English," she said as she propped the door open.

They took her to mean that they should stay quiet; it was the only language they had in common, after all.

Cara wondered if it was the type of place where Americans were charged double. It looked like a bar at first glance; patrons sat around wooden tables drinking, animal pelts hung from the rafters, and a hearth was lit in the far end. The cacophony of voices enveloped them as tangibly as the heat did when they entered. Ada, who was half-expecting a sampling of medieval fashion, was rather disappointed with the jeans and sweaters that abounded.

Amit approached an elderly woman reclining in the corner

of the room and spoke in quick French. She handed the woman a slip of paper, and the woman, in turn, fished a key out from deep in her pocket to give to her.

Once upstairs, Amit opened the second door on the left, revealing two twin beds crammed into a small room. The girls had no energy to question her. Cara closed the door behind her and said, "Bedtime?"

They pulled open their bags, rifling through for pajamas and toiletries. The bathroom was at the end of the corridor and shared with other rooms, but they didn't see anyone else on their way in or out.

Maneuvering into bed, Ada wondered aloud, "I reckon Amit's in the room next door, right?"

Just then, there was a knock at the door. It was Amit, appearing as if summoned.

"Are you two okay?" she asked. She was met with two blank, sleepy stares. "Do you want to talk about what happened tonight?"

Cara and Ada's eyes met, and they understood each other intuitively.

"Thanks for checking in on us," Cara said, "but we're really tired."

Ada slouched deeper into the covers and muttered, "Can we talk about it tomorrow?"

They had just watched a man die; killed him, really. At that moment, Cara felt that more frightening than the act itself was how little she was lingering on it. In Ada's eyes, she had seen a familiar uneasiness—and exhaustion.

It looked like Amit might say something more, but then she nodded and closed the door behind her. They heard the sound of the key turning in the lock. Cara switched the light off. They would sleep while they could. Nothing was haunting them yet.

* * *

A red sky. Looming white towers. Cold, hard stone burning into her side, her leg, her cheek. A horrible ringing in her head. Ada strained to open her eyes. Instead, she awoke.

She craned her neck up to see Cara still asleep. Letting her head plop back onto the pillow, she tried to drift back into sleep, only to hit a wall. Ada had never been an early riser, but she was a vivid dreamer. The elaborate settings, characters, and plots could rouse such intense emotions as the night transpired that she would sometimes be jolted awake in the early morning hours with a feeling of having left behind unfinished business.

To her chagrin, even the most complex storylines would slip from her grasp, dissolving back into the archives of her subconscious brain, usually never to resurface again. Ada was left feeling like a dreamless sleeper, never able to tell her nocturne adventures over the breakfast table like her sister often did, and left with the nagging sense that her part had been cut short. A sense she had been yanked abruptly from a race, not unlike the anxiety of forgetting the last task on your to-do list.

Just then, she heard the sound of the lock clicking.

Ada sat up. The doorknob turned. It was Amit.

"Good morning," she said.

"Hey," Ada replied, smoothing her unruly dark hair back. Her voice was hoarse and unfamiliar.

"There's breakfast downstairs."

"I'll wake Cara up."

They showered first, coming down to find the tavern practically empty. Amit was sitting in the back corner, a large plate of viennoiseries in front of her. The girls were woozy with hunger, having skipped dinner and had an early lunch the day before.

"Are these for us?" Ada asked, already reaching for a croissant aux amandes.

Amit nodded, but didn't look up from the open laptop in front of her.

Cara considered her between bites of a brioche. They rarely found Amit on the computer.

"Are you on the database?" she asked.

"I'm re-arranging your curriculum," Amit replied and finally glanced up. "We have neither privacy nor resources; the methodology must be revised."

Ada nodded, more preoccupied with the bread than her answer, but Cara could tell their guardian was on edge since arriving in Paris. Not only that, her appearance was slightly off. It was the first time they had seen her astounding mane of black hair slicked back, tied into a tight bun; they had assumed she didn't own any hair ties since she always haphazardly twisted and knotted it around itself. She wore her usual black-on-black, but the clothes were more form-fitting, tailored.

Her posture had been what tipped Cara off initially, though. Amit was prone to slinking and sliding, prowling and lurking, skulking, slipping in and out of shadows, blending into corners, melting into walls. It was like a gravitational pull emanated from her navel, pulling the rest of her body down into it.

Today, she sat tall, shoulders broad and spine straight, her chin raised, looking over her high nose bridge at the computer screen. It wasn't that she was at ease, precisely, but like she was trying to give the impression of ease.

Cara went out on a limb, figuring Amit wouldn't go out of her way to impress them.

"Are we meeting someone?" she asked.

Amit's eyes narrowed as she replied, "Why do you ask?"

"Really?" Ada said, perking up. "Is that why you dressed up?"

"I'm not dressed up," she snapped. More calmly, she added, "But you're correct. We're seeing some of my old acquaintances."

"Your friends?" Ada gasped.

Her sister interjected, "I thought we were in hiding."

"You are," Amit said. "But no one knows you're traveling with me. We'll lie to them about who you are. It will be too suspicious if any of these people discover I'm in Paris and didn't reach out."

"You said we can't speak English…" Cara started to say, but Amit was already shaking her head.

"It's fine," she said. "Unless they bring someone I don't know, you can speak."

"When are they coming?" Ada asked once she was done licking the sugar off her sticky fingers.

The front door opened, and a gust of cold air momentarily lowered the room's temperature.

"Now. They're here," Amit said, then stood and said something in French.

The girls twisted in their seats to see three people entering. A woman led them with a confident gait and an easy smile.

She exclaimed when she saw Amit, opening her arms as if to embrace her from across the room. To her right was a tall, thin man with a brown beard and a big yellow coat. He also smiled, his eyes hidden behind glinting glasses. The third man was much larger, a half head taller than his companions, and almost as wide as the door. His head was shaved on the sides, but his hair grew long and blond at the top pulled into a bun at the nape of his neck. As he approached, Cara noticed white markings on the bare parts of his scalp. Thanks to Amit's lessons, she could tell they were Nordic in origin.

The woman grasped Amit's hands when she reached them, kissing her on both cheeks and prattling on in French. Amit replied in English, a wry twist in her voice, "It's been so long."

The woman glanced at the girls, who were still seated at the table staring, and let herself be led. "A long time, indeed!" she said. "The last time I saw you, we were in the Wasteland two feet deep in mud, trying to ward off a hippo with confusion charms." They all laughed. "Who are these precious girls?"

"We're her nieces," Ada said and extended her arm for a handshake. "I'm Lola."

Cara resisted the urge to roll her eyes. Her sister had named all her favorite dolls Lola as a child. She went with "Carmen." It was their paternal grandmother's name.

Amit didn't miss a beat.

"Their parents are attending a massive Spring Equinox ritual and weren't keen on leaving them behind on their own in New York, what with all that's been happening," she said with a raised an eyebrow, and her friends nodded.

The girls put on somber expressions, trying their best to hide the curiosity the conversation inspired.

"Of course," the woman replied knowingly. "Terrible things

have been happening everywhere lately. It is bizarre!"

The words sounded different, rolling off her French tongue.

They took a seat, Amit settling between her friends and the girls.

"How have you been?" she asked the group broadly.

"Marthe and I have been well," the man in the yellow jacket said. "Paris is also going through tough times, but we have done our best to keep a low profile. Otto almost got caught up in one of those mass executions the other day, however." He gestured at the other man, Otto.

"Mass executions?" Cara asked, her eyes widening. They had only been in hiding a month, and the world had descended into such chaos?

"Eh, he means the battles," Marthe said with a shrug. "But the difference in strength is really, how do you say." She turned to the man who spoke earlier.

"Unfair?" he suggested. "Mismatched?"

She turned back to Amit as if forgetting Cara had been the one to ask, saying, "It is one-sided slaughter."

"Why are they battling?" Ada asked.

Marthe gave her an odd look, and Amit jumped in to smooth things over, "Excuse them, they're not familiar with Parisian traditions." Turning to Ada, she explained, "It's a long-standing practice that, should a practitioner be challenged to a duel in certain settings under select circumstances, they must face their opponent or risk being exiled from Paris forever. There are historic factions that began as familiar alliances centuries back—"

Marthe interrupted, "They've become institutions. Feudal lords trying to control everyone and everything."

"They're a mafia," Otto said bitterly. His eyes grew distant, as if recalling bad memories.

Amit made sure to finish her point, "When the factions challenge each other, it's a battle rather than a duel."

"And Paris is their battleground," the other man added.

"Emile," Amit said with a frown. "Don't be absurd. Battles are always carried out in negative space, are they not?"

He shook his head, leaning in, and said, "Their warfare extends beyond the battles, Amit. They conduct terror campaigns against each other and the city. Especially la Pucelle d'Orleans."

"You mean Jeanne D'Arc?" Amit asked, chuckling. "Has she returned from the dead?"

No one else laughed.

"She might have," Emile said.

"With her brain all scrambled up, perhaps." Marthe muttered.

"Speak clearly," Amit replied sharply. "We all know no one would have dared desecrate her ashes. What is it you mean?"

"Of course it's not Jeanne," Emile said with a huff. "She calls herself Ariel, the Lion of God. It's probably not her real name, but she has no kin to reprove her. Nobody knows who she is or where she came from, just that she is extraordinarily strong."

"How strong?" Amit asked.

"Strong enough to have defeated seven of the eight first factions." This was Marthe.

Cara and Ada didn't have enough information to contextualize what they were saying, but they could tell from the atmosphere that it was grim.

"So she has strong companions," Amit started, but she was

interrupted by Marthe's wagging finger.

"Ariel does not belong to a faction."

"What?"

Emile was the one to reply, "She fights alone."

"That's impossible. She must be convening with dark forces." Even as Amit said this, he was shaking his head.

"Dozens have tried to prove that, but they've all failed to produce evidence. She claims to receive her strength from prayer and proximity to God," he said.

"The Catholic one," Marthe clarified.

"Well, has anyone proved *that*?" Amit asked.

They both scrunched up their faces and shrugged, turning their palms up.

"It's debatable," Emile conceded.

"Complicated," Marthe added. "Nothing has been demonstrated beyond a shadow of a doubt, but no one would put this past the Catholic god, either."

Emile seemed to disagree, but Otto spoke before he could. "She has wielded the holy lance of Saint Maurice."

"The one in Vienna?" Amit asked, smirking.

"No," Otto said. "The real one. The archbishop confirmed it."

"Well, he would." She scoffed.

"The Catholic church has done everything in its power to discredit Ariel," he said as he shook his head. "Including testing her sacred artifacts only to reveal that they have genuinely been blessed by their God and wielded by their saints. They're not too happy about a nameless woman appearing suddenly, claiming to be their Lord's envoy and the sole executor of his will. After pushing misogynist rhetoric for millennia? Their God sent a woman?"

The table was silent. Cara took the chance to say something she had been thinking about for a while. "Is she supposed to be, like, the second coming or something?"

Nobody said anything for a moment. Then Emile smiled a humorless smile. "Of the son of God, you mean?" he asked.

"No. Maybe a Horseman," he said, alluding to the apocalypse. "Maybe Death."

* * *

The girls spent their first day in Paris much like they had spent their first day in Nebraska, locked up indoors with a long list of words to memorize. Amit had meant it when she said that the location they chose to escape to was unimportant. They would be restricted just the same wherever they went.

"Do you have any chips left?" Ada asked.

They were sprawled on their beds, shins resting on the headboards. As usual, she was finding it hard to focus on the page in front of her.

Cara glanced at the pile of empty bags and wrappers to her left, and said, "No."

"Damn," Ada huffed, then pretended to review her list silently. "I can't believe she just left us here."

Cara rolled her eyes. "She probably has better things to do than watch us study," she said. "Now shut up. I can't concentrate."

Ada did shut up—for a few minutes. She glanced up to see Cara still pouring over her notebook, then looked out the window. A small bird was perched on the narrow ledge outside. She stared at her scribbled notes, then peered back at

Cara, who didn't bother looking up despite feeling her sister's gaze. Just as she was about to open her mouth to voice some other irrelevant thought, a hard thud resonated through the room. Her head snapped back toward the window.

"What the hell?" she cried.

Cara finished reading the page deliberately slowly, then turned a beat later to ask, "What was that?"

"I'm not sure."

Ada had risen from the bed and was standing by the window. There didn't seem to be anything amiss except that the bird was gone. She pressed her hands against the glass, closing the short gap between them and said, "I don't see anything."

"Let me see." Cara nudged her aside, turning her head this way and that. "It was probably just an animal or something."

"Outside our window?" Ada asked and scrunched her nose. "This is the second floor."

"We're not that high up," Cara said. She shrugged, returning to the bed. "Stop getting distracted."

Ada groaned and leaned her forehead against the window pane. Her eyes drifted downward and paused on the ground directly under them, processing the image. Legs? A person? She straightened.

"I think there's someone down there," she said.

Cara didn't even look up before replying, "There's nothing down there."

"Wait," Ada said, her tone changing. "I think someone's hurt."

Her sister sighed, pushing herself back. "Are you sure?" she asked.

"Well, I can see legs and blood…"

Cara pushed her out of the way.

"Shit, you're right."

"Should we go down there?"

They stared at each other, each waiting for the other to decide.

* * *

The boy used to have a name, among other things.

In the infinite vastness and merciless heat of the desert, his family would set up their house. A few wooden poles and fluttering cloth were enough to shield them from the sun that sought them out from its perch in the sky. In the evening, when it lowered, their house would be gone, packed away as they continued on their arduous journey. But in that time, when they lounged under the multi-colored fabrics, exhausted from walking and hiding and hoping, his mother would smooth his coarse hair with her coarse hands and tell him that he was beautiful and would have a beautiful life in a beautiful place. She would stroke his face and call him her favorite boy.

He knew he wasn't. Her favorite boy had been taken from her seven years ago by the militias that came and ransacked their village, taking everybody's sons to use as cannon fodder in their never-ending war. Her second favorite boy had stepped on a landmine on his way to the creek a few years after. He should have known to stay on the path, but saw a colorful bird perched in the field to his left and thought the feathers would go well in one of the necklaces his mother made. Her third favorite son was a daughter. She would never speak about what happened to her, although, sometimes…No, it is better not to. Even so, he was happy enough to be her fourth favorite son. He was happy enough to be cherished so much that she would leave her home—her terrible, terrible home that she loved so dearly—to ensure she would never need a fifth.

In the merciless heat and infinite vastness of the desert, he had his mother. He had her love. He had a little water, some salted fish, and a small village that moved with them, and he hoped that one day he would have even more. This was his mother's hope, at least. To him, this was enough. To him, it was everything.

12

Amit was walking back to the inn, just a block away, when she saw two familiar figures near the entrance. They glanced about furtively and ducked into an alley. She picked up the pace. As she grew nearer, she started to hear voices arguing faintly.

"Can't we, like, hover him up or something?" one was saying.

"And then what? What do we tell Amit? That we picked some guy up off the street?" This was Cara, obviously. "We should just call in an anonymous tip or something and let the authorities take care of him."

"There's no such thing as an anonymous tip, remember? We can't just leave him here!"

"What kind of trouble have you gotten yourselves into now?" Amit asked, having come up behind them.

They flinched violently and stumbled back. She saw they had been standing around a heavily injured man propped up, unconscious, against the wall. She threw her head back and sighed. "There's nothing we can do. You know that, right?" she asked.

"Yes," Cara answered readily, compliant always.

This shouldn't have irked Amit, but it did. Her sister was

12

quiet for a moment, looking down at the ground between their shoes.

"Ada?" Amit pressed, scowling.

"I know we are in no position to be helping others," Ada said. She was picking her words carefully. "And I know this sounds stupid, but I can literally feel his pain."

Her eyes pleaded with Amit to somehow understand.

"What are you talking about?" Cara groaned and rolled her eyes.

Amit leaned down to get a better look. Up close, she could tell he wasn't much older than Miriam's daughters were. She reached out a hand to touch his face but pulled it away at the last second. It was like a field of magic surrounded him, likely what Ada had sensed. His clothes were in tatters, and his short, tightly coiled hair was matted with blood. A pang of sympathy bloomed in her chest.

"He's probably a refugee. I heard Ariel is not kind to them," Amit said and stood back up. "I'll speak with the innkeeper. Stay with him for now, and—" Ruffling through her coat pocket, she produced a small notepad and pen, scribbled a few lines into it, and handed it to Ada. "Here. This should help a little in the meantime."

Amit had written down a couple of charms phonetically. The sisters shared a surprised look.

"Thanks," Ada whispered, but their guardian had already started walking back.

* * *

The boy awoke to something cool and damp on his forehead. He furrowed his brow, and the sensation disappeared.

139

"I think he's waking up," a voice said.

"No way," another chimed in, coming closer.

They weren't voices he recognized. He could feel a soft surface beneath him—a bed? He couldn't remember the last time he had been in one. The air was warm. He forced his eyes open. Gasps. Two girls stood above him.

"You're awake! How do you feel?" one asked.

They looked alike. Sisters? Cousins?

He felt like someone had cast a body-swapping spell on him. It had been years since anyone had concerned themselves over him like this. He stared back, stunned until he realized they were waiting for his answer.

"I...I'm—" he said as he tried to prop himself up on his forearms and found he felt much better than expected. "Not bad."

He sat up and looked at his hands, his arms. The injuries that had dotted them were gone, as was the grime that seemed like a permanent fixture recently.

"Did you heal me?" he asked and looked up at them with wonder.

"Well, duh," the one in the front exclaimed.

He couldn't make sense of this response before the other girl started bombarding him with questions, "What's your name? Where are you from?"

"Cara!"

* * *

Nothing had been the same for the boy since he was separated from his mother—torn from her grasping hands, thrown into captivity. His magnanimous captors decided what his life was going to be for him: where he could live, for how long, with whom, while doing what. And his mother? Deprived entry, the boy sometimes wondered if she was still trying to get in or was her mission was fulfilled? She had delivered him over the border into the warm embrace of luxury and plenty and so could now resign herself to a lonely existence amidst the dust. He sometimes hoped she never made it through and saw what she had sacrificed everything for. It would be a mercy.

* * *

"What do you mean you don't have a name?" Cara frowned. "Everybody has a name."

"Yes, Cara," Ada stressed, widening her eyes dramatically. "And we can only imagine the types of circumstances that would lead to someone not recalling their name."

Her tone dropped to a whisper, "I mean, do you really believe that—"

Ada let out a sharp breath. "You want to do this right here right now?" she asked.

The boy watched from the bed, then swung his legs over the side and stood up. He was long and lean, with gold flecks in his eyes. He looked much better not covered in mud.

"I think I've overstayed my welcome," he said.

Amit entered, speaking Arabic, "Sit down. You need your rest."

The familiar rhythm caught them all off guard. The girls were instantly reminded of their mother, who sang them lullabies and told them stories in her native tongue when they were children. It had been years since they'd heard her

141

use it, but they still remembered how it sounded. Miriam had the English language down to pat, but in Arabic, she had poetry. Their mother switching from English to Arabic was like jumping from a tautly balanced tightrope into a sea, preening with color and with life.

To the boy, it was also familiar but not as moving. The tongue he was raised in was a wanderer's dialect, recognizably different but sufficiently similar. He had heard Amit's accent a few times when they made camp outside a big city and went in during the day to sell their wares at the market. Even then, it didn't sound as clean as this woman's, not as refined.

"Who are you?" he asked, his shoulders shrinking.

"What does it matter?" Amit asked as she put down a tray she was carrying on the bedside table.

"Are you from Damascus?"

"No." She handed him a steaming mug.

It was too late when the boy realized the cup wasn't filled with tea. The thick liquid oozed down his throat like slime, but he couldn't stop once he started drinking—it jumped out of the cup and into his mouth as if it had a mind of its own. He banged the cup down hard when it was finally empty, coughing to get his breath back.

"What was that?" Ada asked, stepping closer to pat his back.

"Is he okay?" Cara asked.

"It's just a rehydration potion," Amit said. "Some call it—"

"Water slugs," the boy said and wiped his mouth with the back of his hand.

"Couldn't we have gotten him a Pedialyte?" Ada asked.

"Maybe practitioners don't have Pedialyte," Cara suggested.

"We do," Amit said simply.

142

Someone knocked on the door, and they all fell silent. Amit threw a comforter over the boy before cracking it open. The girls settled on the bed around him, grabbing books and looking bored. Rapid French revealed it to be the innkeeper. She had news for Amit, a visitor.

"It's Otto, he's downstairs," she told them, grabbing her coat.

"I'll come with you," Cara said and stepped forward.

"You'd leave me here alone?" Ada gasped.

Amit interrupted the argument before it could start, "Stay. Play nice."

The girls turned to look at each other as the door clicked shut. Then the boy spoke, his curiosity winning out over his trepidation, "Are you in some sort of trouble?"

"No," Cara replied defensively. "Are you?"

"Lots," he admitted sheepishly. "I'd probably be dead if it weren't for you."

Ada was feeling more apprehensive toward the boy than before—there was a stranger sitting in their cramped hide-away all of a sudden—but his candor was comforting. Even though the pain they shared that had drawn her to him was gone, his tortured gaze softened her defenses.

"Was it Ariel?" she asked.

A moment of silence.

"It was. She dislikes people like me," he said.

"People like you?"

"Immigrants. Africans. Vagabonds. I check all the boxes."

"Why do you stay in Paris?" Cara asked quietly.

He took a deep breath. Rich people never understood.

"The chance of getting accepted as an asylum seeker here was already under one in a thousand," he said. "I am productive and follow their rules, so they allow me to stay. What are my options? Take a trip and overstay my welcome somewhere else? And spend the rest of my life dodging torches? Go back home to die?" His voice trailed off. After a moment he shrugged and added, "If I'm going to live a bloody life anywhere I go, might as well stay in the city of lights."

Cara and Ada were quiet. Their parents were also immigrants; from different corners of the world but with the same desperate longing for a better future. They were learning that the practitioner's world wasn't so different from their own. They seemed to mirror each other in all the worst ways.

"To be fair, I don't think we're here legally ourselves."

There was a moment of stunned silence while Cara stared at Ada, trying to ascertain whether she had just confessed their crimes to someone who wouldn't even tell them his name. Then, she turned to the boy, saying, "She's joking, of course. We're here visiting from New York with our aunt."

"I might not know exactly how things work here," Ada said after rolling her eyes. "But arriving through a rift doesn't scream official port of entry."

The boy couldn't control his expression. Healing spells. Rifts.

"Who are you?" he asked.

Cara did her best to salvage their anonymity.

"We're nobodies," she said. "Nobodies in a little trouble, just like you."

"Anyone who travels through rifts is a somebody," he replied, scoffing. "And anyone who heals others for free is a saint. So, who are you? Hagars? Manassehs? Aarons?"

The girls flinched at the last one.

"I don't know what you are talking about," Ada said calmly.

She wasn't lying. Neither of them knew what it meant, what it could possibly mean, that their mother's maiden name had come out of his mouth. They weren't used to being somebodies.

"If you don't, then that's even stranger," he said. A skeptical smile played on his lips. "Practitioners that powerful must go to an academy."

Cara's ears perked up. "Academy?" she asked. "Like a school for practitioners?"

He waved her away. "Don't act like you don't know. Even in the desert, we knew. Everyone speaks of them. People like you would have been required to go."

"Why?" Ada asked.

"Too strong," he said with a shrug. "To be left alone."

Goosebumps pricked her skin. The door opened. Amit was back.

"We have to go," she said.

She had a duffle bag under her arm. Crossing the room in two strides, she shoved the elements they had been using for practice into it. The girls watched, stunned.

"Let's go."

She didn't have to say it a third time. Even the boy leaped to his feet, scrambling to find some way to help.

"What's happening?" Ada asked. She had to put her body weight on her suitcase to shut it. "Are we leaving Paris or just the inn?"

"Paris," she answered breathily. "They were right; it's a battlefield."

As if on cue, a blast louder than anything the girls had ever heard before rattled the walls. They both fell to the floor, hands cupping their ears.

"Damn it," Amit hissed. "Come on."

They filed out of the room and down the stairs, but Amit headed toward the kitchen instead of the main entrance. Past the cluttered counters was another door. It was inconspicuous enough that their eyes almost slid straight past it. Amit pried it open and gestured. The girls crossed over silently, but the boy hesitated.

"You don't have to take me," he told her.

She opened her mouth to say one thing but said another, "You can come if you want."

They followed closely behind her as she weaved and turned through narrow alleyways, blasts sounding sometimes nearer, sometimes further. Despite being surrounded by tall stone walls, they felt the floor shake beneath them, the gusts of air and dust hitting them sharply each time one went off. Slowly, the air surrounding them was becoming heavy with debris. Their breathing became shallow and labored.

Amit paused for a second and held out her hand, palm up. They stared at her quizzically, so she grabbed Ada's wrist and drew a symbol on it—suddenly, she could breathe normally. She did the same with Cara and the boy, who had come along after all. It was some sort of filtration spell, and with it, they could see a few more feet through the grime, as well.

Cara could make out blurry figures at the edges of her vision lying on the floor and propped against walls, much like the boy when they had found him. She was thankful for her obscured sight, which shielded her from the real carnage.

It must have been about twenty minutes before Amit slowed to a tentative crawl, sticking closer to the walls to their left. She traced the cold stone with her gloved hand and stopped. Pressing her cheek close to it, the girls barely saw her lips move before the surface rippled below her fingertips, and she sunk into it. They followed her through and heard rather than saw the wall close behind them. The fighting sounded faint now, as if several blocks away.

"There's bound to be fighting even in the catacombs," the boy said.

Amit met his eyes and said, "Not this deep in."

She turned and went down a darkened stairway. At the bottom, they stopped. She looked this way and that.

Cara had to ask, "You do know where we're going, right?"

"Of course," she said, but still didn't move. "I'm deciding what the best move is."

They stood in silence for another moment, then Ada asked, "What are the options?"

Amit took a deep breath, then turned to them. "I don't think we'll be able to leave Paris tonight."

"Can we not open rifts down here?" Ada asked.

"No," Amit said and grimaced. "The catacombs are heavily enchanted. Even if you could find a rift to travel through, it would drain your energy immensely. The issue is that every faction will be monitoring the rifts above ground to track those that escape."

"Let's just hide a little longer," Cara suggested. "Why did we leave the inn?"

"Emile gave us up," Amit said and pressed the heel of her hand to her forehead. "He knew I was lying, but he didn't know why. He doesn't actually know who you are or why I am hiding you."

"Why would he do that?" Ada exclaimed. What had they ever done to him?

Amit shook her head; she had spent way too much time in

her youth trying to understand those who had wronged her.

"Someone could have threatened Marthe," she said. "Who knows? Otto came to warn me."

"Is someone after us now?" Cara asked. The hair on the back of her neck was standing on end. Suddenly, she felt watched.

"Maybe. We can't be sure if they're pursuing the lead or not, but it was no longer safe for us there."

"Where can we go from here?" This was Ada, quietly trying to stay optimistic.

Amit took a moment. "I'm not sure, yet."

"We could leave on foot," the boy said.

They all turned to him, who had been silent until then.

"I know a way out," he said.

13

As they walked deeper into the catacombs, the walls to either side started to fill with bones. At first, they looked like elongated pieces of rock until the girls noticed the cracked, dull skulls set on top some of the piles.

Cara had known of and expected this, of course, but it was different to see it in person. She shivered again, crossing her arms to keep warm. Even the brisk pace at which they were walking wasn't enough to keep her temperature up. Paris hadn't felt so cold on the surface.

The boy was leading the way despite Amit's initial reluctance.

"I have a perfect sense of direction," he assured her.

Incredulous, she demanded a demonstration. "Which direction is North?"

The girls fidgeted.

"Ah, so easy," he said, pointing to the wall. Not yet impressed, she asked about a bakery on Rue de Lille. He only had to think about it for a second before saying, "It should be about ten kilometers north from here and maybe five to the east."

Amit glowered; he was right. Cara wondered if she had lived in Paris before. They walked for so long that the bottoms of her feet began to hurt, and her stomach began to rumble.

"Are we out of water already?" she asked and licked her dry lips.

Despite their efforts to ration it, they were.

"We're almost there," the boy assured them.

He explained his plan to them earlier. The veil that covered the city was impenetrable. At least, this is what locals believed. Immigrants knew better. Because the veil was maintained by a spell stone in a tower in the thirteenth arrondissement, the effect tended to be stronger and more consistent to the south. In the north, the veil spread thinner and wavered, creating temporary chinks through which people would sometimes sneak in and out.

"How would we even find them?" Ada had asked.

"There's an old woman who lives at the edge of Porte de Clichy. She keeps track of the openings and helps ferry people across. It would be humiliating for the city to even consider the possibility of a gap in their armor, so they don't," he said.

"Sounds about right," Amit muttered. "The fighting shouldn't reach that far anyway. Factions don't stray too much from the city's center."

She was right, of course. It was rare to find an initiated member more than two kilometers from the city center, but Ariel was not an initiated member. Some thought—but didn't dare voice—that she might not be from Paris at all. Was it such a wonder that she could be found near the city's borders, following the voices of God in her head to find innocent sinners to smite in His name? Not until they surfaced to a scene of chaos did Amit realize she had made a grave miscalculation. It was late afternoon. The sun should have still been up, but it was hard to see. Smoke filled the air. Cara could just make out the outlines of figures moving ahead.

"That's the old woman's house," the boy cried, looking at the source of the fire. The veil rippled bright pink and orange above them, disturbed.

"Cara," Ada hissed, crouching by the tunnel's entrance. "Stealth spell."

Amit let her cast it but warned them to "Stay low anyway. The spell might not work on her."

She led them slowly around the smoldering remains of the house, tentatively sneaking closer to the border. Cara's skin was crawling, and she couldn't help but feel it would be better to turn back and hide in the catacombs until the conflict died down.

Then again, if Ariel had made it all the way out here, would the chinks in the city's armor ever be unguarded again? There was also the chance she would hunt down any remnants that took cover underground.

Ada was coming to the same realizations besides her. Now in the middle of a battlefield, their situation seemed bleaker and bleaker. If only she had been more sensible when choosing a destination, she thought, wracked with fear and guilt.

A bloodcurdling scream shattered their reverie. Instinctively, they turned their heads towards the sound. As if on cue, a gust of wind cleared the smoke for just long enough for them to see that in the clearing, surrounded by piles of *something*, stood a girl dressed in medieval armor.

Her long blonde hair wafted behind her, matted with blood.

Two swords stuck out of her torso, one buried deep between her shoulder blades, another in her abdomen. She was looking down at a hand that grasped her foot. They followed her gaze down to the bodies that lay at her feet.

Cara froze like a deer in headlights. Ariel's head lifted and turned, and their eyes met. Smoke billowed between them once more.

"Quick!" Amit shouted.

Before Cara knew what was happening, they were sprinting. She stepped on something soft, stumbled, and fell, coming face to face with an unconscious man. The smell of blood was overwhelming. A whimper caught in her throat. She didn't look for long enough to ascertain where it was coming from. The boy half-dragged her to her feet and forced her to run again.

In the distance, she could see it. The veil was the brightest around it, bright like neon lights. It was closing. Ariel must have fixed it. They were just a few meters away. Then, a few steps.

Amit skidded to a stop, letting Ada lunge through first. Cara turned again to look back, but the boy blocked her view. He said something incomprehensible, and then Amit yanked her arm hard, sending her falling again.

* * *

Ada was screaming. Cara's ears were ringing, and she couldn't hear anything, but she could see that Ada was screaming. Amit was standing in front of her, trying to calm her down. She said something that got Ada to stop, and they both looked at her. Amit came closer and knelt down by her

152

side.

"I can't hear you," she told them.

Amit cupped her ears and murmured a spell. The warmth of her hands made the action feel intimate in a way that made a knot grow in Cara's throat. She missed her mother.

"Are you hurt?" she asked.

Cara shook her head but then realized she was.

"My knee, I think," she said.

Ada stood a few feet away, staring pointedly at a spot in the distance. Cara realized it was the same direction they had just come from: the veil.

"Shouldn't we move away from here?" she asked.

Amit took a breath, then got to work healing the bloody gash on Cara's leg. Her eyes were fixed on it as she spoke, "She's very upset about the boy. He didn't make it through."

Cara was shocked into silence. She could practically still feel the pressure of his hands pulling her up, pushing her through.

"Is he going to be okay?" she asked, her voice barely a squeak.

Amit stood up before replying, "He's in Paris legally, at least. Even if they find him there, I don't think there's much they can prove against him."

Cara recalled the state of the boy when they had first found him. Standing up, she went to Ada's side. Then, looking to Amit, she asked, "Is there anything we can do?"

"I'm afraid not," she said. "We should respect his choices."

He had chosen to help them, Amit told herself. He had chosen to stay.

Cara was thinking of what to say next when Ada turned, facing away from the peaceful lot where the wreckage used to be.

"I'll come back for him," she said. She met Cara's eyes; no one spoke. "I can't just leave him there. Not like that."

The image of Ariel standing on a pile of corpses flashed through Cara's mind. She nodded, saying, "When we're stronger, we can come back. When we are not in danger anymore."

"Yeah," Ada said, then paused. "Where do we go now? Please don't make me choose again."

Amit chuckled, picking her duffle bag up off the ground.

"I won't," she said. "Unfortunately, the whole world seems to be aflame. I think it would be best to go somewhere remote, far from Western practitioner centers." She looked around, then said, "Come on. Let's find shelter first."

Shelter turned out to be a little bed and breakfast a few blocks away with a café on the ground floor. They settled into a table in the back and ordered lattes. Ada found it counterintuitive. She would be too wired to sleep anyway. After exchanging a few words with the waitress, Amit pulled out her laptop and started typing.

"What are you doing?" Ada asked.

Her voice was hoarse from the dust and the smoke and the screaming. Only after sitting down had she realized how tired her feet were.

"I must admit, I wasn't expecting to find turmoil literally everywhere we go. I'm trying to quickly catch up on current events," she replied.

Ada remembered the giant's words. *I see it in the distance, again and again, covering space like rain clouds.*

"Do you think it could be the same..." she started to ask, then stopped.

154

Amit stared at her, waiting. "The same what?" she asked.

Ada hesitated to get into it. She had forgotten the giant's words with purposeful conviction. Even when she had called Cara that night, she had only told her the need-to-knows of the situation. To her, the giant's warning sounded too dire to be true. So grim, she would rather not acknowledge it. And yet...

"I don't know how much my mom told you," she began to say.

"Hopefully, everything," Amit said with a raised eyebrow.

"Yeah..." Ada took a breath. "I guess I was the one that didn't tell her everything. When I went to speak with the giant, she told me Hope Springs wasn't the only place."

"The only place that what?" Cara asked.

Ada avoided her gaze as she continued, "When the Mist-landers were there, it was like this dark fog over the city, but thicker. It was really hard to go through when I projected. She said it wasn't the only place, that there were clouds of it everywhere around the world, and they were multiplying. So, I don't know..." She paused, hoping someone else would fill the silence. They didn't.

"What if the Mistlanders are going everywhere those dark clouds are and taking advantage of the chaos to steal other practitioners' magic?" Ada finally said.

"That would have to be a big deal, though," Cara replied and leaned her elbows on the little round table between them. "I think you would have heard about that, right?" she asked Amit, who was deep in thought.

"I should have," Amit said slowly. "But not if they're going after outliers—practitioners living outside of central society, far from the Committee's watchful eye." She thought of the bodies lying prone under Ariel's foot. "Or those that get ignored and discarded anyway."

Ada's voice lowered to a whisper as she asked, "Could there be that many Mistlanders in the Midlands now?"

"That's the thing." Amit's brow was deeply furrowed as she said, "Mistlanders live in a tribal society. They lack the ability to organize centrally, which is why they have never presented much of a threat. Except about two thousand years ago." The girls stared back at her blankly. "Oh, I keep forgetting—"

"That we don't know anything?" Ada said and rolled her eyes. "Yes, we know. What happened two thousand years ago?"

"The Great Eclipse," she explained. "One of Babylon's kings in the twelfth century BC was a seven hundred-year-old practitioner known by the name Nebuchadnezzar in modern books. He disappeared after his reign only to suddenly come back five hundred years later and violently reclaim the throne. He captured Jerusalem, destroyed its temples, and expelled all practitioners from the city. Of course, there were ancient practitioner houses with roots there that refused to leave. He killed hundreds but eventually was exiled to the Mistlands. They expected him to die there without any human sustenance, but he was so powerful, he cast forbidden magic on his body, forcing it to survive off of Mistlander nourishment and effectively becoming a Mistlander hybrid himself.

"It took him almost a thousand more years, but he eventually cracked the veil open like an egg, spilling millions of Mistlanders into the Midlands and leading to catastrophe after catastrophe. It was an Aaron, actually," she said pointedly, meeting both girls' eyes, "that ended the war, killing not only them but millions of others with one of the most terrifying displays of magic ever accomplished. Suffice it to say, darkness encompassed the world for years to come. It was another Aaron who rallied whatever practitioner strongholds remained and regained some semblance of order. The practitioners that were around back then are what we call the Old Families, the ones that helped rebuild the world."

"And we're the same Aarons?" Ada asked, her skin prickling with goosebumps. "Our mom is?"

"Miriam Aaron," Amit confirmed.

"Why did she leave all that?" Cara asked.

Even as the words left her mouth, she had a feeling Amit wouldn't tell them.

"I told you," she said with a sigh. "You have to ask her. I left years before she did. But is it really that hard to understand? When you're an Aaron, that is all you are, not Miriam or Cara or Ada. I don't know when she met your father, but there is no way she could have married him if she had remained in the family. They would have never let her corrupt their blood that way."

The words hung heavy in the air. The girls had never been so aware of their half-ness. They had never thought much about what ran in their veins except when it had spilled on the sidewalk. They had never considered that anyone else would.

Their lattes arrived, and they sipped them in silence. Amit went back to her computer. They sat there for about a half hour, their frantic heartbeats counting the seconds. Slowly, their shoulders started to relax, and their breathing slowed. She shut the laptop.

"Let's go."

"Where?" Cara asked as she followed her out to the sidewalk. They ducked into an alley and stood behind a rancid-smelling dumpster.

"South Africa. I know someone."

14

The rift left them in the middle of a burgeoning sandstorm. The wind threw fistfuls of earth at them, stinging their exposed skin and preventing them from opening their eyes. The girls thought surely Amit had made a mistake. There was nothing in sight but dunes.

Then, they stepped forward and saw the bar, a lone structure with flickering neon lights. Getting down from the hill from there was tricky; Ada gave up a few minutes in and slid the rest of the way. By the time they reached the entrance, they felt more parts sand than person and hoped Amit knew a spell to get it out of their clothes. Before they could put their thoughts into words, they pushed the door open, and a gust of wind, as fierce as the ones outside, rushed past them.

"Now, isn't that much better?" Amit said, then sighed, pushing past the frozen girls and into the building. Turning to look at them, she asked, "Is something wrong?"

"Oh," Cara realized, standing taller. "The sand is gone."

"The owner doesn't like it when people trail in piles of sand," Amit said.

They followed her deeper in. The narrow hallway was lit with dim red light and lined with frames. Many housed portraits of remarkably ordinary-looking people, but Ada could see out of the corner of her eye that others were mirrors; they darkened as she passed, briefly blocking the scarlet glow. Surreptitiously trying to check her hair, she looked straight at one only to find it swirling and blurring, indecipherable. She tried again in others to no avail.

The hall opened up to a large room, its walls lined to the left with bottles. A person in a suit vest lazily wiped glasses down behind the bar and didn't look up even as three bedraggled customers walked in from a sandstorm. To the right were pool tables, dart boards, and more portraits.

Amit kept walking past it all to a platform at the back of the room. She pulled out a chair, and the girls joined her at a table, following her gaze to the stage. As if they had been waiting patiently for them to take their seats, the red curtains parted.

* * *

The first time Amit met the Mantis, she was beaten half to death and left to dry in the shadow of a hedge in the middle of the desert. After successfully ducking her brothers' henchmen and avoiding their hired eyes, it was ironic that her assailants had neither known her name nor gained anything from the assault—aside from a few bruised ribs and a crippling curse she drew in her own blood seconds after they walked away.

Was it actually better this way? As long as she didn't lose against *them*, had she won? As long as they didn't deal the final blow?

A rumbling laughter. A shadow fell briefly over her feet.

Who's there? As fiercely as she thought it, Amit couldn't bring her tired lips to form the words.

"Would you really consider this a victory?" Something slithered against her ankle. The voice seemed to move from outside to inside her head. "After all you've suffered, don't you think you deserve a second chance? Or should I say a third? Fourth?" Another sleazy chuckle. "What's a few more for a little Phineas made low in the dirt?"

A tribal spirit, no doubt, tugging at my fatigued mind, Amit thought. *The protection spells must be dead.* She had no energy left to give them.

The loudest laugh yet. "Child, you are amusing. Your measly charms can't repel me, creator of the eland, the darkness, and the moon."

A tribal god, then.

"Perhaps, but a tribal god is still a god on his tribe's land. Here, the forces of life and nature bend to me. If you'd like, I can hide you from death and all else who seek you. If you'd like, I could hide you forever."

* * *

Blue light. A deep trumpet. A quick beat. The backlit figure was hard to make out. A large animal skull obscured the silhouette of their face. Then, they turned. Cara gasped. She knew the word for this. *Theriocephaly.*

"Come for another second chance?" the figure asked, standing from a barstool.

Phantom voices harmonized. There was neither band nor instrument in sight.

This person knows how to make an entrance, Ada thought. "Is that your friend?" she whispered.

"No," Amit answered dryly.

"The last time I saw you, I was but a louse in your ear. I assume you've come to pay back your debt?" The figure crossed the room in two fell steps and settled, smoke-like, into a chair close by. "Have you brought these lives as payment?"

Cara and Ada could only assume the skull's empty eye sockets were looking at them.

She hissed, "What lives do I owe *you*?"

"Oh Amit," a new, high-pitched voice intervened. "Haven't you learned by now to not let IKaggen get you all riled up? Ever since you first met, down in that ravine—I swear, you're always at each other's throats."

"Sethu!" Amit cried as she turned in her chair.

"Sethunya," IKaggen echoed, less enthusiastic. "You have arrived."

The music flickered like a light and died.

Behind them, a dark-skinned woman had appeared in jean shorts and flip-flops.

"Sorry I'm late, but you did only give me like five minutes' notice," she said and dragged another chair over, plopping down comfortably at their table. "Are these your cousins?" she asked with a smirk.. "I can see the resemblance."

"Right," Amit shot back sarcastically. "How much do you know about what's happening in Paris?"

Sethu's eyebrows shot up before she asked, "You mean with Ariel? I mean, I read the news."

"What does the news say?"

"That she's a tyrant; hundreds of immigrants are unaccounted for, and the rest of Paris lives in fear. That few are "let in, and none are let out," Sethu said.

"If everyone knows, why hasn't anyone done anything yet?" Ada demanded.

When she leaned forward, the small table between them wobbled. IKaggen, who had all but melted into the shadows around them, laughed.

"What terrible things happening in the world today do you know of that anyone has done anything to stop? War? Famine? Drought?" Sethu asked, shrugging. "Paris will have to solve her own problems just like the rest of us." She leaned back, saying, "Why do a couple of Americans care either way?"

"We were there just an hour ago," Amit explained. "Left an unpaid debt behind."

Sethu hmphed. "Have you come here to hide?" she asked.

"Perhaps," Amit conceded. "We need somewhere to lay low while we figure out what's actually happening."

"With Ariel?"

"No," Amit said, then hesitated. "Something else."

Seeing that she was carefully choosing her words, her friend leaned closer and asked, "Why were you in Paris?"

The girls watched Amit weigh her options, feeling oddly vulnerable. They were slowly realizing the extent to which their fates lay in her hands. So was she.

"Has anyone been talking about the Mistlands?" she finally asked.

"Not for centuries." Sethu noticed she didn't answer the original question. Suspicious, she probed, "Why?"

"There have been sightings."

"Sightings of what? By whom?" Sethu asked sharply. Such claims were hard to believe without evidence.

After a moment of silence, Ada spoke up, "Me."

The god laughed harder, invisible now.

Sethu didn't join him, but she looked skeptical when she asked, "Where?"

Ada glanced at Amit, who nodded, before saying, "Oregon, in the United States."

"What were they doing?" Sethu pressed.

"They were trying to steal my brother's magic."

"Why would they want your brother?"

This time, it was IKaggen who answered, suddenly congealing from the shadows, mouth pressed to Ada's ear, "Cause he's an Aaron."

Sethu's arm shot forward, piercing through the place he had appeared in, but he was already gone.

"That's enough from you," she said. "Enough from you, too." She shot Ada a look. "I think it's time we made it back to my place."

"Rude of you not to include me," IKaggen's disembodied voice jeered. "You were rude when you grabbed the Phineas child from under me, and you're rude now. You'll feel my irritation against you one day. You'll be sorry for it."

Sethu laughed loudly and said, "You should be happy we still visit you at all."

They rose from the table and headed for the front door, past the bar, and through the hall. The girls braced themselves as Sethu reached for the handle and turned it, but instead of the expected blast of sand, they opened their eyes to a beautiful beachside street.

"Welcome to Cape Town!" she yelled above the busy clamor, stepping out first and extending her arms above her head. The view was illuminated by the sunset's last light and

164

streetlamps. Music throbbed on the street.

"It sure is loud," Cara complained as she eyed the skimpily-clad people milling on the sidewalk.

"It's Friday night!" Sethu cheered. "My apartment's this way."

They weaved through languid throngs and turned into a less populated street.

"Camps Bay is fun," she continued. "But so expensive. I found the best little place a couple of blocks from the beach, but I bet I could get double the space if I sacrificed the location. I'm always debating if it's worth it." She abruptly turned left into a corner building and headed up the stairs. "And then I see this view again."

They all turned toward the receding daylight. Most of the sky had gone dark blue, but streaks of fiery orange remained, reflected again on the ocean. Sethu turned away first and crossed the balcony to the first apartment.

"Welcome to my humble abode."

* * *

Sethu was right. If she moved ten blocks east, she would get the same space for half the price. What her apartment lacked in square footage, though, it made up for in taste. Every other item was fashioned from colorful prints or into unique shapes. Her kitchen table stood on hooved legs, cutting off midway through the thigh. The chandelier over the study had glass tentacles that twisted like a sea creature. A mushroom-shaped lamp in the girls' room glowed from within.

It was eclectic, but Sethu had a talent for toeing the line of chaos without stepping over it. It spoke to the girls as soon as they set foot inside, especially to Ada. She asked where Sethu had picked up a couple of pieces, only to receive enigmatic responses. A market on the outskirts of Accra. Somewhere in Indonesia. A gift from a shaman after she rescued his dog. Their cryptic origins only made them seem more stylish.

As for Cara, she could appreciate Sethu's aesthetic but would never think to emulate it. The multi-lingual collection of books was more to her taste. She landed on a zebra print chair and came face to face with a pile of tomes about South Africa. Grabbing one, she flipped to the abstract. Then, her brow furrowed. "Mermaids? I thought this was a history book."

"It is," Sethu said, looking over from the entrance, where she had let a mountain of shoes pile up. She now sifted through them, trying to find a semblance of order, cowed to reveal her mess to her newly arrived guests. "What?" she asked. "You think mermaids have no place in history books? They've been erased for long enough!"

"Oh, I'm sorry," Cara said after quickly realizing her mistake. "I've never seen a practitioner book before, other than spell books, I mean. I thought it was fiction."

"All history books are fiction," Sethu replied. "Or, at best, a mix of story and fact."

Ever the academic, Cara was ready to launch into a spiel about sources and references when Amit interrupted, "Enough teasing. Cara and Ada didn't attend an academy, and they're just catching up on decades of learning."

"Our mom gave us a basic education." Cara meant to defend herself—surely it wasn't decades—but even to her ears, it sounded like she was agreeing with Amit.

"I don't blame her," Amit said with a shrug. "She was never

the best teacher."

"Really?" Ada asked. She had been examining the knick-knacks on the shelves, but this caught her attention. "She wasn't?"

"She was terrible at explaining things. Everything came too easily to her." Amit's gaze grew spacey as she spoke, as it always did when they spoke about their mother. Miriam lived not in her present but in her past.

"I don't know who would get more frustrated during our lessons," she said, laughing. "I suppose theory doesn't matter as much when you have that much talent for practical magic. It might be because you inherited that ease for casting that she didn't concern herself with your formal education."

"She did concern herself with our formal education!" Cara exclaimed and sat up. "She might not have taught us practitioner history, but it didn't seem like there would be a need. We didn't encounter any other practitioners until recently."

"Wouldn't you have liked to learn anyway?" Ada asked. She had a tingling sensation in her chest. Her question was but the tip of the iceberg. The inoffensive conversation had veered into sensitive territory, or perhaps the time had come to let the words running laps in their heads spill out. Perhaps it didn't matter what topic preceded it. Perhaps the pressure had built up, and now something had to explode.

"We did learn," her sister barked back. Ada could almost hear the silent *'idiot'* punctuating that sentence. "She gave us lessons every week for years. We didn't take them seriously, so neither did she."

"Is it our responsibility as children to take our lessons seriously?" Ada sneered. Just talking about their mother made it feel like someone was pressing their finger into a bruise.

Cara stood. Her tone was venomous when she said, "Can't you take responsibility for anything in your life?"

She couldn't believe her sister was being so unfair. Their parents had always put them first and did everything they could to give them the best lives. To keep them safe. She trusted that their mom's decisions had been in their best interest, and she couldn't blame her even if they hadn't always been the right ones. Maybe if she had said this to Ada, it could have soothed her troubled feelings.

Instead, she let her indignation speak, "Our mother works all day every day to finance our college tuition, the house we live in, the food we eat."

"And for that, I am grateful," Ada replied in a measured voice. She usually hated being abrasive. She was *usually* very conflict averse, but she couldn't stop halfway this time. She had a lot more to say. "But she lied to us our whole lives. She lied about her name. She lied about her family—our family! Where she was born. Where she grew up. We don't even know who we are."

"None of that changes who we are," Cara said, her tone of voice final. "I know who I am. I know who my mom is. She has been there for us our whole lives, given everything for us."

"She kept us in a bubble!" Ada snapped. "Now, we don't know how to protect ourselves. We're not prepared to face the world. She didn't trust us enough to talk to us about anything. We're not children anymore."

They fell silent.

Amit and Sethu exchanged a glance. The sisters' outburst

had caught them off-guard, but they recognized the rawness for what it was: vulnerability rather than aggression. They once had nerves like exposed wire, too. Surely, they were yearning for their mother now more than ever. Or perhaps they were grateful not to have her in front of them.

"You girls should get some rest," Amit said as she stepped forward, popping the tension in the room like a balloon. They both deflated. "I know you have a lot to talk about, but this isn't the right time."

Cara wiped a tear from her cheek and said, "I'm sorry, Sethu."

They had only just walked into her house and already made a scene.

"Nothing to be sorry for," Sethu said with a shake of her head. "You've been through some shit, but it's too late tonight to get into it."

Ada was still crying. Her words came out broken when she said, "Literal creatures from hell tried to kidnap our brother."

"And more," Amit said. She came closer and laid her hand on Ada's shoulder. "You might still be in shock. A lot has happened, some very bad things." She stopped herself in her tracks before she could accidentally dredge up those very memories.

"Your minds must be reeling," she said. "I hope we'll have a second to breathe here at Sethu's. Some time to think and talk, but tomorrow. Okay?"

They nodded, but their heads were still bowed, their shoulders still hunched.

Amit, too, had suffered and squirmed under fate's thumb, fought against it, and ran from it. She was slowly beginning to relate to Miriam, her urge to protect these fragile existences.

15

A mit set out to teach the girls what practitioners learned over many years within a matter of weeks. There was no immediate reason they would be forced to leave the refuge of Sethu's home, who insisted they were no intrusion, but Amit knew the dangers of staying anywhere for too long.

They would wake up around seven, eat breakfast, and often take a walk down the shore—Amit had taught them to cast disguises on themselves so no person or device could see their real faces. Then, she would instruct them on spells and potions until the sun set, when they would settle into the living room to study. Even at the dinner table, they would be talking about charms and casting, and Amit would sometimes find them in the morning sleeping with books and notebooks splayed around them on the sofa bed.

Amit was sharing Sethu's bed. The latter flitted in and out of her apartment, ostensibly going to work or to meet with friends, always at odd hours. She chimed in during their discussions, sharing her experience with certain charms or delightful stories that involved gods more often than not. It seemed like there were gods everywhere she went.

The girls were mesmerized just watching her go through

170

her daily routines. She would charm pots and pans in the kitchen to start their breakfast. An invisible hand would stir and flip and adjust the flame. When she lounged outside on the balcony, she would cast a shadow over her face, laying only her legs out in the sun. Even when reading, she'd splay over a chair, head in hands, and have the book float above her, pages flipping on queue. Never had they seen such casual magic. It was fascinating.

"I'd never realized this before," Cara said one day. "But you really don't use too much magic, Amit."

Amit crinkled her forehead, hand shielding her from the sun. They were out on the beach, learning about tidal magic.

"All magic can be traced," she said somberly. "Sethu has nothing to hide from, and if she stopped casting all of a sudden, her friends would probably notice and worry."

"Is it safe for us to practice?" Ada asked. "Won't they trace us?"

"I've taken precautions to hide our trail," Amit replied cryptically.

The truth was, the Committee didn't have a sample to match their scent to, and they had been using only low-energy spells and enchantments. There was no reason for the Committee to detect them, but Mistlanders were another matter altogether.

Ada felt queasy, a physical aversion to being hunted. She had become hyperaware of her surroundings lately and often felt watched. Glancing at dark corners or alleyways, she expected to find a pale, featureless face staring back at her— but it was always shadows. She wasn't the type to dwell on the past but thought a lot about the future. About how strong she had to be to find the boy, face Ariel. How strong she had to be not to die.

Cara, on the other hand, was thriving, as she always did when studying was involved. She would spend most of her waking hours reviewing past lessons and memorizing new ones. Ada also did so, albeit with less zeal. It was a welcome distraction for both.

Amit talked to them about dealing with trauma the day after they arrived, after their argument. Cara admitted that her mind would often wander if she let it, always returning to Deer Creek. The barrel in the attic. The sigil on the severed foot. Cormac closing in on Ada. Black maggots. It motivated her to learn faster, thinking if only she had known this spell then...

Ada surprised her sister and herself by keeping up.

Amit had been working on something else since they arrived: a way around the complex mechanisms that governed the magical communication network. She promised Miriam they would check in every week, but they didn't get a chance in Paris, and it had been nearly ten days. The issue was the colonial-era infrastructure that Dutch practitioners had implemented in South Africa in the eighteen hundreds. It was incredibly restrictive and allowed the Committee access to all communication coming in and out of the country.

Despite becoming obsolete decades earlier, nobody had bothered to fully dismantle it, instead letting it remain dormant overhead. The Committee insisted that no one monitored the airwaves any longer and the system was as good as gone, but locals were wary. The disappearances had toned down in recent years, but in the collective memory, they were still raw and tender wounds. Most young practitioners used alternate communication methods passed down from pre-colonial times and were painfully aware of what they said on official channels.

"What if you go into the Wasteland?" Sethu suggested.

"What's that?" Ada asked through a mouthful of pap.

"Nothing," Amit grumbled. The idea had obviously been brought up before, in private.

"Come on!" Sethu exclaimed, holding her silverware up in the air. "I thought you were trying to educate these girls!" She lowered her voice dramatically as she said, "There is rumored to be in the Great Karoo, a clandestine city built by rebels. They say the veil is two miles thick, and only they know how to train practitioners to traverse it."

Cara didn't like the sound of a rebel city, but her curiosity got the better of her and she asked, "What are they rebelling against?"

Amit interrupted before Sethu could continue, in a mocking tone, "And in the Sahara, there is the Kingdom of Sand, which is a world in itself like the giants' and the Mistlands. These are but stories."

Her friend scoffed. "She would certainly like you to believe that, wouldn't you, Miss Rebel?" she asked.

"A rebel? Amit?" Ada said, raising her eyebrows. "What did you say you were rebelling against?"

Sethu was clearly delighted with the flow of conversation. Amit tried to turn the tables. "Why don't you tell them about it? Wasn't that where we first met?" she asked.

"If I well recall, we met *outside* the Wasteland. Have you ever seen me step foot past that veil?" Sethu demanded.

"Then what were you doing there?" Ada yearned to get one over on Sethu.

She was a prankster, after all. When Amit met her, she

grew suspicious of her relationship with the trickster god Ikaggen and, at the peak of her paranoia, accused Sethu of conspiring with the deity to set her up in their first encounter. Her theory had so many holes that they both agreed to forget it and move on.

Since arriving in South Africa, Ada had her hair turned purple—it washed out a couple of days later; a pair of shorts came out of the dryer in a completely different print—didn't wash out, but gave Amit the chance to teach a simple magic-reversal charm; and a bite of chocolate ice cream turn into a mouthful of savory droëwors, which she promptly spit out.

Cara nearly fell for it when a headline in the newspaper announced that the beach had been infested with rabies-carrying jackals, then she saw Ada in stitches. She wasn't the best sport, so Sethu mostly stuck to messing with Ada and Amit instead. Except when she felt Cara was taking herself too seriously, then she would brave her ire to play the teeniest, tiniest joke.

"I was taking a walk," Sethu replied then. Simply. Pointedly.

"You were taking a walk *out in the Great Karoo*?" Amit imitated her, leaning forward and spreading her hands theatrically.

Sethu laughed the hardest among them but stuck to her guns, saying, "You can laugh and joke. I've never set foot in the Wasteland. That is no place for a lawful committee-abiding practitioner...but you." She raised an eyebrow. "How long has it been since you can call yourself a committee-abiding practitioner? Were you about fifteen?"

"What happened when you were fifteen?" Cara asked.

She had noticed that Amit was too adept at avoiding the Committee, skirting the rules, hiding their trail. Her skillset suited their current situation, but under any other circumstances, Cara might've steered clear of such a shady character. "You grew up with our mom, right? Were you still together?" she asked.

Amit's reaction was less severe than when they asked about Miriam. She groaned, leaning back, and said, "We were together until that day. What happened? Your mother and I were raised under a strict code of conduct. I committed an unspeakable offense and was exiled from my home. Not that it mattered to me. It didn't feel like home." She hesitated suddenly and left it at, "I haven't seen any of my relatives since then, including your mother."

"Is our mother your relative?" Cara pounced.

Amit's smile was uncharacteristically gentle. "Not quite," she said. "Not by blood, but she might as well have been my sister. She was closer to me than any blood relative."

"And you never saw her again?" Ada asked. How lonely that must have felt, she thought.

"Not until that day in Hope Springs."

"Did they really have to exile you?" Cara asked, her expression beginning to droop, as well. It all sounded so archaic.

"Yes, although they would have much rather I died," Amit said, and her face visibly hardened.

"What did you do?" Ada asked in a soft voice as if she hoped no one would hear her.

Amit's determined gaze made her feel a little better for asking something she shouldn't have.

"I refused to keep pretending to be someone else," she said.

Sethu snorted and broke out into laughter. "A Phineas that didn't want to pretend!" she cried, slapping her thigh. "Like a fish that refuses to swim. I can see why your family would disown you."

"Is that your name? Phineas?" Cara asked as a confused smile played on her lips.

"It isn't anymore," their guardian said.

There was no sadness in Amit's voice, no regrets, no doubts. If she ever had them, they had long ago come to terms.

"Alright now," Sethu said and clapped her hands loudly. "Enough of this somber atmosphere. Back to the Wasteland and other fun stories."

"I'd hardly call that a fun story," Amit said, grimacing. "All you need to know about the Wasteland is that you should never go anywhere near it. The rebels are merciless. If they don't know you, they'll kill you or jumble your mind so you can never lead anyone to them again."

"And a jumbled mind," Sethu intervened. "Like a wrinkled piece of paper, can never be quite made right again."

"When did you live there?" Cara asked.

"Only a few years after leaving my home. I must have been eighteen, younger than you."

"That's wild," Cara said with a sigh. "That's too young to be tied up with a militant rebel group."

Here, both women laughed. Cara's cheeks flushed pink.

"I think the average age in the Wasteland must be about nineteen," Sethu said. "It's really just children ordering other children around, isn't it?"

"Looking back," Amit said, shaking her head. "I feel like we could have really used some adult supervision."

"What are a bunch of children doing in a rebel encampment in the desert?" Ada asked. She was frowning, trying to make the pieces fit. "Behind a two-mile-wide veil? Did they really set that up?"

"It does take a lot of magical energy to sustain the veil," Sethu said. "But it's doable if you have enough mediocre practitioners to lend a little effort."

"I want to point out that the Wasteland has been around for what?" Amit met her gaze, seeking confirmation. "Hundreds of years?"

"Since before colonial times," Sethu validated. "It may mostly be children now, but it was the most powerful tribal practitioners of the time that set up the veil. That's why the Committee has never been able to find it."

"What were colonial times like for practitioners?" Cara asked. She couldn't even imagine.

"You really should consider picking up some of those books," Amit said as she gestured to the living room, the mermaid book. "I think you'd find them quite interesting."

"To answer your question," Sethu spoke over her. "They weren't too different for practitioners than for normal folk. If anything, we had to deal with double the genocide, non-magical persecution, and the Committee imposing their ways upon the diaspora of locals, trying to homogenize us."

"Did they lend their power to the colonial effort?" Ada felt she knew the answer. Everything she learned about the Committee made her dislike them more and more.

Sethu had a devilish twinkle in her eye. "This is a contentious topic in the practitioner community."

"Pff." Amit rolled her eyes. "Amongst the Western practitioners, perhaps."

"Somehow," Ada said. "I feel like practitioner history mirrors normal history in all the worst ways."

"You're not wrong. The Committee has never had a real

army," Sethu began to explain. "They assign forces locally to ensure order and—" Using her fingers to draw quotes in the air. "Peace-keeping. Obviously, practitioners didn't initiate colonialization efforts—"

"That we know of," Amit grumbled.

She carried on, "But they have always been present in non-magical branches of government and, often, in their military. Not only was there never a movement within the Committee to oppose the colonial efforts—or, if there was, it was easily stifled—but practitioner soldiers have been known to use their power to subdue indigenous populations and, especially, the local practitioner community.

"So, no," she concluded. "Officially, the Committee never even released a statement regarding their stance on colonialism. They just turned a blind eye and allowed every person to take part in it as they wished with no repercussions."

"It's funny how an institution born in the Middle East, with such deep ties to Africa, has been overtaken by colonizers for the last centuries," Amit spat.

It was obviously a sore topic.

"Arguably since the fall of Constantinople," Sethu said matter-of-factly.

"Any semblance of honor that institution had, any real sense of purpose it served, has been corrupted for generations," Amit said. "It's only been downhill since the True Aaron's days."

"True Aaron? What are there, like, a bunch of fake Aarons roaming about?" Ada joked.

"No fake Aarons," Amit said with a smirk. "The True Aaron was the one that—" She stopped.

The smile fell from her face, her eyes pierced Sethu's.

178

"Had you really not thought of this before?" Sethu asked as she stared back. "I mean, the minute you told me they were Aarons and Mistlanders are after them…I thought it was a logical connection to make."

Amit dug the heels of her hands into her eyes. She suddenly felt so tired.

"You're right," she said. "I have been blind to what has been in front of me all along. Is this why—" She looked up, remembering where she was. Miriam's daughters stared back at her. She couldn't finish her question. *Is this why Miriam called for me?*

Sethu's tone was uncharacteristically dark when she said, "I would have thought you knew the full extent of the risk you were taking."

Amit heard an accusation in her words, but it was her own guilt. "I didn't mean to involve you in anything—" she started to say.

Sethu began picking up plates, rising from the dinner table. The clattering drowned out her friend's voice.

"You'd be wrong to think *I* don't know the danger I invite into my home," she said.

Cara had bit her tongue until then, bearing with her confusion, but she had to ask, "Are we true Aarons?"

Silence. Amit closed her eyes, brow furrowed. "That's not how it works," she said.

Sethu's chair clattered loudly as she nudged it back with her leg.

"Well, that was delicious," she proclaimed loudly. "It's getting quite late, and Amit and I have many things to discuss."

Cara started to protest, but Sethu just spoke louder.

"Many boring, boring things that have nothing to do with you or you." She gave both girls pointed stares. "Off to bed, it is. Don't forget to study your elemental variables. Good night!"

Before they knew it, she dumped the dirty dishes in the sink—where a phantom hand began rinsing them—grabbed Amit's arm, and yanked her out the front door. Cara ran after them, but only to the balcony, watching them disappear down the street and around a corner.

Ada tried to read the room, whether to broach the subject when she came back in. She looked up at the sound of the door latching shut.

"I'll brush my teeth first," Cara said, grabbed her toiletry bag, and went straight into the bathroom.

There was her answer. Ada started rearranging furniture to fit the pull-out mattress in the living room. She fully expected to go over elemental variables for at least an hour or two but found her sister already under the covers when she finished her nightly routine. She quietly switched off the last lit lamp and lay down beside her.

When Ada's breathing slowed, Cara muttered a spell under her breath—she would be a part of the conversation between Sethu and Amit whether they liked it or not. The connection was dodgy, drifting in and out. Cara covered her ears with her hands and closed her eyes to concentrate on the fuzzy words. She could feel Amit's enchantment around them, blurring their voices. She willed it to clear. It was what she sought, and she would find it.

"I think you're jumping the gun here, friend," Sethu's voice cautioned. "You don't know if there is such a thing."

"You know the truth doesn't matter." Amit's voice was

speeding up, as if she couldn't get the words out fast enough. "All that matters is if someone believes such a thing exists and is willing to do anything—"

Mangled voices. Poor connection. Silence. Cara thought she had lost her link, then Sethu's voice, "Some things are said, but mean little."

"If there's even the slightest chance…How could Miriam think of entrusting her daughters to me? We hadn't spoken in decades."

"Is this not a testament of her faith in you—"

"Unfounded. She no longer knows who I am."

"We hadn't spoken in decades."

"That's different." A pause. "I'm sorry."

The longer Cara listened, the less resolute she became to eavesdrop. She hadn't gained any valuable information. Instead, she felt like an intruder. Wishing she could fast forward.

"You are a sister to Miriam as she is a sister to you. Why else would you go to Hope Springs?" Sethu asked. "After she contacted you for the first time in thirty five years, you neither hesitated nor questioned. You went."

"I owe Miriam my life."

Silence.

"I hope you can admit you love at least once before you die."

With a stab to her heart, Cara released the spell.

16

Cavernous halls. A building like an anthill. Hidden passages, abandoned rooms. Depictions of when the world was one, giants and men roaming together. Don't eat me. Don't eat me. Don't eat me. When was the last time a human stepped foot in this place? Ada awoke in a cold sweat.

Amit was standing by the other side of their bed, waking Cara up.

"Hey, it's time to go," she said.

"Go where?" Ada mumbled, glancing at the neon light of the microwave clock. "What time is it?"

"About three AM. It's time to go," Amit repeated.

Ada held her gaze for a second. *Oh.* "Okay, I'll wake Cara up."

It took them twenty minutes to pack up and get dressed. Sethu stood by her bedroom door, backlit by a dim orange light, arms crossed and silently watching. It wasn't until they approached the front door that she stepped forward.

"You could stay here," she said.

"Stop it already," Amit said, shaking her head.

Sethu gave each one of them a tight hug. The girls could hear her muttering under her breath, a spell in a language they did not recognize. When she broke away, she smoothed her hand over their forehead and smiled softly, saying, "You'll be safe."

Her words were like a prayer, a promise they tried very hard to believe.

"Thank you," Ada said.

A knot was forming in her throat. She shut the door and followed her sister down the stairs to the street, wondering if they would meet again.

"Where are we going now?" Cara asked and quickened her pace to catch up to Amit.

"We need to contact your mother ASAP," she replied over her shoulder.

Both girls perked up at this.

"Really?" Cara asked. "How?"

Amit was silent for a moment. "We're going to visit some of my old stomping grounds. See who we find," she said furtively. "Here." They stepped into a dark alley. "I asked Sethu to trade this spell for me. Put your luggage on the ground."

The girls stepped out of the glare of the streetlight and placed their duffel bags and backpacks between them. She unfolded a sheet of paper and took a piece of chalk from her pocket, then crouched down on the floor and started drawing symbols on the pavement. When she muttered an incantation, their luggage shrunk and disappeared.

"I should have done this so long ago," Amit murmured.

"Where did it go?" Cara exclaimed, widening her eyes.

"Just think of them as being in storage," Amit said. Then, she took out two more pieces of paper and handed them out. "So you can get them back on your own when you need to."

Ada's brow furrowed as she took in the rows and rows of symbols, each combination leading to a different outcome. *I'll just let Cara do it*, she thought to herself and pushed it deep into her purse.

They must have been walking for less than twenty minutes when Ada felt a familiar chill run down her spine. She stiffened. The warmth her body had built trying to match Amit's pace seemed to drain. Sure that it was only her paranoia kicking in, and not wanting to alarm anyone, she took a deep breath and glanced over her shoulder. Her heart jumped. She thought she saw a figure in the middle of the street.

"Wait," she tried to say, but she was out of breath, and it came out as a whisper. "Wait!" This time, she was louder. Her legs had slowed to a stop. She turned to look back properly. There, illuminated by the lamplight, was a person. "Are you seeing this?"

Amit grabbed her arm hard, yanking her forward, and said, "Run."

It was a flurry of activity. Ada turned briefly to see Cara panting beside her, Amit bringing up the rear. She couldn't see the person following them any longer, but the hot, humid air of Cape Town suddenly felt cold. She quickly realized, "I don't know where I'm going!"

"It doesn't matter," Amit yelled from behind. "Just keep going."

Amit didn't know who they were running from either, but the moment she had laid eyes on the person behind them, the hair on her arms stood on end. Terrible thoughts entered her mind. Fears she thought she had long banished had somehow resurfaced. She could feel magic, like a dark cloud, hanging over them—it made her feel ten years younger and helpless again. Recognizing their surroundings, she instructed, "Go right! All the way down to the park."

The girls complied, and when they hit the park, Amit charged forward, overtaking them and heading for a building across from it. It had a portal that let out near the border with Mozambique. It wasn't the first time she had used it to escape Cape Town.

"Amit!" Cara shrieked. "Stop!"

Before she could, she was knocked off of her feet by what felt like a rugby player slamming into her. She grunted at the impact, then spat out a curse, and the body flew off of her, the creature's featureless face coming into full view.

"Mistlanders," Ada said, paling.

There were more of them, maybe five. Three were in the park ahead, including the one lying writhing on the floor a few feet away from Amit. Two others stood across the street, blocking their way out.

The girls stood behind Amit, looking back every few minutes to make sure there was no one behind them. Ada searched for the person from under the streetlamp. She knew it wasn't a Mistlander. She would have been able to tell, even from that distance. "Where are you?" she muttered to herself.

"I'm here," a voice whispered in her ear. An arm closed around her waist. She turned her head only to find a man's face two inches from her own. Reflexively, a scream welled up in her throat.

"Ada!" Cara's voice was much further away than it should have been.

When she looked back, the park was no longer in sight. Within a split second, she remembered Amit's curse and repeated it. A burst of sound. She fell to the sand beneath her, her ears ringing. Looking up, she realized they were back at the beach.

Ada jumped to her feet and spun in place, looking for her assailant. A million different spells and curses ran through her mind, all of her studies jumbling into a confusing mix of symbols and meanings. She could hear Amit and Cara yelling her name, but they were blocks away now, making their way toward her. That's when her eyes spotted movement on the periphery. Ada quickly turned, narrowly dodging the hand that reached for her again and coming face-to-face with her enemy.

She was right. It wasn't a Mistlander, but she could tell he wasn't fully human, either. His eyes glowed yellow in the dark. His voice reverberated deeper than it should have. She could feel the vibrations in the air around her. His black clothes seemed to blend into the night. It was hard to tell where one began and the other ended.

"No need for alarm," he said. "I'm not here to hurt you."

"Who are you? What do you want?" Ada growled.

When he smiled, his pearly white teeth stood out against the darkness.

"I'm going to help you."

"I find that hard to believe." The words left her mouth before she could help it.

Amit's voice interrupted them before he could reply, still in the distance but closer than before. Ada turned her head to see them approaching the beach, Cara trailing slightly behind.

"You should come with us," the man said then, any trace of amusement evaporating. "You will only bring them trouble

186

if you stay."

This caught her attention. *Me? Bring them trouble?*

"Go where?" she asked.

He glanced at her quickly approaching companions and clicked his tongue. "I'm afraid we've run out of time." In an instant, he was by her side, whispering in her ear again, "But I'll see you soon."

Cara and Amit were already close enough by then that Ada could see the panic in her sister's eyes. A familiar sensation of wind and pelting sand overwhelmed them. How, Ada wondered, did they find themselves in the middle of a sandstorm while standing on a beach? This and many other questions went unanswered as the edges of her vision blurred, darkening as she fought to maintain consciousness.

Richard was disoriented now that the house on Willow Street was half empty. He often found himself calling for Cara, picking up Ada's favorite cereal at the grocery store, popping his head into their vacant room.

Miriam wasn't much better. She had called the university only days after the girls had left to pull them out of class but still went to wake them up for a week afterward. The few phone calls they had made in the last month were nowhere near enough for parents who had never let their children out of their sight.

Gage felt their absence, too. Suddenly, he found himself the focus of their parents' surplus attention. It was a nuisance, especially now that he was dating Riley.

His schedule had become difficult to handle with school, soccer practice, and the additional practitioner training. Thankfully, he was in his last semester of high school and had already been accepted at the local university; he only had to cruise through his classes on a C+ average. A couple of his friends on the university team floated the idea of inviting the coach over to watch one of their next big games—they were sure he'd be interested in speaking with Gage if he saw him play—but Gage wasn't sure he wanted to make that sort of time commitment. If he did, it would definitely be for the scholarship money. Cara had gotten full rides for her undergraduate and Master's degrees, but he knew Ada's tuition hadn't been cheap.

His parents never let on if they were struggling for money, but Miriam had taken on some extra work from her network of practitioners who often reached out for help formulating spells and potions. When Gage agreed to resume his magical practice, he started assisting her at the club.

They were in the middle of choosing elements that would help a gardener keep gnomes out of their strawberry patch that day. At this point, Gage didn't even blink at the existence of gnomes, just accepted whatever his mother said as fact—when he remembered what the werepeople said the night they moved in downstairs.

"Where does this practitioner live?" he asked.

"Down in California. Why?" Miriam said. It was rare for Gage to show interest in anything pertaining to magic.

"Do you know any other practitioners in Oregon?"

His mother was quiet for a moment, eyes fixed on the stalks of lemongrass she was prepping. Her deft fingers brushed away the remaining traces of dirt, snapped off the leafy ends, cut and discarded the whitish bulbs.

"Yes," she finally replied.

"Then they were wrong?"

Miriam's busy hands paused. "Who?"

"Jed and Bo," Gage said. "They said they couldn't find any other practitioners in Oregon."

It was like the air in the room had shifted. Miriam was quiet for another beat before saying, "I don't know where they are."

This wasn't alarming at first blush.

"People travel," Gage suggested.

She pursed her lips, bracing herself for the conversation to follow.

"I replicated the scrying spell they used, and it wasn't faulty," she said. Her son stared at her expectantly, waiting for her to continue, to set his mind at ease. Instead, the severity of her tone made the pit of his stomach ache. "I couldn't find any practitioners within a hundred miles."

He regretted bringing it up, but it was too late. He had to ask, "Are you sure the spell works?"

"I used other spells," Miriam said. She wasn't planning on talking to Gage about this, didn't think there was any use in worrying him, but once she started, it was hard to stop. The words left her lips faster than she could think, "Practitioners seem to be disappearing left and right. I sent out messages to our database's users, many didn't reply. I wouldn't have been so alarmed, but when I looked into it, most of the unresponsive users were in remote areas, in and outside the US. I asked the ones I could get in contact with to check in with practitioners in their communities, and at least a dozen reached back out worried that someone they knew was nowhere to be found…"

Gage didn't know what to say. His eyes scanned the table between them as if expecting to find the answer there, hiding between glass jars and discarded stems.

"Do you think someone is, like, hurting them or something?" he asked.

The way Miriam looked at him made him feel like a small child.

"I don't know, Gage," she admitted with a shake of her head. "But it seems that the world is becoming less safe by the minute. I sent your sisters away so they could get away from danger, but I'm not sure it worked."

The longer it took to hear from them, the more anxious she became that she made the wrong decision. Ada had spoken about darkness building, dotting the horizon far in the distance.

"It was partly my fault for being so out of touch with the world, but I don't think anyone saw this coming," she said, then shot him a reassuring smile. "It looks like we're going to have to hunker down in Hope Springs a bit longer. Weather out the storm."

Gage instinctively glanced past the railing, picturing the young girls doing their homework below. A pesky thought that had been lodged in his mind for weeks finally made its way to his mouth.

"But they know we're here," he said quietly. "They know who we are and how to find us. Should we really stay in Hope Springs?"

Miriam's smile didn't reach her eyes when she asked, "Don't you trust your mother?" His dissatisfaction must have registered on his face because she reached her hand forward, brushing his cheek. "If the Mistlanders ever break through my barriers, we'll leave Hope Springs for good."

Her words offered cold comfort.

* * *

The high school's prestigious party planning committee would pick a prom theme each year, and this year, it was

Smoke and Mirrors. The cheerleaders heading up the committee had landed on it while brainstorming ways to escape their chaperones' hawkish eyes. They would get the theater kids to set up smoke machines and mirrored corridors across the school gym, creating multiple spots students could hide in to get handsy.

The prom Queen and King would be picked based on their matching costumes, and Riley had tons of ideas. She knew most of her friends were going for the magician and sexy assistant duo and wanted to do something different. She suggested taking the theme more literally, and Gage, not nearly as emotionally invested, agreed. They set a date a few weeks before to visit local shops and check out the selection of black and gray-toned clothes. Then, she wanted to stop by her uncle's hardware store to pick up some broken mirrors he offered to donate to their cause.

Gage was feeling a bit off lately, distracted, but if Riley noticed, she didn't let on. Little oddities had begun to catch his attention. His room had always been messy, but he was finding things strewn around that he didn't remember pulling out of drawers. When walking outdoors, he would see movement in his peripheral vision but caught nothing more than a shadow when he turned. It was always when he was on his way to another location, so he'd never had time to examine the phenomenon closer.

Except once, when he spotted one behind the dogwood on his front lawn as he was heading in. The longer he stared, the darker the shadow seemed, but then his mom opened the door, having seen him through the window, and it was gone.

Gage had also witnessed four car crashes recently, which could have just been a coincidence, but he had been raised by a practitioner to never think of things as coincidences. He still hadn't told any of this to his mother, even though he knew she would want him to. None of these occurrences had seemed alarming or threatening somehow, and he could already picture her face upon hearing about them. Miriam had a special way of making him feel inconsequential, even if he knew that wasn't her intention.

Gage was used to being overlooked. He preferred it really. He had never felt quite *right*. Anxiety grew inside him like a tumor. He often regretted things after saying them and was convinced his friends didn't like him as much as it otherwise seemed. He felt pushy and awkward and dumb. People's kindness felt like pity. His victories seemed false and undeserved. The better he did—in school, on the soccer team, with Riley—the more he felt like he was teetering on the edge, like someone would lift the mask any second and see who he really was. An imposter. A loser.

His nightmares revealed fears he wouldn't dare utter, that his family would one day realize that he was not like them, that he would never be as brave or as strong as they needed him to be, that they would leave him behind. No, Gage never felt quite right. If only he knew there was no such thing as *right*.

Even Riley felt out of place in her own life. Her family was loving but oblivious to who she really was. Her friends were dear to her, but their interests differed. Her older sister, whom she was close to, didn't really seem to understand her train of thought. With all the positive energy surrounding her, she couldn't conceive of being anything but good, but sometimes the sadness inside her was overwhelming.

As she looked around, she would feel like the only person

hiding sorrow in plain sight. Negative feelings would pool and fill her up inside if she wasn't careful, mixing with her baseless grief until it started leaking, leaving dark, oily stains on the floor around her. On the walls. On the people who touched her. Try as she could, she couldn't justify her feelings, her bad moods, why there was sadness in her at all. So blessed she was, and yet there was water building inside her, always looking to burst.

It was almost because of this that she had asked Gage out. Her friends were against it—they wouldn't outright admit it, but they found his family strange. Gage and his sisters shunned societal norms those close to her held dear, standing out for better or for worse. Riley wondered if that was why, when she was with Gage, the pressure inside her didn't feel so strong. He didn't expect a carefully crafted persona, and she found herself relaxing, slowly becoming herself more and more.

She wanted to become that person for him—someone he could be himself with—but she knew that wasn't the case. Riley had been crushing on him for a while and could tell that something had recently changed. He had become more serious, shifting from goofy and careless to quiet and thoughtful. It was like he had grown older all of a sudden, and she wondered why.

"I was looking at my horoscope earlier," Riley said, glancing at Gage from the passenger seat when they were heading downtown. "What sign were you again? Your birthday is coming up, right?"

"Taurus. You believe in that stuff?" he asked.

Gage had to laugh. Astrology was a very legitimate practitioner field, but it didn't extend to the daily horoscope apps his girlfriend liked.

"Listen, I don't make fun of you for wearing the same shirt to school when you have a big game, so don't make fun of me," she huffed.

The shirt thing was a team tradition, but he let it go, saying, "I'm not. What does mine say?"

"Taurus, Taurus, Taurus," she muttered as she scrolled. "Don't get caught up in the little things today, Taurus," she recited. "The answers you are seeking are right under your nose. Just take a step back and take a look at the bigger picture. Stop trying so hard, and things will flow."

"Got it," Gage said and pulled into a parking spot along the main strip.

"So lucky!" Riley exclaimed. "This is a great spot."

As they headed to the first shop of many to search for their monotone outfits, Gage's mind stuck to the whole *horoscope* concept. He remembered a few years ago, his mother partnered with a practitioner somewhere in the Pacific Islands who wanted to advertise their astrological services on the database.

While Riley sifted through racks and racks of dresses, he took a seat inside the store and pulled out his phone. It took a few minutes of sleuthing through database archives, but he managed to find the link he was looking for. It re-directed him to a site asking him to input his birth chart and credit card details. It was fifteen bucks, and Riley was trying on dresses, which only required a few seconds of his attention every now and then, so he went for it. The page said he would receive his results in the next twenty-four hours.

Their shopping trip was uneventful; they ran into a few friends, had a burger, and headed back home. He pulled up to her block and parked just out of sight from the kitchen and living room windows. They tangled together like couples do, then untangled and said goodbye. This left Gage's mind delightfully blank for the rest of the night as he brushed his teeth, undressed, and slept a dreamless sleep.

* * *

The next day was gray and cloudy, Meena's favorite type of day to go to the park. Richard had taken her and was watching her play alone when she called him over to help build a sandcastle. Squatting down, he saw she had placed her dolls strategically around her. "What's going on here?" he asked, pointing at the ones she had placed at separate corners of the sandbox.

"It's Cara and Ada," she replied.

He felt a pang in his heart. "Did you put them over here because they're far away from us?" She shook her head and kept playing. "Are you upset that they're not here?" he tried again. The answer was no again. "Then why are they the only ones all alone?"

"That's just where they are," she replied. "There's a lot of sand."

Chalking it up to an overactive imagination, Richard let it go and focused on the castle. It was one of Meena's favorite parks. It was next to a decrepit cemetery some found unsettling, and not many people came by. That was one of the things Meena liked best.

Miriam once joked that she was playing with the ghosts of the children buried nearby, and Richard wondered if she would really have a different dynamic with the dearly

196

departed than the living. He once asked Miriam if he was strange for thinking of those things, but she just laughed, shook her head, and said, "If you knew the things I think of on a daily basis. No, babe, you're not strange." He welcomed her kiss and felt a little bit closer to his wife afterward.

When Richard first learned about practitioners, he found it difficult to relate to Miriam's world. Little did he know, they would both be challenged years later to understand a completely different perspective, a new way of relating and communicating, of loving.

It was clear from the moment they met her that Meena saw things in a different way. Miriam pored over both magical and non-magical texts, devouring books on neurodevelopmental and psychiatric disorders. She had never trusted doctors, who failed to provide much clarity in this instance as well, so she set out to educate them and their young family on how to make Meena as healthy and happy as possible.

Meena's mother was Miriam's first friend when she arrived in the United States, and for a long time, she was Miriam's only friend. An American-born practitioner who took a sheltered foreign girl under her wing when she had no one and nothing to her name, it was through her that Miriam met Richard, the love of her life. If she hadn't given them Meena, an endless source of love and joy, Miriam would have named their next child after her. Aparajita.

Richard and Meena headed back to the house when fat raindrops started falling on their heads. Gage and Miriam were huddled over a computer at the dining room table. Their voices dropped to whispers when they heard someone walk in, then stopped abruptly before Miriam got up to greet them, kissing her husband and leaning down to ask her daughter about her time at the park.

Richard walked over to Gage and patted his shoulder.

"What's up, champ?" he asked.

Miriam cut in before Gage could reply, "I'm going to help Meena pick some coloring books and will be back down in a minute to explain."

Richard took a seat by his son, who started with some context, "I decided to get an astrology reading yesterday after Riley and I were joking about horoscopes, and this is what I got today."

He turned the laptop toward his father, revealing a five-page PDF. Only the first was text. Scrolling past it, Richard recognized some widely-known Zodiac symbols and imagery but was surprised to see them amongst lines and lines of complex mathematical formulas. He quickly ended up back at the top.

Chaos rears its head again. What is bound must be unleashed. Blood seeps through the sand, elastic extends and extends and snaps back. Shockwaves shatter glass. Glass impales skin. Demon plants his seed. Return home. House in flames. Smoke and shattered mirrors. Chaos rears its head again. What is bound must be unleashed. House in flames. Enemies in the woods. Underground passage. Malignant growth. Rotting façade. What is bound must be unleashed. Chaos rears its head again. Elastic extends and ruptures. A scattered nest, a house in flames. Clear the mold. Purge the pest. Burn the rot. The darkness must be defeated before. The world must be set right before. If the cancer spreads—until it is gone, there will be no such thing as home.

Jupiter makes his way East. So should you. A comet passes closely by Asteroid Lilith next week. Take care not to touch any platinum barehanded. The remaining paragraphs carried on in this fashion, listing out heavenly occurrences happening as far as three months in the future. They were followed by what Richard assumed were the celestial bodies and equations involved.

"What does this all mean?" he asked.

"We don't know," Gage murmured.

"The language is very violent," Richard said. "How concerned should we be about this?"

He caught Miriam's eye as she came down the stairs across from them, and instantly knew the answer from her stony expression. *Very.*

She tried her hand at dark humor, saying, "One thing we know for sure is that our house is going up in flames."

Richard sighed, lifted his glasses, and pinched the bridge of his nose.

"I thought horoscopes were meant to be metaphoric, allegorical, one could argue," he argued, letting her wrap her arms around him, her hand coming to shuffle Gage's hair where he sat beside them.

"They are," she said softly as she rested her head on his chest.

He could tell she was tired, so he put his glasses back on and straightened up before asking, "Does this change the plan?"

"What plan?" Gage asked, suddenly alert. It was the first time he'd heard about a plan.

"I've been setting up safe spots for us around the city, safe spots in case of an attack."

"Oh," he said, then paused. "I thought it would be a little more fleshed out than that."

Miriam sighed, bringing her hands up to massage her

temples.

"I wasn't sure exactly what we were supposed to be preparing for, but clearly, it's something that's going to drive us out of our home," she said.

"We need to figure out where to go," Richard said, placing a firming hand on his wife's shoulder. "My cousin in Toronto—"

This caught Gage's attention. To the best of his knowledge, his dad didn't keep in contact with any of his family.

Miriam breezed by it. "Too predictable. We need to locate or create some safe houses, à la Amit."

"And the girls," he started.

"It sounds like they're going to end up in Hope Springs again anyway, if I am reading that correctly," she said, muttering the last part cautiously. "If we're all in hiding, we might as well be in hiding together. I'll try to contact Amit. Tell her to head back soon."

Richard nodded, deep in thought, then said, "I can pack some grab-and-go-type duffels for us in case of emergency... Do you think we should put some of our stuff in storage? I'm just thinking...if we want to prepare for our house potentially burning down?"

Miriam pursed her lips. She could put as many fire-proofing spells over their house as she wanted, but—if it had been written in the stars—there would surely be stronger spells that could break through them. Unless she was physically present and able to combat it when the house was being attacked, she could not ensure it would stay intact. And there was no way to guarantee that she would be.

"I definitely want to put some of my stuff in storage," Gage said. He was thinking about his favorite albums and books.

"I'm still hoping our house won't burn down, but…Yeah, I think it's better safe than sorry, right?"

His mom caught his eye, then nodded and said, "I agree. Let's put the stuff we value most in storage, just in case. If it does happen, we'll have to resign ourselves to losing a lot of it; we still need our furniture and everything while we're living here, and I don't plan to go anywhere else until I'm forced to…" She trailed off, gaze suddenly blank. It was the first time she had entertained the possibility out loud. "Or would it be better to just leave? Pack our stuff and go?"

Richard and Gage were both silent. They all waited for someone else to decide.

"The girls will be coming back here, won't they?" Richard asked, his voice not much higher than a whisper.

"We could get like a rental or something. Say the house is under construction, move all our stuff there," Gage suggested.

Miriam thought of all the spells and protections she had cast around their Willow Street home, all the work she would have to do anywhere else they went. She realized she would have to do these things again and again when they went on the run. Always, thoughts of this lifestyle led her back to Amit. She who lived her life in the shadows, moved within the hidden undercurrents of their world.

It was funny; Miriam used to think that, for two people who grew up like siblings and went on to spend most of their lives trying to escape their past, their lifestyles had veered drastically apart. Now, it seemed like they were on a collision course again. Maybe funny wasn't the right word.

"I don't know if it's a good idea to get a rental for an indefinite period of time…" she thought out loud. It wasn't just the money but the logistics. They would need to find a month-to-month lease, rare in a town like Hope Springs. "I also own a construction company, so saying my house is under construction and not actually doing anything to it isn't going to work."

"Can we remodel the kitchen?" Gage said, picking a random room.

His mother sighed, thinking of her colleagues sinking their time into a project when she knew the whole place could very well burn down. Plus the cost of a rental.

"I'd rather replace what we lose in the fire," she said at last. "Let's get a storage unit for essentials. Things of sentimental value."

Now that this had been decided, they had the monumental task of defining what essential meant to them. This would take weeks, and the hardest part would be the girls' room. How do you decide which of your daughters' items to save and which to let burn?

Meena helped. It only took her ten minutes to rustle through some drawers, pull out some trinkets. Watching her, Miriam and Richard were reminded of Aparajita, her birth mother, who could divine the future and the past with the touch of her hand.

What do you feel? Miriam would always ask her, fascinated by her ability. It wasn't common. Aparajita, amused by her strange friend, would answer differently every time. *A life. Grief. Living memory. Overwhelming love.* Impending doom?

This time, too, Miriam leaned down and smoothed Meena's dark hair, asking, "What do you feel?"

"Cara," she said, placing a book in her hands. "Ada." A faded photo album.

What do they feel like? She wanted to say, longing to feel it,

202

too. Instead, she asked, "Can I give you a hug?"

Yes, Meena nodded. Yes.

18

Ada opened her eyes to a crowd of women standing over her. Pushing herself up on her forearms, she noticed the ocean was nowhere in sight. The women were wearing long, draped clothing and hijabs, and she could see a few standing further down the street in niqabs. For a delirious moment, she wondered if this was a place without men, then a few emerged from a building nearby. The women seemed to straighten as if going about their usual business, and the men continued down the street without notice.

One said something to her that she didn't understand.

"I'm sorry," Ada said. "I only speak English."

Looking down, she realized she was painfully underdressed in bike shorts and an oversized t-shirt.

The women chattered around her, and one broke off, jogging down the street. Another helped her sit up, handing her a water thermos and motioning for her to drink. Still in shock and trying to process the events that had just unfolded, this small act of kindness threw her off.

She had been tensed like an animal ready to run, which now made her feel vulnerable and stupid. Thankful that she didn't need to speak for now, Ada took a swig. The tightness in her throat made the simple act of drinking uncomfortable. The woman that had run off only took a few minutes to return with another in tow. The newcomer was carrying a bundle in her arms.

"You speak English?" she asked.

"Yes," Ada responded hoarsely.

"Here," the woman said and handed her the clothing she had brought. "You should put these on. My name is Sara; my husband is Rifat, but you don't seem like you would know who that is. How did you come to be here?"

Ada stood up, pulling the long dress over her shoulders and holding the other item in front of her quizzically.

"I don't know. The last thing I remember is being on the beach in Cape Town. A strange man showed up and…" She trailed off, unsure of how to continue.

The women chittered around her—she wondered if they understood more than they spoke.

Sara took the cloth from her hands and wrapped it around her head, saying, "It sounds like something terrible has happened to you. Perhaps it is better that you don't remember. For now, it will be best if you don't stand out. We will find a way to take you to the embassy. My husband is away at work, but maybe when he returns, he can help us come up with ideas."

Just feeling Sara's fingers brush against her hair and her face as she adjusted her hijab made Ada's eyes sting. "Thank you," she tried to say, but her voice was strangled and as foreign to her as the words everyone spoke around them. "My name is Ada."

"Ada," Sara repeated, smiling warmly and brushing her tears away. "What a nice name. Let's walk over there to my house. You can lay down in my nieces' room."

Trying her hardest to stay stoic, Ada took the chance to look around. She had been lying in the middle of a small plaza if she could call it that; some buildings surrounding it must have been shops since they had signs and advertisements propped up against their walls.

She could see now that many of the women had been there waiting for their turn at a nearby well. As she watched, three of them grabbed onto its rusty rig and pushed down hard, making it budge a few inches. None of the roads were paved, and she could clearly see where the row of houses ended ahead, only a mile or so away.

"Where am I?" she asked herself softly.

Only a couple of feet ahead, Sara stopped, turned to face her, and said, "We're in Syria. This village doesn't have a name. It doesn't exist on any maps. We built it a few years ago after militias destroyed our home; it was called Tmek. All the surviving families live here now, so in a sense, these are the remnants of Tmek, even if we're more than a day's trip away now."

Ada pressed the heels of her hands into her eyes. Syria. Should she try to escape through a rift? She'd need some privacy first; too much could go wrong if someone saw her. She definitely couldn't just arrive at an American embassy and pretend to have been kidnapped—especially not out of Cape Town when her last known location was Oregon.

Just the prospect of being interrogated by human authorities like the FBI made her feel sick to her stomach. After all this time dodging the Committee and Mistlanders, thinking about the more familiar consequences of the human realm, prison, for one, seemed like a slap to the face. How would she find Amit and Cara? Were they even together still? Was

Cara alone like her? Suddenly, she felt a warm hand on her elbow.

"Ada." Sara's voice was gentle and sad as she said, "First, let's get some rest. Then we can figure out what we'll do next."

She let her hands fall from her face and nodded, following her into a building nearby. It was a small rectangular home, like all the others in the village. Inside, children were piled into every corner. *Oh*, Ada thought, stepping into Sara's nieces' room. Blankets and pillows were sprawled out on the floor, a few more folded neatly to the side.

"Ah, they didn't all fix their beds today." Sara clucked. "I'll forgive them this time since you can just lay down here," she said, smiling warmly and leaning down to smooth the sheets. "Here, lie down."

Ada complied, feeling her throat tighten painfully again. Before she knew it, tears were streaming down her face much faster than before. She buried her head into her arms. Sara knelt down by her and helped remove her hijab, then pulled the long dress from over her shoulders. "Sleep," she said, and eventually, Ada did.

She woke up because of the heat. Her shirt and shorts were soaked with sweat, but she still grabbed the clothing Sara had given her earlier when she spotted it folded in the corner of the room and pulled the dress over her head. She folded the blanket, placed it neatly near the others, and stepped out into the house's kitchen area.

"Ada!" her hostess exclaimed, apparently in the middle of a lesson. Several elementary school-aged children sat around her on the floor, crowding over a book she held in her hand. "How are you feeling?" Sara asked. She handed the book to the kids and rose to greet her, saying, "Come, let's sit at the table. I have good news."

"I'm feeling a bit better," Ada assured her and sat down. "What's the good news?"

"My husband, Rifat, he was supposed to return Thursday, but one of the women convinced her husband to use his cell phone to send him a message. He said he would return tomorrow with a car, then drive us to Damascus, where you can take a bus to Lebanon and the American embassy in Beirut. It will be a long journey, but we can go with you half-way, and we have a cousin there who goes to Beirut every two weeks for business who can help us figure out the right bus route."

"Sara," Ada whispered. "How can I ever pay you back for your kindness? You have saved my life. How can I repay you?"

"No, Ada," Sara said as she grasped her hand. "It is Allah who has saved you. Also, because you're here, we've had a much better turnout for class." She winked, gesturing at the children who gathered around her kitchen, taking turns sneaking curious glances.

Fighting back tears again, Ada nodded and said, "Sara, I'll pray for you for the rest of my life. For your family's safety and prosperity."

Sara seemed to like this. She laughed heartily, then turned to the children and said something in Arabic.

"I've been teaching them English," she told Ada. "As much as I can. My husband used to work at an international company before, so he taught me and our children. I only have that book left now, and they don't have a lot of opportunities to practice, but I think of how many opportunities knowing

English could provide them in the future..."

A few of the kids stood up and gathered around the table, trying out their fledgling foreign language skills on Ada. She smiled, picking up phrases and words and trying her best to keep them engaged. She turned to Sara to ask, "Which children are yours?"

Sara smiled sadly. "They're not here," she said. "The last time I saw them was in Tmek."

Ada struggled to find something appropriate to say. "I'm sorry," she started, but then a girl started tugging on the sleeve of her dress, demanding attention.

Sara shook her head, her expression wavering. They didn't do much for the rest of the day. Ada watched the children play outside in the street while Sara was whisked away by neighbors asking for help. By the evening, some young women came by and collected their children, thanking Sara for looking after them. When nighttime came, they shared some bread, and she apologized for being unable to provide more.

"My husband is returning with more food and some seeds. We want to become a self-sufficient community, but we also know that militias could find us here any day. It's hard to decide how much we should invest into our life here, whether we should plant the seeds or wait for our forever home," she said.

Ada thought of Sethu's place, how she wished time would have stopped there. It was the third time they had been forcefully driven out of their place of refuge since leaving Hope Springs, but even so, her only regret was not savoring every moment of peace and letting them slip by inconsequentially.

She bit her lip, then replied carefully, "It's not my place to comment, but I think you should plant them now. Make your life as beautiful as you can every day. We don't know if we'll get another chance to."

Sara smiled and said, "That's what I've been thinking, too. In this world, everything you have today can be gone tomorrow. We should plant our seeds now." She added more resolutely, "The more we wait, the longer they will take to grow."

That night, Ada waited until all the children were asleep and then sat up quietly, cross-legged. Her mind drifted back to Paris, to the boy, and she wondered what his life was like before he was forced to leave it. Leaning her back against the wall, she felt the depth of the world's injustice more deeply than ever before.

She had never shied away from learning about global conflicts and the senseless death they engendered. At twenty-two, she was familiar with outrage and shock. She had signed petitions, given donations, and attended protests organized in and around her university. But the sadness and indignity that surged within her when she thought of Sara's children, forever exiled to their mother's memory of their hometown; when she wrestled with the reality that they would never know the comforts that she and her siblings had been granted only because they were born in the right place at the right time, was unlike any vestiges of empathy she had felt in the past. Ada was overwhelmed by her humanity. How it made you unable to look away from those who shared in it.

She let her head fall forward and closed her eyes, envisioning the village in her mind, all that was left of Tmek. *This village will be safe*, she thought. *Sara and her family will be safe. The seeds they plant will grow strong and plentiful. This village will be safe. This family will be safe. They will be happy and have plenty of food to eat.*

Slowly, she began tracing a circle on her thigh, willing her magic to encircle them. *This village will be safe. Sara and her family will be safe.* Not confident enough to attempt a sigil, she willed this to be enough. Her fingers traced symbols on her skin. *Allow me to protect them*, she begged a silent God, slowly drifting into sleep.

The next morning, she could feel the anticipation in the air. Sara and her nieces, Amal and Fatiha, waited anxiously for Rifat to return home—he texted his friend to expect him around nine. Ada lost count of how many times she glanced at the living room's blue clock. "It's a few minutes slow," Fatiha told her.

"Usually, so is our uncle." Amal giggled.

Despite the jabs, Rifat was almost exactly on time, the clock trailing him just barely. His nieces jumped on him the minute he appeared at the door, throwing him off balance and clamoring in their mother tongue. His eyes fell on Sara, and he said something that made her laugh.

Rifat presented the bag off his back almost like an offering, stuffed as it was of all the things Sara had mentioned: food, seeds, clothing, even a new cell phone, which the girls snatched from his hands to go play with in the living room. Ada felt like an intruder, a voyeur staring in at a heartwarming scene she had no business being a part of.

Yet, when he finally turned to where she stood sheepishly in the kitchen corner, he planted his hands firmly on her shoulders and said, "Welcome, Ada. I hear you've been through a lot. Please, I hope you can find some respite in our home."

Ada smiled and nodded, feeling her lip tremble despite her best efforts as she said, "Thank you. I have."

That day, Sara whipped up a feast. Apparently, it was customary on the days that Rifat returned. A number of neighbors stopped by to snack on the varieties of cookies and spreads she produced, playing musical chairs with the limited seating available.

Ada found her mind quieting as she helped chop, stir, and assemble. She missed working silently alongside her father in the kitchen and the magical chaos of cooking at Sethu's. This was something entirely different, filled with colorful characters from the village that entered and left the house freely, all with their own stories they wanted to share. Rifat and Sara translated them obligingly. The laughter of children filled the house again.

"People here don't meet strangers very often anymore," Rifat told her. "It is nice to have a pair of fresh ears to listen to our stories. Everyone around here has heard them hundreds of times."

Ada smiled and said, "I love learning about other people's lives, especially when they seem so different from mine."

"You know, Ada," he said. "I've met many people in my life from dozens of countries, and I've never found humans from anywhere to be that different."

"I think I am learning that now," she replied, nodding.

"Of course," Sara chimed in, setting a fresh bowl of muhammara in front of them. "Humans everywhere want love and safety and to not be afraid."

"And money!" Rifat added. She frowned, but he pressed on, "I think in this world, most humans want money, too."

"Okay, okay!" Sara conceded, her frown half turning into

laughter. "But I think most people want money because it means security."

"Except for those who want power," her husband countered.

"Those are the bad ones!" she replied.

Ada smiled at their bickering, feeling more at ease than she had in days. The sun snuck down quicker than she expected, and soon, she was back in the dark room with Amal and Fatiha sleeping soundly beside her. She slipped out of her covers again, pressing her back against the wall and shutting her eyes tight. She thought of Cara and of Amit, tried to see them on a map in her mind's eye. How she wished to have Cara's talent for scrying. Instead, she imagined string connecting them and tugged at it with her magic, pulling them to her. Nothing happened.

I'm out here, she thought. *Where are you?*

S and whipped Cara's skin. She had been just steps away from Ada—close enough to reach out and touch her—before the wind knocked her straight off her feet. In a moment of weightlessness, she questioned if they were the victims of a freak hurricane.

Piecing together a few of the active and passive words Amit had drilled into their brains while in Nebraska, she muttered a spell to go down and soon found herself falling. It didn't take long for her back to hit the hot sand with a thud. The brightness of day threw her off; it had been dusk in Cape Town.

There were no buildings in sight. In fact, there was nothing in sight. Just like the day that they arrived in South Africa, she found herself in the middle of an infinite desert, but this time with no dive bar to shelter in.

"Ada!" she yelled. "Amit? Ada!"

Cara instinctively knew that she was alone. This hadn't been a natural occurrence; the Mistlanders and *that person* must have hurled them into random corners of the desert to pick them off one by one.

Still, she yelled their names until her mouth was dry, the glaring sun scalding her skin and making her sweat through her clothes. Frustration brought tears to her eyes. What if something happened to them?

"Okay, Cara, think," she said out loud. "We need to find water. Civilization."

The key word was *find*. Scrying.

Having thrown her bag into Amit's magic storage unit, she had nothing but the clothes on her back, her phone and headphones, and a few dollars she kept on her person just in case. She had the spell to access their things, but there wasn't a good surface to draw a sigil on; the sand wouldn't hold the shapes.

Her phone had battery still, but she could only use it on Wi-Fi outside of the United States. It was, in short, useless. She decided to turn it off to preserve the battery just in case.

Such was Cara's talent for scrying that she could usually find the things she was looking for without performing a spell, but desperate and shaking from exhaustion and heat, she decided to play it safe.

She concentrated, willing her words to mean something, and shouted out what Amit had called "the seeker's rhyme," a four-lined Arabic poem that immediately opened her higher mind. She crouched down, grabbed a handful of warm sand, and let the grains slip through her fingers, asking, *Where can I find shelter and water?*

Despite the still air, the sand spun up in rivulets, floating to her left and into the distance. She followed. It must have been an hour before she stopped again, her calves and knees aching from walking in the slippery sand. She was grateful to have worn pants that covered her ankles, but the sleeves of her shirt left the bottom half of her arms exposed, and her skin was already bright red. Her head was pounding, both from dehydration and presumably lack of sleep. She plopped down on the sand and decided to try again.

What is the fastest way to get to water?

The sand fell through her hands and was carried out in front of her once more, not seeming to change directions in the slightest. Cara sighed, her resolve hardening again. Without further ado, she set off across the dunes. As she did, a myriad of questions passed through her mind, most pertaining to Ada and Amit. Were they together? Were they safe?

It was hard to tell time in the scorching heat. She could have been walking for two hours or just thirty minutes. She didn't want to turn on her phone to check. It was difficult to even know how far she had walked. In the midst of identical sand dunes, space seemed to compress. Like running in a nightmare, she couldn't tell if she was making progress at all.

Her mind drifted back to that night, to the silhouette of a person she had vaguely made out in the darkness. Amit surely could have rescued Ada from them. All Cara could see were glowing yellow eyes and a bright white-toothed smile. They had leaned in close to Ada's ear, and Cara's stomach had churned. If she was stronger, she wouldn't have let anyone that close to her sister.

As the sun finally started making its descent, her legs grew slower, and her consciousness started slipping. Never having been known for her endurance, she normally would have been proud to have made it this far. Not now.

"I swear to God, if you don't get up this instant, we are going to die out here," Cara muttered to herself. She was fully lying on the ground, no longer bothered by the sand that invaded every corner of her body.

"Get up, you stupid bitch," she hissed, pressing her hands into the warm sand and pushing herself up to her knees. Her fingers were numb by now, cracked and raw. "If you have to crawl, you'll crawl."

And so she crawled for a little while, then lay down for a while more. The sun started lowering further, and cold winds began to blow from afar. At first, she thought it was a nice break from the heat, but then she began to shiver.

Making her way up another hill, her legs started to buckle. If she let herself collapse, she would slide back down the dune the same way she had come from, wiping out any progress. Sometimes, while living with Sethu, it was easy to forget what they were running from. Falling into the sand once more, she curled up into a ball to preserve body heat.

Everything hurt, and the pain served as a stark reminder that there were people out there who wanted her dead. She had been dropped into this desert to die.

Sobs wracked her body. Was Ada suffering like this somewhere, too? Cara missed her mother, her father, Gage, and Meena. She held the image of their faces in her mind for a moment, and it filled her with strength. She was a practitioner, Goddamnit. She could magic her way out of this situation for sure.

What had she been studying so hard for all of these weeks—no, years? Even with renewed strength, all Cara could think of at the moment was sleep. Her eyes refused to stay open for more than a few seconds, so she told herself she would try scrying one last time, then take a short nap before trying every other spell she could think of.

Unlike Ada, Cara didn't like mixing her own spells and sigils and potions. She was weary of practicing magic without detailed instructions, always taking her mother's warnings of everything that could go terribly wrong to heart, but this was a life-and-death situation, and she could afford to put it off no longer.

Weak, she stretched out her hand and grabbed one final fistful of dirt. By now, it was cold to the touch and grated against her blistered skin. *Please,* she begged it. *I need help.*

As the sand drifted from her fingers and up from the ground, she heard something she hadn't until then. The grains pitter-pattered as they collided with the hard leather of a big black boot.

"Help," she tried to say, but her body didn't seem to be responding any longer.

* * *

The sudden sandstorm left Amit wounded and disoriented. She had almost reached Ada when a powerful impact threw her back across the street—banging her shoulder and the side of her head against the pavement and momentarily shocking her. She tried to push herself up to her feet, setting off an intense wave of vertigo that blinded her.

The Mistlanders were nearby, and she had no time to waste. She put up a defensive barrier and yelled for Ada and Cara. No answer. Nothing ran into her barriers. Once her vision was restored, she could see that there were no longer any Mistlanders or practitioners around her. She was alone.

Amit tried calling out for the girls a few more times, but still in the middle of Cape Town, she didn't want to attract unwanted attention. Five or six hide-and-seek charms and heat-seeking spells later, her frustration got the best of her.

Turning to a nearby post, she kicked it until it dented and bent. Then, while catching her breath, she tried to figure out her next move.

Sethu's wasn't an option; they had been found so easily. She was tempted to go back and check on her friend's safety, but that would undeniably endanger both their lives. Still holding out hope that Miriam's daughters couldn't have gone far, Amit hesitated to stray from South Africa. She wracked her brain for allies in the area. Someone who could bypass the magic blocking her from divining Cara and Ada's coordinates.

Her mind conjured memories that hadn't been unearthed in years, in no small part because of the dark aura that had enveloped them when they were being chased earlier. Like condensed fear, it had oozed in through her ears and into her brain, reaching deep into her subconsciousness to find long-forgotten insecurities. Images of alien-looking helmets and futuristic buildings flashed before her eyes. It might be time to check in with her old friends out in the Great Karoo.

She had to be careful not to be seen in Cape Town, but ran the risk of being recognized anywhere she went. That meant she could only afford to show her face once and needed to get the most bang for her buck. No friends or acquaintances; other than Sethu, they were all dead or long gone anyway. Rather, she had to venture down the rabbit hole. At four AM, she knew all she was going to find down there was filth, the kind she usually had to bend closer to the gutters to hear. That's exactly what she was going for.

Someone started laughing as soon as she walked through the door. There were more people in the bar than she expected, but not a dozen altogether. They were all the type that couldn't be outside once the sun was up, the type to burn under the red-hot rays. The one that was laughing looked melded to the chair he sat in, almost like he had died and been left to rot. His skin was stuck to the seat, and the legs would clatter, banging the floor as he hacked. "It's been a while since we've seen you in South Africa," he called, jolly in tone.

She tried to pick out a face from the bloated features, saying, "So you say, Oom. Have you missed me?"

"Not the trouble you always bring," he replied. Amit figured they must have met before. "Too old for the Waste now, are we? Has Katlego thrown you out? Sweet Katli," the old man spat, his words dribbling down his chin. "Katli won't leave us behind." His voice went high, like he was imitating someone else. "The Wasted will save us all! Ha!" He tried to laugh again but choked and coughed instead.

"It's good to know Katlego is alive and well," she said and positioned herself behind a seat at his table.

In her youth, she had grown used to listening to older practitioners ragging on the Wasteland. They took to calling the youths that frequented it the Wasted.

"Alive and well and surrounding himself with children still," the man said between breaths. This caught Amit's attention.

"That's suggestive," she prodded. Incited. She remembered Katlego as a young man, maybe a few years older than she was. He was charming and authoritative. Indeed, he must have reached middle age by now.

"I only say what I hear."

"Have I asked for more?" Amit drew the chair in front of her and sat. "Where do you suggest I find him?

"Where do you think?"

220

"Oom, you know I haven't been to the Waste in years," she lamented.

"And you're no longer welcome." He laughed, enjoying the power his knowledge brought him. That is why he sat, after all, in this chair. "If I knew, I might tell you, but the Wasted children have become more careful than ever, especially with the Committee hounds and all."

"So the Committee has been looking for them? That's nothing new."

"Oh, girl." He shook his head, rotting teeth on display once more. "The Committee has infiltrated."

Amit left the establishment feeling just barely more informed than she had before. Yet it was a start. She remembered a trick she used when the practitioners trained to transport people across the Wasteland's notoriously thick veil weren't available to shuttle her over. At best, she'd be able to jump into their library, take a book, and leave. At worst, she'd be spotted by some teenagers and have to escape before her mind got jumbled.

Something her informant mentioned stuck stubbornly in her head, *still surrounding himself with children.* The old man had been insinuating, if not outright accusing... Under normal circumstances, she wouldn't hesitate to verify and discipline—under normal circumstances, she was the judge, jury, and executioner—but she had to prioritize Miriam's girls. She had promised to.

Amit slinked through the busying streets like a pickpocket, avoiding everyone's eyes. Using an old trick to escape the bus's fare, she rode an hour out of the city and hopped out at one of the line's less frequented stops. "You got a ride?" the bus driver confirmed before letting her off.

"Yes, sir," Amit assured him.

She waited for him to drive off and walked out into the desert. The heat was stifling. She didn't remember it being quite this bad when they were young, but she did remember her clothes being drenched in sweat all of the time. Sethu would make fun of her, not understanding why she went to such great lengths. There were ways to help the world without sweating, she would say.

What have you done to help the world lately, my friend? Amit would ask her.

I help you, and you are part of the world.

Indeed, Sethu's hands were full with her own problems. She said Amit was only looking for a way to get back at her parents.

Amit approached a familiar hill and found the rock she sought within minutes, its unusually smooth curved surface almost glinting in the sun. She pressed her hand against the stone and felt the whole world compress so painfully around her it felt like all the space was being squeezed out of her body. Unlike rifts, which took seconds to cross, this sensation lasted over a minute, each moment less bearable than the next. Then, she was in.

The rebel youth inherited the facility they dubbed the Wasteland from the original South African practitioners who raged against the Boers, the British, and eventually the forced and separate Republic—ancient practitioners from the San, the Khoikhoi, the Bantu, and the Zulu. The library had once been their crowning jewel. Now, it stood empty in comparison. The shelves were disheveled and not half-full. Some books lay, damaged, strewn across the floor.

It wasn't unusual for the Wasteland to change over the years.

Around the time Amit was involved, some architecturally gifted practitioners had begun remodeling the outside of the building, shaping it into futuristic structures drawn straight from their favorite science fiction novels and comics. But the library and other facets at the core of what the Waste stood for, its history, those things were sacred.

Amit materialized between some bookshelves and peeked out. She could see a table that looked like it had been recently occupied, an iced drink sitting unchaperoned, condensation building up on the cup's surface. She snuck a bit closer. The room was quiet, and the air felt undisturbed, but the residents would surely be back soon. The evidence that the Committee had infiltrated the Wasted was so clear, Amit first doubted whether someone had planted it. But there was no one left in the Waste to play such a trick on her.

As if playing a twisted game of *Where's Waldo*, she quickly picked out two pieces of Committee propaganda on the table: the biography of a war criminal idolized by traditionalists and a plastic pouch of what looked sickeningly like mermaid scales. It was a two-punch combo; finding out a once impenetrable revolutionary force had been corrupted by the very entity it sought to dismantle and seeing it now trafficked in mutilated body parts.

This would have never happened in the Wasteland a few decades ago, not just because of the towering moral implications, but also because every member of the insurrection was flat-out broke. Where was this new generation of Wastelanders getting money to buy mermaid scales, she wondered. If anything, that was the third tell-tale sign. People with money profited from the establishment. They didn't oppose it. She took advantage of the emptiness of the room to make a calculated dash through the bookshelves.

When she was but a few rows from the main door, straining to see past it and into the corridor, a group of four teenagers walked in, each more sixteen-year-old looking than the next. Amit was about to throw on a stealth spell and bolt out when one of the girls started talking about her friend. And Katlego.

The nausea intensified. White hot rage bubbled inside her, making her see red. Her resolve wavered. Maybe she *should* deal with things in the Wasteland before she left. She promised herself she'd be on her way to the girls within the hour.

20

Many mythical cities have risen from the deserts of Alkebulan, the mother of mankind. Some, like Aoudaghost, have been found. Plenty remain hidden amongst the Kalahari, the Sinai, the Namib. The gods and spirits sometimes reveal them—coquettishly flashing an ankle—only to bury them in the sands once more for centuries. They find nothing more pleasing than tangling an expedition. Nothing more satisfying than seeing a man go mad trying to retrace his steps.

In the dunes, there are no steps to retrace. You will never walk the same path again. This was a promise the desert made to its people. That's why it stung the people of Kitara when the white man found them. Long worshipped as demigods, they cultivated the wisdom of the Dogon, fostered the Yoruba's wealth and culture, and healed the people, ridding them of evil spirits. They would barter with the gods for a plentiful harvest and just enough rain and would often birth blessed children who could float through the air or speak to others with their minds. All this glory, they thought, would surely be enough to protect them.

The people of Kitara would have never let the ugly, pale-faced stranger inside their walls, but he came to their king

225

Omukama Winyi III in a dream and showed that he, too, was favored by the gods. He showed that he could perform the holiest magic only their priests could master, and he preached unity amongst the blessed.

The man's flashy tricks wooed the hearts of Kitara's practitioners but frightened the city's elders. They pleaded with Omukama Winyi to remove the man at once, jumble his memories so he could never return, but he was not swayed. The man had promised to show him the most powerful magic of all, that which could decimate armies and turn empires to ruins. Entrancing the court with frivolous displays, he made sure it was too late by the time they realized that the empire he would turn to ruins was theirs.

Overcome with hatred and despair, Omukama Winyi vowed to never let an outsider inside Kitara's walls again. He gathered his surviving peoples to the capital city, the last bastion of his once great empire, and ordered the practitioners to hide them so that no one could ever stumble upon them again. That day, the Empire of the Sun disappeared amongst the sands only to be recounted as a subject of tales and myths.

* * *

Cara woke up to a blunt object prodding her forehead. "Wake up," someone demanded. "Your presence has been requested by the king."

This sounded like nonsense, and she would have assumed she was still dreaming had she not opened her eyes to find four tall, armed men glaring back at her from beyond bars.

"Get up, demon," one spat, so she did, bad as always at

resisting authority.

He opened the door to her cell and ordered her to follow.

Flanked on all sides by intimidating military types, Cara contemplated her options. She could continue doing as she was told and hope that the knack for obedience that had gotten her this far in life would once again prove useful, or she could try to escape and probably die.

Had she been with Ada, she might have considered the latter. Had she been with Ada, she might not have had a choice. Her sister would have gotten them in trouble one way or another, and they would have had to escape to survive. Ada wasn't here, however, and Cara's penchant for sucking up had seldom failed her, so she would stick to what she knew.

They emerged from the dark prison and into the dawn. She tried to regain her bearings, and then, as the events of the last twenty-four hours came rushing back, realized she'd never had them. She could smell the musk of the stables nearby. Only a sliver of light radiated from the east. The earliest birds were starting to chitter.

There was no one in sight besides the soldiers. They turned onto a larger road, at the end of which sat a monumental structure. She wondered how she could have missed its colossal clay pillars until then. They held up painted ceilings and flanked intricately carved gates. Small houses lined the path, decorated in colorful patterns and shrouded in greenery.

Cara ventured a peek over her shoulder, avoiding the eyes of the men behind her, and caught a glimpse of a city that stretched out for miles. The palace ahead sat upon a steep hill, and the closer they got, the more massive it seemed.

She felt her legs shaking beneath her, exhausted from a day traversing dunes.

Great, she thought sarcastically. The last thing she needed was to pass out in front of the king.

They entered the building, and the temperature dropped a few degrees inside the clay walls, sending a shiver up her spine. Torches lit the cavernous hallways, making shadows dance in their periphery, keeping her on edge. Cara wondered what crime they thought she had committed to call her a demon. Would they believe her if she told them she had committed no crime at all?

They stopped in front of a closed set of doors, which opened to reveal a pair of hypnotic black eyes.

The voice was high and sweet, like a birdsong. "So she has awakened. Bring her closer."

Cara's heart was pounding, her eyes glued to the ground. One of the guards prodded her forward, and she glanced up, meeting the king's eyes. They stared at her unwaveringly. Her mouth was dry. Her stomach twisted. Was this fear? It felt different. Unlike the darkened streets of Cape Town. Unlike Paris or Nebraska.

They stopped a distance away from the king, and the guard ahead bowed, stating, "The intruder, your Glory."

Cara stood behind awkwardly, debating whether to copy him.

The king didn't look much older than she was. "How did you find us?" she asked.

Cara decided it was best to bow. She replied carefully, "I was wandering the desert blindly, begging God to survive. It must have been His endless mercy that led me here."

"My soldiers say they found you scrying."

"I don't know what you mean," Cara fielded. Witches didn't receive the warmest reception in many cultures. Was this why they were calling her a demon?

The king seemed to have no patience for these games. When she stood, her embroidered robes shimmered, the light reflecting off them like sunlight on waves. Cara could almost feel the ocean breeze. Smell the salt. "Are you a practitioner?" the king asked.

It wasn't just her dress's fabric. Cara suddenly felt the whole room thrumming with magical energy. Behind the king, she spotted a long table stacked up with books and elements: herbs, preserved insects, what looked like dry lizards. Beyond that, a strange apparatus pointed at a skylight—some sort of telescope? The questions in her mind morphed into something new, the fear converting quickly and recklessly into anticipation. "Are you?" she asked.

"I asked you first," the king said.

Two guards in her periphery pawed their weapons, ever so slightly positioning them toward her. The burst of excitement faded, and Cara remembered that being amongst practitioners didn't mean she was safe. If there was anything she had learned since leaving Oregon, it was this.

"I am a practitioner," she said, realizing that without Ada, it was up to her to take the risks. "And I did find you through scrying, but everything else I said was true. I was lost in the desert trying to survive."

"You don't seem like the type to be wandering the Sahara."

Cara hesitated, debating how much to reveal. "It wasn't of my own free will," she finally admitted, hoping to come across as weak and pitiful. Non-threatening.

"Who chases you?"

"I don't know."

"How did you find us?"

Cara was surprised by the question. Hadn't the king said it herself? "Through scrying," she answered.

The guards tensed again, unable to control their anger. They angled the tips of their spears toward her. "Enough with your lies," one hissed.

"Scrying doesn't work here, demon," another added.

The king didn't flinch, instead coming closer. "Yes, the issue is that you have found an unfindable city. Not even the Committee could scry their way to our gates, and yet my men saw you crawl your way through the dunes only to collapse at their feet. If you are a spy, you're not a very good one, and we have no doubt you must be colluding with treacherous forces within our walls. Now," she said, her long fingers traversing the space between them and landing on the sunburned skin of Cara's forehead. "Tell me who brought you here."

Cara felt the magic first. Like a teabag dipped in hot water, it seeped through her brain and numbed her senses. Then, a series of memories flashed by her eyes, like flipping through a scrapbook. Here she was laughing, then she looked over her shoulder at a dark street, wind whipped her hair, her eyes shut tight against the sand. Finally, back out in the dunes, she lost consciousness and woke up with a gasp.

"Who is it, your Glory?" one soldier asked. "Was it Kyabambe as we suspected?"

"Say the word, your Glory," another clamored. "We will end his bloodline where it stands."

Cara's breath steadied, and she ventured a glance upward. The king stared down at her, her gaze unreadable and unwavering. After a tense silence, she said, "She was merely a pawn. Of course the ringleader would not show their face to her." She turned, and Cara could feel the men hanging on every word. "One person I did see was Iguru Mugenyi II."

Iguru. Cara latched on to the name. Had such a person really been in her memories? Could this unfindable city have something to do with her family's recent misfortune? Their current pursuit? The guards had a visceral reaction to the name and filed out of the room, presumably to find this Iguru person.

"Now that it's just you and me, Cara," the king said, walking back toward the table. "Come, have a seat."

Surprised at the sudden change of tone, Cara ascertained that they were indeed alone. She considered declining but was already at her limit. Her head had a fluffy cotton-like feeling that meant she wasn't far from collapsing. Her knees gave way as soon as she bent them to settle into one of the cushioned chairs, the relief eliciting a long sigh from deep within her. Immediately, her eyes began to close again. She forced herself to straighten and stay awake.

"I apologize," the king said, catching her completely off guard.

"Did you read my mind?" Cara aired her suspicions.

"I can't read people's minds, only their memories," the king said, took a bowl from a nearby table, and set it in front of her. "Here, have some broth. It will help."

Cara took the bowl with both hands and sipped it slowly. The clear liquid felt like life force pouring in through her cracked lips, moistening her tongue, clearing her throat, and warming her stomach. The quest for water is what had led her here. As much as she wanted to chug, nausea overwhelmed her, and she had to pause.

She took the chance to ask another nagging question, "Who is this Iguru person? Where did I meet him?" Was it the man who chased them two nights ago?

"Iguru Mugenyi is a lieutenant in Kitara's third regiment," the king explained. "He's been riling up lower-ranked guards and village folk, trying to get them to riot and interrupt a ceremony I will be performing this month." Cara did her best to follow along, waiting for the part where her family came into it. "His patron, a High Minister in my council, wants to dethrone me by angering the gods. He believes only I will fall from their grace."

"And you saw him in my memories?"

Her answer took Cara completely by surprise.

"I did not, but no one will believe your word over mine."

The brain fog made it hard to process her words. "You were lying?" Cara asked, then chafed at how childish she sounded.

"I'm the king."

"And me? What happens to me?"

The king had little to say before sending Cara away. *I have yet to decide.* She waved her dismissively, as if they were discussing what to have for lunch or what to wear the next day. Cara couldn't ignore the irony. Her desire to live might have led her to a more certain death.

The attendant who guided her was silent, weaving through dark and narrow corridors. Cara had to assume they were purposefully taking a less frequented route because they didn't encounter another soul. When they approached a plain wooden door, she was hopeful that there would be somewhere to lie down on the other side—whether a prison

232

cot or the floor. The broth had helped, but she was still lightheaded and not completely in control of her body.

Instead of finding another jail as she expected, the door led to a cavernous suite. There was a mesh-veiled bed against the far wall, a sitting room in front of it, and what looked like a practitioner's den to the right. Intricate woven blankets and carved artwork adorned surfaces and walls. Cara looked for a holding cell within the room, but there was nothing of the sort.

"The king orders you to wait in her room," the attendant said, stepping past her and showing her to a chaise in the sitting room. "I suggest you rest here. The king has duties to attend to and will arrive at her leisure."

Cara would be hard-pressed to stay awake five minutes after she lay down, so she took the chance to ask, "Why does everyone here speak English?"

The attendant had walked back to stand by the wall.

"The king will answer your questions," she said.

That was that. Cara lowered herself onto the soft, suede-like chaise and into the quiet darkness of her dreams. When she opened her eyes—who knows how much later—two obsidian orbs greeted her. The king was sitting across from her on a wicker armchair, her feet dangling over one side, popping dates into her mouth. "Would you like some?" she asked. "They will help replenish your sugar."

Cara sat up and hugged her knees in, leaning against the back of the chaise. She eyed the plate on the table; it was packed with dates, figs, crackers, and honeycomb. She knew she must be hungry, having not eaten in at least a day, but she just felt nauseous and groggy.

"Why does everyone here speak English?" she asked again.

Her voice was hoarse, her throat painfully dry.

"Why do you think?" the king asked before sitting up and nudging a tall wooden cup toward her.

Cara took it, drinking almost half of the sweet coconut water before answering. The liquid found its way through the labyrinth of her body, reminding it of its basic needs. Of course she was hungry.

"Colonialism?" she ventured, then grabbed a cracker to nibble at.

"No," the king said with a smirk. "We are hidden precisely to shield ourselves from that." Cara wondered if she was supposed to guess again. The atmosphere was less intimidating than in the throne room; the king's posture much more relaxed. "None of us speak English. I put a spell on you so we could understand each other."

"Oh." *Fascinating.* "I wonder if—" She stopped short. Others didn't usually share her level of interest in these things.

The king watched her with those eyes, then prodded, "Yes?"

"It's nothing, really," Cara said preemptively. "I was just wondering about the word 'king.' What does it mean in your language?"

"It means that I am the ruler of this land."

"Of course," she said, nodding. "Is it the same word for male and female rulers?"

"Yes." The king frowned. "Why would it matter if I'm male or female?"

Cara laughed, saying, "I mean, you're right. I don't know why, but in English, there are different words for them."

The king didn't smile. It was difficult to gauge her thoughts.

"What would you call me?" she asked.

"Probably a queen."

"Were you expecting a man then?"

"Yes, I suppose I was," Cara admitted somewhat hesitantly.

"Were you disappointed?"

What a cryptic question! What an unsettling, burning gaze.

"No, I can't say that I have been," she replied.

The king stood and stepped slowly toward the den. Cara watched her as she walked, wondering if she should follow. Then, the king said, "You must have so many questions, young Aaron."

"Even you know the Aarons?" The words slipped out of her mouth before she could stop them.

"The Phineas was right." She couldn't see the king's expression now that she faced away from her. "You have a lot to learn."

"How far back in my memories did you go?" Cara asked. She was suddenly uncomfortable.

"As far back as I needed to make sure you weren't a threat. The one time Kitara let a foreigner inside her walls, it led to this," the king said before turning and gesturing around them vaguely. "Centuries upon centuries in hiding. Isolated from the outside world."

Cara stood and walked closer. Her voice barely rose above a murmur when she said, "Will it be this way forever?" *Do you wish it were different?*

There were questions she didn't dare ask even if the king seemed to suddenly trust her—know her.

"It is what's best for my people," the king said.

Maybe she was trying to even the playing field. Cara hated being the only uninformed one in the room. Her mind had been casually perused like a photo album, if not precisely against her will, then certainly without permission. It brought out a brazenness Cara didn't know she possessed.

"And for you?" she asked.

She knew she had gone too far, but the king humored her, saying, "What is best for my people is best for me."

By now, they weren't too far apart. The king's hands rested on the large wooden table that took up much of the den. Glass-guarded shelves covered the back wall, filled with what looked like every component a practitioner could dream of. Cara resisted the urge to ogle, instead asking, "Would you answer my questions?"

"Have I not been?"

"I never like to assume."

The king smirked again. Cara was starting to interpret the slight upturn of her lips as a smile. "Don't expect me to share any classified information," she said.

This wasn't an issue; her questions didn't pertain to Kitara. Yet, Cara didn't even know where to start. "Do you know what a True Aaron is?" she asked.

"Of course," the king said. "So do you. Amit told you the story of Nabu-kudurri-usur and the Great Eclipse. The Aaron who defeated him is what we call the True Aaron. Really, that was just the start of your family line. Not everyone agrees, but some also consider the other Aaron who helped rebuild the world after her sister tore it apart a True Aaron."

"They were sisters?" Cara asked. The parallel was hard to ignore.

"The Aaron lineage has always leaned heavily female. I suppose that's why they are governed by a matriarch," the king mused.

Cara realized that even this was common knowledge in the practitioner world. The more she learned about the Aarons, the more terrified she became of them. Why had her mother been hiding from them all these years? *Could they be the ones after us?*

The king must have caught a hint of the turmoil roiling under the surface because she said quietly, "It seems we are always caught in this cycle. Searching for our mothers."

Cara looked up. Just as quietly, she said, "You are young for a king."

"Do you want to contact your mother?"

The abruptness of the offer stunned Cara for a second. It was appealing enough to make her completely lose the thread of their conversation. Her answer was a resounding, "Yes! Is there a way to do that?"

Even though the king had brought up the idea, she seemed to hesitate. Then, she took one of the books on the table and flipped it open. The writing was incomprehensible to Cara, but she recognized some of the symbols Amit had drilled into their brains.

"Are these from African tradition?" she asked and pointed at a row of elemental variants.

"Yes, much of modern magic draws from pre-eclipse African tradition," the king said. "It's not just the cradle of mankind but of magic."

Cara remembered something Amit had said when they had first met.

"Is that why Aarons usually specialize in pre-historic magic?" she asked.

"Indeed, many consider that to be the secret to Aaron's power. They have many primary texts passed down from the True Aarons, which no one else in the world can access. This allows them to communicate with forces in the universe that many practitioners have no way of getting in touch with. The Spirits of the Earth, Gods of Time and Space; I've heard they have methods of easily traversing veils and realms of life and death."

Thinking of her sister, Cara commented, "I've met practitioners who can traverse veils."

"A skilled traveler," the king said with a nod. She had seen Ada in her jaunt through Cara's memories. "Of course there will always be intuitively gifted practitioners, and the Aarons can't monopolize these powers. But they are amongst few who don't need natural talent."

"I see," Cara said. She was getting distracted scanning the rest of the writing on the page. Excitement started growing inside her, a feeling not unlike anxiety. Her heartbeat quickened in anticipation. "Is this for contacting my mother?"

A pause.

"Yes."

"What do you need me to do?"

The sky was still dark blue when Ada hugged a sleepy Amal and a teary Fatiha goodbye. She was reminded of the last goodbye she had to say, only days ago, and how Sethu had cast protections for them on their way out. She silently did the same for the girls.

Rifat had a blue two-door car on loan from one of his friends in town, who would let him use it every month to stock up on supplies. He would trade some of their village's wares, deliver mail, and run other miscellaneous errands. Since these things take a few days, his friend wasn't expecting his car back until the end of the week, leaving him with enough time to drive Ada to Damascus and come back within the allotted time. He and Sara would see her off at the bus, then tie up some of the business he had left unfinished on their way home.

The car was small, and Ada could see how the goods Rifat transported could take up the entire back seat. Sara hesitated to go with him since their nieces couldn't come along, but she didn't want Ada to go unaccompanied either. She asked one of the village women to keep an eye on the girls while they were away.

Ada would have struggled to stay awake—she had a tendency to fall asleep on long car rides, and this one would take close to five hours—but Rifat was interested in learning more about Oregon and Hope Springs. Too young to care, Amal and Fatiha had changed the topic when they tried to hold a conversation about Miriam's construction company over dinner the night before. Now, with a captive audience, he asked myriads of questions, some that Ada didn't know the answer to. They chatted away as dawn broke, the sky painted with bursts of color and light, until they made it to the highway that would lead them to Damascus.

It was around eight in the morning when they hit a bad bit of traffic. The road was narrowed due to construction, and there seemed to have been an accident ahead. Rifat stuck his head out of the driver-side window and asked a neighboring driver what was going on. Ada listened intently to the conversation but could pick out little more than *Damascus* and some sounds of concern.

Sara translated for her, "He says a car exploded, but no one knows why yet. It might have been a bomb."

Ada gasped. "Was anyone injured?" she asked.

"They think there was a family in the car," Sara said, nodding, then added, "Allah yerhamo."

Rafit supplemented a few details. Soldiers were looking into the circumstances, but no one could connect the victims to any militant group or figure out a motive. Nothing had been officially confirmed, but a child was rumored to be in the car.

"He says it happened about three kilometers ahead, so there will be traffic for a bit longer," he said, then thanked the driver he talked to and rolled his window back up.

The little car's air conditioning system was louder than

it was effective. The mass of cars trapped the heat between the sun and the sizzling pavement, their shells providing just enough of a barrier from the undulating heat waves to make a difference.

Sara took the chance to pass breakfast around—a type of open-faced meat pie. Ada settled into her seat again, having been perched at the edge, and finished it within minutes.

Looking out the window into the cabs of neighboring cars, listening to them talk to each other in Arabic, the car lurching forward a few feet every couple of minutes, she found herself being rocked to sleep. Her dreams were like a radio, and a phantom hand was flipping through the channels.

She struggled to decipher what she was seeing and hearing before the scene changed, all of it feeling as intimate as the glimpses she had caught of strangers alone at the wheel, with their children, on their way to work. Then the incoherent flashes started linking together, like someone was whispering a story to her, just not in words, but in images.

* * *

A young girl sitting on a shaded porch, her mother and aunts chattering around her. She tires of weaving yarn and, not entertained by the gossip, turns her eyes elsewhere. A tug at her mind, and she drops to the dirt beneath them. Like a voice, a seed calls to her beneath the ground. *Let me up*, it says. She does. Her mother tries to beat the witchcraft out of her.

Now a budding adolescent, she is sent to gather roots and wild berries by the riverbed when they are in season. Years tighten the supply of food, and her family grows somber and

241

thin. She prays and prays that she will find food by the banks and thanks Allah when she does for his mercy and his grace. But she is too blessed—her father grows suspicious. Where was she getting these unseasonable wares? He starves her until she admits to flirting with a shopkeeper in town. She names him Mohammed, and, in her mind, she imagines he has a kind, kind smile.

Years pass, and the girl is married. She lies and tells her husband she doesn't know much about agriculture or horticulture. She shuns plants, does not approach a flower, a fruit tree, but she is bursting at the seams. She moves into her husband's home, and the greenery in their garden grows lush through the drought. Her mother makes excuses to come visit and throws salt on them until they die.

When the woman becomes pregnant, the strange occurrences stop. She likes to pretend she is using the energy that sprouted within her youth to grow the child in her womb. When he is born, he is everything she could have ever asked for. She prays for him each minute of the day and blesses him with her thoughts. She feels the same *feeling* every time.

One day, he notices her admiring a picture of a rose and makes one for her out of thin air. Her mother notices the signs soon after. The woman begs her husband not to let them take their child, but her mother has convinced his family that this is best. Her mother says he is sick, that she cured her daughter of this disease before. It takes five years to get her son back.

Like a steady stream, the woman is filled with what feels like anxiety. It sloshes in her head and fogs up her view. It fills her stomach and expels the little food she eats. She wishes she could ask to be sent to her father's house, but she knows her husband's family would never allow it.

She feels fortunate to have a husband loving enough to wait until she is nursed back to health, who doesn't take another wife. This is partially because of his work, which takes him close to conflict and makes him stay there for days at a time. He has no time to take a new wife. Five years later, she is pregnant again, and her health begins to improve.

The woman and her husband pile into his uncle's red car and wave goodbye to his family, expecting to see them in two days. She beams and fawns over him on their way to her parents' house, dreaming of their family reunited again, trying to ignore her worries—what if she grows ill again, what if their second child bears her curse, what if, what if, what if, what if, what if, what if.

Running through endless scenarios, she braces herself for whatever disappointment she could encounter next. Yet, she could have never expected this. The woman assumed her mother would raise her grandson the same as herself. She didn't take into account that her mother viewed her as a failure. A failure to suppress. A failure to submit. A failure to conform. A risk to her family's reputation. One she wouldn't take a second time.

What if her son is a stranger? What if his eyes are cold and dull? What if her mother hands him smugly back to them? *He is cured.* What if the pressure was building up inside of him? What if *he* was bursting at the seams?

Back in the car, the woman sits in the backseat with her child, begging him to speak to her. She touches his hair tenderly, his hands. He is gripping his bag so tight, his knuckles are white. She begins to cry and apologize.

With her vision blurred, he looks much like she did as a

child. *You are safe now. You don't have to go back. You will never see them again.* His grip slowly normalizes, he begins to understand. But repression is not control. You can only hold back an overpowering tide for so long. Then, it swallows everything.

* * *

Ada woke up submerged in magic and gasping. Her skin tingled, every inch covered in goosebumps. The air felt crisp, and her thoughts were racing, like she had drunk one too many cups of coffee. Sara turned back at the sound.

"Are you alright?" she asked. "We are just going to pass the explosion. Do you see it? There?"

Ada followed the direction she was pointing in with her gaze. There, nestled between military jeeps and hazard tape, was a burned-up car, gutted and with some fixtures splayed around the ground: the mirrors, a cut-up tire, some charred belongings. She pressed her hand to the window, trying to get a better view. Thankfully, the bodies had been removed long ago. If she squinted, she swore she could make out streaks of red paint.

"Were you having a bad dream?" Sara asked, bringing her back to the present. Her eyes were gentle and understanding.

Ada wondered if she had PTSD, not because of human traffickers in Cape Town like Sara thought, but everything else. She had no other way of explaining the tears gathering at the edges of her eyes, especially as they grew heavier and dropped down her cheek. She nodded.

With her senses heightened, the wet warmth felt uncomfortable. Ada dragged the heels of her hands across the

244

bottom of her eyes again and again. She wished she knew this practitioner's name, if only to honor her in death. She didn't understand what had happened. Had the magic built up until it burst, like a dam flooding all it was built to protect?

The mother's face would not leave her mind. Soon, it was conflated with Miriam's, and it was all Ada could do to stifle the homesickness in her chest, her stomach.

Hope Springs seemed like a distant dream at this point. Like an unattainable reality. Without Cara by her side, she felt untethered, a directionless existence. She took a few breaths, reaching for the tethers she envisioned led to Cara and Amit— reaching for someone, something she could anchor herself to. The exercise calmed her down, her tears started to wane, and she settled back into the present.

"What was it you said before, Sara?" she asked, clinging to rituals where she could find them. Her throat was hoarse, but the sheer amount of magical energy permeating the air had jolted her awake, energizing her down to her bones. "Allah yer—?"

"Allah yerhamo. May Allah have mercy on him."

"Allah yerhamo," Ada repeated shakily as she sunk further into her seat and hoped this strange feeling would subside sooner rather than later. It left her jittery and on edge.

But, as if an atomic bomb had gone off, this child's energy left radiation for miles.

A mit figured she could get everything she was looking for in one place: Katlego's room. It was the best room available in the Wasteland; he would have surely continued to monopolize it through the decades.

Hidden from sight with a simple light reflection charm, she skulked through the hallways, keeping an eye and ear peeled for any nuggets of information she could gather. So far, nothing too useful had come up—much of the usual teenage gossip—except a ceremony someone brought up around the Summer solstice, a few months away. If the old informant was correct and the Wasteland was indeed in the Committee's pocket, whatever Katlego was planning would surely line up with institutional objectives.

Her own objectives were as follows: pull a spell from the library to find the girls, find out more about the upcoming ceremony, and kill Katlego. Amit had accomplished the first, nicking a number of books from the derelict library and stowing them in the storage space she and the girls shared. It was hard to shake the feeling of desecrating something sacred, but looking around at the decrepit shelves assuaged her conscience.

Once she reached safety, she'd be able to search through

them for the right spell, applying an indexing charm for speed, but this was not the time nor place. The other items on her list had to be struck out quickly. If she employed the right methods, dealing with Katlego could enlighten her on a myriad of topics. Amit just needed privacy and time.

The layout of the Waste hadn't changed over the years, and with each step, her memories came flooding back. This place had once been her haven, her home—and for many others. It was a collective based on mutual aid and the belief that practitioners should be free to organize in their local communities, have sovereignty over their traditions, and operate as removed from the system as they choose.

It was paradise in a world where many thought it was impossible to speak, cast, or sleep without the Committee breathing down their neck. Young practitioners got the chance to experiment with their magic outside of the academies' strict traditional training, remember the magic of their ancestors, and deeply explore their relationship to that astonishing, harrowing, god-like energy they wielded and carried inside them.

It was hard to judge by just the snippets of conversations she caught on her way, but the kids now reminded her of the ones she had gone to attended the academy with before leaving home, curt and mean-spirited. She no longer sensed the same camaraderie she had so valued as a discarded youth.

As someone who had no one and nothing in the world, this place had taken her in and shown her that sometimes it was better this way. Sometimes, you need to break free. So it did pain her to kill Katlego. He was a touchstone, embodying tender memories from her past.

When she found his room, she ascertained it was empty

and slipped in, searching for undeniable evidence. One of the books she recently acquired centered on truth spells; she fished it out and commanded the space to reveal its past. There, all his secrets were, playing out in front of her like a movie. Any attachment she had felt for Katlego perished.

Amit would wait for almost an hour, taking the time to find the most painful entry in the truth book for her old friend and scouring his quarters for the smallest clues. When he arrived, she stunned, bound, and forced him to spill his guts. About the Committee—yes, they were financing the Waste now; the mermaid scales—just one of the things the Wasted provided in the partnership; the children—he swore it was consensual; and the ceremony.

They arrived at this last topic at a point in the conversation in which Amit didn't think she could be more horrified by the human sitting in front of her. She was wrong.

"I never knew you could be so soulless, Katlego," she said. "I should have killed you long ago."

His once charming brown eyes stared back at her. Desperate, he appealed, "I know you wouldn't kill your comrade, Amit. Not your fearless leader."

It had the opposite effect. If anything, Amit felt more desensitized and disassociated with the situation. He of all people should know that violence was nothing if not second nature to her. That the world they lived in was dog eat dog. *He must think I've gone soft*, she realized, hardening further. "You are no leader. You are a child abuser. Whether I kill you or not, the Committee surely will. You told me all their secrets."

He laughed darkly and said, "Amit, the Committee hasn't told me a single one of their secrets."

She should have just killed him; it was foolish to stay longer than she already had. Maybe it was the sentimentality clouding her judgment. "How did you end up this way?" she asked, but she also knew that if he was this way now, he likely had been this way from the start.

A girl came in through his door, two other practitioners close behind her, people Amit recognized. Not children. She cursed under her breath and ended Katlego's life with the flick of her wrist.

A nearby window was the perfect escape; she launched herself out of the room, propelling herself with another spell. Amit had to get back to the girls no matter what. She had to tell Miriam about the ceremony.

She felt a sudden, searing pain in her right side and crashed down hard. Dust billowed around her. Her arms were scraped and bleeding from dragging on the ground. Her knees stung despite the fabric that covered them. There was dirt in her mouth. Still, she felt lucky. She hadn't hit her head or lost consciousness. There was no way she was going to die here.

The sun was setting now. She took advantage of the long shadows it cast, melting into them, and catapulted herself into the desert, far away from the main building. She could already hear the Wasted trickling out, putting together search parties to find the intruder—the assassin. After a half-hour trekking through the wilderness, Amit found what she was looking for: the counterpart to the stone outside the veil. She wondered if people still used it, if it was the first place they would come looking. She needed to move fast.

Although the pain in her side had subsided, if she didn't treat the wound before traveling, she risked worse injury or death. She stuffed her shirt into her mouth, hoping no one would hear her whimper, then lifted a red hot finger to trace the gaping flesh, cauterizing it.

Similar situations had taught her basic healing spells, which she drew on her abdomen with bloody fingers. Amit wasn't a healer, and without natural talent, the spell would take a few hours to have a noticeable effect and a few days to regenerate the skin. The wound would surely reopen, but this would have to do for now. She pressed her hand to the rock and bid adieu to the Wasteland one last time.

* * *

The king and Cara set up the spell together. The king read the instructions out loud first for Cara, magic translating it automatically, then transcribed the symbols onto parchment, explaining the power each one channeled. They laid the circle out on the den's table, passing by each other again and again, now standing shoulder by shoulder, now leaning close to check continuity.

Cara had never noticed how intimate it was, drawing a magic circle with another practitioner. She had never done it with a stranger and was suddenly self-conscious of her calligraphy, the neatness of her strokes, the speed at which she drew, the silence. With two sets of hands, they were done in ten minutes.

The king turned to her practitioner's pantry. Setting out some sprigs and incense, she warned, "You will only be able to speak to her for fifteen minutes. But count yourself lucky. You can only speak to the dead for five." Under other circumstances, Cara might have lingered on this comment longer, asked herself who the king was conversing with in the afterlife. They stood at opposite edges of the circle.

"Repeat after me," the king said.

For a simple five-line spell, the energy that rushed through Cara's body was shocking. It seemed to channel her magic more effectively than any other she had cast before. The feeling was exhilarating but frightening, like something you could give yourself over to entirely.

Cara braced herself, concentrating her power at her core. She pictured her mother's twinkling eyes, felt her soft hand brush against her cheek, and could practically smell her perfume. Suddenly, there she was.

"Cara?"

23

The night before, the king was plagued by convoluted prophetic dreams. Colossal waves crashed over mountains. The earth cracked open, revealing cavernous fissures from which beast-like men and men-like beasts crawled out and bellowed in pain. Three moons inched closer together in a red sky on a collision course. The king stood at the top of a hill, staring down. The desert curved and dipped like a prone body; here, it looked like a clavicle, there like the rise of a hip.

A young girl appeared, walking toward her, and she tensed. It was the woman she would soon come to know as Cara but years younger. On her stomach was a coiled golden serpent, and on her chest was a colossal seed.

They stood in stillness more than an arm's length apart. The girl's presence was suffocating, the radiance of the snake blinding, the objects at their periphery blurred. The king remembered all the myths about snakes creating and destroying and tried to decipher whether this one would do the prior or the latter.

Are you here to end the world? she tried to ask. It wasn't clear if the girl heard her—she replied cryptically, *We are always searching for our mothers.* In her mouth, the word mother became a woman, and the woman was a sister and a warrior, and it was the king, and it was the girl, and it was a burnt carcass clawing its way out of the ashes.

The girl was suddenly closer than the king remembered anyone ever having been; she could feel her warm breath as she whispered in her ear. At this distance, the king could see that the girl was not a girl but a million seconds stitched together. Instead of words, images flowed from her throat, her figure becoming transparent as the memories emptied out into the king's mind. The memories weighed her down like lead, and her feet began to sink into the sand. She looked down and saw that she, too, had a seed on her chest, and her hands were also a child's hands.

As she sank, darkness closed in around her, and she saw a beautiful city spring up above. Loud voices flooded lively markets and streets, sturdy walls stretching up as high as the eye could see. It was Kitara.

The girl had sunk, too. Their hands were tightly entwined. They began to blend with dunes, blend together. The seed in the girl's chest grew roots so long they wrapped themselves around their bodies, cracked the foundation of the buildings above them, and siphoned all the nutrients from the earth, suffocating and starving every living thing in the land. The king's heart lurched, and she fought to disentangle herself. When she did, the roots shriveled and died. The girl finished fading with them, a steady stream of images flowing into the king's mind until she was no more.

* * *

"Mom!" Cara lurched forward, her hands reaching for

253

something she realized she couldn't touch.

Standing in front of her, flickering and translucent, her mother looked like a ghost. Her arms were extended, mimicking Cara—as if she could catch her if she fell. As if they could hold each other.

"Where are you? And Ada? Are you with Amit?" Miriam asked rapid-fire.

Cara assumed that, like her, her mom had a limited view of her surroundings.

"We got separated. Someone attacked us," she said.

"How were you able to set up this spell? What is it? Some sort of communication portal?" her mother asked. Her expression was suddenly studious, the way it always was in front of intriguing magic.

"A practitioner saved me. She helped set this up," Cara said. She was fudging the truth but didn't want to risk angering the king. The trust felt fragile.

"Cara, I don't like you out there alone," Miriam pleaded. "You have to find Amit and your sister."

"I'll find a way."

"You will have to come home soon," she added. "There have been some...new developments."

Miriam may as well have started her sentence with *don't freak out, but*. Her eldest immediately sensed something was off.

"We only have fifteen minutes. Tell it to me straight."

The king watched with mild interest from the nearby chaise as they discussed Gage's horoscope. She was still trying to decide if the snake in Cara's stomach was one which created or destroyed. Her first instinct when the guards reported a foreigner crawling up to their gates was execution, but seeing the face from her dream made her stop short.

She hadn't been granted the gift of prophecy, so her suspicion didn't wane until she ascertained Cara's innocence through her memories. The king was quick. She took the chance to rid herself of a thorn in her side but was left at a loss of what to do with her destiny-laden visitor.

If her dream was to be believed, their entanglement could lead to catastrophe for Kitara. The king had to understand why. She confined Cara to her own chambers for privacy and nearly laughed when she found her fast asleep—it gave her plenty of time to probe her mind for clues.

When she went back a week in her memories, though, the situation was unfathomable. Cara was in South Africa using spells to disguise herself while she practiced magic on the beach, coming home to a practical stranger's apartment every night.

Only two months back, she was living an idyllic life in America, attending university and living with her parents. Confused, the king decided to retrace the steps that led this seemingly inoffensive practitioner to her doorstep. After combing through some uneventful weeks, she found the night of Ada's encounter with the giant, the Mistlanders' attack, Cara's magic forcefully wrung from her body. It became harder to stay disaffected.

It was the deepest the king had ever ventured into another's memories. Her ability was usually reserved for criminal judgment, requiring only confirmation of an act committed. Her noble mind had matters of state to attend to, lofty goals to plan toward, and tens of thousands of mouths to feed.

Painstakingly conceived through rituals, sacrifices, and lunar planning, she was a blessed child in every sense of the word, fated to carry the weight of her people on her shoulders. It had taken many years for her mother to bring a pregnancy to term, trying and failing and trying again until her body was tired and broken, and the young consort didn't recognize herself any longer.

The ghosts of her siblings crowded the womb, and the king was born with a twisted neck from being pressed against the bloody walls. The third child to make it through labor, she quickly broke her siblings' records by living past her first week—but the shadow of death was inescapable. It had been written in the stars. Her mother took her last breath, relieved to have accomplished her purpose.

Her father mourned his consort's passing—he valued her kind and gentle nature—but there was an overarching air of celebration. He had an heir to secure the throne and could finally get his advisors off his back. He didn't marry again, which some took as a sign of devotion to his late wife, who toiled so hard to give him what he wanted.

When she was older, the king would understand that her father had no interest in love or romance. He was completely devoted to the one some called UMvelinqangi, Mawu, or Magec, the only divine and eternal source of light that gives life to creation and does not recognize time, change, or pain. As a devotee, her father could not concern himself with earthly matters like food, sleep, or personal relations. He had no intention of becoming the ruler of Kitara and would have dedicated his life to religion if his siblings hadn't murdered each other, leaving him the only successor to the crown.

The High Ministers happily took on the role of puppet masters for their last apathetic liege. They ran the country so efficiently without him that no one noticed when King's father, consumed by his fervent devotion and having reached a state of closeness to his god previously unattainable—rumors listed iboga, kwashi, and voacanga amongst the hallucinogens he sourced from a shady black market shaman—locked himself in a room for three weeks and starved to death.

After an opulent funeral for which no cost was spared, business carried on as usual. The only difference being his now orphaned seven-year-old daughter had inherited the throne and had to show her face at every council meeting.

The High Ministers hadn't paid much mind to the child until then and wouldn't for five more years. The king neither shared her opinions nor weighed in on meetings. The few times she did, the ministers feigned deafness and spoke louder, drowning her out. They assigned soldiers to guard her whose loyalty lay elsewhere and would control what information reached her ears.

Every successor received exhaustive tutelage until their coming-of-age ceremony, but the Ministers disparaged the traditional curriculum and rewrote it, cutting it down to only a few hours a week. Instead, the king spent her days in the Northern Temple with the Gatekeepers, the practitioners who powered Kitara's impenetrable veil.

The written record detailed how scores of practitioners first gathered to set up the kingdom's barrier, but there was no mention of those who maintained it. No one could fathom the Gatekeepers' age or their immense power. They took the young king under their wing, imparting wisdom they withheld from past rulers and their tutors.

It was there that she grew to understand the power of knowledge, how to attain it, and how to wield it. On her twelfth birthday, the king put it to the test, purging the army from enemy sympathizers before accusing all council members of treason. The evidence she presented in the trial was unequivocal, her judgment inexorable. All save two of the ten ministers were executed.

Even without having met her father, the king emulated him in the most uncanny way. She held herself to an impossible standard and was oblivious to her needs, often pushing herself to exhaustion. They were big-picture thinkers and could lose sight all too easily of the little things. Most of all, she inherited his fervor—or her mother's devotion. Either way, the shared zeal that attracted them to each other in the first place was inescapable. The king spent every waking moment thinking about Kitara, the issues currently facing her people, the threats looming over the horizon, the harvest, the gods, the veil, prophecies.

Any free time was spent gathering more knowledge, whether from studying books or the astros. She didn't see the need for personal relations; they would only siphon time from her political and strategic alliances. The orphaned king never knew lack of affection, so loved she was by her people, but an emptiness she couldn't name snuck into her bedroom late at night and sat next to her as she read, creeping under the covers with her when she couldn't sleep. It was an intimate relationship, hers with loneliness. A loneliness not unlike that of a god.

Like a god, the king could come off as cold and distant, but she wasn't devoid of empathy—it was just usually reserved for her citizenry. She attributed her inclination to help Cara to this empathy, although it felt decidedly different from when she heard of a family in strife.

She told herself it was normal to want to help the less fortunate, noble even. Anyone would have been concerned at seeing the Mistlanders' attack. Anyone's heart would have ached to see the abrupt end of the happy days at Sethu's. The king found herself lingering on those memories, laughing at their practical jokes, replaying them in her head, feeling an unidentifiable warmth. It was puzzling.

She had never wanted to be anywhere else but where she was. She had never encountered such uncertainty, such difficulty in deciding what to do. The gods had sent her that dream for a reason. Why?

* * *

The sun was still high in the sky when the little blue car reached Damascus. Rifat found a place to park near the bus station, bought Ada a ticket and a plate of dolma, then stood with her for thirty minutes waiting for the bus to arrive. Sara cried as they hugged goodbye, and Ada made sure to get Rifat's email address before leaving. She promised to get in touch with them when she got home. She promised herself she would repay them.

On the bus, Ada resolved to hop off after a few stops. She figured a moving target would be more difficult for Amit and Cara to find. They passed a market, and she got off soon after, doubling back to the plaza and blending in with the crowd—she wanted to nick some materials for a spell. Not that Ada had a particular spell in mind. She wasn't good at memorizing them the way Cara was, but she remembered some of the elements Amit had brought up in communication and scrying sessions and hoped whatever she gathered would be similar enough.

Ada had never stolen anything except a few marbles from her classmates' desks in second grade—which she still felt guilty about to this day—and sensationalist headlines floated in her head detailing how women and thieves were punished in religiously conservative countries. She wasn't certain if that was the case in Syria, but it was hard to shake the feeling that she was about to risk her life again. It was a feeling that never got easier to swallow. Her first thought was to find some cover.

A narrow alleyway partially obscured by a vendor's cart proved a deserted dead end—jackpot. Ada slipped in when the merchant was distracted and crouched near the back. She dipped her finger in the dirt and tried to draw an invisibility spell on her hand. No dice; the sand fell right off. She needed more adherence, which meant ignoring all the social conditioning that taught her playing with spit was gross.

She gathered as much saliva as she could and made a little mound of mud. It wasn't the best ink, but she could make it stick long enough to draw a jumble of symbols on her forearm; some she remembered from their lessons, others she wasn't so sure about. Chuckling to herself, she wondered if her mother would still threaten her with a magic-blocking spell if she saw her now.

Regardless of whether her spell was drawn perfectly or not, Ada felt the key was her will. She felt circles and elements were just there to provide some guidance, and her mind would do the rest. She infused the symbols with magical energy and willed herself to be invisible, unnoticed; for light to avoid her and eyes to pass right by her; to inconspicuously blend with the air and the walls and the wind; for no living being to notice her; for no person to catch her; for her hand to be deft as she swiped things; for the things not to be missed; for fortune to fall on those she steals from.

Having run out of ideas, she threw one last item in for good measure. *And please let me find Cara and Amit again.* Thus, the spell was complete, and she set out to test it.

Ada started small, angling up to a merchant selling clothes and standing still in front of the store. He gave no sign of having seen her, but she wondered if he could be ignoring her. She went a step further, picking up a beautifully embroidered coin purse. The vendor still didn't react. She felt a jolt of pride. The spell must have worked.

Ada moved on, straining her memory as she considered the effect that different elements would have on her spell—the acidity of citrus, heat, and earthiness of various spices. Had the moon been a waning or waxing gibbous last night?

It was these complicated calculations that had made her shy away from studying magic in the first place. It felt like she was back in high school chemistry, except, instead of her GPA, her life was in the balance.

Thinking of the days old flowers her dad would often bring home, Ada purposefully chose bruised fruit and a chipped bowl to lessen her guilt about stealing from small business owners. Rounding off her crime spree by swiping a perspiring water bottle sitting unattended on a counter, she made her way back to the alley and spread out her sorry loot.

Trying to channel Cara, she thought of all the times she'd seen her sister scry, but it proved useless. Cara made it look way too easy. Ada persevered, assembling the closest approximation to a spell circle she could. She decided to start by looking for Cara, hoping their blood would make her easier to find than Amit. Ada focused on her sister's face, her voice, the way she stood and walked.

Soon, she entered a trance-like state, her breath drowning out the sounds of the busy street nearby. Her heartbeat made her think of Cara's heart, the blood they shared pumping through her veins. *Where are you?* she thought. *Reveal your location.*

A house flashed before her eyes, not unlike others she had walked by that day. It was in Damascus, only five blocks away. The spell showed her the way. Ada's eyes flew open, and she scrambled to her feet, leaving the spell circle behind. She was worried she would forget the directions and set out immediately to follow them. Weaving her way through the throngs of people on the street as unobtrusively as possible—still invisible—she wondered if Cara could really be in the same city as her. Had her sister found her first? Was she with Amit? Ada didn't want to consider what it meant if she wasn't.

It took Ada at least twenty minutes to find the right house. Even having seen it in her mind's eye, it was hard to distinguish it from the other tall houses on the block. Upon closer inspection, she noticed it lacked the slight dilapidated look many other buildings in the city had. The tile that lined the bottom half of the house gleamed in the sunlight, the white paint on the arches above was pristine, and a shock of bright pink flowers peaked from a windowsill on the second floor. Ada was nervous to approach and walked around the block instead, devising two entrances—a main doorway and a side door on the adjoining street.

She stood across from the latter for ten more minutes, questioning whether Cara could really be inside. Then she noticed the shadows getting longer; the sun was slowly descending. Ada had nowhere to sleep that night after ditching the plans Rifat and Sara had arranged. If worst came to worst, she figured she could sleep in the alley, cloaked in invisibility, but if she wanted a roof over her head, there was no time to waste.

There was a big window next to the side door. She snuck up to it, angling to the side to look in. It was a kitchen, and she saw an older woman bustling inside. Ada felt her stomach shrivel with anxiety. She didn't know how much to trust her stopgap stealth spell—in her head, she repeated the chant she had come up with, or at least the parts she remembered.

Invisible. Unnoticed. Light bounces off. Eyes pass through. Blend with the air, the walls. Find Cara and Amit.

The woman in the kitchen picked up a tray and exited the room. Ada knew her courage would falter if she thought too hard. She immediately reached out and jiggled the doorknob. To her surprise, the door swung open without resistance.

Once inside, Ada tried to calm down the banging in her chest, scared someone would hear it. She made her way to the door that led out of the kitchen and held her breath, listening. She could make out faint voices, but they seemed to be coming from upstairs. She peeked out to see a huge open space, tall pillars holding up the roof—a beautiful sun-drenched parlor sat at one side while the other housed an elaborate dining room. They were both empty. A staircase wound around the right wall, doors lining the space beneath its veranda. The décor was sparse but elaborate; it smelled of old money.

Ada resisted the urge to dash across the tiled floors and throw open the door to every room until she knew for certain whether Cara and Amit were there. Instead, she tiptoed toward the sitting room, which was nearest to the stairs. As she approached, she noticed that the tall windows looked out into a courtyard. Clear water ran out of the fountain at its center, elegantly trimmed greenery surrounded it.

Captivated, she moved closer, coming to stand by a wooden bookcase with pictures and trinkets crowding its surface. She glanced down and paused, the garden forgotten. Ada felt she recognized the people in the pictures.

There was something familiar about the shape of their faces. Their smiles. Her eyes darted from one to the other, trying to figure out where she had seen them before. Then, they landed on a face she could never mistake for anyone else, and her heart skipped a beat. The air left her mouth involuntarily.

"Mom?"

24

Cara and the king ate dinner in silence: lamb and plantains and other things Cara wasn't sure she could name. It was delicious, but the call with her mother had left her vibrating and not in a good way. Cara felt frazzled and reactive and knew that one wrong word could end in tears.

She had always been the sensitive one and often got caught up in her own head, making it difficult to communicate with others. Her inflexibility and tendency to hold grudges didn't help her avoid conflict either. She had mapped out her academic and professional careers until retirement, leaving little room for improvisation. If marriage and children happened along the way, then great, but she wouldn't alter her plans to find them. Those things came second.

When Miriam told them they had to take a sabbatical, Cara had a full-on panic attack locked in the bathroom where no one could hear her. Suddenly, survival came first. She had to remind herself that as long as she had her life, her plans could get back on track, or the sense of drifting—like being stranded in the open ocean—became overwhelming.

Cara hadn't felt this way since she arrived in Kitara, though. She was otherwise preoccupied. The object of her attentions was sitting across from her now, at the other end of the table.

"It sounds like your brother has found himself some trouble," the king said after noticing Cara's stiffness.

There was no response. She took in Cara's furrowed brow, the way her hands were gripping the silverware so tightly that her knuckles had turned white and her eyes were fixed ahead. The king felt for her—her path seemed as treacherous as her own. She stood and walked over, placing a hand on her shoulder. This was enough to make Cara look up from her stupor.

"I'm sorry," Cara said. Her gaze was dazed and vulnerable. As her forehead relaxed, so did her grip. "Did you say something?"

The king's chest tightened uncharacteristically, but she didn't know what it was to comfort, to console. She only knew how to rule and provide, so she said, "Cara, this has all only just begun. You must be prepared—it will get worse before it gets better—but you can make it through. Your family can make it through together. I can't help you, not outside Kitara, but I know someone who can find your sister."

Cara's voice barely rose above a whisper when she asked, "You do?"

This has only just begun. The words rang in her ears. Cara had known deep inside that until they faced their problems, they could only keep running from them, but it made her want to curse and scream and break things. She managed to keep a straight face.

The king nodded, then said, "But we'll have to wait until tomorrow. There's a festival on the palace grounds, and the guards will be occupied. It's a risk for you to leave this room otherwise."

266

"What if someone asks where I went?"

"I'll tell them you've been executed," she replied with a wry smile. "I'm not someone you need to worry about."

"Right."

The king's confidence set her at ease, at least enough to stave off the oncoming panic attack. She rose from her chair, and they were suddenly standing very close together, not far apart in height. Cara let her eyes linger on the king's face, her onyx eyes.

"Thank you for dinner and for everything," she said.

"Before bed, I consult with the astros," the king told her. "Ask their thoughts."

For the king who had—for a moment after reading her memories—felt like she knew Cara inside and out, it was strange not to know what she was thinking. To be reminded of this stranger in front of her.

"Don't let me get in the way," Cara said, mustering a smile. Something that under normal circumstances would have her jumping out of her seat to learn barely elicited the smallest spark of excitement.

It only took a few words from the king to fan it into a flame.

"Would you like to see how?"

Was there anything else she could say but yes?

Cara felt like she was vibrating with energy again, but not necessarily in a bad way. She leaned against the table while her ethereal companion calibrated instruments and calculated complex measurements. The colossal telescope sticking out of her room moved incrementally by millimeters until she was satisfied with the view.

"Look," she said. Cara leaned in, expecting to hear about how the next day's festival would go or something about

Kitara's harvest. The king's next words caught her off guard. "This cluster of stars represents your family." *My family?* "I can see the turbulent actors Summer." Her last words made Cara feel as warm as somebody wrapping their arms around her. "Based on their trajectory, one might venture that things will turn out okay."

Cara suddenly felt grounded, peering through the looking glass at the seemingly indifferent cosmos as fate whispered in her ear. Whereas before, she was but a wisp of herself, a vague idea of a person struggling to come into being, now her body solidified around her. Her heart began beating again, demanding attention; there is life in here, it said.

Even if her head was failing her, there was more to her than that. It felt like the static inside her was being displaced by new emotions. It spilled out through her eyes, wetting her cheeks and then her hands as she brought them up to cover her face, trying to regain her breath.

Thank you, she tried to say through ragged inhalations, but it sounded like she was drowning, and she wasn't sure if the king could hear her. Then she felt a hand smoothing down her hair, guiding her to a bench.

The king sat next to her, waiting until she dried her tears. She handed Cara a cup, saying, "This will help you sleep. I'll have somebody draw you a bath and give you clean clothes."

Cara couldn't help but feel self-conscious. Her face felt puffy; she hadn't showered in days and barely slept. The person in front of her was shockingly stunning. As kind as the king was, there was an uncrossable distance between them.

"Does anyone ever call you by your name?" Cara suddenly asked.

If the question caught her off guard, the king didn't show it.

"No, for a citizen of Kitara, that would be treason."

"But you do have a name?"

The king laughed, the twinkle in her eye, saying, *really?*

"Yes, I have a name. My father gave it to me."

"Is it too precious to you to tell me?"

It was an odd way of asking, but everything about Cara seemed odd to her. That's what kept things interesting. The king wouldn't have gone through all this trouble for someone boring.

"No," she said. The only precious thing her father gave her was the divine right to rule Kitara. "My name is Tambika, which means offering in our language. He was a very devout follower of the gods."

"I see." Cara chewed on the inside of her cheek, thinking, then said, "My mother gave me my name. It means beloved. My dad wanted to name me Claudia." She rolled her eyes, not feeling in the slightest like a Claudia. "I wonder what name your mother would have given you."

It wasn't really a question but a thought. Yet, even when Cara was called for her bath, the king lingered on it. She had never dwelled on her given name before—it was but a formality in the written record—but she was suddenly painfully aware of a deep, dark pit in her stomach that could only be filled by a name, and the name her father gave her wasn't enough.

Cara dreamt of scrying that night. When she looked down, there was a blue string tied to her wrist that led off into the distance. She ignored it, instead following a trail in the ground that guided her to the king. She sat by her on a tall mountaintop and interlaced their fingers.

A dark-skinned woman appeared, glowing like she was illuminated with a sun from within, and leaned in close to the king's ear to whisper, *Lakicia, the favorite amongst people, my miracle, my love.*

Light started pouring from the king's—Lakicia's—eyes. Cara would never know that the king was having the same dream, but a few feet away.

* * *

The next day, the king led Cara through the palace's deserted halls. The bustling sounds of the festival wafted in through the windows, along with various smells. They were making their way to the Northern Temple, where the Gatekeepers resided.

Their footsteps echoed loudly as they weaved through the corridors, going from grand rooms to narrow halls like the ones Cara had first approached the king's chamber through. The place was massive. It took about twenty minutes of power walking to reach the temple.

"Will they really be okay with helping me?" Cara asked. Her nerves were catching up with her now that she wasn't worried about being spotted.

"They are loyal to me," the king replied confidently. "And see all that happens within Kitara's walls. They already know we are coming."

"What?" Cara thought it was a joke for a second. Surely, they weren't on their way to meet a pair of omniscient beings?

The king didn't smile. "We're almost there," she said.

The temple was adjacent to the palace—they wouldn't

have to sneak out like Cara expected. Huge wooden doors came into view; one swung open when they walked up to it, beckoning them inside. Cara's eyes lingered momentarily on the carved masks and statues populating the entrance, hollow eyes glaring at her from every angle. Voices greeted them, but for the first time since arriving in Kitara, she could not understand what they were saying.

The king's reply still sounded like English to her, "Hello, Aunties, I trust you know why I've come."

It took a second for her eyes to adjust to the dim lighting. The temple was just as big as the doors had suggested. Other than the walls near the entrance, the space seemed to go on forever, edges disappearing into the darkness. The main source of light came from a skylight straight ahead. Below it stood two people. A hearth was built into the floor behind them. The furniture that surrounded them was stacked with books.

The king led Cara closer, and the Gatekeepers' features became easier to distinguish. One was very tall, and the other quite short, with a voluptuous figure. In all other ways, they were alike, from their shimmering robes, glossy dark skin, and mischievous look in their eye. They spoke again, one voice lower and more raspy than the other. The king glanced at Cara but was met with a blank spell. *Ah, the translation spell.*

"Will you not let yourselves be understood?" the king asked.

The answer was unintelligible. Cara was about to resign herself to being left out of the conversation.

Then, the tall keeper spoke, translating the words she had said in her native tongue, "She has arrived, the one who was not supposed to be here."

The statement was cryptic—to say Cara had understood her would be a stretch, but she knew what each word meant. "Am I not supposed to be here?" she asked timidly, holding the keeper's cat-like gaze.

"Not to worry," she said. "Things that aren't supposed to happen do happen all the time. Even though we ask the astros what they think the future holds, we can only hope they're not too far off!" The keeper punctuated this with a cackle that dissolved into a bit of coughing.

Her partner slipped between them and took Cara's hand, turning the palm to face her and saying, "It's really no wonder that you ended up here, so slimly have you missed Kitara at other times."

"Me?" Cara asked wide-eyed. She hadn't left Oregon state lines until a couple of months ago.

Indeed, for Cara, it would have been hard to understand the keepers. For them, there were no certainties, too many absurdities. The stars provided a steady stream of information, but only a part of it came true—at least in their corner of the chaotic universe...Perhaps in another...They gave each other a look and laughed good-naturedly.

"It's too bad that you have to go," one said.

"I hope to come back someday," Cara said. She was painfully aware of the king standing to her left.

The keeper's eyes softened. "That won't be possible, young one," one said. "You either stay inside Kitara's walls or beyond them. That is our blessing and our curse."

"But I—" she began to say.

"Unprecedented," the other cut in and placed a hand on Cara's shoulder. She had a small bowl nestled in her palm.

"We will be closely inspecting the circumstances that allowed you to find Kitara and ascertaining that this will never happen again."

Then, she dipped her finger in the bowl, coating it in a brown clay, and pressed it across Cara's forehead. The coolness made her flinch.

If they were really all-seeing, Cara had to ask, "Didn't you see me coming?"

The keeper paused. It was almost imperceptibly; she resumed her ministrations immediately before saying, "Just because we are able to see everything doesn't mean we can see everything at once."

Cara found the vagueness unsatisfying, but before she could come up with something to say, the king stepped closer. Her clothes brushed Cara's arm as she said, "I've taken this line of questioning many a time, but they've thought of every justification and rationalization for their shortcomings."

"We regret that we cannot be perfect for our king," the keeper replied gruffly.

The king rolled her eyes, surely having heard this before as well, and Cara laughed. The conversation reminded her of her family, and it made her happy to see the king had people she could let her guard down with. The relief she felt surprised her. She hadn't realized until then how worried she was about leaving the king behind alone. Cara shook her head at the absurd thought. The king wasn't alone. She was King.

"It'll take a few minutes to set up the portal," she said after a brief discussion with the keepers. "You must be relieved."

Cara mustered a smile but felt it falter. "It seems we will not meet each other again after this," she said. "I can't express how grateful I am for what you've done. I wish I had the chance to repay you."

"Life can be—No, how should I phrase this?" the king said. The hesitation in her voice gave Cara the courage to look up again. It was a rare sight; a person normally so full of conviction, uncertain, and grasping for words. "It's easy for someone like me to live without being challenged or having my opinions questioned."

"I didn't question your opinions," Cara said. She wasn't sure where this was going.

The king smiled, grasping her hands, and said, "But you challenged them. It's hard to explain, but I am also grateful to you." Cara shook her head, and she squeezed her hands tighter. "You were like a breath of fresh air in these stale palace grounds. I've never had a friend before, someone I can talk to as an equal."

How painful gratitude felt. The warmth that blossomed in Cara's chest at the word *friend* was enough to make her spill the tears she had so dutifully been keeping back. Her lip quivered as she spoke, "I think we're very similar people. We would have probably got along."

"We did get along, Cara. Just because it has come to an end doesn't mean it didn't happen."

"Ah, I feel like an idiot," she said and wiped her tears with both hands. When she looked back at the king, her expression was peaceful, if somewhat melancholy.

"The spell is ready," the king said. They walked over to the spell circle the keepers were huddled around, and the king spoke softly, as if revealing a secret, "We aren't supposed to say goodbye."

Cara laughed humorlessly, saying, "Yes, I suppose so.

We weren't meant to meet, and so we aren't meant to say goodbye." She stepped into the circle as the keepers directed. "But just because I can't come back doesn't mean we can't keep in touch."

"Perhaps," the king said as she followed her into the circle and interlaced their fingers. The keepers now stood around it, waiting for the king to step out. She stared into Cara's eyes, trying to decipher what she was feeling. "I wonder if in another life…"

Cara's eyes were gentle as she leaned in closer to say, "Maybe the reason I wasn't fated to come here is because I would have stayed."

The king smiled, torn by the images from her dreams. "Perhaps."

She stepped away slowly, letting their fingers disentangle until their hands fell back to their sides where they belonged.

Once out of the skylight's luminescence, Cara could no longer make out her expression. She tried not to think about it, about what could have been. It felt unfair that she would never know, but there were more pressing matters to attend to. She couldn't lock herself away behind Kitara's walls and ignore the rest of the world forever, leaving her loved ones to fend for themselves.

One of the keepers spoke, "Concentrate on your sister."

Right before the room disappeared, only a second before the vertigo kicked in, she heard the king say, "May your future hold what the stars have shown us."

25

The Gatekeepers' spell thrust Cara into a disorienting existence where there wasn't up nor down nor upside down. The ground solidified under her feet within a minute, and her knees buckled. When she looked up, a familiar face greeted her. "Cara?"

Ada's voice was music to her ears. She stumbled toward it and landed in her arms, giving her a brief hug while the vertigo subsided. She broke away when her vision returned to look at her sister's face.

"Oh my god!" Ada exclaimed. "How did you get here? Are you okay? What's that on your forehead? I was trying to gather ingredients for a scrying spell to find you, but I definitely got the spell wrong. I went to this house, and they had a picture of Mom. Isn't that wild?"

While she rambled, Cara took stock of the situation. They were in an alley by a busy market. Ada was wearing a long skirt she had never seen before and a messy headwrap. At their feet, there was a random assortment of objects and two leather-bound books. She didn't recognize the covers or titles.

"Really? That *is* weird. I'm fine," Cara finally said. "I got thrown somewhere in the middle of the desert and found this, like, hidden city. The king actually helped me find you and let me talk to Mom."

"No way! What did she say?" Ada asked.

She was a little bit jealous. A hidden city in the desert, a king, and a call with Mom sounded a lot better than her time in Tmek, but she reminded herself to be grateful that Sara and Rifat had found her in a world full of unsavory characters.

"Ada, Mom said we have to get back to Hope Springs as soon as possible," Cara said. "We need to find Amit and go. Is she here?"

"No, I was hoping she would be with you."

They both deflated at the realization.

"Why would we go back to Hope Springs? Is it safe now?" Ada asked.

Cara bit her lip before answering, "No, quite the opposite. Gage got a terrible horoscope reading that said the house is going to burn down, so they're going to go into hiding, too. Mom said if we're all going to be on the run, might as well be together."

"Wait, a horoscope?" Ada asked, frowning.

"But like a legit one, from a real practitioner that Mom knows. She said this guy's usually super accurate."

"And he said our house is going to burn down? Are they going to save our stuff?"

It was dawning on Ada that she had said goodbye to a lot of things in her childhood home that she may never get to see again.

"Honestly, I didn't even think to ask about that. We only had fifteen minutes and were trying to form a game plan," Cara said with a sigh.

The speed at which events were happening was barely

giving her time to think. Her eyes still felt puffy from her earlier farewell, but she needed to shift her brain into gear.

"What's the game plan then?" Ada asked.

"Find Amit, get back to Hope Springs, and rendezvous with the rest of the family."

Her sister had been expecting a bit more detail than that, but they had learned over the last two months that even the best-laid plans are often overturned. Ada had her own theories on what they should be doing anyway. A little side quest, to put it that way.

"I see," she said and looked for a segue into her spiel. "Well, remember that house I mentioned earlier that my failed scrying spell led me to?"

"Yeah?" Cara said absentmindedly. She was squatting down to examine the variety of foodstuffs and damaged goods her little sister had accumulated.

"I thought that you might be inside," Ada started carefully. "So I broke in."

"Ada!" Cara's neck snapped back towards her, her face contorted in shock.

"What?" She opened her eyes wide, both trying to look innocent and daring her sister to condemn her at the same time. "I thought someone had kidnapped you and was holding you hostage. I think breaking in to check is the least I could have done!"

Cara groaned and said, "Fine. It's just, when you say it like that, it sounds so bad."

"I mean, it is pretty bad, but the good thing is you weren't kidnapped!" she said. "And I found these books."

"I was meaning to ask you about them. You stole them from that house?" Cara fretted. *That* she couldn't justify.

Ada expected this reaction, but she had a bigger bomb to drop. "Cara, I saw a picture of Mom in there. I think it's our grandparents' house, the one she grew up in." She had formed this hypothesis by looking closer at the pictures—between the gaggle of kids, one looked particularly like a young Miriam.

"Mom said she grew up in New York, not…Where are we right now?"

"Damascus. I actually landed in a small village a few hours away, but a kind couple took me in and drove me there. They wanted to help me reach an American embassy."

"What did you tell them happened to you?" Cara hadn't considered the complexities that relying on a non-practitioner's kindness would have.

"I said I couldn't remember, so they thought I had been drugged and fallen victim to human traffickers."

"Dark," Cara said with a sigh. Thinking back on the last few days, their reality wasn't that much better. "There was a moment when I thought I would die lost in the desert."

Ada was visibly perturbed. She gave her older sister a one-armed hug. "I'm glad you're okay."

"Me too."

Ada picked back up where she left off, "We both know Mom hasn't told us a single truth about her life before she met Dad. She definitely didn't grow up in New York. I always knew her accent was suspicious."

"She barely even has an accent, and it's because she moved to New York when she was a kid," Cara said.

"Cara, I really sympathize with your need to believe that our mother hasn't been lying to us our whole lives, but the evidence is damning."

"You haven't shown me any evidence."

Cara's eyebrows were furrowed. She was getting annoyed, as she usually did when anyone contradicted her, much less Ada. Their mutual stubbornness had been the seed of many fights throughout the years.

"Then look at this," Ada said, then flipped open one of the thick leather-bound books in her hand. "It's the history of the Aarons, an abridged version." Cara took in the cover, the title page, the glossary. Ada grabbed the other one. "This one." She opened the other book to the place she had been reading before Cara arrived. "May hold the key to defeating the Mistlanders."

This caught Cara's attention. "That's a lofty claim," she said.

"It's a full history of Mistlander research and has compiled biological information about the vessels they inhabit in the Midlands," Ada stated and handed it to her.

For what it was, the book was certainly not very large. Only one hundred and seventy pages without subtracting the index et al. If this was all they had to go off of to defeat the Mistlanders, Cara felt the situation was bleak—but this edition was published in 1997, and she held on to hope that the practitioner community had upgraded the literature on the topic since then. "How did you even find these?" she finally asked.

"They were the only two books I could find in English," Ada said conspiratorially. "Coincidence? I think not! I wanted to take the picture too, but I thought they would notice that for sure."

It was definitely a coincidence, Cara thought, laughing softly. But then again, she thought of Kitara. It was all already starting to feel like a dream. "Things that shouldn't happen, happen all the time," Cara murmured.

"I feel like we've been caught up in things that shouldn't have happened for months," Ada replied.

It wasn't really what she meant, but Cara nodded anyway. Ada observed her for a second while she flipped through the book. "I hate to get in between you and a good book, but we need to figure out where we're going to stay tonight," she finally said.

"You're right. The first thing we should try is finding Amit," Cara said, already wracking her brain for useful spells.

"Do you think Amit may be on her way to us?" Ada asked. Their eyes met as they both considered the possibility. "It won't be easy to find a moving target," she pointed out. "Instead of going to her, we should try to let her know where we are."

"I don't know, Ada." Cara shook her head. "She could be injured or worse. It's already been, what? Three days? We can't wait for her forever."

"It hasn't been a full three days," Ada insisted. She remembered the tethers she had tried forging between their consciousness and breathed some energy into them. "I definitely think we should try to communicate with her before making any moves," she said.

"Fine," Cara muttered. "Let's get our stuff."

She pulled out the sheet of paper Amit had given them with the spell to access their magical storage space.

"I lost mine when I lost my purse," Ada lamented.

The girls looked closely at the ground and chose a spot where the dirt was a bit looser to replicate it. Ada used the cap side of the bottle of water she had long ago emptied, and

Cara a rock shard she found in the alley. It was difficult to draw precise symbols—the end result was big and awkward—but when they channeled their energy into them, the portal glowed and materialized as meant to. Cara reached her hand into the emptiness and willed her notebook to appear. It did.

"Let me try something," Ada said. She reached in and brought out a liter of water. "Yes!"

Cara was relieved to know that water would have been at her fingertips even if she hadn't found Kitara. "Do you think she has food in here? Are you hungry?" she asked.

Ada wasn't very hungry, but she checked anyway and found granola bars, jerky, and dried mango for dinner later. Cara quickly flipped through her notes and rattled off a few objects and ingredients at Ada, who cloaked herself in a stealth spell again and went into the market to gather them. Cara wasn't willing to sit and wait while others did important tasks, so she followed her sister into the unfamiliar streets. The sounds, smells, and crowd in the market accosted her senses, locked away with the king as she had been for days.

On occasion, Miriam acknowledged her Syrian roots, and Cara recognized some foods and items from the research she had done throughout her life. By the time she got back to the alley, her heart was beating fast. She felt she had grasped a sliver of the soul of the city, a grain of dirt in the massive desert of its history and culture. As new as it all was to her, the warmth was familiar and nostalgic. It comforted her enduring homesickness in the most subtle way. Thinking her mother might have grown up here made her feel both closer and further away from her than ever.

They scavenged materials close enough to the ones they were looking for and regrouped in the alley, dumping them onto the floor. The magic was layered and complex—they would have to imbue ordinary objects to mimic high-energy elements like crystals and herbs—and they were foregoing animal elements, which would make the spell unstable.

A few months ago, they wouldn't have hesitated to provide their own blood, but Amit had since drilled into their heads that there were very few exceptions in which a practitioner should use their own body parts to practice magic. Protection spells, curses, and hereditary or mass charms were included, as were select summoning rituals. Communication and scrying spells were not. She made it seem like a dangerous rule to break.

As they worked through the steps, Ada felt a little ashamed about her prior scrying spell. No wonder it had failed so spectacularly; according to Cara, citrus and spices had less than a tenth of the energy required. She thought briefly of her tethers, now doubting she had created even the slightest connection with Cara or Amit. Her sister hadn't brought anything up, and she was too embarrassed to do so herself.

It must have been twenty or thirty minutes until they took a pause.

"Is there anything left to do?" Ada asked.

Cara had put together a spell using notes from Amit's lessons. She ran through the prep one more time; they hadn't missed anything. "If this doesn't work, I'm scrying," she warned.

They sat at each side of the spell circle and recited the chant she came up with—a combination of the active and passive words they learned in Nebraska. The energy started flowing quickly; Cara had once more proven her astonishing instinct for magical design. Surprisingly, as Ada concentrated on

Amit, she felt the tethers in her mind strengthen, feeding off of the spell's energy.

She willed the person at the other end, Amit, to hear them and heed their call. Ada imagined the spell's energy traveling toward Amit, guided by the tether. Just as they seemed to be making progress, she felt something strange happen; like a blocked pipe, the spell had hit an obstacle. It proved an insurmountable wall. The spell was too weak to break through. The magic started to drain from the spell. Ada opened her eyes. Cara was grinning.

"We did it!" She held out her hand for a high five.

Ada hesitantly reciprocated, weakly tapping it with her own hand. "Are you sure? Something seemed off on my end."

"What are you talking about?" Cara said as she stared back at her blankly. "Didn't you hear Amit?"

"No, I didn't…" Ada said.

She was reluctant to go into detail about her experience, unsure of how much weight to give it after her botched experiments from earlier. She hardly considered herself a gifted practitioner, and Cara was more likely to be right— statistically speaking.

"I heard her clearly," Cara said with a shrug. "She said to meet her tonight at some mountain."

"A mountain? Why?" Ada asked. She had goosebumps on her arms despite the balmy air. Her mind was running a thousand miles a minute. She thought their spell had been intercepted, that it hadn't reached Amit, but Cara was convinced otherwise.

She seemed so sure as she spoke, tensed with a sense of accomplishment. "She tracked down someone who might be able to help us."

"Amit said that?" Ada asked.

"It's strange that you couldn't hear her," Cara finally said with a tilt of her head. "I'll show her the spell when we get there and ask what we did wrong." She moved on quickly, saying, "Can you open a rift?"

Her sister gaped at her, unable to follow the thread of the conversation. "Where are we going?" she asked.

"Mount Hermon."

Cara told her to wait while she pulled up the storage portal once more, producing from it a world atlas. Ada was impressed there was even one in there.

"Amit wants to do some reconnaissance before we go halfway across the world back to Oregon," Cara said. "She was doing some research and found a clue to how the Mistlanders may be entering the Midlands."

"Really?" Ada said.

The explanation made sense—and it would be great to find out where the Mistlanders were coming from—but she couldn't shake the feeling that something was off.

Cara found the page she was looking for and leaned in to inspect the map. When they activated the spell, Amit told her she had narrowed it down to three possible spots, including the Mount of Olives in Jerusalem and Mount Tabor in Israel. She said it had something to do with Jesus's transfiguration. And it got weirder.

"We're meeting Amit here," Cara said, pointing. "Mount Hermon, where most biblical scholars think the fallen angels made their entry into Earth."

"Angels? Like from the Bible?" Ada asked, then shook her head. "What are you even *talking* about?"

An hour ago, Cara may have said the same thing, but

she heard Amit's instructions loud and clear. Irritated, she snapped, "Shut up, okay? I once asked Mom about Jesus, and she didn't rule anything out, saying he may have been a practitioner. Who knows? We've encountered the craziest shit so far. If there can be a god of chaos in South Africa, why are you so sure that angels never existed?"

Ada recognized the tone in her sister's voice and knew that once in this state, it was useless to disagree with her; she had already made up her mind and would have a retort for any argument you made. Even so, she had to try.

"Cara, please, listen to yourself," she said. "We practice magic, not miracles. This is literal gibberish."

"I suppose you know everything now, do you?"

There was the venom Ada was used to when she got into altercations with her sister. The words themselves were hardly an insult, but the way she would throw them in her face seeped in disdain would sting like nothing else could. Instantly, she felt disinterested in anything Cara had to say.

"Fine. Do whatever you want."

They turned away from each other, fuming in silence. Ada tried to distract herself, picking up the book on Mistlanders and scanning it for any mention of Mount Hermon. Nothing. She did the same in the other book, just in case.

Cara's voice interrupted, "Are *you* going to open the rift, or should I?"

Ada was bitter, but she wasn't petty.

"I'll do it," she said, then knelt down to draw a few symbols from memory.

Hundreds of portals materialized before her eyes, bright streaks of colors shimmering iridescently. She stepped through first.

Prom was a week away, and the school was buzzing. Last-minute dates were agreed to, people were freaking out about their outfits, and close friends were bickering. The frenzy and paranoia peaked after a tenth grader accused her boyfriend's ex of copying her idea of dressing like a sexy disco ball. Now, the fad was keeping outfit details top secret to guard against espionage. Gage was having a strange one, and not just because of the eccentricities of his peers.

After the doomsday horoscope reading, he grappled with which items to prioritize amongst his belongings. The image of a carefree teenager, he tried to avoid introspection as much as possible and had certainly never confronted the banality of material possessions to this extent. Were clothes worth saving? Was a book? He could always buy another one, but the ache he felt when he thought of everything he owned burning to the ground was hard to ignore.

He settled on his CD collection, which took years to build and now numbered in the hundreds; his video games and console; and some sketchbooks. Gage drew often when he was younger, but not anymore. He flipped through one now, seeing how his drawings improved over time, then threw it back in the box. Even thinking about picking up his old charcoals felt intimidating and burdensome knowing that he would not be as good as before.

There was something else Gage had been looking for without success in the piles in his room. He couldn't get it out of his head, a pendant he found once at an away game in a neighboring town. The team was hanging out in a park behind the hotel drinking warm liquor, and his roommate headed back early, warning that their shared bathroom would be inhospitable for the foreseeable future. Gage got the urge to break the seal not long after and went to the restrooms in the lobby. When he turned to wash his hands, something glimmered in the dull fluorescent lights.

He could have sworn it wasn't there when he walked in, but it wasn't like he took a close look. To this day, Gage wasn't sure what it was meant to be. The whole thing was about the size of his thumbnail. It was hard to tell if it was made of a precious metal; its dark sheen was corroded with time and neglect. He could make out the shape of a lithe, dog-like animal with a long face and ears.

A straight line ran across it, bending into a T on one end and forking into an upside-down U on the other. He brought it to the front desk on his way up to his room, but the concierge said that no one had used that bathroom in a few days. They were the only hotel in that little Oregon town and didn't get many guests. If someone had lost it, they weren't missing it. Gage could keep it if he wanted it. Otherwise, it was getting thrown out.

Gage had kept it but never shown it to anyone. If they had asked why—why he kept it, why he hid it, why he wanted to safeguard it along with his most prized possessions—he wouldn't have known what to say. It just seemed neat to him. It appeared in front of him, and now it was his.

Yet now he had rifled through every drawer and bag in his room and could not find it for the life of him, nor could he remember the last time he saw it. In the past, it always just happened to be there in a pant pocket or backpack compartment.

After an hour or so of reacquainting himself with his room and belongings, a frustrated Gage welcomed the distraction of Riley's call. She was out front.

He slipped on some sneakers, grabbed his wallet, and then thumped down the stairs, taking them two by two.

Richard was on his laptop at the kitchen table ordering some inventory for the flower shop and looked up at the sound. "Where are you headed, champ?" he asked.

"Riley's picking me up," Gage said, already halfway across the living room. "We're going to get some decorations for prom."

"Oh, is she on the committee?"

"No. Her friend is, but she doesn't have a car. So Riley told her she could pick them up for her."

"That's nice of her. Will you take the recycling on your way out?"

"Sure," Gage muttered, only slightly annoyed. He back-tracked to the kitchen and sped out.

Riley was parked at the curb. He waved and held up a trash bag before making his way to the side of the house, where the bins sat. Just as he was about to turn to meet Riley, something moved in his peripheral vision. The hairs on the back of his neck prickled, and goosebumps rose on his skin.

Not one to be easily startled, Gage turned toward to look

at it directly. It seemed like someone was peeking around at him from the backyard, but now all there was were shadows. As he continued to stare, though, some parts of the shadows started to distinguish themselves from the others, becoming darker and more solid as if they had more substance than their surroundings. Then, his cell phone buzzed in his pocket, breaking his daze and reminding him that his girlfriend was idling a few steps away. He didn't want to make her wait.

* * *

"Good morning, honey," Miriam said when she saw him coming down the steps the next morning. "Happy Monday!"

Gage mumbled something in response, his hair still sticking out in every direction after wrestling mercilessly with his pillow all night. He melted into one of the dining room chairs, struggling to keep his eyes open.

His mom leaned against the kitchen counter, nursing a coffee and skimming the morning newspaper. "What would you like for breakfast?" she asked.

The reply was another barely comprehensible grumble. She laughed lightly, peeling herself off the counter and walking over to her son. She ruffled his hair, and he opened his eyes fully to stare back at her. "Eggs?" He nodded. "Scrambled? Toast?" Two more nods. "Okay, I'll let your father know."

When she reached Richard, he was kneeling next to one of their many indoor houseplants, inspecting the leaves closely. She squatted down next to him, laying a hand on his shoulder, and waited for him to look up.

"Will you go wake up Meena?" he asked and glanced at his

290

watch. "She has swimming lessons at eight."

Miriam nodded, then said, "Will you make some scrambled eggs and toast for Gage? He's at the table."

They shared a smile like an inside joke—the kind only shared by those who have loved each other for decades—then went on with their respective tasks.

Meena had been dreaming about water like she usually did when her mom woke her up. Her dreams were always vivid and hard to forget when she awoke, often blurring the boundaries between dreamscape and reality. She spent that night flying through the sky, cold winds stinging her face and clouds leaving her covered in dew if she didn't dodge them in time.

A glistening blue sea gurgled and misted below her, spreading out as far as the eye could see. Sometimes whales, dolphins, and fish would breach the surface, breaking its uniformity, but travel as far as she would, no island or land would appear. Her mother's warm voice and hand, gently patting her head and her shoulder and calling her back home, offered welcome repose.

"Rise and shine, sweetie pie," Miriam said while smiling gently from the edge of the bed. "You need to wake up if you want to get to swim class on time." Meena burrowed her head into her mother's legs and wrapped her arms around her torso, eyes still shut tight. "Shall I ask Daddy to make you some breakfast?"

She nodded, her hair ruffling against Miriam's shirt, then let go of her locked arms and stretched them overhead. "Pancake, please," she whispered.

Half an hour later, both kids were fed, and Richard was waiting for Meena by the door. She grabbed the backpack he had prepared for her and followed him to the car. It was only a fifteen-minute drive to the community pool, and since the class clashed with regular elementary school hours, it was a small and varied group that attended.

There were two other kids around Meena's age, a twelve-year-old girl and a ten-year-old boy, both homeschooled. They barely interacted except when the coach paired them together for exercises. Other than them, there was a young Russian woman who spoke little English when she first arrived and an elderly man who said one of the items on his bucket list was to learn how to swim.

Usually, classes would be divided by age when they took place during Summer or on the weekends, but there were so few people interested in weekday classes that the community center had decided to group them together to avoid incurring the costs of a second class.

The group got along well despite their differences and had already been practicing together for a few months. The young woman's English had improved significantly in that time, and the old man had announced he would be discontinuing his lessons in the not-so-distant future. He had already mastered the breaststroke and was working on breathing techniques with the coach.

Meena loved the pool. She was her usual quiet self during the lessons—occasionally pointing something out or giggling when a particularly funny thing happened—but in the water, she was fast and could turn sharply, always following instructions to a T. The coach had approached Richard and Miriam about signing Meena up for competitive swimming, but after attending one of the matches, they saw that the noise and atmosphere could be overstimulating.

Once she got in the water, she would be fine, but they didn't feel it was worth the added stress when she could just continue her usual semiweekly pool sessions. Meena hadn't shown any particular interest either.

That day, Meena enjoyed how her dreams blended into her lesson. As she held her breath underwater, aquatic beasts would emerge and disappear at the edges of the pool. Prehistoric armored creatures would accompany her on her laps, obscuring the other humans swimming alongside her and prompting her to speed up to keep up with them.

By the end of the hour, she was exhausted but satisfied and ready for a snack and a nap. Her dad greeted her, holding a towel wide and wrapping her tightly like a burrito. Meena ran over to the changing rooms to rinse off the chlorine and wash her hair. Always one to get distracted in the water, by the time she was clean and dressed, both female participants from the class had left.

Meena stuffed everything back into her backpack except for her bathing suit and cap, which she had to wring the water out of. With the mirror in front of her at the sink, she could see the entire changing room in its reflection, from the entrance to the lockers to the bathroom stalls. She wouldn't have noticed anything unusual had it not been for an odd metallic sound that rang through the empty room.

Although Meena was reluctant to break her concentration on the task in front of her, an odd feeling crept into her stomach and up to her head. It wasn't exactly like the glimpses of past, present, or future she sometimes received, but more like a hunch. Looking up, she was relieved to find the room was still vacant. Then, the utility closet at the far right corner of the room caught her eye. It was always locked;

the coach was the only person she knew who had a key. She had never even seen the door open. Until now.

Still looking at the reflection in the mirror, Meena could tell that the door was slightly ajar, a sliver of darkness wedged between its frame. She wondered if it was related to the strange noise from earlier. Removing herself from the sink, she hastily wrapped the damp garments in a bag and crammed it into her backpack, slinging it across her shoulder to meet her father outside.

Trying to dismiss the creeping sensation that plagued her, she ignored the closet on her way to the exit. As the doors stood on adjacent walls only a few feet apart, it proved harder to do than she had hoped. In order to exit the locker room, she would have to pass quite close to the unlatched door.

Richard was immersed in a particularly tricky sudoku puzzle when high-pitched shrieks jolted him out of it. Knowing Meena was the only person left in the pool area, he jumped to his feet and ran through the door so forcefully it hit the wall behind it, producing a loud bang. Inside, his eyes were immediately drawn to an open door to his left.

Not seeing Meena anywhere, he rushed in to find her curled up with her arms around her knees and her head buried between them. There were puddles of water across the entire room—his feet splashed as he approached her.

In his haste, he grabbed her shoulders and tried to look at her face, crying, "Meena! Are you hurt? What happened?"

Meena lashed out, hitting his arms and wriggling out of his grip. Coming to his senses, Richard let go and backed off.

"I'm sorry, honey," he breathed. "I'm so sorry. Please just look at me. It's Daddy, I'm here, and you're fine."

Meena didn't seem to be hurt. He looked around the room

294

to ascertain the cause of her distress. Other than the unusual amount of water on the floor, it was dark and humid to the point of being unpleasant. The two windows illuminating them were high and below a ledged roof, which didn't allow much sunlight in. Richard was worried that the room itself was troubling Meena; he swallowed his fear of being disliked and tried again.

"Meena, my love? Are you listening? Can you hear me?" He was greeted with more trembling. The sight of her backpack on the floor gave him an idea. He rifled through its contents and found the towel she had used previously. It was still damp but not soaked. He wrapped it around her. "Meena," he said gently. "I'm going to carry you outside now."

Outside of the changing room, Richard set her down on a bench by the pool and sat down at a short distance to wait for her to come back to the present. It took a while, but eventually, she uncurled and sat up, still shaking and catatonic.

"Hi, baby," he said and edged slightly toward her. "Whenever you're ready, we can get in the car and go home."

A couple of minutes passed before she reached her hand out and gripped his arm. Richard breathed a sigh of relief. He didn't want to press her about what happened until she had time to calm down and process the events. They drove home in silence, Meena still wrapped tightly in her towel, but her breathing slowly returned to normal.

At home, he swapped the towel out for a blanket and gave her a few options of snacks until she showed interest—her stomach had growled loudly on their way back. She sat silently at the dining room table, staring straight ahead while he brought it over, but reached for the peanut butter and jelly sandwich immediately. Feeling like the worst had already passed, Richard took the chance to step out into their yard and call Miriam.

* * *

When Gage got home that evening, he was in a bad mood. It was only Wednesday, but the week felt like the longest in his life. Ever since the first encounter with shadows by the trash bin, it seemed like everywhere he went, there were dark figures lurking in his peripheral vision, try as he could to ignore them.

Any time he would accidentally or purposefully look directly at them, they would condense and consolidate, becoming more and more humanoid until someone snapped him out of his stupor. He was thinking about telling his mom about the things he had been seeing, but when he walked into his house that day, he could tell her expression was off.

"How was school?" she asked before holding her arms out for a hug. She kissed his temple and let him extract himself to put his backpack and gym bag down.

"It was fine," he muttered. "How was work?"

Miriam shrugged and said, "Same old." A pregnant silence followed, but he pretended not to notice. "Gage, darling," she finally said, "something happened today to Meena."

"What?" Gage's head snapped up. That wasn't what he was expecting. "What happened? Is she okay?" he asked.

"She's…fine now," his mother answered, but the pause left a bad taste in his mouth. "The issue is that we don't know exactly what happened. Your father took her to swim lessons and heard her scream inside the locker room, but when he went inside, she was alone and very scared."

His eyes were wide, his thoughts etched on his face. "And you don't know what happened?"

His mom shook her head somberly. "She hasn't said a word since."

"Is Dad upstairs with her?" She nodded and kept her gaze on him. "What can we do?" he finally asked.

Miriam had been waiting for this question, or, more accurately, she had been waiting for the chance to ask her own. "There is a way to find out exactly what happened," she said cautiously.

The way her tone shifted set alarm bells off in her son's head, but he grit his teeth and played along, saying, "Magic?"

"Yes."

"It's good that you'll be able to figure it out."

"Well, I can't figure it out by myself," his mom said with a sigh. "The only spell I found that can reveal what happened in that room today requires two practitioners."

"I'm not a practitioner," Gage said reflexively. They both knew he wasn't going to get anywhere with that. They had continued their weekend lessons in the club, often with an audience of little girls cheering them on.

"Babe, just because you don't want to practice doesn't mean you're not a practitioner. That's like saying you're not human," his mom replied. She always took a gentle tone when they spoke about magic like he was five years old again. It was annoying.

"I feel like neither," Gage said with a scoff.

"Oh, honey." Miriam recoiled at his spiteful tone, making a mental note to follow up with him on the topic, but they had more urgent matters to attend to. "Will you help me help your sister?" she asked.

There really was no other answer that Gage could give but yes. He rolled his eyes but nodded.

"Good, thank you," she said, then walked over and cradled his face in her hands, making him meet her eyes. "Thank you," she repeated.

After dinner, they set the TV on to Meena's favorite channel and convened by the front door. The spell would work better on more recent events, Miriam explained, and there was a chance the assailant would come back to erase their traces. They had to go tonight.

Richard saw them off with a smile, but alone in the house with a still catatonic Meena, ugly, familiar feelings reared their head again for the first time in years. Voices in his head reminded him of how useless he was, incapable of protecting anyone. He would be fine by the time they got back that night—he liked to think he had matured since the days he let those thoughts affect him.

Miriam had spent hours researching that afternoon, but most of the spells she found had to be cast on Meena. Having seen the effects of a botched memory spell firsthand, they still haunted her to this day. She refused to cast on her daughter's mind no matter how harmless the spell claimed to be.

Practitioners would usually need the Committee's authorization to cast the sort of spell she was planning on using with Gage that night, although some preferred to commission a certified psychometrist to unearth a room's secrets. Miriam had to start the night with several magic containment spells to avoid detection by those same Committee-certified practitioners.

Gage was still getting the hang of writing out magic

circles—he could draw two symbols per minute, maybe more if they were straightforward enough—but his mother picked up the slack with her quick movements. There were ways to improve his speed, and teaching him the elements that collectively made up each symbol would be a good way to start, but they were only meeting a few hours a week.

Because of his strong aversion to practicing magic, she was gradually introducing him to what she thought would be most useful: the basics of self-defense, healing, and escaping danger. Like all her children, he had a strong affinity for magic and would pick up spells easily during practical lessons. Despite that, he quit their periodic lessons as soon as he could, around thirteen, purportedly too busy with school and extracurriculars.

Miriam had noticed his adverse attitude toward magic before that but could relate to the feeling all too well. She, herself, had once disliked it so much she wanted to pretend it didn't exist—but that was in the past.

Her children had enough raw power to protect themselves if push came to shove, and that comforted her. But spells were specially crafted to help practitioners wield power more carefully and precisely. It worried her that they would someday hurt themselves or those they wanted to protect without meaning to. That's why she insisted they only practice magic in the club under supervision, especially when trying something new.

Those rules became obsolete when Cara and Ada left Hope Springs, but then again, they were who the rules had been geared toward. They showed much more interest in magic than Gage or Meena.

It took an hour to get everything in place, squarely within

Miriam's expectations.

"Come stand over here," she instructed. "I'll stand on the opposite side. You need to concentrate on the circles we formed and the symbols within them. Remember what we're trying to achieve. We need to see what happened to your sister here today. Once we activate it with our magic, don't break your focus until we're finished, alright?"

Gage nodded, a little nervous. He didn't want to mess up and be the reason they didn't find out what had happened to Meena tonight. His anxiety reminded him why he agreed to train again with his mother. Up until now, his magic had only been a nuisance—drawing out feelings and questions about himself he would rather avoid—but it had recently become the only way he had of protecting others. At the very least, he didn't want to become deadweight to those he cared about.

Thankfully, the power flowed easily from him, and the room filled with cool white light. He only had to hold his breath for a minute; the figures started taking shape quicker than the shadows that had been recently plaguing him did. Realizing that his mother was probably exerting more influence than he was, he decided to relax and pay closer attention to what was going on around them.

The dark room was transformed. They could make out the most minute object on the shelves as everything reverted to how it was hours prior.

The air was still for a moment. Nothing happened. No one entered or left. Then, like a vortex, a rift opened up in the middle of the room, and two Mistlanders emerged. Gage recoiled, only having seen such creatures once and under dire circumstances. He remembered the one that had spoken to him, how he had silenced it—an action so uncharacteristic that he had erased it from his recollections.

It wasn't until this moment, watching two awkward Mistlanders lumber around the community pool's utility closet, that it dawned on Gage that he had killed one of these beings before. Not long ago, in fact. Looking at them now made his blood curl.

He was the type to catch bugs alive when his sisters freaked out and asked him to kill them. The type that cried that one time in sixth grade when his buddy invited him out to a hunt, and he saw an animal killed in front of him for the first time.

How had it been so easy? How could he have forgotten it until now? The thought seemed so preposterous that he wondered if it had really happened. There wasn't exactly someone he could ask. He wouldn't be able to explain why he did it, why he hid it, or why he only thought of it now. Keeping his irrational behavior hidden was becoming a theme in his life.

The Mistlanders were at the door of the closet. The frame was jammed and made a metallic clang when they pried it open, just as it had when Miriam and Gage arrived. They left it ajar and waited. A heart-wrenching sound left Miriam's lips when she saw them reach out of the room and come back with a shrieking Meena in their arms. They threw her backpack to the ground and tried to pin her down.

Suddenly, torrents of water started streaming into the room and hitting the Mistlanders head-on. Unfamiliar aquatic animals floated in and circled the room. A second later, everything was gone, leaving a trembling Meena on the wet ground. Miriam deactivated the spell when she saw Richard run in, left standing in the pitch-black room with her son.

"The water was probably Meena," she said. Her voice was fragile and unfamiliar.

"What did they want?" Gage asked. His frame was vibrating; his hands were clenched tightly into fists.

"It's hard to say. They may have wanted to kidnap her or take her magic."

Her calm tone only made him angrier. Later he would notice the bloody half-moons his fingers left marked on his palms. "Those fuckers."

Miriam lay a hand on his tensed shoulder and promised, "They're never going to touch Meena again. I'll make sure of it."

He remained in the room for a few moments after she walked out. Overwhelmed with rage, standing in the dark, he could certainly understand how he killed one Mistlander before. It wouldn't be difficult to do it again.

* * *

As an Aaron, Miriam underwent Spartan training from infancy on detecting magic. In their childhood, she and her siblings would be locked in a windowless room for hours, straining their every sense to feel what their parents described as a change in the atmosphere, a prickling of the skin, a shift in the air.

Later lessons on how to deal with invisible enemies, detect curses and unrestful spirits, and find a good plot of land to build on would be reminiscent. The Elders would frame it as a game when they were younger, but the older they grew, the longer the hours became, the more insignificant the amount of magic was, the more difficult it was to leave that cold dungeon.

Sometimes, the children, desperate with thirst, hunger, or the intense pressure from their bladder if they had resisted so long, would suspect that there was no spell. It was rumored that someone had gone mad during his last lesson, a twenty-four-hour session in which two spells would be deployed and had to be identified. Now, he would lose his sense if magic was practiced in his vicinity, dream it when it wasn't there. A great uncle who had left the main house at fifteen and lived alone in an isolated village in the mountains. He was in one of the pictures on the mantle.

The method was efficient, if inhumane. By the time an Aaron hit puberty, they could detect whether a person was a practitioner from a distance.

Miriam had been in the middle of her workday when she felt the enchantment breach the wards she had placed on the building. She reflexively deflected it, but the urge to close her eyes and let it take over was alarming. She managed to fend it off for long enough to convince her colleague of a sudden migraine and lock herself in her office's private bathroom, a feature which had seemed excessive when they closed on the space over a decade ago but was coming in handy now.

Miriam's office had a large window, and the blinds wouldn't have fully blocked the unnatural white-blue light Cara's apparition gave off. She wasn't in the habit of closing them, either.

Fifteen minutes later, Miriam was surprised at how short fifteen minutes could feel. She was also impressed at the potency of the magic Cara had cast. *Where could she possibly be?*

Miriam couldn't let her mind linger; there were still three

hours left in the workday. That her daughters had been separated…No, she couldn't linger. They established that they would meet back in Hope Springs to regroup and go on the run together as a family. Then she wouldn't have to worry about them so much.

Now, she had to think of what came next.

27

Mount Hermon was misleadingly named, Cara explained before they entered the rift. It was actually a cluster of mountains between Syria and Lebanon that included the highest peak in Syria. Called Jabal-al-Shayk, Jabal Haramun, Har Hermon, Saphon, the gray-haired mountain, the eyes of the nation, it had hundreds of names before Gilgamesh defeated Humbaba, splitting it from Lebanon. A sacred enclosure indifferent to the borders of transient nations slashed into its Jurassic rock, the behemoth refused to be segmented by man or anyone.

When Semjaza and his legion of angels landed on earth, risking God and heaven to sate their all-consuming libido, they landed on Hermon. From there, they would taint the human bloodline, spreading forbidden knowledge, celestial secrets, and science. Azazel brought welding and taught how to make knives, swords, shields; Penemue introduced writing with ink and paper; Sariel and Shamsiel passed on the signs of the moon and sun. Scholars would surmise all of this from a few words carved in the limestone of Qasr Antar.

Most snow on the peaks had melted by this time of year. The runoff made the mountains and surroundings dark green and lush. When the girls stepped through the rift, the bright light of the afternoon sun illuminated the dust in the air, creating a haze. Despite the heat, Ada's skin immediately broke into goosebumps, her hair standing up on end. She crossed her arms tightly and looked around, scanning their surroundings for prying eyes.

Even if she thought something was wrong, it was hard to convince her sister. She hoped things would clear up when they saw Amit.

"I'll find out where Amit is," Cara said. She was in good spirits; things were going smoothly.

She walked to a nearby sapling and snapped off a twig. Even gifted scryers benefited from using traditional mediums like these. Amit had taught them that commonly used elements were identified through centuries of research by practitioners looking for effectiveness and efficiency.

Indeed, it took Cara less than a minute and no spell to start walking, following an invisible path only she could surmise. Ada trailed slightly behind as they traced the edge of the mountain, sticking close to its curving foot. They walked more than twenty minutes before Cara came to a stop.

They hadn't reached their destination per se, but she had caught sight of it and had finally experienced some of the dread her sister had been harboring for a while. A few feet in front of her, there was a dark gaping opening in the rock, a large cave where the light seemed to get swallowed steps in. On the floor to the left of the entrance, there was a familiar backpack.

"Amit!" Ada cried, then launched herself past Cara and across the ominous chasm. She came to her knees in front of the bag and picked it up. It seemed full, but she hesitated to check the contents.

"Open it," Cara said, suddenly at her shoulder.

* * *

Amit was somewhere in Nigeria when she heard that Miriam's girls were in Mount Hermon. She didn't mean to end up in Lagos when she left South Africa, but mustering all the energy she had left to open the rift meant she had less control. The spell brought her back to the same place it had deposited her hundreds of times before.

Amit considered herself a nomad and lived in fear of being pinned down by the Committee—or worse, her family—so she stubbornly refused to call Lagos home. If you tallied up the months, weeks, and days, though, she had spent fifteen of the last twenty-five years between a low-key apartment on Lagos Island and her friends' places around the city.

She knew the city like the back of her hand and thrived off the energy of the diverse communities. Amit didn't think she would stop running before the day she died, but when she let her mind wander and fantasized about creating a life for herself, she imagined it in Lagos.

When she stumbled out of the rift, the wound on her side had reopened, and she was close to passing out. She had instinctively routed herself to the sixth-floor studio apartment she rented on and off and was now propping herself up on the wall outside the door, praying to no particular god that the place be unoccupied.

She debated whether to overextend herself and use a spell to find out. In the state Amit was in, even this kind of magic could knock her out, and if there were people inside, she would be screwed. First, she knocked. Determined to wait a few minutes, she sunk to a squat, back still against the wall. Closing her eyes, she willed the walls to stop spinning. She knocked again.

Her consciousness started slipping. She couldn't wait any longer. She sent a burst of magic through the doorknob, unlocking it and coming in. Her knees buckled, but she managed to reach the nearby couch before losing consciousness.

It was the next day when Amit awoke. Her injury was throbbing, but she could tell her healing spell was still working—its effect was weak, but she wasn't getting worse at the very least.

After a good night's sleep, she felt strong enough to reinforce it, willing her body to regenerate and heal as fast as it could. It did little to reduce the pain, but she had built up a high tolerance over the years and knew she could make her way around even in this miserable state. She checked the bathroom cabinet as a last hail Mary and found some ibuprofen a previous tenant had left behind. After reading the label, she took the maximum dose and pocketed the rest.

At least in a familiar city, she knew where to find the answers she was seeking without alerting people that she was around. She headed to her most frequented spots beyond the veil.

Since non-practitioners' global encroachment, most magical creatures that remained in the Midlands did so in a network of veiled communities across the planet, seldom having any reason to venture out. Every city, town, or village in the world with a big enough practitioner community had a veiled side of it that non-practitioners couldn't access. The veiled sector of Paris, for example, was established hundreds of years prior. Lagos's veil was put up sometime in the colonial period, as was often the case with settler states. Prior to that, practitioners lived in harmony with locals and had no reason to hide their powers.

Across the world, most cultures considered their practitioners indispensable to their communities and relied on them for communication with gods, spirits, and ancestors—not to mention for ensuring good harvests, ridding themselves of pests, and for healing.

Genocide meant Europeans not only physically murdered tens and sometimes hundreds of thousands of practicing and non-practicing humans; they thoroughly decimated settler states' history and culture and tried to impose their own. That included persecuting anyone who dared speak of magic and driving the mention of practitioners in written histories to near extinction.

The Committee pushed veiled spaces as safe havens and epicenters for magical society, but they monopolized research on how to establish them and imposed strict censuses and recordkeeping inside them. Veils, which previously had been rare within the Midlands, were established en masse.

In their haste to unite practitioners as a homogeneous demographic, many were cleaved from their cultures and deprived of interconnectivity with their land and non-practicing neighbors. Even then, a veiled sector didn't mean refuge for every practitioner; not all were equally welcome.

Amit had participated in and listened to debates many times about the benefits and costs of keeping practitioners behind a veil. As with most things the Committee did, she opposed it and could work herself into a bad mood if she let her thoughts linger too long.

Today, especially, she had to keep her mind focused on the

task at hand. She needed two things to find the girls: their location and more strength. She knew how to hit both birds with one stone, but the interaction leading up to it would not be pleasant.

In their winding history, they had offended each other countless times and even left one another for dead. But at the end of the day, he was one of the few people she could go to for help under almost any circumstances. While she knew many people who hated the Committee, he was the only one who was as dedicated to disrupting their hegemony as she was.

Everyone knew him as the Peddler—names became both lethal and unnecessary in their line of work. He was a slight man and could blend into a sparsely populated room as well as if it were a crowd. He was unremarkable and even a little ugly, which meant people's eyes didn't linger and easily forgot him.

The irony was that Amit wouldn't trust him in most situations but could, on occasion, leave her life in his hands—like now. She ducked into the dingy shop behind which he kept his secretive locale, giving the attendant a short wave and walking straight to the back.

The place was grimy by design, meant to keep away a certain type of person, but patrons like Amit knew that the Peddler's wares were unrivaled.

He didn't greet her when she jammed the door open by force; the lock had been broken ever since she could remember. Instead, he silently kept working on whatever was in his hands, turning it this way and that. His back was hunched over his work, making it impossible for Amit to see what it was.

"Hello," she said. "Can you stop whittling and pay attention to me?"

"What do you want?" the Peddler asked in his usual near-whisper.

She sighed, coming closer to the table he was sitting at, pulling out a chair, and saying, "I doubt you want the details, but I need to find someone and am willing to stake my life for it. Unfortunately, I am also nearer death than I prefer to be, something I am hoping you can remedy."

"Someone you are willing to give your life for?" This gave him pause, then he laughed and said, "It must not mean much with how little you value yours."

Amit understood why he would think so, but it exasperated her anyway. Pushing her hair back with one hand, she snapped, "Can you take me seriously for once?"

"What are you offering?" he asked with a sneer.

She held his gaze and said, "I'll give you anything you want."

* * *

"Do we go in?" Ada asked, toeing the imaginary line that delineated the entrance to the cave.

Rifling through Amit's backpack had given them few insights. It held little other than a map, some money, first aid items, and a signal flare. It shouldn't have been surprising that Amit carried so little on her when she could store nearly everything behind a spell portal—in fact, Ada questioned why she carried these things with her at all. Judging by Cara's expression, she was not in the mood to discuss it.

The girls had been hoping to find a clue about where Amit was. Ada thought the cave was an obvious choice, but Cara disagreed.

"What are we going to do in a cave? We don't even know if she's in there," she said sharply.

Ada kept a straight face, trying not to let her frustration get the best of her, and said slowly, "When you were scrying, did the trail go somewhere else?" Cara frowned and remained silent for a moment. "Well?" her sister pressed.

"The trail ended here," she muttered.

"What?"

"There is no trail. The trail ended here," Cara repeated, emphasizing each word.

Ada realized it was dread underpinning her sister's anger. Fear. It had crept into her mind, too. A terrible thought popped into her mind: *what if Amit wasn't in the world of the living?*

"What does that mean?" she asked.

"It means something is blocking my scrying spell," Cara said as she looked deep into the depths of Mount Hermon. "I think it's the mountain."

At this point in her life, Ada would believe anything, but she still had to ask, "The mountain? Can mountains do that?"

Cara let out a deep sigh, rubbing her eyes hard with the heels of her hand, leaving them seeing stars. "Mom once told me that natural formations like mountains, rivers, and forests can have their own effects on casting," she said. "Mount Hermon has also historically been associated with magic, so I wouldn't be surprised if magic is distorted in its vicinity."

"I don't have a good feeling about this, Cara," Ada told her.

They stared at each other for a moment.

"You don't think we should go in?" Cara asked.

Ada knew her sister well enough to know that she was

looking for an excuse not to, but Cara didn't want to be the one to make the decision. "I think we should go in," she replied honestly. "But I don't have a good feeling about this. What precautions can we take?"

Now she was speaking Cara's language. "We should definitely tether ourselves to something outside the cave and cast a stealth charm."

"But we want Amit to find us," Ada protested.

"Amit and no one else."

Their eyes met.

Seeing Cara so serious made Ada's mouth dry.

She asked, "Do you think there's other people inside the cave?"

"We have no way of knowing."

Ada said what they were both thinking out loud, "We may be walking into a trap."

Cara wanted to say something reassuring, but nothing came to mind. Instead, she said, "We don't have many choices."

There was nothing left to add. They set up the spell circle faster than ever, able to anticipate each other's movements after months of training. By the time they were done, their earlier prickliness was forgotten. Standing in front of the gaping chasm, they could see up to a hundred feet of dirt path flanked by jagged rock walls. The entrance was wide enough for four people to stand shoulder to shoulder, but there was no telling if the walls narrowed further along. The light only reached a few steps in. The rest was pitch black.

Ada swallowed, then asked, "What about flashlights?"

Cara snapped her fingers; she knew they were forgetting something. "I'll get a couple from storage."

Now armed with flashlights, extra batteries, a tether to the outside tied to Cara's wrist, and stealth spells, there was no more delaying the inevitable.

"You can hold my hand if you want," Ada offered.

Cara frowned, asking, "Do you want me to hold your hand?"

"No."

"Me neither."

They both let out humorless laughs, diffusing some of the tension, then took their first step in.

The inside of the cave was unremarkable—that was Cara's impression ten minutes in. Natural light had puttered out, and they could barely see a few steps in front of them with their flashlights, but she wasn't too on edge. So far, they hadn't heard anything except for their own footsteps and had yet to see anything other than rock.

She attempted scrying repeatedly within that time, but the interference remained. Cara could sense it acting upon her magic more clearly now that they were inside.

When she spoke to Amit in Damascus, she said she ended up in Nigeria after they got separated. She had linked up with one of her friends, who told her about Mistlander sightings across Africa and Asia. They had originally been clustered around the Middle East, especially the countries surrounding Mount Hermon, but then became sparse. His theory was that someone had used ancient knowledge carved into one of Mount Hermon's temples to open the rift to the Mistlands. Amit wanted to go down and investigate.

The logic checked out for Cara, and nothing during their conversation stood out to her as odd or uncharacteristic, but she couldn't help but notice Ada was ill at ease, and it had started to affect her, too. She knew that as soon as they were reunited with Amit, their worries would melt away, so she kept trying to scry despite multiple failed attempts. From her perspective, walking through Mount Hermon was just as scary as walking through a dark hallway. Enough to make the back of her neck prickle but wholly manageable.

Ada couldn't say the same. She admitted to being easier to startle than her other siblings, always embarrassingly susceptible to jump scares in movies or from those hiding behind corners. This felt different.

Not only did she get the sense they were being watched, something about their current reality felt completely off. She had the nagging sense that their surroundings were being manipulated, blocked off, tampered with—like the rules of nature were bent around and inside Mount Hermon.

She had shed the extra layers of clothes Sara had gifted her, putting them away in the storage space, but now wished she had kept them on. The goosebumps on her skin wouldn't go away.

Instead of a haunted house, where she waited with bated breath for monsters to pop out from every corner, this reminded her of the ghost tour their family took once in Portland. Back then, unaware she was a traveler, she had taken the odd whispers and cold gusts of wind for figments of her overactive imagination or her siblings messing with her, but looking back at it now, she wondered how much of it could have been real spirits.

"This place is creepy," she finally said. The only words they had exchanged so far were *careful* and *watch out for this*, and she was hoping that some idle chatter would disrupt the foreboding atmosphere.

"It's not too bad," Cara said with a shrug. "But I know you've always been afraid of the dark."

"I'm not anymore," Ada grumbled. Not since she got into the habit of sneaking in and out of their house at all hours of the morning around sophomore year in high school. She couldn't be busting out her phone's flashlight, so she had learned to navigate their childhood home in pitch darkness. Yet the image was harder to shake.

"Right." Cara sounded unconvinced. "Well, you can always hold my hand if you need to."

As well intended as Cara's offer was, Ada felt a bit annoyed. She chose not to respond. A wise choice, it would seem. If they had continued speaking, would they have heard the disembodied voice of Amit, muffled but steadily emanating from somewhere to their left?

"Cara," Ada hissed. Her fingers closed around her sister's arm and stopped her in her tracks. "Do you hear that?"

Cara furrowed her brow, concentrating on the sound. "Is that her?" she asked.

"I think so. Who is she talking to?"

Standing closer together, their arms tightly intertwined, they could see each other's expressions clearly in the darkness. Cara frowned and said, "I don't hear anyone else."

"Neither do I," Ada said while releasing her grip on her sister's arm. "Do we follow her voice?"

They had lowered their voices to a hurried whisper. "Let's check if there's openings in the rock. You know, other hallways or turns," Cara said.

"Are we splitting up?"

She recognized the alarm in Ada's voice. "No, let's start with the left. That's where it seems to be coming from."

316

Sure enough, when they approached the left side of the path and shone their lights on the wall, there was not one but several openings that branched out, going deeper into the mountain. As they approached the one closest to them, Ada thought she heard more than just Amit. Her fingers closed again around Cara's lower arm, vicelike when she said, "I don't know if we should go in there."

"What?" Cara asked and narrowed her eyes. "Didn't you just hear Amit's voice? We're so close, Ada."

"I know," she said, grip loosening. "But I think we're far from alone here."

As if to prove her point, a loud sound pierced the air a few meters ahead of them. Their heads snapped in the direction they had just been going, but the darkness was pristine and undisturbed.

"The more reason to come this way and find Amit," Cara hissed, then pulled them both toward where the stone walls fractured. They heard what sounded like a large object landing roughly, followed by a labored breath.

"Which path?" Ada asked. She wasn't happy to be right.

Cara quickly paced up and down about ten feet, shining her flashlight down the three paths to their immediate left. None of them stood out to her in particular, but they didn't have time to explore further and check for more paths ahead, so she picked one at random and pulled Ada's wrist behind her, saying, "Let's hide in here for now."

It was unmistakable now. The first sound had been brief, but it was replaced by a noise halfway between the squelching of a wet mop and something much heavier dragging on the rocky floor. It sounded like it was coming closer, and the girls didn't want to stick around to figure out what it was.

Cara started jogging down the path she had selected, keeping close to the wall on their right. Each time a new trail opened to the side, she shined her torch to check it out. Ada averted her eyes each time, afraid the next would not be empty, and tried not to trip on the tether dragging behind them.

They stopped ten minutes later, the uninterrupted darkness behind and ahead of them starting to give both girls vertigo and nausea. The halo of their flashlights seemed thinner than before, as if the dense blackness were constricting them with its pressure.

They would have chalked it up to their imagination, except they could feel the pressure themselves, weighing on their shoulders and making their legs sluggish. One second, they could feel it so acutely that it was like walking through water. The next, it was subtle enough to make them questioned if they had been overreacting before.

"Cara?" Ada said, then pulled on her sister's arm until they stood shoulder to shoulder. "We should get out of here. Let's go back."

"Wait." Cara held up a finger to her lips.

She could no longer deny the eeriness of the cave— it sent shivers down her spine—, but she had a feeling Amit would be just around the next bend. If only they could go a little further.

"Don't you hear that?"

28

Amit was in disbelief. Even standing in front of Mount Hermon, she held out hope that she wouldn't actually have to go inside. She thought the Peddler was joking when he told her where to find Cara and Ada.

He had said it a few seconds after she downed his regeneration potion when she was bent over, coughing her lungs out. The potion was nicknamed Liquid Fire and not in the fun, alcoholic way. As it traveled through her throat and made its way through her body, it left a trail of burning flesh and organs.

I thought this shit was supposed to help me, she said at the time. Now, she could certainly feel the difference. While she wasn't as good as new, it was like her wound was a month old; she only felt pain after certain movements.

Mount Hermon was the equivalent of the boogeyman for young practitioners. Misbehave and you will get locked away there, mothers and nannies would say. Wild stories about the mountains abounded, almost as many fake as true.

No, her father had told her, practitioners are not the offspring of angels with humans. But yes, a powerful god had been born in the Fertile Crescent from the local peoples' collective consciousness millennia back. A powerful god that could create angels, half-giants, and great floods to wipe out his mistakes.

It wasn't a unique god, though, and its giants weren't to be confused with the titan-like ones of the Highlands. It was created the same way every other god and spirit and ancestor is created, through the pooled will of the people.

This was not something Amit's father had taught her. It was Miriam's mother who had sat the children down one day and answered their questions on gods. An unusually generous moment of hers.

You see, she said, *we live in a magical universe.* Every rock, tree, and animal on this planet was born with a tiny bit of magic inside it. Even non-practitioners, with their useless rituals and foolish traditions, have the power to make their will a reality—and in the Aaron household, willpower and magic were often interchangeable words.

As a Phineas, Amit was taught to equate will to power in a different way. Regardless, she had never forgotten that day. Before then, she knew gods existed but didn't understand their relationship to practitioners. Miriam's mother framed them as a tool for practitioners to call on, powerful allies capable of bending the rules even practitioners had to abide by. The Old Families like theirs often called on them to make deals and trades. Their existence wasn't sacred to them.

To put it in simple terms, gods were born when enough people believed in them. A single non-practitioner had only a trickle of magic power in their being, too little to do anything noticeable with. Granted, sometimes, when they focused enough on a problem or desire, miraculous things could happen and did. However, many went throughout their lives with no knowledge of how to direct this power toward anything useful.

Enter the world's first organized religion, far before when Vedas guided life in the Indus Valley. It is hard to ascertain whether early tribal leaders knew what their periodic prayers and sacrifices could accomplish, but most prehistoric communities managed to form at least some environmental spirits or call on ancestors to aid their survival. It wasn't until relative modernity that the really powerful gods started arising, though, when religions managed to spread across continents either organically or through conquest.

Suddenly, as empires grew, their local gods became fearsome entities with seemingly unlimited power. The more people believed in them, the more powerful they became; the more often they could travel outside their temples and epicenters of worship; the more they could meddle in human life and answer devotees' prayers.

The god of the people that lived around Mount Hermon was no exception. Amit had often heard people warn against equating that god to the current Christian or Catholic ones, which varied greatly and were by no means the same being. In fact, it was the segmentation and fragmenting of the churches into various Lutheran, Methodist, and Presbyterian branches that led to such a decline in the Fertile Crescent god's power. People were worshiping completely different beings described in sacred texts of wildly varied translations and with sometimes polar opposite teachings.

Amit followed the scent of magic to the entrance of a large cave. She couldn't be sure if the magic belonged to Cara or Ada. After all, the whole area was intensely charged with energy. After the local god smote his unruly subordinates and the unfortunate byproducts of their transgressions, he imprisoned the treasonous angels deep in the bowels of Mount Hermon. Therefore, they were known as demons or devils.

It wasn't until centuries later, when the jailer had practically forgotten about his convicts, that the Alliance of Jacob co-opted the space as a convenient high-security prison. The god had made it just short of impossible for anyone confined inside to escape, and it wasn't difficult for some of the most talented practitioners of the time to decipher what spells and sacrifices had to be made to manipulate his seals.

Over the years, Mount Hermon had amassed a colorful collection of gruesome mass murderers, magic researchers who had taken their experiments to callous and grisly extremes, and political prisoners of the Committee. Meant as an eternal jail for immortal beings, time did not seem to move once inside, and captives would find that they, too, did not age. It was truly Hell on Earth.

Amit knew there was only one reason why Cara and Ada would be here. They had been lured by the Mistlanders or whoever was leading them. As time passed, anxiety built up inside her. They could be anywhere. In any state. She had to find them stat.

Miriam's face had been haunting her for days. Not as she had seen her most recently, middle-aged and cleanly put together, but as a teenager in Damascus. As Amit took her first steps into Hell, she was accompanied by her most beloved childhood friend.

* * *

Miriam and Amit didn't have a choice but to become friends.

322

For practitioners, Damascus was just a hop, skip, and jump away from Cairo. Their parents would feast together on Saturday nights, discussing Committee business in cryptic terms and ignoring their children to the best of their abilities.

Amit had three older brothers, and her mother had just welcomed a surprise fifth when Amit turned fifteen, making it a solid twenty-year age gap with the firstborn. Miriam got lost in the crowd of her seven siblings, squarely caught in the middle as the fourth eldest; just like her own mother had been.

When their uncles and aunts joined for more formal festivities, the children gathered would number in the forties. Not to mention when they met with their contemporaries from the other Old Families that established the Second Seat. More often than not, that meant convening with the Jallow, the Qeb, and infrequently with their European counterparts—the Oudinot's appearances were even rarer than the Olgivoch's or Howard's despite France's relative proximity—or Eastern ones, who would only appear when the scale of the event justified it.

The children of the Old Families were predominantly home-schooled until they were old enough to attend specialized lessons at the Committee headquarters in their early adulthood. While it was a perfect funnel into leadership positions in the practitioner world, the limited and often contrived social interaction with other children left many descendants with stunted communication skills and under-developed capacities for empathy when they hit adulthood.

It was no wonder each family stuck to their corner of the world. Their millennia-long association wasn't without rivalry or grudges. The tension could be palpable when too many of their inflated egos filled a room. Everyone was used to being the biggest fish in their pond. It was due to their similarities that they clashed with one another, but it was also within the Old Families that the closest inter-generational alliances were formed.

Amit had remarkably clear eyes from birth. Many things bothered her in childhood that she could not quite explain, and by the time she was six, her parents were sick of her kicking up a fuzz.

The Phineas were snake-like people with an unparalleled gift for shapeshifting running through their veins. In ancient times, they were worshipped as demigods, but over the years, their strategy changed as they chose the shadows over the stage. When the True Aaron banished Nebuchadnezzar, the Phineas offered the strength of their clan in exchange for a place at the Second Seat. The families had been deeply intertwined since then, with some intermarriage but mostly through loyal partnership and friendship.

Once the Phineases tired of Amit, they delegated the task of raising her to various maids and nannies at the main house. The women would struggle to fit a young Amit into her stuffy button-downs, drag her to her lessons—and help hide her worst sins from her parents. But none were kind enough to let her indulge in her transgressive ways.

Everything Amit saw troubled her. She didn't like how her family treated her caregivers or their dismissive attitudes toward practitioners unaffiliated with the Committee. Her parents were unscrupulous when disciplining their children, and her brothers inherited their violent tendencies. Thus, it was a palpable fear that motivated her to conform.

A Phineas like her shouldn't be so interested in cooking.

Instead of hanging around the women, she should go outside and play. She should wear the right clothes. She should read the right books. Cut her hair short. Ignore the beautiful, delicate items that caught her eye. Act like the little boy the world wanted her to be. It was so hard. Yet she bared it.

Miriam was born blind, but the Aarons quickly restored her eyesight through a series of rituals and sacrifices. If they had failed, it's hard to say if she and Amit would have ever met. The Aarons weren't in the habit of advertising their anomalies. Luckily, they weren't in the habit of failing either.

Miriam would later wonder if it was due to her blindness that her mother acted so coldly toward her, perhaps having emotionally detached at the time. It was clear through other people's accounts of her mother's temperament that she was not always as dry and disinterested as she was during Miriam's childhood. No, Layla Aaron used to smile and run around with other children and read trashy English novels her older siblings would make fun of her for. At some point, she had been chosen as the successor to their father, partially due to her outstanding magical abilities but also because of her siblings' various missteps and digressions.

Layla's eldest sibling was embarrassingly caught in a bad deal with a djinn. The second lost her sense of smell first while pillaging an elven treasure, then half her face in a gas explosion in Madrid years later. The third, enthralled with the Hindu framing of manifested will as siddhis to be attained through sadhana, detached from Aaron's materialistic way of life and retired to a last known location near the plains of the Indus River by the border of Sindh and Rajasthan.

Her younger siblings were candidates as well, but the fifth and sixth hardly showed interest in the ongoings of their massive ancestral estate. The seventh, well, Miriam hardly knew anything about her except she was killed by people rebelling against the Committee in what should have been a harmless visit to Timbuktu.

Later, in the comfort of her home on Willow Street, Miriam would let herself feel sorry for her mother, who carried the weight of their world on her shoulders. But as a child, when she wasn't busy pining for her love and attention, she only ever felt resentment.

Amit was two and a half years older than Miriam, which meant she experienced everything first and could warn her friend about what to expect. Of course, the Phineas training was different from the Aaron's, but it was just as hellish. Most of their brothers and sisters chose to internalize their suffering and put on invincible facades, refusing to discuss their pain or fear, pretending nothing fazed them. Always ready for more.

But Miriam was different. She was unconvinced of the Old Families' methods and slowly stopped seeing her pain as a badge of honor. By the time she was an adolescent, she felt passionately that there had to be a better way—a better way to train and a better way to live. A way to minimize suffering instead of maximizing it. A timid teenager, she didn't dare speak back to her elders, but in Amit, she had a captive audience.

* * *

Amit had never been to Mount Hermon before, although she had heard her parents discuss matters concerning the Committee's prisoners at a young age. It was widely known as a labyrinthian space that could twist the natural rules of physics and magic, a testament to the power gods wielded in ancient times.

Wary of entering such a place, she wracked her brain for useful information but only came up with an exchange she once had with Miriam in their early teens. It was a wonder she remembered it at all. Miriam was fascinated by all sorts of obscure topics that blended together in Amit's memories.

Miriam must have been around twelve when a biblical scholar came to stay temporarily at her house. The Committee had given him a grant to study the effects of Mount Hermon's mountain range. This meant they would not only provide funds but access to a trove of spells, information, and other tools unparalleled in the Midlands, as well as their permission and protection. The scholar needed the most sensitive detection spells to reveal veils, sophisticated methods of testing the limits of the space, and safeguards to document his observations without losing his life or mind.

The adults talked loudly about his bravery and persistence, but the man seemed rather cool-headed to Miriam, displaying no sign of his supposed exploits. In a lull of activity, when the room's attention had drifted to another subject, the young girl approached the scholar and asked how he had emerged unscathed when so many of his companions from the excursion were unable to attend the party, institutionalized.

She found the man's answer unsatisfactory at the time, and it proved of very little use to Amit decades later—the day she understood what fear of god meant. The man had tapped his temple, the look in his eye suggesting he may not have left as unmarked as she presumed.

The mountain is a prison of the mind, crafted to contain angels and sinners for eternity. We are no angels, but we are sinners. If you wish to escape its bowels, you must lay down your sins and keep God in your thoughts. Then Hermon won't have the power to confuse or distract you.

Amit hadn't been there, but she imagined Miriam scoffing at this. It was rare to find a religious practitioner—given their awareness of the symbiotic nature of deity-believer relationships, most refused to worship and grant gods more power. Although she wouldn't admit it aloud, Amit could see the appeal of having an ally that seemed larger than life, especially for such a small price.

Mulling this advice in the present day, she took it to mean that the magic acting within Mount Hermon would show her illusions and try to throw her off, but she had to focus on something bigger than herself to make it through.

Unfortunately, the gods she was most familiar with governed things like trickery and secrecy, and she didn't trust any of them to guide her way. Instead, she continued thinking of her childhood with Miriam.

* * *

The girls heard Amit's voice again.

"But who is she talking to?" Ada asked.

Her unease was on a steady upward trend, her hand still gripping Cara by her upper arm. It felt like hundreds of eyes were watching them. The more time they spent in the cave, the more it felt like a trap.

"It's Amit," Cara exclaimed in frustration. That's all they needed to know, in her opinion. "I don't know, maybe she got some backup, someone to show her the way."

328

She forged forward, and Ada was forced to follow, carefully avoiding the tether sliding by her ankle. A few minutes later, they could still hear her voice, but it didn't seem any closer.

"Are you sure we're going the right way?" Ada asked. "What if the acoustics are just really good in here?"

Cara ignored her. Even if scrying didn't work inside the mountain, she could feel herself getting closer to what she was looking for.

Behind her, Ada questioned everything. They saw no break in the darkness other than their flashlights.

Then, Cara stopped so suddenly that her sister almost ran into her. She turned to the left and whispered *this way* in the smallest voice. Ada thought she had imagined it until Cara turned and headed down another unmarked tunnel.

Surprisingly, the blackness ahead became a dimness instead. Ada started to gain confidence in her sister. Then, both flashlights shut off.

Ada almost jumped out of her skin with fright, coming close to dropping the torch altogether. Cara flinched, too, pressing her back against the wall and reaching out to grasp her sister's hand. Linked, they inched forward toward the light.

Neither noticed, but Amit's voice had stopped.

When the path veered steeply to the right, they stuck close to the corner, gathering their courage to peek around it. Cara did so first. To her relief, the place was empty save for a couple of lit candles. It was a small room with an intricately painted wall. She crossed toward it in a few steps and said, "Look at this mural."

"Someone must have lit these candles," Ada said with a shiver.

"How old do you think this is?" Cara asked a she got a closer look. "Could this be the Nebucha-whatever guy Amit said caused the Great Eclipse?"

The mural did seem to portray a Mistlander invasion. A large dark hole represented a rift in the veil between the Midlands and the Mistlands. Countless faceless figures emerged from it, spilling across the landscape and terrorizing villages, setting houses on fire, battling with practitioners. Some lay presumably dead, while others filed into a cave in a mountain remarkably like the one Cara and Ada had walked through earlier, emerging with other mysterious figures.

"Is that Mount Hermon?" Ada asked. She was starting to tremble. Everything felt so horribly wrong. "This is ominous."

Cara agreed. Her curiosity had diverted her attention for a moment, but her sister's tone reminded her where they were. She straightened, saying, "Let's get out of here."

When they turned to head back to the main tunnel, they found their path blocked by shadowy figures.

"I didn't expect this all to happen so quickly," one said.

29

For Amit, the hallucinations started just a few minutes into the cave. Familiar voices at first, then figures out of the corner of her eye. Soon, her father stood in front of her with a belt in hand. He was attuned to some non-practitioner tendencies, too. Her family was savvy that way, one of the few Old Families that regularly ventured outside of the Committee's system of veils.

Many Committee-affiliated practitioners found the unveiled Midlands low brow, not worth their attention or energy. It was a sheltered view, ignorant of the delicate balancing act the Committee's intelligence and external commerce arms had to manage with a foot in each world—for example, to procure the non-magical goods practitioners consumed en masse. Most of all, it glossed over approximately a third of the practitioner population that resided in unveiled areas.

The Phineas, who led the intelligence branch of the Committee, easily slid in and out of these worlds despite their stature. They were the first practitioners to buy cars, televisions, motorboats, the kind of items more conservative practitioners would look down upon as silly trinkets, far less efficient than any spell. A few years later, the same items could be found in the house of every Committee official, and later still, they trickled down to other ranks of society.

Even so, Amit's parents maintained some habits other practitioners could only consider eccentricities, like their collection of gunpowder weapons and love of the silver screen. They had given up on finding others to share their interests with—for most practitioners balked at non-practitioner social norms, had a hard time following the plots, and would be bored halfway through—so they conditioned their children to enjoy their kind of entertainment from a young age.

Amit wasn't sure why she was lingering on one of the few happy memories she had as a child—soundly tucked between her brother and mother watching old French films—while the specters of her nuclear family hurled abuse at her. It had been some time since they last had the pleasure of spitting and cursing at her, digging up the most demeaning insults at their disposal and holding her gaze so that she knew they meant them.

She had grown past this already and didn't let them slow her down. She had to find Miriam's girls. But as she pushed through, their faces and bodies morphed, showing off her family's signature ability. Some donned the appearance of her beloved nannies, her teachers, even of the Aarons.

Amit did her best to ignore them, but then, a young Miriam was standing in front of her. She looked startlingly like she did the day Amit broke into her house at the earliest hours of dawn to say goodbye when things had truly become unbearable. She was saying things Amit hoped the real Miriam never had the misfortune of hearing. This did bring a lump to her throat, but it was neither new nor unusual.

Images like these haunted her dreams for years. She kept moving.

To distract herself—or better put, to improve her focus—she thought of what Cara and Ada must have been like as children. The girls had shown her pictures of Gage in his sports uniform and Meena at the pool, both of whom she had briefly met during the night she spent in Hope Springs, and Amit imagined the family gathered together.

It had been immediately apparent to her that Meena didn't carry Aaron blood, but she refrained from raising the topic. Personally, Amit had never understood the purpose of elevating blood ties and inherited traits other than to further the sense of tribalism and segregation between humans. Likely due to her own rejection by and rupture with her relatives, she spent years mulling over the significance of such relations and questioning where these loyalties came from.

Was it a survival instinct? Grasping for the allies most readily available when faced with an uncertain world? Or were humans just prone to caring for and being loyal to those they were forced to be in close proximity with for years?

Either way, Amit considered worship of the nuclear family as societal programming and was proud to consider herself deprogrammed. Throughout the years, she had formed stronger and more long-lasting bonds with people with far different genetic material than hers compared to the ones with her Phineas brothers. Yet, she could imagine a family like Miriam and Richard's being different.

She didn't go so far as to think most families were as flimsily bound together as hers. Nucleic acids proved remarkably unreliable predictors of interpersonal relationships countless times throughout history. There had to be more than just that—a true concern for each other's well-being at a minimum—to keep people together. And sometimes even that wasn't enough. She thought of Miriam, agonizing over the absence of her eldest two.

Then, like a drunk suddenly sobering, Amit was jolted out of her reverie by an unmistakable proximity to death. To a practitioner, walking into Mount Hermon was like walking into a fog of white noise. It was a fuzzy, staticky environment where you couldn't feel magic energy even two feet in front of you. Amit had already resigned herself to this reality when the air rippled palpably, and she felt a bolt of magic about to hit her square on the chest.

With a split second to react, she slid her feet forward and called upon the quickest shield she knew how to cast, her back scraping against the ground as the attack whizzed overhead. Amit, far from a novice dueler, started moving automatically.

A quick propulsion spell got her back up on her feet within seconds, and she released a barrage of electric bullets to pinpoint where her enemy was attacking from. Her shield held against a second attack, but it made her painfully aware of her body's subpar condition. She wasn't as young as she used to be, and the barely healed wound on her abdomen threatened to reopen if jostled enough.

Thankfully, her strategy worked, and two Mistlanders were soon revealed to be casting from the shadows of nearby tunnels. Amit might have captured them alive under other circumstances, but she didn't have the energy to spare. Instead, she used one of her favorite, if rarely deployed, spells, completely frying their minds until they dropped to the ground.

"That's a sign I'm on the right track," she muttered to herself.

Taking advantage of the temporary lucidity the adrenaline had granted, she crouched down to the ground and channeled all of her will into a single question, begging it not to backfire. It took more time and much more energy than usual, but eventually, she felt the semblance of an answer. *Left.*

Thinking of the number of identical tunnels she had passed so far, she pressed for more specificity. After a minute of silence, she decided to conserve the rest of her power to get the girls out of there and approached the left wall to investigate.

The compactly packed ground left no room for footprints, however, and no markings in the cave indicated the presence of inexperienced practitioners. Amit couldn't help but consider the hellish destinations the wrong path could lead to, the possibility of getting trapped forever in the labyrinthian prison, and the disastrous consequences Cara and Ada could face because of her mistake.

She was unable to decide between several indistinguishable tunnels that flanked her on the left, walking back and forth between them to find any discernable differences. She lingered by their entrances, fully knowing Mistlander reinforcements could be on their way.

Amit felt her anxiety growing each second she delayed her decision, an infuriated voice inside her head demanding she make a choice. But her mind couldn't stop cycling through the endless ways everything could go wrong, seemingly tapping into the parallel timelines where demons devoured her soul and all three women rotted within Mount Hermon forever.

The more she pressed herself to go, the harder it seemed to be. The soles of her feet felt like they were filled with lead. From one moment to the next, her body started to go numb. She tried lifting her hands to examine them but failed to move.

Had the Mistlanders cast a spell to keep her immobile?

Or was this the mountain feeding on her weakness?

* * *

For the first time since entering the cave, Cara and Ada were not alone. Two hooded figures stood ahead, speaking in hushed tones.

This is a bit cliché, Ada thought, but the predictability didn't stop her heart from picking up speed.

The girls had dropped into a crouch, sticking close to the shadow-draped wall. These people did not seem like allies. It was hard to make out full sentences, but they were speaking English and loud enough for the girls to catch bits and pieces. The taller of the two was complaining about something they had dealt with. The shorter one referred to Mount Hermon.

Cara and Ada had almost gotten their nerves under control, soothed by the fact that neither shadowy character was noticing or pointing out their presence, until one of the voices grew loud enough for them to hear their words clearly.

"I didn't expect this all to happen so quickly. I guess it's true what he said. You should never underestimate an Aaron."

Then, they both pointedly turned towards them, heads angled downwards toward where they were crouching.

The sisters jolted up in terror.

"Run," Ada said and pushed Cara forward.

They darted in the direction they came from, toward the main tunnel, but a group of Mistlanders blocked their way. Cara turned to assess the situation. They were flanked from behind by two men with cartoonish evil grins. Their magic created menacing auras around them. *Slash*. They turned to find that their tether had been cut. Ada's voice still rang in Cara's ears—*run*.

"Come on!" she called out as she reached for Ada's hand. Her fingers slipped on the fabric of her sister's long-sleeved shirt.

Instead, when Cara dipped to the left of the practitioners, Ada bounded to the right to confuse them.

Cara cast a spell meant to stun their assailants, but they easily deflected it. Ada zapped the men herself and successfully caught one of them off guard, but it only took a minute for him to recover. Soon, a tether wrapped itself around Ada's arm.

Cara, who was ahead, ran deeper into the mountain. She thought her sister was at her heels and was planning to veer into a random tunnel to lose their pursuers. When she turned and realized that Ada was nowhere in sight, her breath caught in her throat.

Hoping it was just the darkness that separated them, she whispered, "Ada?"

* * *

One of the practitioners had cast an invisible vice that was now biting into Ada's upper right arm. The pain was searing—she could practically feel her skin bruising—and the grip was still tightening.

It was hard to fight her initial instinct to pry the force away; her attempts would be useless after all. Instead, she concentrated on the practitioner who faced her. He had come close enough to touch. He looked like he could be any other person in the parking lot of the mall.

Ada had never been more terrified of another human being. Her whole body was shaking. Her teeth were chattering. Not only was Cara gone, the other man was hot on her heels—Ada saw him take off after her. No one had her back.

Things had been going downhill from the moment that giant had arrived in Hope Springs. Ada's nerves were so frayed at this point that she felt exhausted and numb. When their attackers first appeared, her fear had been blinding, but somewhere along the way, a new feeling had blossomed, just as overwhelming and disorienting as the first. Anger.

Maybe it was the gang of Mistlanders that watched them from a distance, conveying faceless disinterest. They had ruined her life. They had endangered her family. And for what?

Does it matter? she thought. This nameless evil had cracked her world open like an egg and dropped it into a sizzling frying pan. Before, the panic had made her surrounding fade and blur, but the anger brought everything into sharp focus.

She gnashed her teeth and snarled, "Why can't you just leave us alone?"

White hot rage overpowered her senses. Her core started to warm. It was a familiar sensation, that of a spell activating her magic, but she hadn't recited any incantations. Afraid her power was shooting off erratically—the way her mother always warned it would if she didn't practice meditation enough—Ada immediately closed her eyes and focused on her center.

Rather than try to contain it, she redirected it. In her mind's eye, she envisioned her captor collapsed. His magic dispersed. Her arm free. No pursuit. When she opened her eyes, her will was done, but it was a rude awakening to see half a dozen Mistlanders approaching his prone body.

Ada attempted to redirect her magic to them, but she was walking backward and couldn't see the bumpy path. A stone caught her heel, and she stumbled back, losing focus and almost toppling to the floor. Ironically, a lifetime of clumsiness made her a pro at catching herself; she quickly regained her balance and turned to sprint down the path Cara had taken.

Now separated, she couldn't help but imagine the worst-case scenario. Her sister was facing the other practitioner alone. Reuniting was the priority.

As she ran into the pitch darkness, Ada realized she no longer had a flashlight. She didn't want to run into a wall, but she could hear the Mistlanders not far behind her. Desperate, she figured creating a little magic light couldn't be that difficult. Only a small glow.

* * *

Cara started rushing back before pausing. She didn't want Ada to be on her own, but she would be no use to her by walking into enemy hands. She couldn't just run in there without a plan.

She took a good look at the tunnel in front of her, took a deep breath, then turned off her flashlight and started inching slowly in her sister's direction. Her main advantage was the element of surprise. It was only a few minutes later that a torch illuminated the path ahead of her. A glass-half-empty person by nature, Cara trusted this was one of their pursuers and wracked her brains for useful spells.

When the halo of his flashlight reached the ground ahead of her, she aimed carefully for his head and fired what could only be described as an explosive. While he took a moment to deflect it, she had already deployed a second spell to bind his feet and a third for the ground to open up and bury him. The uneven floor rippled, but even as he fell, she became acutely aware of a burst of power emanating from his body. He was trying to catch himself before getting swallowed.

Unsure of how to deal with it, Cara tried pushing him down into the chasm that had opened through brute force. Everything slowed down for a moment as the man struggled against the push of her magic. The force of the propulsion he had cast meant he was stuck as two invisible walls closed in. As soon as his spell stopped, he dropped momentarily and cast an attack as he did. Cara felt it coming at her like a bullet and quickly raised a shield to defend herself.

The spell she had been holding against him until then deactivated, and he straightened, casting one attack after another. Cara found herself faltering under the sustained barrage. The force of the hits rocked her back, but she dug her heels in.

Her hands were shaking, and no matter how hard she tried to remember the last few lessons with Amit, her mind was drawing a blank. To think it had only been a few days since they sat at Sethu's kitchen table.

After an hour of wandering through Mount Hermon's twisted bowels, even Kitara felt like a distant dream. The desperation she was feeling now was reminiscent of when she crawled through the dunes, feeling the sun sucking her energy dry. Once again, she was stuck in the type of situation she disliked most: chaotic and ambiguous.

Cara steadied her breath, quieting the voice in her head. She would have to rely on her instincts instead.

* * *

Casting complex magic usually requires drawing detailed spell circles, and the elements needed range from several to a record-breaking ten-thousand and forty-three. Together, they act as checks and balances to avoid the catastrophes caused by rampant energy, but gathering them could prove impossible under time constraints or the threat of death.

On the other hand, spoken incantations have little nuance and can't be relied on during duels or battles, so practitioners formulated tricks to facilitate complex casting while bypassing these issues.

That's why after reviewing the basics of spell circles, which Miriam had taught Cara and Ada years ago, Amit pivoted their lessons to more practical applications, explaining that when there's no time to gather the elements or draw a circle, complex magic doesn't become impossible, just more difficult. It requires absolute focus regardless of surrounding distractions.

Cara and Ada had been casting mentally since infancy. At first, it was accidental, then erratic, and after a few years of Sunday school with their mother, it became deliberate and increasingly rare. Slowly, practice became more like a chore, a task to cross off of their weekly to-do list.

The older and busier they got, the harder it was to find time to review the meaning of flowers and herbs, memorize common symbols and the correct order of drawing them in, remember the effects of each phase of the moon.

Magic became like a second language they didn't practice often enough, an odd part of heritage passed down on their secretive maternal side of the family. Cara felt she would have done things differently if she knew the types of situations that would arise in the future—if she had known that she would have to rely on magic to survive.

She closed her eyes and slowed down her breath. The blood rushing past her ears was deafening. Turning her focus inwards, she could feel how disorganized the magical energy in her body was acting, only partially filtering into her shield.

Concentrating on her pulse, she envisioned the energy pooling together and pumping throughout her body like blood, following the path of her veins. Suddenly, she could sense exactly where her opponent stood, merely feet away. Not only was she more aware of her own power, but she could see the flow of magic in his body and how it would take shape before he launched each of his attacks.

Cara felt more like herself. In control. Organized. Efficient.

Even her adversary noticed when her shield strengthened; it was no longer faltering under his continued blows. Cara once again wracked her brain for their most recent lessons with Amit. She had memorized the three minimum elements needed to cast without a spell circle—an elemental shortcut, an action word, and a directive—but she had no idea what would happen when she just threw a random combination together.

Under normal circumstances, Cara would have never done something so reckless, but she had no other choice. Anything could have happened to Ada by then. What if she was their only hope of seeing the outside world?

Steeling herself, she muttered what she hoped was an aggressive offensive incantation and pooled her power behind it. Through squinted eyes, she saw the man launch backward, slamming against the cave wall and slouching to the ground. For a few moments, she remained still, shield erect, taking calming breaths. Without warning, a tear rolled down her cheek, stinging her badly sunburned skin.

Just as she was about to move, the man let out a groan.

He's alive, she thought with mixed feelings. *Please stay down.*

Before she could do anything about it, another light peeked over the edge of the corridor, and she braced herself for the other practitioner or Mistlanders to appear. Instead, the light only intensified, growing brighter and brighter until it was blinding—as if the sun itself had descended into Hell to find them.

A mit's body was paralyzed, decidedly due to Mount Hermon's ability to maximize suffering for all those who entered. That her paralyzing anxiety of making the wrong choice led to this was not lost on her. It seemed she had already made the worst choice of all.

Not only was she struggling to move so much as a finger, her eyes could only see as far as her peripheral vision. She marveled at the fact that no foes had found her in this vulnerable state. If they weren't here, they had to be with Cara and Ada, and as the minutes ticked by, they had more opportunities to hurt them.

Oh, Miriam, Amit lamented. *You should have never let them out of your sight.*

Inside her head, Miriam always looked fourteen, almost fifteen—her birthday was two months away. This was the face Amit expected when she showed up on Willow Street at her friend's request a couple of months ago—the last face she had seen before leaving the Phineas name behind—but that was not the case.

The grown Miriam looked even more like Layla Aaron than the fourteen-year-old version did, not that Amit was about to bring up Layla unprompted. Miriam's message had been brief, but she emphasized that she had cut ties with her family and was living off the grid.

Despite knowing this, Amit was still surprised by the intricacy of their concealment. As far as the Committee knew, there were no practitioners in Hope Springs. She couldn't help but wonder what had driven Miriam to such lengths. Amit had imagined how Miriam's life had turned out many times, but she had never imagined it like this.

Was it because of her daughters' extraordinary magical abilities? No, she seemed to have cut ties with her family much earlier than that. Plus, Amit figured, wasn't it a given that Miriam's children would be extraordinary? If Cara and Ada had received the training she and Miriam had...The girls would surely not be the people they were today.

As practitioners, they would be stronger, but at what cost? Amit let her thoughts trail to darker, rarely frequented places. Reminding herself of her upbringing, she allowed the pent-up self-hatred that was always stewing under the surface, waiting for the right moment to break through and emerge.

You call yourself a Phineas? A real Phineas would never look as pathetic as you do now. How difficult can it be to conquer a mere illusion? To think we wasted so much time and money on you. Aren't you ashamed? Time to prove how worthless you are again? Move. Move! How dare you disobey me? Move!

The voice was her father's.

* * *

Being unable to control her strength was nothing new to Ada. She was taller than every other girl in her grade since kindergarten and big-boned at that. Even so, she never expected the theme to extend to her magical abilities, as well.

What had meant to be a light only strong enough to illuminate her way turned into a floodlight worthy of a stadium. While she had initially been taken aback, it unexpectedly worked out in her favor. The Mistlanders seemed blinded, a fact she ascertained after managing to dim the brightness hitting her face.

Ada took the opportunity to chase after Cara and the practitioner who followed her, hoping she could stun the latter long enough to make a run for it in the other direction. Thankfully, they hadn't gone far, but the scene was different from what Ada had imagined. Cara was standing, unharmed, a few feet from the unconscious practitioner.

"Cara," she shouted and bent the light so her sister could see beyond it.

Cara was in tears, and the relief upon seeing Ada made the knot in her throat grow. They hugged, but just for a second. "He won't stay down long," she said, gesturing in the man's direction.

"Let's go," Ada said with a nod.

Running back the way they had come, the path seemed steeper and longer than before. A few minutes in, they were both starting to breathe heavily, and beads of sweat formed on their foreheads.

"Shouldn't we have encountered the Mistlanders by now?" Cara asked.

"Yeah," Ada panted. "This seems like a completely different road than before."

They stopped and stared at each other.

"There's no way we're going down the wrong path, is there?" Cara asked. She didn't believe it to be the case. All the other tunnels were noticeably narrower than this one.

Ada frowned. She didn't think so either. Or did she? She thought of the road she'd come through and said, "It was definitely not this steep."

Cara gnawed on her chapped bottom lip, a metallic taste filling her mouth when she drew blood. "I think we should keep going up. I mean, up is a good sign, isn't it?" she said hopefully.

Ada couldn't explain why, but she wasn't convinced. Even so, she nodded, saying, "Let's keep going." Cara didn't move. "Hey, let's go," Ada repeated.

When her sister turned, she looked as confused as Ada felt. "Is that Amit?" she asked.

Indeed, now that she could concentrate, Ada could also hear Amit's voice, but she couldn't tell if it was coming from behind or in front of them. At this point, Ada was hesitant to keep chasing after a disembodied voice. "Do you think that someone could be playing tricks on us?"

Cara's eyes were haunted when she replied, "So we just leave her?"

"We don't know that she's back there," Ada said. After a moment of silence, she asked, "Do you want to go back?"

Cara remained still and quiet.

"Fine, what about this," her sister said with a sigh. She gestured in the direction they were headed. "You keep walking that way for five minutes. I will walk back the way we came for five minutes, and we will meet back here in exactly ten minutes. If we're going the right way, you should see the Mistlanders. I will make sure there was no other possible path we could have gone down."

"I don't think we should split up," Cara said uneasily.

"What do I do if I meet the Mistlanders? And what if that practitioner woke up already?"

Ada held her sister's hand; it settled in hers like a foreign object.

"Try to make a light like this. It will blind them for long enough to run back," she said to more silence. "It would be the worst if we walked for an hour in the wrong direction. It's worth taking at least five minutes to check."

Cara nodded. Ada let go of her hand. They stepped away from each other.

* * *

When light shone from deep inside the tunnels, Amit gave one last push to break her trance. As unhealthy as her family's method of overcoming weakness was, it was still scarily effective to this day.

Once she allowed her mind to revert to the past, shattering the paralysis became relatively simple. Perhaps when it came to her childhood scars, the sway they held deep in her subconscious was much stronger than even Mount Hermon could hope to achieve. Was this her twisted version of God?

Amit had no time to ponder such questions as she sprinted down the tunnel. There, she found half a dozen Mistlanders following the now-receding luminescence. She cast a barrier ahead of them, blocking their path and trapping them with her. The Mistlanders didn't notice until they crashed into it with full force.

They recovered from the pile-up quickly, spinning to zero in on their new target. Amit put up another shield to defend herself, sharp attacks ricocheting and chipping off pieces of

348

the stone walls surrounding them.

Despite the state of her body, she was confident she could stave off this many opponents—she'd faced worse. Even so, it required laser focus. Rather than waste her energy on feeble jabs, she focused on more complex casting, high-damage spells that could take out one or two opponents at a time.

It was satisfying to see the Mistlanders buckle, but by the time the third did, the exhaustion was catching up to her. She felt her shirt sticking to her wound and hoped it was due to sweat rather than blood, but the mismatched battle didn't give her a second to check.

Just as she was considering pooling her remaining power into a single, explosive attack—one that would have likely incapacitated her as collateral—something across the barrier distracted the Mistlanders, working them into a frenzy.

Amit looked past them; Cara was on the other side. She cursed as her vision began to flicker. Why now, when maintaining the barrier was more important than ever? Suddenly, the room tilted on its axis, and she was closer to the ground than ever.

She was on her knees, her eyes barely making out shapes. Something lunged toward her, a Mistlander. The others must have gone for Cara. Her discombobulated mind cycled through thoughts. The shields. Cara. Ada. Miriam.

The voice of her father wormed its way in through her ears once more. *Is this really all you can do? Pathetic.*

Amit concentrated on the sharp rock biting into her knee, the pain of the pebbles searing into her skin. It had been a long time since her body had felt so foreign. Only seconds had passed; she could still save Cara, that blur of brown hair just feet away.

Before she could carry out her kamikaze attack, a burst of energy blew through the room, knocking her on her back. Her ears were ringing.

Have you reached your limit, Amit? Amit? Amit. Amit!

"Amit!" Hands collided with her shoulders. Her head came to rest on a soft body. "Amit, what's wrong? You're bleeding! Are you okay?"

"Cara." The voice that came out of her mouth was raspy, and weak, like she hadn't used it in weeks.

"Oh no," Cara said. She sounded like she was on the verge of tears.

Amit was holding on to consciousness with all her strength. The face of a fourteen-year-old Miriam behind her eyelids blended with Cara's face in front of her. They did look alike.

Please, someone pleaded, *you have to be okay.*

She felt the words seeping into her skin. No, not words— bright golden energy. Magic. As it filtered into her blood, her organs, the pain started receding. Slowly, she was getting her strength back.

Amit's hands tightened around Cara's forearms. Her eyelids fluttered open.

"It's alright," she tried to say. Her words were slurred but intelligible. "I'm going to be alright."

Cara helped her sit up and then stand. She looked flustered, but when Amit took stock of the situation, she found all six Mistlanders knocked clean out.

Cara started rambling, as she always did in stressful situations, "Ada went to check that we were on the right path. The road was really steep and confusing. We split up and agreed to meet up in ten minutes. Have ten minutes already passed? I have to go get her!"

350

Amit grabbed her arm before she could turn away, saying, "Wait." She closed her eyes and took a deep breath. When she opened them, she looked more alert. "I'll go," she said. "Mount Hermon is like a sentient labyrinth. It will do all it can to trap you inside."

Goosebumps rose on Cara's arms. Her suspicions were confirmed.

"But you're hurt," she protested. "You almost passed out."

"I'm fine," Amit assured her. "Whatever you were doing a second ago really helped me. Do you think you can do it again?"

Cara was confused when she asked, "What was I doing?" *Crying like an idiot?* she thought, embarrassed.

"Cara," Amit said with a frown. "I felt you share some of your magic with me. The reason I collapsed is because I've overexerted myself and don't have energy left, but if you can give me some of yours…"

"Oh, well, yeah. Of course," Cara said, then stared at their feet. "H-how do I do that again?"

"Here."

Amit grabbed both her hands, wrapping her fingers around her wrists. The truth was, she had never heard of a practitioner transferring their magical energy to another so easily, but she only needed a little more power to get them out of there. If Cara had done it once, she could do it again.

"Control your magic," she instructed. "Close your eyes, concentrate on your breathing, visualize the flow of energy."

Just like that, familiar golden bursts of energy started shooting from Cara's fingertips and into Amit's wrists. The effect was immediate. Amit's jelly-like knees solidified, and her headache subsided. She was starting to feel like a human being again. She directed some of the magic toward her injury, hoping traces of the healing spell still lingered. After a minute, Amit felt as strong as when she first entered the cave—not perfect, but good enough.

She let go of Cara's hands before saying, "This will have to do."

Cara was torn; she wanted to give her more power, but Ada was waiting. Seeing that some of the color had returned to Amit's cheeks, she nodded and said, "Ada shouldn't be too far."

"You go back and wait for us outside," Amit told her, cutting her off with a sharp glare before she could protest. "There's no such thing as safe inside this mountain, Cara. I don't want to come back with Ada to find you have been whisked away by one of its tricks, okay?"

"Alright," Cara reluctantly agreed. "Be quick."

* * *

Two-hundred and fifty-two. Two-hundred and fifty-three. Two-hundred and fifty-four. Two-hundred and fifty-five. Ada counted silently in her mind, tracking the three hundred seconds that meant five minutes had passed and she was due to turn back. She had decided on this method in the absence of a watch and found it to be quite effective.

That being said, with forty seconds to go, she was starting to feel like she might as well turn back now. No other path had rivaled the one she and Cara had been following. Figuring her beam of light was an effective beacon for her enemies, she had dimmed it to a weaker glimmer.

Now, alone in the semi-darkness, the craggy tunnels

seemed creepier than ever. Not only could Mistlanders and evil practitioners be waiting for her past every corner, but other sinister creatures could be lurking just beyond the shadows. She shuddered to think about it.

Two-hundred and seventy-seven. Unfortunately, she did have an obsessive side to her, albeit in a different shape and form than her sister's. Once she started counting to three hundred, it was hard to stop just short.

Plus, they had heard Amit's voice. It was worth twenty more seconds of aimlessly wandering to make sure she wasn't somewhere behind them.

The way had leveled off not long after Ada turned back, strangely losing its previous steepness. There had been no signs of life since passing the unconscious practitioner Cara had dealt with about three minutes in. *Two-hundred and eighty-five.*

Prone to speaking to herself out loud, Ada didn't even notice when she started muttering under her breath. At first it took great mental dexterity to not lose track of her inner timer, but it became easier the longer she kept it up. Now, she could afford to get lightly distracted.

"It doesn't seem like anyone has been down here in a while," she mumbled. *Two-hundred and ninety.* "Oh?" *Two-hundred and ninety-two.* Ada leaned down to get a closer look at the ground. "Are these footprints?" *Two-hundred and ninety-four.* "Could they be Amit's?"

She heard a quiet scuffle a few feet ahead of her and froze, debating if she should make her presence known. *Two-hundred and ninety-six.* Her heart was pounding hard. She turned her light off completely. *Two-hundred and ninety-seven.*

Even if it was Amit…*Two-hundred and ninety-eight.* It would be better if she went to get Cara first. *Two-hundred and ninety-nine.*

Then, a man's voice came from beyond the shadows, "Three hundred."

The surprise was enough to knock Ada backward. Not about to stand around and wait for this mind reader to appear, she turned on her heel and sprinted back to Cara. To her dismay, she could hear heavy footsteps following closely behind.

"Cara!" she shouted and hoped her sister was close enough to hear her.

"Ada!" someone called back. Not Cara, but…

"Amit?" Ada shrieked, the relief only displacing some of her fear. "Come on, there's someone behind me." She grabbed Amit's arms and pulled her forward.

Amit dug her heels into the ground. "Ada. Ada, stop," she said calmly.

"We have to go," Ada gasped. "Let's find Cara and get out of here."

Their pursuers were so close, the ground around them was vibrating.

"Cara is waiting for you at the entrance of the cave," Amit said as she gripped her shoulders. "Go find her. I'll hold them off."

"What? No! How can I leave you here alone?"

When Ada looked back, three figures had appeared at the edge of the tunnel, each bigger than the last. In the dim light, their shadows stretched and twisted into horned silhouettes.

"Ada, listen to me," Amit said. She had put up a barrier by now and was waiting for them to tire themselves out clashing with it. "They won't be able to leave Mount Hermon, so all you have to do is get outside."

"All *we* have to do," Ada corrected. "We'll be waiting for you. We won't leave without you. You have to come."

"I will," Amit said. "Now go."

In near darkness, Ada hadn't seen her blood-soaked side. If she had, perhaps she would have argued more forcefully. Tired, confused, anxious, and afraid; instead, she went up the way Amit had come.

To Amit, this was a relief. The creatures they faced were no mere Mistlanders—they were the very prisoners Mount Hermon was tasked with confining. They had no doubt taken advantage of their pause to size up their opponents.

Cara had managed to staunch the bleeding and postpone the inevitable, but Amit was under no illusion of guaranteed victory. Then, a voice sounded so close by that she snapped her head to the side to ensure there was no one standing behind her.

What a wretched fate you march so willingly toward.

Before she could linger on the words, the dwellers of Hermon launched their attack. Not only was their individual strength formidable but their blows were synchronized. This was not the first time they had fought together, and they knew how to complement each other's weaknesses. They were in a different league than the Mistlanders.

Again, it felt like someone spoke into her ear, *And if I could offer you a chance to escape, a helping hand if you will...*

Amit wondered if it was one of the prisoners playing tricks on her but quickly dismissed the idea. They didn't seem preoccupied with anything except demolishing her shield.

Would such a proposition interest you, my mysterious friend?

"Who's your friend?" she growled. Her body was tensed, waiting for the first attack to pierce through.

I apologize if I overstepped and offended you, dear magician We might not be friends yet, but I don't see why we shouldn't seize on the opportunity presented. An alliance would be immensely favorable to both parties.

Amit responded with silence; the entirety of her mental and physical energy was being funneled into the battle. She knew exactly how it felt when her power started taking a toll on her body, demanding too much from the tissue so that it started to accelerate the cycle of cell death. It was a phenomenon much studied by practitioner scientists but still very little understood. If she continued in this manner for too long, her lifespan would be significantly shortened.

If you would just entertain me for a minute, the disembodied voice pressed on. *You might be interested to know that the girl you just sent away is tittering on the edge of a trap. Dancing by the chasm of the abyss, so to speak.*

This did catch Amit's attention, even as she began to disassociate from reality. The immense amount of power she was expending forced her into a trance-like state where instinct overruled conscious thought.

"What of Ada?" she managed to mutter as the edges of her vision faded and her hearing distorted.

Ah, I see. It is not your life but hers that matters. I'm sure you'll understand that I can save only one—

"Yes, not mine but hers." Amit clenched her jaw hard, pushing for a moment of lucidity. Her breath shuddered when she realized she might have lied to Ada. They might not meet outside the cave, no matter how long the girls waited. "What do you ask of me?"

I only require a small favor, dear practitioner. An assurance of sorts.

"Spit it out."

She had no time to dawdle on formalities, already having come to terms with reality. One of her three enemies had folded, crumpling to the ground, but the others persisted. She could sense how close they were to distending her barrier, precariously held up as it was with sheer willpower.

Her body had started deteriorating. Her wounds had reopened and likely worsened. Amit was no stranger to Death, having brushed by it countless times before. It was a wonder she didn't feel its presence sooner. Now, it permeated every breath she took.

It had been decades since Amit allowed herself to indulge in reminiscence. Perhaps that's why she couldn't stop herself from doing it now, or perhaps it was a trick of the mountain. Her mind, like clockwork, turned to Miriam.

She may not know it, but she saved Amit's life when they were children—by virtue of her existence. If Amit hadn't known someone like Miriam, that such capacity for kindness was possible, she would have lost hope, seen no reason to endure the endless suffering that was all she knew life to be. Despite feigning indifference and refusing to seek her out in adulthood, it was without hesitation or regret that Amit derailed her life for her.

Although, perhaps Amit did have one regret. Try as she did, it was difficult to conjure the image of the Miriam she last met in Hope Springs: the texture of her hair, her voice, her gaze. Amit had hoped to see her again, though she would never have admitted it.

She was looking forward to dropping off the girls sometime

soon. Miriam had left her a message Amit planned to reply to when they were back outside. Yet now, here she stood, hopeless and alone as she hadn't been in ages. Except, maybe not alone.

"What is it that you want?"

31

These days, Miriam would return home no earlier than eight at night. The tension in the house was palpable despite the normalcy they tried to project for Meena's sake. Gage did his best to stay out, either at practice or with Riley. It wasn't hard with prom just around the corner.

There was much to prepare, and his parents were glad he had something to get his mind off things, but Gage's anticipation was slowly converting into something that tasted more like dread. Not just prom, most things in his daily life started to seem frivolous and pointless. Everything except Riley.

"Are you okay?" she asked when they met up after class. Her car was at the shop, and they were carpooling when their schedules overlapped. Coach Byers gave the team the day off. Prom was only a night away. "You seem a little distracted."

Riley's perceptiveness was one of the things he liked about her, but Gage could not tell her the truth. Sometimes, he wished she didn't see him quite so clearly. "It's not a big deal," he muttered. "Meena's sick is all. I'm a little worried about her."

"Oh no." She pouted sympathetically. "Is it serious?"

"Nah." Gage continued lying through his teeth. "Just the flu. My dad's staying home with her, so she should be good."

"Let me know if there's anything I can do," Riley said and smiled, laying her hand on his shoulder.

"I will," he replied, but kept his eyes on the road hoping to staunch the guilt.

Riley's parents weren't home yet, so he turned off the car and walked her in. After a steamy, leisurely goodbye, he found himself back in his car and on his way to Willow Street. Unused to having free time before dinner, Gage made his way up to his room and settled in front of his console, ready to blow off some steam.

To his frustration, his favorite games all seemed to be glitching, showing player IDs floating in empty air, his audio connection getting disrupted, making him miss out on his teammates' conversations more than once. When the screen started going dark on the right side, completely obstructing his view of the targets he was supposed to be gunning down, he finally threw his controller across the room, texting his friends that his console was shit and he'd see them tomorrow at school.

Meanwhile, Miriam was leaving the office and doing what had recently become her regular rounds. The closest stop was the flower shop, then the community pool, the high school, the club, and the art supply place where Meena had painting classes.

Only when she had reinforced the barriers around each, checked the safe spots she had set up in their vicinity, tested that her alarm system was still intact, and enacted any additional defenses she had fantasized about during the workday—only then would she head home.

Gage, whose stomach had started communicating with him, migrated down to the kitchen to watch Richard cook. Meena's favorite mermaid movie played on the flat screen when their mother walked through the front door, plopping her briefcase onto the entry table and making a beeline to her youngest, who waved silently and allowed her to place a kiss on the top of her head.

From there, she ruffled Gage's hair and gave her husband a peck, asking about their days. Richard was making pasta. They agreed on a red, and she poured them both glasses. The evening seemed quiet and peaceful until a knock sounded at the backdoor.

***

When Ada found the exit to Mount Hermon, Cara was sitting by it, huddled against the chilly dusk. Drawn in the dirt in front of it was a spell circle, perfectly composed to open a rift and undeniably in Amit's handwriting. She had been planning a fast escape.

"Where's Amit?" Cara asked.

Ada explained, still out of breath. She had run up the path feeling like a killer was at her heels. Then, she lowered herself to the ground next to Cara, expecting Amit to appear any minute.

Instead, they found themselves sitting side by side for hours, watching the sun finish its kaleidoscopic descent through the sky. The temperature cooled, and the wind picked up, sporadically slapping debris into their faces. It didn't take long for Ada to lose her patience; sand got into her eyes and mouth.

She pulled her shirt all the way over her head so it covered her face completely, her midriff exposed in the process. The fabric was thin enough to be breathable, and now shielded, she fell asleep. When she woke, the sun had returned, peeking shyly over the horizon. Cara was alert by her side, her watchful eyes never seeming to have left the cave.

Taking initiative, Ada pulled out the instructions to access the storage space and set up the spell circle in the ground beside her. She fished out a couple of bottles of water and granola bars on her first try but couldn't find other sustenance in subsequent attempts—Amit must not have expected them to need that many emergency rations.

A few hours later, the sun had made its way to the top of the sky, its scalding rays landing on their exposed skin like irons. Sitting by the cliff face, there was no refuge to be found except around the corner, hidden from the glare.

The sisters could only turn their backs to the light, fanning their hair over their necks so they'd be somewhat protected. They were reluctant to let the cave out of their sight, as if they feared Amit could emerge at any minute, villains hot on her heels, and—not seeing the girls anywhere in sight—would activate the rift and leave without them, none the wiser of their parallel trajectories.

When the sun inched down and disappeared behind the mountain, the shadows stretched in a burst of unreality. Ada, who had so successfully kept her thoughts at bay thus far, felt her throat tighten. Her head was pounding, and her stomach had been turning for hours. Her voice caught in her throat when she spoke, "I'm not feeling very well."

Cara finally tore her eyes from the cave and said, "We're definitely dehydrated. What should we do?"

Tears started spilling down Ada's cheeks. She didn't want to be the one who suggested they leave without Amit.

"What if we go get help?" she asked.

Her sister assented, "Who? Sethu?"

She shook her head, wiping her runny nose on her sleeve, and said, "Amit didn't want to get her involved."

"We have no choice then."

* * *

Miriam was tensed as she approached the backdoor that night. The only other entrance to the yard, a gate by the bins, had been jammed and unopenable for months. She had never gotten around to fixing it, so whoever their visitor was must have either jumped the fence or magically appeared.

To her surprise, instead of an unwelcome guest, Miriam found a familiar face when she swung the door open. Her skin was sunburned; the griminess of her hair apparent, even pulled back. Regardless of the unfamiliar, steely look on her face, this could only be—

"Ada!"

Pulling her daughter into her arms, it was hard to ignore the smell, but it was harder to let her go. Her appearance was so sudden that Miriam felt she would be gone with a blink. Even so, she forced herself to pull back, bringing her hands up to cup Ada's face, and asked, "Where's Cara?"

"She's waiting for us through that rift," Ada replied, then gestured to the middle of their yard, where an iridescent, glowing portal awaited them. "We need your help. Can you come with me? We'll explain everything once we're there."

"Ada?"

Miriam looked back, remembering where and when they were as if waking from a dream. Richard was standing behind her, visibly emotional.

"Dad." The word was enough to choke Ada up. "We need to do something really quick, but we'll be back soon. I promise."

Richard's eyes migrated to the rift behind her and then to Miriam, who held his gaze reassuringly, saying, "Start eating without us. I'll make sure we're back within the hour."

She forcefully interlaced her fingers with Ada's—who resisted the unfamiliar, tender touch, visibly uncomfortable—before walking through. Miriam suddenly realized that her two eldest had never been very affectionate with each other. She hoped they had at least been kind while away from home. It was with Ada's hand still tightly held in hers that she threw her arms around Cara when they materialized on the other side, so reluctant she was to let go.

"Mom," Cara said as her whole body shuddered. "We've been waiting for Amit for over a day now, and she hasn't appeared." Here, Miriam intended to reply, but she babbled on, "She said Mount Hermon is like a labyrinth that traps you and that we shouldn't go look for her. She would buy some time and meet us out here. We originally thought of tying a rope to ourselves and following it back, but the Mistlanders cut it. If someone waits out here, don't you think—"

"Cara," her mother soothed her, running her hands up and down her arms. "Cara, my love, calm down." Tears had started streaming down Cara's cheeks, and Miriam wiped them away, the moisture smearing the dirt caked on her face. She hugged Cara again, pressing her head into her shoulder, and said, "You're not going into Mount Hermon."

Cara was docile in her embrace, her shoulders shivering

as she sobbed. Ada, on the other hand, sprung back at this declaration.

"Mom!" she cried. "What do you mean? Amit is in there. We need to find her. What if she's in trouble?"

Cara straightened, wiping her own tears this time and saying, "We can't just leave her."

Miriam clenched her jaw. The shock was wearing off, and an undercurrent of anger that had been throbbing below the surface was taking center stage. Never mind the fear and guilt that accompanied it, she refused to focus on them now. "How in the world did you end up in Mount Hermon anyway?"

The girls were startled and visibly cowed by her sudden change of tone. After a second of silence, Cara spoke, "It was my fault."

"It wasn't," Ada interjected.

"It was," she repeated, not a trace of tears left on her face. "You didn't want to come, but I insisted."

"That's not what happened," Ada said with a shake of her head. "I think we were duped. This was a trap from the start."

"A trap I led us straight into."

"Enough," Miriam said and held both hands up in front of her. "I'm not looking for someone to blame. Tell me what happened, play-by-play."

And so they did, starting with their botched escape from South Africa, the ambush, and separation. It was the first time Ada heard a detailed account of the Kingdom of Kitara and Cara of Tmek. When they got to the part about Damascus, Ada hesitated but told her mother about the house she found and the picture of someone who looked just like her.

Miriam was silent throughout, her brow furrowing when

she heard of the dangers they faced, her hand squeezing theirs. When they got to the communication spell, the one where Cara heard Amit but Ada didn't, they paused.

"That must have been the Mistlanders," Cara muttered.

"Not Mistlanders," Miriam said, shaking her head. "But whoever is leading them."

"When we got to Mount Hermon, we thought Amit was waiting inside," Ada continued. "We tied the tether to Cara and went in slowly, but there were two practitioners and, like, ten Mistlanders waiting for us instead."

"Amit still found us somehow," Cara said. "We had separated for a few minutes, and she told me to go ahead while she found Ada. I waited outside for maybe thirty minutes before you appeared."

"Yeah, she found me after that. Someone was chasing me, and she wanted to stall them." Ada paused, debating how much detail to go into.

Before she could say any more, Cara stepped in, saying, "She was injured."

"What?" Ada's eyes, previously trained on the ground, darted up. This was news to her. "Where?"

"Around here." Cara gestured to her lower abdomen. "She was bleeding."

"Why?" Ada was horrified. How had she not noticed?

"I don't know. It was like that when I first saw her."

They were both silent for a minute, feeling guiltier by the second. Miriam stepped forward then. She had made them relive their trauma long enough.

"Amit was right," she said. "Mount Hermon is not somewhere you can easily go in and out of. You said you've been waiting for a day?"

366

They nodded.

"It was daytime when we got out," Cara said. "We waited a night and a day. Then we got you."

Miriam felt her throat tighten before saying, "You've done enough, girls." She placed her right hand on Cara's head and her left on Ada's, smoothing down their hair. "Let's go home. I'll take it from here."

"We can't just go home," Ada said, her voice barely a whisper.

"I'm not going to abandon Amit," her mother said and forced her to meet her eyes. "I'll drop you off at home with your dad and your siblings, and I'll come back to get her."

Cara gripped her hand tighter before saying, "We're not letting you go to Mount Hermon by yourself."

"I'm not as reckless as you are," Miriam joked, but her attempt to lighten the mood fell flat. They stared back at her with haunted eyes. "Oh, my loves," she said as she pulled them both in for a hug. "Oh, my darlings, my little girls. I'm sorry. I'm so sorry you had to go through this."

When they all calmed down, Ada reopened the rift, and Miriam shepherded them through it. She told Richard to get them clean towels and food. "Check if they have any wounds," she said once they were in the shower and out of earshot. "I'll be back by morning."

* * *

Ada lay awake for hours that night, the sweet refuge of sleep just out of reach. The water had run brown for the first five minutes of her shower, and she hadn't been able to finish the heaping plate of pasta her dad served her. Beside her, back in their childhood room, Cara breathed deeply. She hadn't napped outside the cave like Ada had and could hardly resist when her head hit the pillow.

When they first got home, Ada's mind had been blank; with the sudden decompression, it was hard to form coherent thoughts. It was helpful when they rehashed the order of events with their mother earlier—borderline therapeutic—but they had cut it off a bit early. With nothing to distract her in the pitch-black room, she began processing what happened to her after leaving Amit.

There were things Ada had not yet said out loud. Things she didn't know what to make of.

After Amit told her to go ahead, it hadn't been a straight shot up. Instead of a steep incline, the road back had twisted and turned, at times dipping and at others tilting up. The tunnels at the side now looked more like forks in the road, and as if this weren't enough, her illumination spell started to dim despite her efforts. As if the darkness had a mind of its own. As if it were forcefully swallowing the light that antagonized it. Soon, it had the brightness of a cell phone screen, and she could barely see three steps in front of her.

Ada must have inadvertently gone the wrong way because, without any warning, the ground suddenly dropped off in front of her. She noticed the sudden chasm seconds before she would have fallen into it, but it wasn't enough. She must have been fated to plummet into the abyss because she did. It was inevitable.

Thinking back on it now, she figured she must have slipped when she turned to go back the way she came. Perhaps the rocky ground had been too smooth, and her shoes could find no traction. There was no discernable sinister force at

368

fault—no sudden gust of wind or unidentified hands to shove her—but seeing where she ended up, it was hard to chalk it up to coincidence.

Not that Ada really knew where she ended up. Her first thought when she found herself in a free fall was that this would likely be it. How was she going to recover after this? But the same answer always came to her in moments like these: magic.

Disregarding both her tutors' insistence on the use of vetted spells, Ada closed her eyes and concentrated. She willed the air around her to become dense and viscous enough to slow her down. By the time her legs met the cold ground, it was as if her body was being placed down gently.

"What now?" she muttered.

This is quite the predicament indeed.

Ada had been operating under the assumption she was alone and nearly jumped out of her skin at the sound of a stranger's voice. She turned in place, trying to reignite her torch, but was unsuccessful.

"Who's there?" she finally asked, feeling a bit silly.

Fear not, young Aaron. I have no intention to harm you. Your companion, the Phineas, and I made a deal.

"Why would I trust you?"

Only an idiot would blindly trust. I'm not an unsuspicious fellow. The truth is I've already failed to uphold my end of the deal with the Phineas and, in the process, been rendered powerless to help you. You'd be happy to learn I cannot harm what I cannot help.

"That's a relief." *If it's true,* Ada thought.

She didn't know what kind of deal this being was referring to, but if she had to be in their presence, she would rather they be powerless.

You wouldn't say that if you knew...We're not where we were before. It is no longer so simple to escape.

"Don't we just have to climb back up there?" she asked, looking up at the homogenous blackness, already grasping at the smooth rock wall for craggy stones she could lean her weight on.

It may be difficult to understand, but there's nothing up there. We've fallen somewhere else entirely. There is more than one Hell in Hermon. We may as well be behind the veil, in the Mist or Highlands.

Ada wondered if this voice was also fabricated by the mountain to discourage her. Ever since falling, she had felt strangely calm and in control. It would take more than a few words to make her give up.

"And you're fine with staying down here forever?" she asked.

They sounded amused when they responded, *Whether I'm trapped in one Hell or the other for all eternity hardly makes a difference.*

"Yeah, well, if you want to stay here, you can," she said, only half paying attention. "You said we're behind a veil—"

I said we might as well be—

"I'm a gifted traveler. Neither veils nor flesh will bind me."

Ada felt warmth spread through her core when her power activated. Her body vibrated with energy, and the air around her began to glow. When she spoke next, she had no doubt her words would manifest—even as she was barely aware of who she was talking to.

"I'm getting out of here," she said just before the magic overtook her senses. "You can come with me, or you can

370

stay."

How careless you are with your words, young Aaron. How dangerous.

In a more lucid state, she would have heard the laughter. Instead, Ada blacked out. When she awoke, she was in a more familiar tunnel, a dimness ahead allowing her to make out a tether to her right. She started running.

His older sisters were still asleep when Gage went to school the next day. He had a short day of classes before prom; the students would be let out early so the organizing committee could decorate.

It was hard for Gage to concentrate for a number of reasons; the image of Cara and Ada walking in through the backdoor, covered in grime and with tear-streaked faces, was one of them. But by mid-morning, all thoughts of that—never mind prom—were pushed out of his head by the fact that the shadows that had been sporadically appearing around him had multiplied overnight. Whereas he used to encounter one every few days, and they would disappear within minutes, today it seemed there were shadows ever-present, lingering in the periphery.

They were showing up in places they never had before, closer than ever. When he woke up, there was one in his bathroom. It disappeared by the time he brushed his teeth, but another was lurking in the hallway of his house as he grabbed his bag and headed out. They were everywhere in school: behind lockers, in the corner of the classroom, by the cafeteria lady as he picked up some lunch. Gage felt his patience wearing thin, long ago having lost any sense of trepidation toward them.

By the end of the school day, he walked straight past one on the way to the exit. The congealed darkness evaporated into the air like it was never even there. For the first time ever, he was hoping *not* to run into Riley. She would clock that something was going on the minute she saw him.

Luckily for him, Riley was a part of the decorating committee in everything but name. Technically, it was her friend who was a member, but Riley had been roped into filling in when three of the students involved came down with mono a week before and had to bow out. Gage wouldn't see her until shortly before prom when they would meet at her place, and her parents would take pictures.

He had mixed feelings about heading straight home after school. The atmosphere had become heavy since last night. His father had been on edge from the moment Ada appeared. Curiosity intermingled with dread at the thought. What exactly had happened to his sisters?

Gage was surprised to find all five of his family members at home when he arrived. They were dispersed across the first floor: Cara and Miriam sitting in the living room, Ada and Meena across from each other at the dining room table, Richard in the kitchen. His mom patted the seat next to her, so he walked over.

"Why aren't you at work?" he asked and let her lay a kiss on his cheek.

"I didn't get much sleep last night, so I called in sick," she said. Then, turning to look in the direction of the kitchen, she called out, "Hey babe, Meena, Ada. Can all of you come here?"

They gathered in the living room—Meena bringing her

drawing to the coffee table and settling down on the rug to work on it.

"We can't stay in Hope Springs any longer," Miriam announced. "I think we should leave on Sunday."

Something within Gage flared up. "If we're staying because of prom, I really don't care if I miss it—" he began to say.

"No." She held up a hand, cutting him short. "We need time to prepare; it's not like we can get up and leave right now. The earliest we'll be ready by is tomorrow night."

"What about Amit?" Ada asked.

Miriam's voice became gentler when she replied, "I can open a rift to Mount Hermon from anywhere, but the next place the Mistlanders are going to check for you is here."

"They probably know we're here already," Cara interjected. "They've had eyes on Hope Springs all along."

The living room was silent, everyone feeling a little more paranoid, until their father spoke up, "Then we shouldn't stand around and speculate. We're taking action. We're leaving Hope Springs as quickly as we can. In the meantime, I don't see any reason why you shouldn't spend some time with your friends, bud." He reached over and squeezed Gage's shoulder.

"I kind of wanted to see my friends," Ada muttered. "But it's for the best if I don't."

"Oh, honey." Their mom clicked her tongue. "You can see your friends."

"Not until everything is ready," Cara said with a frown.

Ada agreed. There was a lot of work to be done, not just packing but things like arranging excuses for their unexpected absences, and Miriam wanted them to empty the club. Without regular reinforcements, the magical barrier could begin to decline, and they ran the risk of someone stumbling across it while they were away.

All its contents had to be packed into plastic bins and stowed in the attic, the overflow distributed throughout the house. Even if she did meet her friends, Ada thought, what would she say about the time she'd been away?

"What about the fire?" Gage asked.

"What fire?" This was Ada.

After Cara spoke to Miriam in Kitara, she was the only one unaware of his horoscope reading. He pulled out his phone and scrolled through the inbox, conjuring and reading it aloud.

"We're inferring this means our house is going to burn down?" she asked. "What's the contingency plan for that?"

"We've been evaluating our options," Richard replied. "But it's now come to a game-time decision. Should we get some off-site storage space for important belongings?"

Ada felt it was a no-brainer. "As opposed to just letting everything burn?"

"We were concerned it might look suspicious if we hide our prized belongings away before our house inexplicably goes up in flames," her mother said, then sighed. "Our absence will be conspicuous enough. Who knows what the insurance company will say?"

A light bulb went off above Cara's head.

"What about magical storage space?" she asked. Miriam stared back at her blankly, so she continued, pulling out the instructions to access it, "Amit gave us this spell and told us we could keep our luggage in it. We've also found emergency rations and things like maps. I don't know how big it is, but couldn't we do something similar for select items?"

Miriam analyzed the composition of the spell circle silently. It was unfamiliar but harmless at first glance. She would need to break it down to its bare components to understand the space's parameters and optimize it for their use, which could take a few hours.

"I'll look into it tonight," she finally said, already itching to figure out where Amit had learned to use this new tool. "You two," she said as she turned to Cara and Ada, "should go through the house and decide what you want to save. We have a pile in the garage you can put it by."

With that, they concluded the family strategy session, and Richard was off to the flower shop to prepare for his extended absence. It was a modest operation that attracted high schoolers and college students as part-timers—meaning high employee turnover—but he was lucky to employ a trusty manager who could keep things running without him.

Ximena was a widowed landscape painter who, when her husband died in the line of duty at the ripe age of twenty-eight, was left with enough benefits that the leisure and fair wages were exactly what she needed to finish raising her two kids. She had been at the shop for nearly twenty years and had no reason to leave when she was periodically offered raises and promotions, to the point of getting to make up new titles for herself.

When Richard informed her that his family would be out of town for a few weeks visiting his ailing father in South America that day, she named herself interim General Manager and reminded him to be back by Gage and her daughter's high school graduation in May. They had promised to celebrate together.

After that, he needed to drop by the various places Meena

took classes to excuse her from them indefinitely, Gage's school, and the university. Cara and Ada had originally gotten permission for only the rest of the semester off, and that was ending soon.

Meanwhile, Miriam would take care of things at the construction company, reaching out to the management team and delegating responsibilities. She called clients to recuse herself from projects and elevated the head of finance, a close friend they occasionally had Thanksgiving dinner with, to acting CEO.

It was early evening by the time they were done, and almost time for Gage to go to prom. If he'd had it his way, Gage would have already been at Riley's sneaking some hits from her vape, but his parents had made him promise they could drive them to prom. They knew by now that was the only way they would see him and Riley together, notwithstanding the pictures her parents would share.

Richard and Miriam pulled up to the house just minutes after each other and got out together, no doubt having spotted each other on the road. Gage watched from his bedroom window as his father reached out his hand to his approaching mother. They lingered briefly before heading in.

He could already tell that this would be a strange night.

* * *

Cara snatched the car keys on the way out, silently indicating that she would drive them to the club. Ada slid into the passenger seat and hooked her phone up to get some extra charge; she had a lot to catch up on after more than a month off the grid, and her battery was drained.

Her sister had been particularly snappy since arriving in Hope Springs, unable to shake the sense that they had come holding a ticking time bomb—one no one was paying attention to.

Ada realized too late that she had inadvertently saddled herself with DJing responsibilities, so she carefully selected albums they both liked in a subtle attempt to ease Cara's nerves. Ada was also feeling unsettled in their hometown; things seemed off-kilter in the most indecipherable ways. She wouldn't be surprised to wake up and find it had all been a dream.

She was debating whether to say something. The employees inside the diner were buzzing around in preparation for the dinner rush when they pulled up. She finally settled on, "Feels weird to be back, doesn't it?"

Cara put the car in park and got out without a word, slamming the door. Ada sighed and followed, opting to keep quiet for the remainder of their time together. She popped in an earbud for their trek through the forest and tried not to take it personally. Years of living with hotheaded siblings had taught her that sometimes it was better to walk away from an argument than confront them.

Gage must be heading to prom, she thought, glancing at the clock on her phone. She hoped he could have some fun.

Their mother had spent the night tweaking Amit's storage spell, presenting them with the updated version in the morning. She spent some time going over the changes at Cara's behest. Then, they swung by the depot to pick up the plastic bins they were now lugging through the woods. Thanks to Cara's magic storage idea, they wouldn't need to carry them back out when they were filled and heavy.

Jed, Bo, and their girls were long gone by the time Cara and Ada showed up. After Miriam ascertained their claims of practitioner disappearances, she gave them access to her server of magical information and advice on how to go off-the-radar long-term.

"I'll do the upstairs," Cara said when they walked in, then took the stairs up two-by-two without waiting for a response.

She had already thought of ways to categorize the various herbs, crystals, and miscellaneous elements their mom kept stocked up. This task suited her methodical personality perfectly, the repetitive movements lulling her into a meditative state and soothing her anxiety.

Ada had no issues organizing the ground floor. Instead of minute artifacts, it mostly held books and trinkets the family had accumulated over time. There were also more utilitarian items like the inflatable mattress Gage had brought out for the werepeople and kitchen utensils.

Despite the club's ample square footage, the space was underutilized and sparsely populated. The items quickly dwindled, and the girls were almost done by the end of two hours. Cara, having calmed down after a nice bout of tidying up, came down to partake in some of the snacks left in the makeshift kitchenette.

"This feels like a goodbye," she said as she looked around at the bare space.

Once they removed all traces of life, only dingy furniture was left—an old couch they had replaced in their Willow Street living room years back, a table scavenged from a curbside dump when neighbors moved out down the road, a bookshelf already present when Miriam stumbled across the empty warehouse after getting lost on a hike.

She couldn't have found a more perfect venue for their magical practice if she'd built it herself. That was just a few months into their life in Hope Springs before even Cara was born. The Leivas always wondered who the space belonged to before they took over, but no one ever came by to claim it. Nobody in town seemed privy to its existence. It was as if Hope Springs had given them everything they needed before they knew they did.

Ada nodded, oddly desensitized. Cara started crying by her side. She patted her shoulder and said, "Let's finish this up, and we can go hang out with Mom and Dad."

Cara dried her tears and asked, "Do you want me to start setting up the magic circle?"

"Yeah, I'll finish up."

Ada put away the miscellaneous items remaining within minutes: a couple of picture frames, a teapot, and some old blankets amongst the stragglers. It took a joint effort to activate the circle and drag all the bins into storage.

The clock hit nine-thirty by the time they were done, and they were exhausted. After double-checking that nothing had been overlooked, Cara swept the remnants of the spell away with the sole of her shoe.

They stepped out into the temperate night, debating whether to pick up food on the way back. "I would kill for some sushi," Cara groaned.

"I'll text Dad and ask what the plan is," Ada said, but something struck her as odd. "Do you have any signal right now?"

"I should," Cara said and glanced at her cell phone. "Oh. Actually, no."

Ada stopped in her tracks, meeting her sister's gaze. Suddenly, the atmosphere seemed charged. She could feel the tingle of magic on her skin. In the air. Magic they had not cast.

* * *

Gage was glad that most of his friends were too wasted to notice that he wasn't. Riley might have, except the cheerleaders were all holed up in the bathroom—one of them had fought with her boyfriend shortly after he picked her up.

Gage stood in the hall outside the gym, waiting for her, accompanied by some of his rowdy soccer team, trying not to tune out of their conversation. He smiled when he heard them all laughing, someone to his right slapping his arm in an *are you getting this* gesture. Shadows congealed by the bathroom door, solidifying just out of the corner of his eye and drawing his gaze toward it. Riley emerged alone, walking in the opposite direction. Gage followed.

"Hey," he said, turning the corner behind her. "Where are you going?"

She jumped, her heart skipping a beat. When she turned and saw it was him, she kept walking, saying, "You scared me. Becca asked me to go get something for her."

"Get what?"

She shook her head, exasperated. "Apparently, Billy is selling molly in the lab, and she—"

"Asked you to buy it for her?"

Riley could hear his disapproval, and her next words came out defensively, "She's my best friend, and she's having a really hard time!"

381

"Can't she buy her own drugs?" he spat.

"She usually does, but you know how she gets when they fight."

Gage could never stay mad at Riley. He started walking again and said, "I'm not doing any."

She hesitated but agreed. "Neither am I."

Billy was indeed in the lab room, his underdressed friends sitting around as he passed around a joint. The window was cracked open behind them, but it provided insufficient ventilation, and the smoke lingered in the air. Gage made a mental note to spray himself with cologne on the way out.

Riley walked up to them confidently, saying, "I heard you've got molly."

Billy had come wearing black on black, perhaps the most on-theme of his posse. However, some residue had fallen on him while rolling the weed, and now the black was peppered with green and ash. It didn't help that his hair seemed to have been gelled in the wrong direction. He generally gave an impression of chaos, and Gage liked him for it, but he didn't like his drugs. They were cheap and cut with God knows what. This molly was unlikely to be the exception.

Billy nodded. "How much do you want?" he asked.

"Fifty bucks' worth," she replied and handed him the bills.

He pulled his backpack out from behind him and fished around before producing a foot-long case. He popped it open to reveal an inside that looked like a miniature toolbox, each segment holding a different species of pill and powder. Identifying the murky, dime-sized bag within seconds, Billy tossed it across the room at Riley, missing her by about a foot and hitting Gage's shoulder. The shadows in the room flared up in a coordinated movement that startled him, but he stifled his reaction. Nothing else seemed out of the ordinary.

"Let me see," Riley said as she leaned against him to get a glimpse. Billy was back in his spot, and no one was paying attention to them. She reached over and pinched the bag between her thumb and index finger, separating the capsules. "Looks legit."

Does it? Gage thought.

He disliked the idea of letting the annoying dark figures that dogged him affect his opinion of things, but it wasn't just their unusual, restless movements in his periphery that felt off. He turned on his heel, grabbing his girlfriend's hand with his free one, and led them out of the hazy fog.

Once out of earshot, he pressed her, "You're not taking any of this shit, are you? It could be meth for all we know."

"I'm not!" Riley snapped, then snatched it out of his hand and forged ahead. He only caught a quick look of her pinched facial expression.

Gage was taken aback, unsure of the reason for her sudden irritation, although he was sure to be the cause. She went back into the bathroom as he headed for the flock of jocks hovering just outside the gym. When she returned ten minutes later, she was accompanied by the rest of the cheerleaders.

The couples fell in line naturally and headed inside. Gage caught a glimpse of Becca handing her boyfriend something discreetly and wondered whether they had already made up or if the whole purpose of the drama was to secure the drugs.

At least the planning committee had curated some good music, despite the school's insistence that they would shut down the prom if they heard as much as a B-word over the stereo. They got some sodas and ventured into the crowded belly of the party, where one of his buddies produced a dingy plastic bottle from his jacket and poured amber liquid into each of their cups.

Gage kept an eye out for the chaperones that lined the dance floor, but the people surrounding them blocked their lines of sight. It wasn't long until he started feeling the buzz, and suddenly, the party seemed like a whole lot more fun.

Riley had let go of her earlier moodiness and danced with him through fast and slow songs, pressing close to him until a teacher warned them once more to keep their distance. For the first time that night, he was glad he came.

Then, a thought flitted through his mind that even the alcohol couldn't banish, his family's impending self-exile. It must have registered on his face because Riley cupped her hands under his chin, drawing his gaze to hers.

"Want to take a break?" she asked.

Gage nodded and let her lead him away. He had to say something.

C ara and Ada stood back to back, putting up shields against still invisible enemies. Ada hoped only Cara could hear her mutter, "Do we make a run for it?"

"The car is too far away."

"And Mom's safe spots?"

Cara wracked her brain. Where was it exactly?

"It's at the back," she hissed while clutching at Ada's arm. "We need to go around to the back of the clubhouse."

"Ready?" Ada asked as she braced herself. In the woods to their left, a bush rustled. A twig snapped. The air was increasingly charged.

"Now!"

The girls took off sprinting, hugging the edge of the cement structure. As they did, the electricity in the air gathered, forming a bolt of lightning and striking the ground where they just stood. Ada looked back in horror, allowing herself a moment of distraction to glimpse the smoldering patch of dirt.

Looking back at Cara, she found herself about to run straight into her back. Their road was blocked ahead by a mean-looking man and three snarling Mistlanders. They were surrounded again. At this point, they had grown to expect it.

Luckily, Cara had spent all her free time that day reviewing offensive spells with their mom, Ada joining between helping Richard and watching Meena. Never again did they want to feel as helpless as they did in Mount Hermon—helpless to save themselves or others.

"I'll take these," Cara said, referring to the Mistlanders that blocked their way.

Ada turned, her stomach twisting in knots as she confronted the ones behind them. Within seconds, they were fielding attacks. The practitioners seemed to be in charge of spell casting while the faceless Mistlanders took advantage of the chaos to inch closer, step by step.

Shit, Cara thought, seeing one just to her right. She was too focused on keeping up an offensive against the practitioner. Then, an invisible force blasted them back—Ada.

"Thanks," Cara muttered, all too aware of their position's strategic disadvantage. "We need to get past them somehow."

Ada was quiet for a second. There was an idea that had been rattling around her brain for days but had been useless in Hermon's twisted magic field.

"I think I can get us out of here," she said tentatively.

"How?" Cara snapped, struggling to divide her attention equally among their opponents.

Ada swallowed, reminding herself magic was as much about self-belief as it was about formulas and algorithms. Spinning to face her sister, she muttered an incantation under her breath and grabbed her hand, shouting, "Run!"

Cara was caught off guard when they hurtled straight toward the group she had been combating with what seemed like no plan. Then, the space in front of them rippled, and the colors started to blur. A rift sliced the air open just in time for Ada to hurtle through first. When she looked up, they were just a few feet behind their assailants, closer to the back of the clubhouse than before. Cara didn't have a chance to think before Ada tugged her forward toward the shelter Miriam had constructed.

"Wait!" Cara yelled. "Once there, then what? We're just going to be stuck."

Ada paid her no mind, and Cara didn't go so far as to resist. She had a point, though.

"Mom will come, right?" Ada asked. "We're alerting her that we're in danger. That they're here."

Their sentences grew shorter as they ran, struggling to catch their breath.

"Will the shield hold up?"

"What about another rift?"

"The barrier's designed so no one can travel across it."

"Then what?" Ada asked between gasps.

They paused by the designated area and looked back at the half-dozen villains pursuing them.

"We can alert Mom while we think," Cara finally said and pushed them inside the barrier's perimeter, effectively sending a signal across the entire network. Her phone immediately started ringing. "Mom," she answered.

Ada only heard her side of the conversation, watching as their attackers caught up, hurling magic and bodies against the shield.

"We're at the club, and there's, like, five Mistlanders here. And some practitioners. Yeah, we're in the safe spot. What, now? Okay, see you soon."

"She's coming?" Ada asked when she put down the

phone. Cara nodded, pushing her hair back. Her impassive impression tipped her sister off. "But you don't think we should stay here and wait, do you?"

The Mistlanders and their practitioner allies had gathered around the barrier by now, only feet away from where the girls stood. The practitioners' mouths were moving, but Cara and Ada couldn't hear what they were saying. Soon, the Mistlanders started milling around, and it became clear they had received instructions. One by one, they knelt down and started drawing intricate symbols on the ground.

"They're trying to tear down the shield," Cara said. "We've only bought ourselves some time."

Ada stared at them, then replied, "We can do that, too." *Tear down the barrier?* Cara thought, confused. Then, Ada squatted down, set up a familiar rune, and it clicked into place. "If we can knock them out or distract them long enough to run out, I can open another rift, and we can meet Mom somewhere else."

"Right," Cara said.

She thought back to the most powerful spells Miriam and Amit had taught them but ruled out the ones she couldn't recreate perfectly from memory. If magic that strong backfired on them because of faulty composition, they could end up doing their enemies a favor.

Before she got through her circle, she heard a blast and looked up to find two of the Mistlanders that had been drawing by Ada's side thrown back on the mulchy forest ground, the bottom of their pant legs singed and smoking. One of their shoes was on fire. When they got up, she heard her sister mutter an expletive.

"I was hoping they would stay down," Ada said. "Guess we

have to use something stronger."

They both worked in silence for a minute, trying to ignore the attacks and subsequent ripples on the barrier. Ada launched another explosive spell, this time effectively knocking four of their assailants over. Three of them stayed down. When Cara offered her a high five, she noticed her sister's hand was shaking.

Swallowing, she put the finishing touches on her own spell and activated it. For a second, nothing happened, and Cara anxiously wracked her brain for anything she might have done wrong—but then, it hit. Everyone standing outside the shelter fell to their knees, clutching their heads.

"Now!" she shouted, grabbed Ada's arm, and sprinted away from the clubhouse.

"I'll open the rift!" Ada cried.

Within seconds, Cara noticed the air start to ripple ahead of them. Once out, they would find their family and get out of Hope Springs immediately. Someone had to check on Gage. What if they had targeted him when he was alone?

Cara was about to reach the portal when Ada gasped behind her. Something whizzed by them, missing their heads by inches. Cara was running too fast to stop, her inertia enough to send her toppling through the roots and fallen leaves if she did.

She looked over her shoulder to see the two practitioners on their feet again, running toward them. "We can make it," she shouted.

Ada met her gaze and nodded, but her expression was stony, cryptic. Even though she wasn't far behind her older sister, she had noticed the practitioners moving at inhuman speeds. They had to be using some sort of acceleration magic.

As Cara passed through the rift, Ada turned once more to see one of them so close she could hear him breathing. She could see the bloodlust in his eyes. There was only one way to lose them. She closed the rift.

* * *

Gage and Riley made their way to the parking lot, rounding a corner of the building to an area the teachers didn't usually check. They settled on a secluded spot past a couple of smokers, far enough to deter eavesdropping. Riley took out her vape and offered it to him, but he declined. She put it away and pressed herself against him, wrapping her arms tightly around him. His throat tightened as he returned her embrace.

His voice was hoarse when he called her name, "Riley." No response. "I need to tell you something."

Her eyes searched his for clues. "What is it?" she asked.

"My grandfather, my dad's dad," Gage started started to say, the lie already leaving a sour taste in his mouth. "He's sick. They're not sure if he's going to make it. My parents want us all to go visit him before..."

"When are you going?"

"This weekend, Sunday."

"When will you be back?"

Gage was quiet for a moment. "I don't know."

This made Riley step back. "What? What do you mean?"

Silence, then, "He lives in Chile. We don't exactly know when he could," a pause, "pass away. It could be this week or next. Or longer."

"What did the doctor say?" she asked, shaking her head.

"He said he had a month to live a couple of weeks ago."

"So you're all buying one-way tickets? Your whole family is putting their lives on pause? What about your parents' jobs?" Riley demanded. She was growing more agitated by the second.

Gage wasn't expecting any less. His story didn't exactly make sense, but it was what they had agreed on, and he had to stick to it. He didn't blame her for being confused when he had never mentioned family in Chile or any of his grandparents.

Gage himself didn't know where the truth ended, and the lies began. Richard had, in fact, been born in Chile—but was his father there still? Gage was so overwhelmed when discussing their plan that he didn't think to ask.

"Look, Riley, I'm sorry," he said and bowed his head. "I wish I could have told you sooner, but this was just decided yesterday. You know I would have said something to you if I had known..." He trailed off, running his hand through his hair.

She was quiet for a minute, staring out at the distance. Then, she nodded, saying, "I get it. It's not your fault. I hope you get to see your grandpa."

She stepped closer again, her gaze on the ground. He felt her hand touch his.

"I won't be gone forever," he said.

"I know."

Gage hugged her, hoping it would make them both feel better. If anything, he felt worse. Maybe he shouldn't have dated her in the first place, but he didn't know back then what he did now. A thought passed fleetingly through his mind, but he swatted it down in annoyance—that perhaps it would be kinder to break up with her then and there.

A shiver ran down his spine, interrupting his train of thought. Something was making his skin tingle, goosebumps rising across his arms. It reminded him of seeing a glimpse of Eden for the first time. Could someone be practicing magic nearby?

He gave Riley one last squeeze. Anxiety crumpled his stomach like a piece of paper.

"We should head back in. Make the most of tonight," he said as he pulled away.

As they rounded the corner toward the school's entrance, they noticed a trickle of people walking out, two by two, with their dates. It was too early for partygoers to go home; the prom had started only an hour and a half ago. One couple passed close by them as they approached the doors, and Riley asked what was going on. One of the girls seemed apprehensive, but the other didn't hesitate.

"We're not exactly sure," she said. "But, like, three people randomly started having seizures. It was scary!"

"Seizures? Are they okay?" Riley asked with a gasp.

The girl shrugged, saying, "I was freaked out, personally. Someone said some of the kids had never had seizures before, so it was super weird. Totally killed the mood."

"Okay, thanks."

Riley turned to Gage after they walked off, giving him a quizzical look.

He tried to seem unfazed, but blood was rushing loudly in his ears. The shadows that plagued him were gathered around the main entrance, pulsating and beckoning him over. "It might be the molly," he muttered, jaw tensed.

She rolled her eyes. "You are *obsessed* with the molly, Gage.

392

I'm sure someone would have called," Riley started to say as she fished her phone out of her purse, then she stopped. "Oh, that's weird. I don't have any signal."

Gage's hair stood on end. Their school was known for having slow Wi-Fi but never for having a bad signal. "I think you should go home," he said.

"What are you talking about?" she snapped. "Let's go in together and figure out what's going on."

He shook his head, meeting her eyes, and said, "I have a bad feeling about this. Can you please just do me a favor and get yourself to safety?"

Riley's chin jutted out, her first instinct that of adolescent rebellion, but she was taken aback by his sincerity. Gage looked genuinely worried. She was confused and a little embarrassed when tears started swelling in her eyes. "Don't make me leave alone. Can we at least go together?" she asked.

He said nothing for a moment, his eyes shifting from pleading to guarded. It felt like he was suddenly further away.

"They might need my help," Gage said.

"I can help, too!" she protested.

"Riley." His tone seemed desperate again, his gaze downcast. "Please."

Her voice came out in a whisper, "Fine." Then, louder, she added, "But don't think this conversation is over."

With that, she spun on her heel to join the crowd marching through the parking lot in search of a cell phone signal. Gage turned back toward the school building to find the trickle of people leaving had turned into a steady stream. As he approached, it became harder and harder to swim against them.

393

The crowd seemed more frantic and at the edge than the initial deserters. One person shot him a funny look when they saw him maneuvering his way through the doorway, stopping just short of elbowing his way in.

"You shouldn't be going back in there," they said. "I don't think they'll let you in even if you left something behind."

Gage, sweating and growing impatient by then, gave them a tight-lipped smile and nodded.

It had taken him twenty minutes to cover a distance that usually took five, and he was only halfway to the gym. The further he went, people's expressions started to change. From impassive to uncomfortable, anxious to frightened. Chatter quieted down to distressed whispers. Things seemed to have gone from bad to worse.

* * *

Ada raced through the forest. Her feet sunk into the damp ground, and her calves burned from the effort. She could still hear her pursuer's footsteps pad, pad, padding close behind her.

She prepared to open another rift—leading to their backyard on Willow Street like the one Cara took just minutes before—when someone grabbed her shoulder, pulling her back. Ada's stomach dropped.

To her relief, the practitioner had been standing slightly too far to get a good grip; the balmy hand slipped off despite his attempt to hold onto her clothes. The rift had opened, but her spell casting had been interrupted and was incomplete.

As she passed through it, she knew it would only take her so far. Once out the other end, she found herself still in the forest, the practitioners now smaller figures in the distance. She almost let herself relax, finding reprieve for a blissful moment, until she noticed figures moving ahead past the foliage. Mistlanders.

One lunged at her from the right, and she instinctively blasted him back. The force of the spell ricocheted and made her lose her balance; she felt herself falling. Ada knew that if she did, she would be trapped—forced to battle a horde of enemies from the most disadvantageous position.

The nearest Mistlander was only feet away, running straight at her like a football player intent on tackling. Her mind raced fruitlessly, but there was only one spell she trusted herself to cast in a split second. Her eyes glazed over as a burst of energy built inside her. She imagined a rift tearing through the space in front of her like a bomb. It appeared within a blink of an eye, and she fell through. Now, she had to make sure no Mistlanders followed.

Ada had never opened a rift that quickly. The spell's inertia was still expanding the portal when she passed through it. Before the magic could settle, she tried reverting the flow of energy and felt the sheer force of it pushing back against her. She had to crush it with all her strength, every muscle in her body engaging as she did. Each second felt like minutes, like enough time for a Mistlander to reach through and grab her.

Then, the rift imploded on itself—disintegrating rather than shrinking like rifts usually did. She fell to one knee, panting like she had just run a marathon. She was in front of the diner, two steps from the Jetta. Still trembling, she remembered an important fact—Cara had the keys. Ada cursed.

Remembering that Gage was alone at prom, she pulled

out her phone and called him. It didn't connect. Her mind raced through worst-case scenarios. No way had this been an isolated attack. Mistlanders had blocked the cell phone signal at the club, and they could surely block it at the high school. Ada texted the family's group chat as quickly and concisely as possible.

Got away from Mistlanders at the club. I'm going to school to get Gage. Meet there? She waited a beat, then added, *The car's at the diner.*

The hair on the back of Ada's neck was standing on end. If she wasn't already being watched, she knew she soon would be. She couldn't wait for a response. Instead, she opened what must have been her fifth or sixth rift of the day and stepped through, strategically depositing herself by the cluster of trees behind the football field, far from where the prom was happening, expecting it to be secluded.

As she walked across the field and up to the school building, she started to hear the sound of voices—too many voices, considering it was an indoor event. As Ada got closer, she saw there was a mass of people milling at the front in the parking lot. Rather than a jubilant atmosphere, the few faces she saw looked confused and unsettled. Most were making their way to the edge of campus.

It would have been impossible to find Gage amongst the crowd, but Ada was convinced he wouldn't be there anyway. She had noticed an undeniable electricity pulsing in the air the moment she stepped out of the rift; magic was flooding out of the school building.

If this was only the overflow, there had to be some powerful spell-casting taking place inside. As aloof as Gage tried to come off, there was no way he would walk away from something like this. She had to look for him in the eye of the storm.

He will be safe, she told herself again and again. *He will be safe*, she hoped.

* * *

Cara found herself outside her house on Willow Street, markedly alone, no rift in sight. She waited for a minute in hopes that Ada would materialize nearby, but it was in vain.

Wracked with guilt at having left her little sister in the midst of a hostile mob, she burst through the backdoor shouting, "Mom? Dad? Are you home?" Her voice cracked as she let out a shaky "Help."

She heard someone thumping down the stairs. Richard materialized within seconds. "Cara, honey? What's wrong? Where's your sister?"

"She opened a rift, but only I came through."

Before she knew it, she was in her father's arms.

"Your mom went to the club to get you two. She should be with Ada soon," he comforted her, running his hand down her hair.

Cara shook her head, fighting the knot in her throat that threatened to choke her, and said, "Won't Ada open another rift to escape? We need to tell Mom."

"Okay, I'll call her. Sit down, catch your breath."

"And Gage?"

"We haven't heard from him since he picked up Riley," he replied and held up the ringing cell phone to his ear. "Miriam? Cara's home. She said Ada opened a rift and can do it again. You might want to confirm she's still at the club before running in there."

Cara jumped in before he could hang up, "We need to get Gage. They won't leave him alone."

Miriam said something she couldn't hear. Richard nodded, saying, "See you at the school, then."

"What about Meena?"

"She's upstairs. We'll bring her. We can't afford to be separated right now."

Cara agreed, starting to feel nauseous.

If the club wasn't safe, that meant nowhere was safe. Not even home. As she had suspected, danger followed them wherever they went.

* * *

Gage didn't know what he was expecting when he rushed into the gym. Students had been mostly evacuated, with some teachers and chaperones following to keep the order. The hallways cleared up toward the end, allowing him to pick up speed and burst in dramatically. Everyone inside was so preoccupied no one turned to look when he did.

At least five bodies lay sprawled on the ground, limbs twisting and contracting in unusual ways. The remaining adults scuttled around, cushioning the prone students' heads, moving tables and chairs away when they got too close. The gym teacher and Coach Byers were going around and trying to turn them on their sides. They weren't the ones that caught Gage's attention. He could see why everyone was so freaked out now.

In the middle of it all stood three boys, all members of

the soccer team; amongst them was Sam, Gage's best friend. The girls outside were right. The victims weren't epileptic. Sam and Gage would carpool to the pediatrician and swap results as unselfconscious preteens—other than dealing with his dyslexia, Sam was fit as a fiddle.

Yet, all three of his teammates seemed to be suffering from seizures, except they were staying upright somehow. They had no vestige of bodily control—their eyes were rolled back to show white, their fingers clenched and unclenched, their mouths hung ajar.

Anyone would have been unsettled; their unnatural movements seemed painful, their skin was pale. The others couldn't see what Gage saw. He stepped closer to ascertain it hadn't been a trick of the light. There was a neon-colored glow emanating from under the boys' skin. Gage could see it pulsating through their bloodstreams; the blip appeared periodically on the inside of his team member's arm. And there it was again.

"Gage!" It was his homeroom teacher, the first to finally notice him. "Step away from them. You shouldn't be here."

"Please listen to me," Gage said as he stepped back, his hands raised. "I think they took some weird pills. My mom can help. You *need* to call her."

"Gage, I know your mother, and she is not a doctor."

"A doctor can't help them, Ms. Kabul—"

"Don't be ridiculous. Coach Yan is out there right now, calling an ambulance. It will be arriving any minute, and you will share any information you have on these 'weird pills' and where they got them. Capiche?" she cut him off, using air quotes.

"Miss," Gage pleaded to no avail.

He mulled over his options—he could try magic if no one was watching, but was there a way to get the adults out of the room? How could he convince them that Miriam could help?

Before he could get anywhere, a piercing shriek split the air. Ms. Kabul's head snapped up, and she ran over to the history teacher. One of the unconscious students had started moving differently, something that had first been tentatively celebrated as a possible sign of recovery. Yet they didn't regain consciousness and remained unresponsive to their name.

Instead, they grabbed onto the history teacher's arm so hard that she fell to the ground as she tried to free herself. The student's hand only continued to tighten and pull her closer. Now, five of eight adults milled around the two, prying fingers and bodies away. Then, a second student started moving. And a third.

Soon, all of the prone students were tossing and turning; some began to babble incomprehensibly. Similar to the first, they were oblivious to external stimuli, failing to react no matter how forcefully the teachers tried to wake them.

The adults looked at each other, puzzled and scared. "Someone should go check on that ambulance," one suggested.

Gage stayed out of sight until they agreed on who would go, afraid that they would use any excuse to vacate him from the premises. He needed time to come up with a better plan.

"Sam?" one of the teachers said. Gage spun to see him standing in front of the soccer players, peeking up at Sam's face. "I think their eyes are starting to normalize!" the teacher yelled.

He was right. The three teenagers were settling down,

making less erratic movements than before. As they found stillness, their posture also improved, their facial expressions neutralizing until they looked nearly normal again. It didn't make Gage feel any better.

The bizarre glow was more apparent than ever. Sam's eyes descended slowly, neon yellow and holding more malice than Gage knew he was capable of. In an instant, it clicked. Gage's heart dropped. "Watch out!" he yelled, but it was too late.

Sam reached forward and grabbed the teacher's shoulders, pulling him in as he slammed his knee into his stomach. Once, twice, three times. The teacher first contorted, curving defensively, then lost strength and fell limp to the floor.

Next to Sam, the remaining two students were coming to. They didn't bother dodging the bodies on the floor when they did, forging ahead and callously stepping on their writhing peers. Their eyes were trained firmly on Gage.

34

A da ran into the empty school building, determined to find Gage and get the hell out. She knew she would encounter resistance—she had grown to expect sophisticated coordinated maneuvers from whoever was behind the Mistlanders—but the earlier spat had steeled her and left her feeling like a blunt force weapon. A club. A hammer. A mace. She had faced these enemies before and defeated them. She knew how to wield her power now better than ever. She wouldn't let anyone touch her little brother.

Three Mistlanders appeared when the gym doors were already in sight, blocking her way. An explosive spell was enough to incapacitate two, but the third was quick enough to deflect it and lunged forward.

Ada put up a shield, finding herself closer to this Mistlander than she had ever been before. Seeing them often had desensitized her to an extent, but she was once more struck by how unsettling their featureless gray face was. Earless and noseless, the light caught on their beady black eyes, their jagged teeth barely visible through the slits in their skin.

The fact that she was battling it in the school hallways was borderline comical; her high school days seemed eons away.

Summoning a shield was like second nature. Ada pushed

it back with relative ease, planning to immobilize them and get her brother.

As she did, a noise at the end of the hallway diverted their attention. The Mistlander's head snapped up, but Ada was slower to look. Judging by the dress, it was a prom-goer running deeper into the school.

Exposing a non-practitioner to magic was problematic, but Ada could hardly worry about it now. She had graduated years prior and doubted any of Gage's classmates would recognize her anyway—other than his close friend Sam. At most, it would culminate in a baseless rumor.

Ada would have stuck to her plan had the Mistlander not ducked out from under her shield and gone after the passerby. For a moment, she watched their retreating bodies. Gage was just steps away. She needed to know that he was okay.

She took three steps before the scream rang through the halls. Ada had heard Mistlanders in pain before, and it sounded nothing like this—they were more guttural, animalistic. It had to be the student.

Gage was her priority, but Ada felt responsible for the Mistlanders descending on Hope Springs—if only she had been more careful...

She turned on her heel and sprinted after them, hoping to atone for her initial selfishness. Dealing with one Mistlander would take her ten minutes max. Then, she'd run back and get Gage.

In the meantime, she prayed that the magic in his veins would protect him like it had her.

* * *

The gym's atmosphere had been frantic from the moment Gage arrived, but now it had descended into madness. People were screaming. The history teacher was crying inconsolably in the corner. "The faculty have lost their faculties," he muttered, chuckling darkly.

His homeroom teacher milled around trying to build a consensus on what to do next, but it wasn't easy. The one parent chaperone who remained up until the assault left alone to "get help" after failing to convince others to come with him.

Of the remaining adults, two teachers tended to their fallen colleague, while the other three stood at a sensible distance from Sam and his buddies, trying to reason with them. A handful of students still lay on the floor, moaning and moving about, but everyone present seemed to have agreed there wasn't much they could do for them at the moment.

"Boys, we know you're in there!" Coach Byers said, but he may as well have been talking to a wind-up doll. The athletes trudged on, forcing him to jump out of their path.

Gage stood with his back to the entrance, watching their approach. They were moving slowly enough to give him time to think—and something about seeing his best friend and teammates wobbling toward him, glowing neon, was kind of unterrifying. He would have made a joke if Sam could hear him, but he knew that despite the flesh they inhabited these were no friends of his.

Another reason his zombified friends couldn't command the full terror they deserved was that Gage's attention had been partially siphoned by the pesky shadows that plagued him. They were conducting themselves in new and curious ways.

404

Minutes ago, they had flared by the gym door like there was something important outside it. Gage wondered if they were telling him to run. Then, they did something he had never seen them do before, wresting themselves from the walls and slithering across the floor to circle around everyone present.

You should command them.

It was his voice. The words couldn't have sounded more clearly in his brain if he had read them off a piece of paper. He shook his head. *Command them? What makes me think they'll listen to a word I say?*

Sam was closer now, two more steps, and he could reach forward to touch him. Gage didn't want to get into a fistfight with his possessed best friend, and he didn't have the confidence to cast spells and charms the way his sisters did. In a matter of seconds, they were face to face.

The teachers trying to stop them earlier had stepped away to convene after the three boys proved inoffensive. One looked back now and gasped, "Gage!"

Sam had grabbed his shoulder, just like the teacher he had kneed in the stomach earlier. Their friends loomed behind him, unaffected yellow gazes planted on Gage, ready to step in as needed.

Previous attempts to speak to them had fallen on deaf ears, but Gage tried anyway. After all, this was his best friend, the guy that was too intimated by the cafeteria workers to ask for extra helpings.

"Hey Sam," he said while still wracking his brain for what to say next and coming up short. Going into auto-drive, he landed on, "Don't you think you've been watching too much anime lately?"

His best friend replied with his knee, knocking the air out

of him and sending his mind reeling.

Fine, he thought, eyes fixed on Sam's leg as it retreated momentarily.

He could hear a scuffle behind them as the teachers tried to intervene, and the soccer players kept them away. The shadows had followed them and weaved in and out between the figures, obscuring his sight.

As the second blow approached, Gage looked at one and muttered, "Help me."

It was a blur. He didn't follow the exact sequence of events, but both he and Sam ended up on the floor.

Disoriented, it took Gage a moment to realize that the gym's doors had been thrown open. A new pair of hands was fuzzing over him while another helped him up. "Gage, my love, are you okay?" When his eyes focused, he saw his mother's face. His dad stood behind her, a death grip on the strap of Meena's backpack.

"What are you doing here?" he asked but immediately thought of countless better questions. "How did you know?"

Miriam looked to the right, and he followed her gaze to Cara, who was casting a boundary around the soccer players to keep them back.

"The girls were attacked by Mistlanders at the club," his mom said. "So we suspected they'd come after you, too. Are you alright, sweetie? Have you seen Ada?"

Gage rose to his feet, saying, "I'm fine." But... "Ada? No, I haven't seen her. Why? Was she supposed to be here?"

Miriam licked her lips before replying, "Yes, she texted us saying she was on her way thirty minutes ago. She must be somewhere on the premises. Cara!" she barked and waved her over. "I'll take care of things here," Miriam told her. "Take

Gage and find your sister. I sensed her magic in the hall. She got here before we did."

Those words were enough to raise goosebumps on Gage's skin. If Ada was in the hall, why hadn't she made it inside?

"What about Dad and Meena?" Cara asked as she stepped toward the door.

"I've got it covered, darling," their mom said and gave her a tight-lipped smile. "Go on now."

"Come on, Gage." Cara touched his shoulder lightly. "We have to find Ada."

Cara walked out confidently, easily tracing a burst of magic to the second corridor from the gym. This was her specialty. She would find their missing sister in no time. If there was one thing she could do, it was scrying.

And yet, thirty minutes later, after scouring the school and football field for clues, they were no closer to finding Ada than before. They had checked the cafeteria, the bathrooms, the music room. Gage had even limbed up the precarious hanging ladder to the roof, just in case.

Cara was having heart palpitations. The only place her scrying didn't work was Mount Hermon—the place where they had last seen Amit, where Amit might still be. Had they taken Ada back there? The thought made her feel like she was gasping for air.

She presented her theory to her mother, who had been intently treating the affected students, but Miriam shook her head and said, "It doesn't make sense. Too many variables are out of their control in Hermon. It's too risky."

Cara had her doubts—the entity behind the Mistlanders seemed entirely at ease using Hermon's magic to their advantage—but she wasn't about to argue with her mother, not before ruling out all other options. To start with, she had to confirm, "Mom, could they purposefully be hiding Ada's presence?"

"Yes, most likely."

"Then, how can I find her?"

"There are ways. I'll show you," Miriam said as she stepped away from the bustle.

Gage stood nearby, impressed. The chaos in the gym had substantially subsided since Miriam's arrival. All problems seemed small next to her. She had wrangled the teachers onto the bleachers, where they sat in an orderly line whispering among themselves. Sam and his teammates now lay on the floor alongside the other students.

They all seemed to be in a fitful sleep, fingers still clenching and jaws clicking. Only one was completely knocked out, lying still. His face was almost too relaxed; with his eyelids slightly parted, a trickle of drool escaping his agape jaw, he looked more vulnerable than anyone was meant to see him. Unsettlingly so.

Gage took a step toward him, bending down. Something moved just past the boy's teeth—one of the shadows. It weaved in and out of his ears, his mouth, squeezing out under his eyes like smokey tears.

Gage's stomach turned; he found it unexplainably revolting. "Mom? Mom!" he called, hoping for once to be proved wrong.

* * *

Ada fought the urge to turn around and retrace her steps. When she chased after the Mistlander, the hall elongated endlessly like in a nightmare. No matter how much she ran, she didn't seem to move in space. It was reminiscent of Mount Hermon but somewhat unlike it. Ada suspected that she had inadvertently followed the pair through a veil.

It proved apparent when the space stabilized that they were no longer in the school hall. The vandalized off-white walls had been replaced with a stony interior and soaring ceilings. She spun on her heel, searching for the Mistlander, the student, or whoever had brought her here. All she saw were darting shadows.

Looking up, Ada realized she was standing in a courtyard overlooked by rows of corridors stretching up as far as she could see. Lights flickered and extinguished high above her. There were two exits on opposite sides of the cavernous ground floor, leading into darkness. It looked like a place where nothing good ever happened.

Ada decided to wait. Someone brought her here for a reason.

"Ada."

There it was, her name coming from somewhere up there. She turned toward the voice but saw only faint lights in the distance.

"Behind you."

Familiar yellow eyes. The practitioner that accosted them in Cape Town stood before her.

"Is this where you wanted me to go with you?" she asked, remembering what he said then.

This man was clearly affiliated with the Mistlanders. Yet, when they last met, he claimed to want to help her, not hurt her. Ada wasn't going to let her guard down, but she hoped there was a grain of truth in his words.

"Not quite what I meant..." He trailed off. "But in a way, yes. We are together now."

The dim lighting allowed for a better look at his face than daybreak at the beach had. Miriam once told her that practitioners didn't age like non-practitioners. Was that why his age seemed inscrutable?

At first glance, she would have placed him around forty or fifty years old, but when he spoke, the folds in his face bunched up and made him look much older. His faint yellow glow may have given the appearance of jaundice—or having fallen into a vat of toxic waste—but his presence was no less intimidating for it. This was no feeble old man.

"What do you want from me?" Ada asked, then got a sense of déjà vu.

"You and I are more alike than you think, young magician," he replied cryptically.

Magician? She had never heard practitioners referred to that way until falling into the chasm in Mount Hermon. To suddenly hear it twice in such short succession was perplexing.

"In what way are we alike?" she spat.

Her nerves made her sound more hostile than she intended. His tone had been cordial so far, friendly even, and she didn't want tensions to escalate. She had to keep her cool.

He smiled, and her skin crawled. "Oh, it goes down to our very core. We're made from something different than everyone else," he said while cupping a hand over his chest. He lifted an eyebrow. "I'll show you mine if you show me yours."

With a flourish of the wrist, something erupted from his breast. A black mass gushed into the room at hundreds of miles per hour, filling it entirely within seconds. Ada suddenly found herself enveloped in it, but a few inches of air spared around her.

Whoosh. Whoosh. Whoosh. The sound of it encircling the room was deafening. Then, it went quiet. When she opened her eyes, there was no trace of the substance left. She almost expected surfaces to be sticky with dark goo, but there was only the man. Standing there. Smiling.

Ada couldn't control her facial expression. She was tired and scared. One of her legs faltered, but she caught herself before asking, "What was that?"

Her voice was barely audible, so he might not have heard it. She got the feeling he did but chose to ignore her.

"It's your turn," he said.

Before she could repeat herself, he appeared closer, hand outstretched. When his fingers brushed her head, the black mass reappeared, but it was different. Stronger. Worse.

Ada fell to her knees, her arms cupped around her head. The wind, like blades, slashed her arms. There was no buffer between them now. She was light-headed and nauseous. The left side of her face started going numb, and she wondered idly if she was getting a migraine.

It must have been a few minutes before the sound subsided. When she came to, her cheeks were wet with tears. Her joints felt like they hadn't been used in days, but she managed to sit back on her hip. It felt like someone stuck their hand in her stomach and rummaged around, leaving her organs out of place.

As she regained feeling in her hands and feet—the sensation of a million pins and needles—Ada became aware of a stinging on her legs. The skin felt like it was pulled too taut against her bones. Shaking, she pushed herself back to standing. It hurt to bend and straighten her knees.

Surely enough, grizzly scrapes extended down to her ankle. The pressure of the black mass had pushed her down onto the uneven ground. She gingerly brushed off some pebbles that protruded from her mangled flesh.

"Ouch," the man said insincerely. "That must hurt. The good news is—" Ada felt woozy, her eyesight dimming at the corners. His smile looked more twisted than the last. "—You are just like me."

As her consciousness faded, she heard him mutter, "Tch! They've always been meddlesome these Aarons. No getting around it."

35

Miriam and Cara found Ada behind the locked doors of the teacher's room, unconscious, bloodied, and drained of magic. When emergency responders finally made it to the gym, they carted out seven very confused teachers and eight unconscious students on gurneys.

All fifteen were immediately taken to the hospital, where one of the students was pronounced brain dead after rigorous testing. The sheriff's office secured the scene and scoured the premises for suspects while they waited for police from the neighboring city to arrive—with whom they often collaborated on narcotics cases.

The next morning, they released a joint statement identifying Billy as the final link in the chain that had brought fentanyl-laced heroin to the festivities, marketing it as MDMA. The deceased student's parents insisted their son would have never touched recreational drugs, but Gage knew the truth. Whether Billy had been given molly, heroin, or fentanyl to sell, someone else had tampered with the pills, lacing them with mind-control magic.

That night, when Gage had called his mom over, it was clear that the Mistlanders' attempt to possess the boy had jumbled his neural signaling network beyond what she could repair. She still tried as hard as she could until Richard came running from down the hall. The authorities had arrived.

"Let's find Ada and get out of here," Miriam said.

Her voice was determined, reassuring—but she lingered after the children had gone. Richard let Meena walk ahead with her siblings, standing by his wife until she looked up and met his eyes.

"A child," she said, the word barely a whisper. Tears were gathered in her eyes.

He nodded, took her hand, and led her out.

They had to leave Hope Springs, but everyone agreed they deserved one last night at home. The whole family sat in the living room while Miriam cast protection spells around them for hours—against intruders, fire, lightning, explosions, flooding, forceful relocation, time jumps, the list went on.

It was midnight, and Meena was asleep, curled under her father's arm, when they were done. Still, they sat in the candlelight silently for a little longer before going upstairs. The rest of the kids were asleep soon after.

Only one light remained on, that of their parents' room. Surveyors of possibilities and protectors from the unknown, alone at dawn, they dared speak that which they could not say in front of their children. Unearth fears. Find strength, consolation. Make difficult decisions that would be painted easy by morning.

They were still awake at four when a mass text made both their phones vibrate. The funeral was being held the next afternoon. The boy's only surviving grandfather was having surgery on Monday, and his mother had to fly out.

Miriam flinched at the convergence of events. She hoped

the family would find rest. It was as close as she had gotten to prayer in a long time.

* * *

The mood in the house was muted that morning—less like the aftershock of disaster than the weary feeling of being in the midst of a crisis. Belongings were packed. Cell phone chimes were ignored. Breakfast was had in silence.

They gathered in the foyer when they were ready to attend the wake. Sitting in the church pews, Gage couldn't help but think of the moment he realized his classmate was dead. The fear and despair made such a toxic cocktail that, for a second, it had felt tinged with disgust. In hindsight, he wondered if the disgust was aimed at himself for letting things get this bad.

The kid was younger than he was, only having made varsity that year. If only Gage hadn't refused lessons from his mother, could he have helped before Miriam got there? The few tears that he couldn't hold back were of guilt. He wouldn't be weak by choice any longer.

Richard, Miriam, and Meena were stoic throughout the service. Ada's lip quivered, and she couldn't help some tears that spilled over, but she had wept most of them into her pillow. It was Cara who found herself holding back sobs. Ada suspected that her older sister was mourning more than this innocent child's life.

She, herself, was still reeling from months of traumatic events, and the evening's cryptic encounter had left her lost and limping. After the service, people filtered out onto the parking lot to follow the procession. There was still a burial to attend.

"Kids," Richard called out. They gathered around him in a half-circle. "Your mom and I are going to load up the car, and we'll pick you up at the cemetery. Can you catch a ride?"

It was odd timing but not an unusual request; their kids were used to carpooling home from school often before getting their licenses. It might have been awkward if they weren't surrounded by close friends and acquaintances.

Cara and Meena jumped into the car of an old family friend while Ada and Gage latched onto classmates they'd known for years. Luckily, no one was concerned with the girls' recent whereabouts amidst the present circumstances, and conversations remained generic.

Minutes after arriving at the cemetery, Ada saw Riley pull Gage to the side, toward the forest line. She didn't want to pry, but it pained her to let him out of her sight. Instead, she glanced to and from them until he walked back, leaving his stunned girlfriend behind.

Ada held out an arm as he approached and patted his back when he stopped at her side, squeezing his shoulder in what she hoped was a comforting motion. She couldn't think of anything to say.

"What is it?" This was Cara, standing to her other side, asking Meena. Their youngest sibling had turned away from the burial and was staring at the road. At the end of her gaze were two figures in black.

"More guests? They're a bit late," Cara remarked.

Meena corrected her, "They're not guests. They're waiting for us."

Ada felt her heart skip a beat before asking, "Are they bad people?" She saw Cara shoot her a look out of the corner of

416

her eye but ignored it.

Meena shrugged. The siblings looked at each other.

Cara sighed, then said, "Fine. I'll go first."

If she meant that they should wait for her, they didn't, instead following a few steps behind. When they got close enough to discern their features, the siblings were surprised to find that they did not recognize these people—an odd occurrence in tiny Hope Springs.

They seemed disinterested in the ceremony, making no move toward the crowd as they waited for the Leivas to come near. One was a middle-aged woman with tufts of dark red hair poking out of her black bolero. She smiled gently when they drew close enough.

"You must be Cara!" she exclaimed in subtly accented English. "What a pleasure it is to meet you."

"And you are?" It always unnerved Cara to meet a stranger who already knew her.

"I am Brooke," she said. Her tongue caught on the *r*, hinting at Eastern European roots. "And this is Dumas. We are from the Committee." Greeted by blank stares, she continued, "The Aarons have sent us here to collect you."

Ada bristled at the combination of words. Committee. Collect. *Aarons.* "Which Aaron?" she demanded as she stepped forward.

Brooke smiled more kindly than ever as if she had been waiting for precisely this question. "Miriam Aaron, in fact." The bewilderment must have been apparent on their faces because she elaborated, "She asked us to come get you."

"Impossible," Ada hissed.

"Can you prove these claims?" Cara asked.

"Dumas?" Brooke said, then glanced at her partner for the

first time.

A tall man at least a decade younger with a head of well-manicured tight curls, he wordlessly produced an envelope from his breast pocket. She took out the letter from within, unfolded it, and handed it to Miriam's eldest, saying, "As you can see, it bears your mother's seal, which would be impossible to falsify."

In fact, none of them had seen the seal stamped at the bottom of the sheet of paper before, much less known their mother had a personal one. Cara read it with bated breath, Gage and Ada crowding around her.

"It's Mom's handwriting," Gage pointed out. "What does it say?"

"It doesn't have the answers we are looking for," Cara replied, defeated, and handed the letter to Ada. She stepped in front of Meena and knelt down to catch her eye. "Can I hold your hand? Thanks," she said when Meena's soft little palm landed in hers. "We're about to go somewhere new, Meena. You, Gage, Ada, and me. Mom and Dad aren't coming with us."

"This is bullshit," Ada muttered, skimming the letter herself, drowning out Cara's voice with curses.

Ada was seething by the time she handed the note to Gage. It felt like their parents had pulled a fast one on them. That they had chosen to hand their children off to a sinister practitioner institution when things got bad, just days after they had finally reunited, was a tough pill to swallow.

It didn't help that her siblings seemed largely unaffected. Gage barely bothered to read the letter before giving it back to Brooke, who shook her head and said, "Keep it. And rest assured, the Committee is doing everything it can to locate

Miriam Aaron and your father. Now, come this way."
Her words were anything but reassuring.

To be continued.

Epilogue

To my beloved children,

I must start by apologizing for the confusion you must be feeling right now. You surely have many questions, and your father and I regret parting with you without answering them or saying goodbye. Please trust that this is not a decision we took lightly, that we've considered every other option, and that separating from you, however temporary, is the hardest choice we've ever had to make.

Hope Springs is no longer safe for us. As heartbreaking as it may be, we must flee for our family to survive. I have guarded you jealously from the dysfunctions of practitioner society until today, but now that it's come to this, we have no one else to turn to. The Committee will do what I have failed to: keep you safe. Their defenses compare to nowhere else in this world. I hope you will have room to breathe and learn about all I have kept from you. I may have no right to say this, but I hope you don't resent me too much.

Your father and I cannot join you, for he will not be welcome behind the veil. For the same reasons I have evaded the Committee for so long, we must now separate. It may be hard leaving the state for the first time, but don't worry— you're strong enough. And remember, our home will always be the place where Hope Springs.

Please, don't look for us. We will find you when the danger has passed. Until then, stay together. Bend, but don't break.

Your father and I long for the day we meet again.

With love,

Mom

About the Author

Meghan Williams grew up on the Caribbean coast of Colombia. She has since lived in the United States, Hong Kong, and France. She started writing *The Sound Carries* halfway through her bachelor's degree in International Business, a culmination of ideas that had been swirling shapelessly in her head for years prior. Prior to that, she had mainly written on online platforms for young authors like Figment (RIP), publishing a steady stream of short stories, poems, and unfinished novels.

Now based in Paris, Meghan is directing her professional efforts toward climate action. She hopes to one day merge this passion with her love for writing. She is currently working on the final installment of the Hope Springs trilogy, which is expected in October 2026. The second book of the series, Into the Machine, is available wherever you get your books.

Subscribe to her newsletter or follow her on social media to receive updates on her work.

You can connect with me on:

🌐 https://www.meghanwp.com

Subscribe to my newsletter:

✉ https://mwilliamsauthor.substack.com